STONE BRUISES

www.transworldbooks.co.uk

STONE BRUISES

Simon Beckett

BANTAM PRESS

LONDON · TORONTO · SYDNEY · AUCKLAND · JOHANNESBURG

TRANSWORLD PUBLISHERS
61–63 Uxbridge Road, London W5 5SA
A Random House Group Company
www.transworldbooks.co.uk

First published in Great Britain
in 2014 by Bantam Press
an imprint of Transworld Publishers

A CIP catalogue record for this book
is available from the British Library.

ISBNs 9780593073285 (hb)
9780593073292 (tpb)

Addresses for Random House Group Ltd companies outside the UK
can be found at: www.randomhouse.co.uk
The Random House Group Ltd Reg. No. 954009

The Random House Group Limited supports the Forest Stewardship Council® (FSC®),
the leading international forest-certification organisation. Our books carrying the FSC label
are printed on FSC®-certified paper. FSC is the only forest-certification scheme supported
by the leading environmental organisations, including Greenpeace. Our paper
procurement policy can be found at www.randomhouse.co.uk/environment

Typeset in 12/15pt Bembo by
Kestrel Data, Exeter, Devon.
Printed and bound by
CPI Group (UK) Ltd, Croydon, CR0 4YY.

2 4 6 8 10 9 7 5 3 1

In memory of Friederike Kommerell

1

THE CAR IS RUNNING on empty. There's been no sign of a garage for hours, and the petrol gauge is needling into red. I need to get off the road but the fields seem endless, intent on funnelling me along to the engine's last gasp. Even though it's still early the day is arid and hot. The breeze that whips through the open windows only stirs the air without cooling it.

I drive hunched over the wheel, expecting the car to die at any moment, and then I see a break in the green barrier. On my left a track cuts out of sight between wheat fields. I turn off, bumping over the rutted surface, not caring where it leads providing it's out of sight. The track dips down to a copse. Branches scratch at the windows as I edge the Audi into it and switch off the engine. It's cooler in the trees' shade. In the ticking quiet I can hear running water. I close my eyes and lean my head back, but there's no time to rest.

I need to keep moving.

I check the car's glove compartment. There's nothing identifying in it, only junk and a nearly full packet of cigarettes. Camels, my old brand. As I reach across the passenger side for them I become aware of a smell. Faint but unpleasant, like meat left out in the sun.

There's something smeared on the rich leather of the passenger seat, and also on the unspooled seatbelt that hangs on the floor.

The tough fabric is nearly severed at one point, and when I touch it my fingers come away sticky and dark.

My head swims to think I've driven all this way with it in plain view. I want to put as much distance as I can between myself and the car, but I can't leave it like this. Branches push against the door as I get out. There's a stream running through the copse, and my hands are shaking as I soak a cloth from the glove compartment in it. The seat wipes down easily enough but the blood has clogged in the seatbelt's weave. I rub off as much as I can, then rinse out the cloth in the stream. Water flares over my wrists like manacles of glass as I scrub my hands, scouring them with sand from the bottom. Even then they don't feel clean.

I splash water over my face, wincing as it stings the grazes on my cheek, and go back to the car. It's coated with dust from the roads, camouflaging the black paintwork. I use a rock to smash off the UK number plates, then fetch my rucksack from the boot. As I lift it out it snags on the mat covering the spare wheel. There's a glimpse of something white underneath. I pull the mat aside and my stomach knots when I see the polythene-wrapped parcel.

I lean against the car, my legs suddenly weak.

It's about the size of a bag of sugar, but the white powder it contains is far less innocent. I quickly look around, as though someone might be there to see. But there are only the trees, and the background hum of insects. I stare at the package, too tired to process this new complication. I don't want to take it with me, but I can't leave it here. Snatching it up, I cram it deep into my rucksack, slam the boot and walk away.

The wheat fields are still empty of life when I leave the copse. I fling the car's number plates and keys out into the tall stalks before taking out my phone. It's broken beyond hope of repair. Still walking, I remove the SIM card and snap it in two, then throw the pieces into one field and the phone in another.

I've no one to call anyway.

The road's grey tarmac ripples and distorts as the sun climbs higher. The few cars on it hardly seem to move, caught in the heat until they flash past in a sudden blare of colour. The rucksack rides high on my back, my own private monkey. I walk for almost an hour, until I feel I've put enough distance between myself and the car. Then, holding out my thumb, I begin to hitch.

My red hair is both an advantage and a handicap, attracting attention and announcing that I'm a foreigner in one single message. The first lift is from a young couple in an old Peugeot.

'*Où allez-vous?*' he asks, cigarette barely moving.

I struggle to switch linguistic gears. I'm more used to hearing French than speaking it recently, but that isn't what makes me pause. *Where am I going?*

I've no idea.

'Anywhere. I'm just travelling.'

I sit in the front passenger seat, the girl having moved uncomplainingly into the back. I'm glad the driver's wearing sunglasses, because it gives me an excuse to keep mine on. They cover the worst of the bruising on my face.

He glances at my red hair. 'British?'

'Yeah.'

'Your French is pretty good. Been over here long?'

For a second I struggle to answer. It already feels like a lifetime. 'Not really.'

'So how'd you learn?' the girl asks, leaning between the seats. She's dark-haired and plump, with an engagingly open face.

'I used to come over a lot when I was younger. And I'm . . . I like French films.'

I shut up then, realizing I'm giving away more than I intended. Luckily, neither of them seem interested. 'I prefer American movies myself,' he shrugs. 'So how long are you over for?'

'I don't know,' I say.

They drop me off at the outskirts of a small town. I dip into my small fund of euros to buy bread and cheese, a bottle of water and a disposable cigarette lighter. I also buy a baseball cap from an open-air market in the square. It's a cheap Nike copy but it'll keep the sun off me and help conceal my bruises. I know I'm being paranoid but I can't help it. I don't want to attract any more attention than I have to.

It's a relief to leave the town behind and head out into open country again. The sun burns down on the exposed back of my neck. After a kilometre or so I stop under a row of poplars and try to eat some of the baguette and cheese. I manage a few bites and then puke everything back, dry-heaving until my stomach's sore. When the spasms have passed I slump against a tree, feeling so wasted I want to just lie there and give up.

But I can't do that. My hand trembles as I flick a tongue of flame from the disposable lighter and draw on the cigarette. It's the first I've had in two years, but it tastes like a homecoming. I breathe out some of my tension along with the smoke, blessedly thinking of nothing for a few moments.

I finish the cigarette, then get to my feet and start walking again. I've only the vaguest idea of where I am but since I don't have any plans that doesn't matter. I stick out my thumb whenever a car passes, but that isn't often. The roads here are all secondary ones, backwaters where there's little traffic. By mid-afternoon, a Citroën and a Renault later, I've covered less than twenty kilometres. The lifts have all been short, locals travelling to the next town or village, but now even they have dried up. The road is so quiet I can believe the rest of the world has forgotten about me. The only sound is the scrape of my boots and the incessant drone of insects. There's no shade, and I'm thankful for the cap's protection.

After I've been walking for what seems an age, the open fields are replaced by a dense wood of chestnut trees. It's fenced off by strands of old barbed wire, but the broad-leaved branches still offer some respite from the sun.

I carefully ease the rucksack from my sore shoulders and take a drink of water. There's only a couple of inches left. Blood warm, it barely touches my thirst before it's gone. I should have bought another bottle, I think. But then I should have done a lot of things. It's too late to change any of them now.

I squint down the road. It runs arrow straight, shimmering in the heat and empty as far as the eye can see. I screw the top back on the water, willing a car to appear. None does. Christ, but it's hot. I feel parched again already. I take off my hat and push my fingers through my sweat-damp hair. A little way back down the road I remember passing a farm gate. I gnaw my lip, reluctant to retrace my steps. But my dry throat decides me. I've no idea how long it'll be till I reach another town, and it's too hot to go without water.

Picking up my rucksack, I head back the way I came.

The gate is trimmed with the same rusty barbed wire that borders the woods. A track runs from it, disappearing into the chestnut trees. A mailbox is fixed to the gatepost, on which faded white letters spell out the single word *Arnaud*. An old but solid-looking padlock hangs from a hasp on the gate, but it's been left unlocked.

I look once more down the road, but there's still nothing in sight. Mindful of the barbs, I push open the gate and go through. The track slopes gently uphill, then curves down to reveal a cluster of roofs through the trees. I follow it and find myself in a dusty courtyard. A dilapidated old farmhouse stands at its head, half-covered by a flimsy-looking scaffold. Opposite it is a large barn, and at one side a stable block in which is set an ancient, one-handed clock. There are no horses, but several dusty vehicles are parked in the open archways in various attitudes of permanence.

No one is in sight. A goat bleats from somewhere nearby, and a few hens scratch around in the dirt. Other than them the place could be deserted. I stop at the edge of the courtyard, reluctant to go any further. The farmhouse door is ajar. I go up to its un-painted panels and knock. There's a pause, then a woman's voice answers.

'*Qui est-ce?*'

I push open the door. After the bright courtyard the interior seems impenetrably dark. It's a second or two before I make out a woman sitting at a kitchen table, a moment longer to see that she's holding a baby.

I raise the empty bottle, hesitating while I marshal my question into French. 'Can I have some water, please?'

If she's discomfited by being disturbed by a stranger she doesn't show it. 'How did you get in here?' she asks, her voice calm and unhurried.

'The gate was open.'

I feel like a trespasser as she regards me. She sets the baby down in a wooden high chair. 'Would you like a glass of water as well?'

'That'd be great.'

She takes the bottle to the sink, filling first it and then a large glass at the tap. I drink it gratefully. The water is icy and has an earthy tang of iron.

'Thank you,' I say, handing her the empty glass.

'Will you padlock the gate behind you?' she asks. 'It shouldn't have been left open.'

'OK. Thanks again.'

I can feel her eyes on me as I walk across the sunny courtyard. I follow the track up through the wood to the road. It's as quiet as before. I lock the gate and keep on walking. Every now and then I'll glance back to see if a car is coming, but there's only the sun-baked tarmac. I hook my thumbs under the rucksack straps to take some of the weight. It feels heavier when I remember what's in it, so I clear my mind and concentrate on putting one foot in front of the other.

The drone of an engine gradually detaches itself from the overheated silence. I turn and see something approaching, a dark speck distorted by the heat. At first it seems to hover unmoving above a reflection of itself. Then its tyres stretch downwards and touch the road, and it becomes a blue car speeding towards me.

I'm already stepping out from the shade of the trees when I notice there's something on its roof. Realization comes a moment later. I vault over the barbed-wire fence, snagging my jeans and landing awkwardly because of the rucksack. Without stopping, I plunge into the woods as the note of the car's engine grows louder. When it sounds almost on top of me I duck down behind a tree and look back at the road.

The police car blurs past. I listen for any signs of it slowing, any indication that they've seen me. But the sound of its engine steadily dwindles to nothing. I rest my head against the tree. I know I'm overreacting, that the French police probably won't care about me, but I'm too jumpy to take the chance. And I daren't risk my rucksack being searched.

There's a bitter taste in my mouth. Blood; I've bitten through my lip. I spit to clear it and take the water bottle from my rucksack. My hands are trembling as I rinse my mouth, then take stock of where I am.

The wood is set on a shallow hillside, and some distance away I can see the glimmer of a lake through the trees. To one side of it are the roofs of farm buildings, small and insignificant at this distance. I guess they must be where I asked for water, so I'm probably still on their land.

I stand up and brush off the twigs and soil that cling to my jeans. My T-shirt is stuck to me with sweat. It's so hot the air seems scorched. I look at the lake again, wishing I could swim in it. But that's not going to happen, and I need to keep moving. Taking another swig of water, I step away from the tree and cry out as something seizes my foot.

I drop to my knees as pain lances up my leg. My left foot is engulfed in a pair of black, semicircular jaws. I try to pull free but the movement sends fresh hurt searing up the length of my leg.

'Jesus!'

I stop moving, sucking in panicked breaths. I've stepped in some sort of iron hunting trap, hidden away in a knotted tangle of tree roots. It clamps my foot from mid-instep to above the ankle, its jagged teeth piercing the tough leather of my boot. They've stabbed so deep into my flesh that I can feel them nuzzling coldly against the bone.

I squeeze my eyes shut, trying to deny the sight. 'Oh, fuck! *Fuck!*'

But that doesn't get me anywhere. Shucking off the rucksack, I shift to a better position and take hold of the trap's jaws. They don't budge. Bracing my free foot against a tree root I try again. This time I'm rewarded by the tiniest sense of give, but not nearly enough. My arms quiver with the strain as the metal edges bite into my hands. Slowly, I let it ease shut and sit back, gasping.

Rubbing the sore patches on my hands, I study the trap more closely. It's crudely made, lightly ochred with rust but not enough to suggest it's been lying here very long. If anything, the oil on the hinges looks fresh. Worryingly so, in fact. Trying not to think what that might mean, I turn my attention to the chain that tethers it in place. It's short and leads to a wooden spike buried among the tree roots. A few tugs are enough to convince me that I'm wasting my time trying to pull it out.

Sitting with my trapped leg stuck out in front of me, I put my

hand down to push myself upright and feel something wet. The
bottle of water is lying where I dropped it, most of its contents
soaking into the dry earth. I snatch it up, even though it's already
spilled as much as it's going to. Taking a careful sip, I re-cap
what's left and try to think.

OK, stay calm. The initial pain has evolved into a throbbing,
like toothache, that extends up my shin. Blood is beginning
to soak through the leather of my boot. Except for the buzz
of insects the sun-dappled woods are silent. I look over at the
distant roofs of the farm buildings. They're too far away for
anyone to hear me shout, but I don't want to do that anyway.
Not unless I have to.

I rummage through my rucksack for my pocketknife. I know
it's in there somewhere, but as I search for it my fingers encounter
something else. I pull it out and a shock runs through me.

The photograph is dog-eared and faded. I'd no idea it was
in the rucksack; I'd forgotten I even had it. The girl's face is
almost obscured by a crease, distorting her smile. Behind her
is the whiteness of Brighton Pier, vivid against a blue sky. Her
hair is blonde and sun-bleached, her face tanned and healthy.
Happy.

I feel dizzy. The trees seem to tilt as I put the photograph
away. I take deep breaths, willing myself not to lose it. The past's
gone. There's nothing I can do to change it, and the present is
more than enough to worry about. I find my pocketknife and
open it up. There's a three-inch blade, a bottle opener and a
corkscrew, but nothing for dismantling iron traps. Jamming the
blade between the jaws, I try to prise them open and fall back
as it snaps.

I throw the broken knife down and look around for something else. There's a dead branch nearby. It's out of reach but I
use a smaller one to drag it closer, then wedge its thickest end
between the jaws. The metal gouges at the wood but the trap

slowly begins to open. I apply more pressure, gritting my own teeth as the iron ones start to pull out of my flesh.

'Yes! Come *on*!'

The stick breaks. The jaws spring together again.

I scream.

When the pain subsides I'm lying flat on my back. I push my-self up and fling the stick impotently at the trap. 'Bastard!'

I can't pretend any longer that this isn't serious. Even if I could free my foot I doubt I could walk very far on it. But I'd willingly settle for that problem, because not being able to free myself is far more frightening.

Happy now? You've brought this on yourself. Blanking out those thoughts, I try to focus on the more immediate problem. Using the knife's corkscrew, I start digging around the spike that holds the trap in place. It's a futile attempt but allows me to vent some emotion by stabbing the ground and tree roots. Eventually, I let the knife fall and slump back against the trunk.

The sun has sunk noticeably lower. It won't be dark for hours yet, but the thought of having to lie there all night is terrifying. I rack my brain for ideas, but there's only one thing left I can do.

I take a deep breath and yell.

My shout dies away without an echo. I doubt it will have carried to the farm I went to earlier. I yell louder, in English and French, shouting until my voice grows hoarse and my throat hurts.

'Somebody!' I half-sob and then, more quietly, 'Please.' The words seem absorbed by the afternoon heat, lost amongst the trees. In their aftermath, the silence descends again.

I know then that I'm not going anywhere.

By next morning I'm feverish. I've taken my sleeping bag from the rucksack and draped it over me during the night, but I still shivered fitfully through most of it. My foot throbs with a dull agony, pulsing to the beat of my blood. It's swollen to above the ankle. Although I've unlaced the boot as best I can, the leather, which is now black and sticky, is stretched drum tight. It feels like a vast boil, waiting to burst.

At first light I try to shout again, but the dryness of my throat reduces it to a hoarse croak. Soon even that is too much effort. I try to think of other ways to attract attention, and for a while become excited at the idea of setting fire to the tree I'm under. I go as far as pawing in my pockets for the cigarette lighter before I come to my senses.

The fact that I was seriously considering it scares me.

But the lucidity doesn't last long. As the sun rises, stoking itself towards a mid-morning heat, I push off the sleeping bag. I'm burning up, and have accomplished the neat fever-trick of being soaked with sweat while I'm shaking uncontrollably. I look at my foot with hate, wishing I could gnaw it off like a trapped animal. For a while I think I am, can taste my own skin and blood and bone as I bite at my leg. Then I'm sitting propped against the tree again, and the only thing biting into my foot is the half-moon of iron.

I come and go from myself, submerged in garbled, overheated fantasies. At some point I open my eyes and see a face peering at me. It's a girl's, beautiful and Madonna-like. It seems to merge with the one in the photograph, racking me with guilt and grief.

'I'm sorry,' I say, or think I say. 'I'm sorry.'

I stare at the face, hoping for a sign of forgiveness. But as I look the shape of the skull behind it begins to shine through, peeling away the surface beauty to show the rot and dissolution underneath.

A new pain bursts in me, a fresh agony that bears me away on its crest. From far away there's the sound of someone screaming. As it grows fainter I hear voices speaking a language I recognize

17

but can't decode. Before it fades altogether, a few words present themselves with the clarity of a church bell.

'*Doucement. Essayez d'être calme.*'

Gently, I can understand. But I'm puzzled by why they need to be quiet.

Then the pain sweeps me up and I cease to exist.

London

THE SKYLIGHT IS FOGGED with condensation. Rain sweeps against it with a noise like a drum roll. Our smudged reflections hang above us as we lie on the bed, misted doppel-gangers trapped in the glass.

Chloe has gone distant again. I know her moods well enough not to push, to leave her to herself until she returns of her own accord. She stares up through the skylight, blonde hair catching the glow from the seashell–lamp she bought from a flea market. Her eyes are blue and unblinking. I feel, as I always do, that I could pass my hand over them without any reaction from her. I want to ask what she's thinking, but I don't. I'm frightened she might tell me.

The air is cold and damp on my bare chest. At the other side of the room a blank canvas stands untouched on Chloe's easel. It's been blank for weeks now. The reek of oil and turpentine, for so long the smell I've associated with the small flat, has faded until it's barely noticeable.

I feel her stir beside me.

'Do you ever think about dying?' she asks.

2

THERE'S AN EYE STARING down at me. It's black but clouded at the centre by a cataract, a grey fog hung with dark shapes. A series of lines spread out from it like ripples. At some point they resolve into the graining on a piece of wood. The eye becomes a knot, the fog a spider's web stretched over it like a dusty blanket. It's littered with the husks of long-dead insects. No sign of the spider, though.

I don't know how long I stare up at it before I recognize it as a wooden beam, rough and dark with age. Sometime after that I realize I'm awake. I don't feel any compulsion to move; I'm warm and comfortable, and for the moment that's enough. My mind is empty, content to stare up at the spider's web above me. But as soon as I think that it's no longer true. With consciousness come questions and a flurry of panic: who, what, when?

Where?

I raise my head and look around.

I'm lying in bed, in a place I don't recognize. It isn't a hospital or a police cell. Sunlight angles in through a single small window. The beam I've been staring at is a rafter, part of a triangular wooden ribcage that extends to the floor at either side. Slivers of daylight glint through gaps in the overlapping shingles of the roof. A loft, then. Some kind of barn, by the look of it. It's long, with bare floorboards and gables at either end, one of which my bed is pushed against. Junk and furniture, most of it broken, is stacked against the unplastered stone walls. There's a musty smell that speaks of age, old wood and stone. It's hot, though not uncomfortably so.

The light coming through the dusty glass has a fresh, early quality. I'm still wearing my watch, which tells me that it's seven o'clock. As if to confirm that it's morning the hoarse crowing of a cockerel sounds from somewhere outside.

I've no idea where I am or what I'm doing here. Then I move and the sudden pain at the end of my leg gives an effective jolt to my short-term memory. I throw back the sheet that covers me and see with relief that my foot is still there. It's bound in a white bandage, from which the tips of my toes poke like radishes. I give them a tentative wiggle. It hurts, but not nearly so much as before.

It's only then I realize that I'm naked. My jeans and T-shirt are on the back of a wooden chair next to the bed. They've been folded and look freshly washed. My boots are on the floorboards next to them, and an attempt has been made to clean the damaged one. But the leather is darkened with bloodstains, and the rips from the trap's teeth are beyond repair.

Lowering the sheet, I try to recall what happened between my stepping in the trap and waking here. There's nothing, but now other memories are presenting themselves. Caught in the wood, hitch-hiking and abandoning the car. And then I remember the events that led to me being here in the first place.

Oh, Jesus, I think, passing a hand over my face as it all comes back.

The sight of my rucksack leaning against an old black rocking horse snaps me out of it. Remembering what's in it, I sit up. Too quickly: I close my eyes, fighting a wave of nausea as the room spins. It's only just begun to fade when I hear footsteps approaching from below. Then a section of the floor gives a loud creak and swings open.

An arm pushes the trapdoor back, and then a woman steps up into the loft. I've seen her before, I realize; at the farmhouse with the baby. Which settles the question of where I am, if not why. She hesitates when she sees me.

'You're awake,' she says.

It takes a moment to register that she's spoken in English. Strongly accented and a little halting, but fluent enough. Feeling rough stone behind me, I find I've backed myself up against the wall. One hand has gripped the sheet into a sweaty knot.

I make myself let go. She stops a little way from the bed, which I've realized is just a mattress lying on the floorboards.

'How do you feel?' Her voice is low and quiet. She's wearing a sleeveless shirt and well-worn jeans. There's nothing threatening about her, but the sluggish computer of my brain seems stalled. My throat hurts when I try to speak. I swallow, try again.

'My foot . . .'

'It was badly cut. But don't worry, it's all right.'

Don't worry? I look around. 'Where am I?'

She doesn't answer straight away, struggling either to understand the question or formulate her answer. I repeat it, this time in French.

'You're at the farm. Where you came for water.' Her voice is more fluid in her own language, but there's still a hesitancy about it, as though she's vetting herself before she speaks.

'Is this . . . it looks like a barn?'

'There's no room in the house.' Her grey eyes are calm. 'My sister found you in the woods. She fetched me and we brought you here.'

I have a fleeting image of a girl's face, then it's gone. None of this is making sense. My head is still so muzzy that I'm not sure how much of what I remember is real or delirium.

'How long have I been here?'

'We found you three days ago.'

Three *days*?

There are vague impressions of pain and sweat, of cool hands and reassuring words, but they could just be dreams. I can feel panic bubbling up in me again. I watch anxiously as she takes a twist of tissue from her pocket and unwraps a large white tablet.

'What's that?'

'Only an antibiotic. We've been giving them to you while you were unconscious. You've been feverish, and the wound's infected.'

I glance at the tent made by my foot under the sheet, all my other fears suddenly relegated.

'How bad is it?'

She picks up a bottle from by the bed and pours water into a glass. 'It's healing. But you won't be able to walk on it for a while.'

If she's lying, I can't tell. 'What happened? There was a trap . . .'

'Later. You need to rest. Here.'

She holds out the tablet and glass. I take them, too confused to think straight. But there's an air of quiet reserve about her that's strangely calming. She could be a year or two either side of thirty, slim but with a fullness of breast and hip. The dark hair is cut straight above the nape of her neck, and every now and again she tucks one side back behind an ear in a gesture that seems more habit than affectation. The only striking feature about her is her eyes, which, above the tired-looking shadows, are a dark and smoky grey.

I feel them on me now, solemn and unreadable as I swallow the tablet. I wash it down with water, first taking only a sip, then gulping it as I realize how thirsty I am.

'More?' she asks, as I finish. I nod and hold out the glass.

'There's fresh water in the bottles by the bed. Try to drink as much as you can. And if the pain gets bad take two of these.'

She holds up a bottle of tablets. On cue my foot begins to throb, the pain only a shadow of its former glory but there all the same. I try not to show it, but there's something about the calm grey eyes that makes me think I'm not fooling her.

'How did you know I was English?'

She answers without hesitation. 'I looked in your passport.'

My mouth is abruptly dry, regardless of the water. 'You went in my rucksack?'

'Only to find out who you were.'

Her expression is grave without being apologetic. I try not to glance over at the rucksack, but my heart is thumping harder in my chest.

'I have to go now,' she tells me. 'Try to rest. I'll get you something to eat soon.'

I just nod, suddenly anxious for her to leave. I wait until she's gone, the trapdoor lowered behind her, then drag my rucksack over. Relieved of its weight, the rocking horse nods backwards and forwards. I open the rucksack and plunge my hand inside, feeling nothing except clothes. Then, just when I'm convinced it's gone, my fingers encounter a crinkle of plastic.

I don't know whether I'm relieved or sorry.

The package doesn't seem to have been disturbed. It sits heavily in my hand, its solid weight like an accusation. I should have got rid of it when I had the chance. Too late now. I wrap it in a T-shirt and tuck it back at the bottom of my rucksack, covering it with the rest of my clothes. I check that my passport and money are also still there. They are, but as I put them back my fingers touch a square of glossy card.

Not wanting to, but unable to help myself, I take the photograph out again. There's a pain lodged under my breastbone as I look at the girl's face smiling in the sunlight, and on impulse

I grip the photograph's edge to tear it in half. But I can't do it. Instead, I smooth out the crease and put it back into the pocket.

Suddenly I'm exhausted. And more confused than ever. The woman didn't really tell me anything, especially not why I'm in a barn instead of a hospital. Belatedly, something else registers. After the woman closed the trapdoor there was another noise, the solid *thunk* of metal on wood.

The sound of a bolt being shot into place.

My bandaged foot throbs as I swing my legs off the mattress. Ignoring it, I stand up and almost fall over. I lean against the stone wall, waiting until the loft has stopped spinning, then try taking a step. My foot shrieks under my weight and I pitch forward, grabbing onto the chair and causing something to rattle hollowly inside its base. It's a commode, I realize, noticing for the first time the pressure in my bladder.

But that will have to wait. It's obvious I'm not going to get far, but I can't go back to bed until I know. Supporting myself on the dusty furniture stacked against the walls, I lurch over to the trapdoor. There's an iron ring set into it. Gripping onto an old bureau, I take hold and pull. There's a slight give, then it sticks fast.

It's bolted.

I fight down a fresh surge of panic. I can't imagine any reason for me to be locked up here, at least nothing good. But there's no question of trying to force the bolt. Even if I could find something to wrench it open, just getting this far has taken everything out of me. I use the commode, glad of that small relief, then collapse back onto the mattress. I'm coated with a greasy sheen of sweat, and my head and foot are both throbbing.

I take two painkillers and lie back, but I'm too fretful to sleep. My foot is starting to quieten when there's a soft noise from the trapdoor. There's a grating whisper as the bolt is eased back, then with a creak the hatch swings open.

It's someone else this time, a girl. I haven't seen her before, but as she lowers the trapdoor the play of light on her face strikes a discordant note of memory. She's carrying a tray, and smiles shyly when she sees I'm sitting up. I hastily drape the sheet over my groin, preserving my modesty like a Renaissance nude. She lowers her eyes, trying not to grin.

'I've brought you something to eat.'

She looks in her late teens, strikingly pretty even in a faded T-shirt and jeans. She's wearing pink flip-flops, and the sight of them is both incongruous and oddly reassuring.

'It's only bread and milk,' she says, setting the tray beside the bed. 'Mathilde said you shouldn't have a lot just yet.'

'Mathilde?'

'My sister.'

The other woman, of course. There isn't much of a resemblance between them. The girl's hair is lighter, almost blonde, and hangs to her shoulders. Her eyes are a paler shade of her sister's grey, and the bridge of her nose has a slight bump where it's been broken; a minor imperfection that somehow adds to the whole.

She keeps darting quick looks at me, smiling all the while. It puts engaging dimples in her cheeks.

'I'm Gretchen,' she says. It isn't a French name, but as soon as she says it I think it fits. 'I'm glad you're awake. You've been ill for days.'

Now I understand why she looks familiar: the Madonna-like face from my delirium wasn't a hallucination after all. 'You're the one who found me?'

'Yes.' She looks embarrassed but pleased. 'Well, it was Lulu really.'

'Lulu?'

'Our dog. She started barking. I thought she'd seen a rabbit. You looked dead at first, you were so still. There were flies all over you. Then you made a noise, so I knew you weren't.' She gives me a quick look. 'We had an awful time getting you out of the trap. We had to prise it open with a crowbar. You were struggling and yelling all sorts of things.'

I try to keep my voice level. 'Like what?'

'Oh, just rambling.' She goes to the other side of the bed and leans against the rocking horse. 'You were delirious, and most of it was in English, so I didn't understand. But you stopped when we got your foot out.'

From the way she talks there might be nothing unusual about the situation. 'Who's *we*?'

'Me and Mathilde.'

'Just the two of you? You brought me up here by yourselves?'

'Of course.' Her mouth forms a playful moue. 'You're not so heavy.'

'No, but . . . How come I'm not in hospital? Didn't you phone for an ambulance?'

'We don't have a phone.' She doesn't appear to see anything odd about it. 'Anyway, there was no need. Mathilde knows how to look after wounds and things. Papa was out with Georges so she didn't want to— Well, we managed by ourselves.'

I don't know what she was about to say or who Georges is, but there are too many other things to think about. 'Is Mathilde a nurse?'

'Oh, no. But she cared for Maman before she died. And she's used to looking after the animals when they hurt themselves. The sanglochons are always squabbling or cutting themselves on the fence.'

I haven't a clue what a sanglochon is and don't care. 'You didn't even fetch a doctor?'

'I've told you, there was no need.' She sounds annoyed. 'I don't know why you're getting so upset. You should be grateful we looked after you.'

This whole situation is becoming more surreal, but I'm in

no position to antagonize anyone. 'I am. It's just . . . a bit confusing.'

Mollified, she perches on the rocking horse. Her eyes go to my face. 'What happened to your cheek? Did you fall when you stepped in the trap?'

'Uh . . . I must have.' I'd forgotten the bruising. I touch it, and the soreness sparks memories that set my heart thumping. I drop my hand and try to focus on the present. 'The trap didn't look very old. Any idea what it was doing there?'

She nods. 'It's one of Papa's.'

I don't know what shocks me more, the casual way she admits it or the implication that there are more of them.

'You mean you *knew* about it?'

'Of course. Papa made lots. He's the only one who knows exactly where they are, but he's told us whereabouts in the woods we need to be careful.'

She pronounces it *p'pah*, two soft expellations that push out her lips. The diminutive sounds more reverential than childish, but I've other things on my mind right now.

'What's he trying to catch? Bears?'

I've a vague notion that there might still be brown bears in the Pyrenees, even though that's nowhere near here. I know I'm clutching at straws, but it's the only halfway innocent explanation I can think of.

Gretchen's laughter kills even that faint hope. 'No, of course not! The traps are to stop people trespassing.'

She says it as though it's all perfectly normal. I look at my foot, unwilling to believe it even now. 'You're not serious?'

'The woods are our property. If anyone goes in them it serves them right.' Her manner has cooled, become haughty. 'What were you doing on our land anyway?'

Hiding from a police car. It's starting to seem the lesser of two evils. 'I needed to pee.'

Gretchen giggles, her temper vanishing. 'Bet you wish you'd waited.' I manage a weak smile. She considers me, running her fingers over the rocking horse's coarse mane.

'Mathilde says you're a backpacker. Are you here on vacation?'

'Something like that.'

'You speak French very well. Do you have a French girlfriend?'

I shake my head.

'An English one, then?'

'No. When can I leave?'

Gretchen stops stroking the horse's mane. 'Why? Are you in a hurry?'

'People are expecting me. They'll be worried.'

The lie sounds unconvincing even to me. She leans back, bracing her arms on the rocking horse so that her breasts push against the T-shirt. I look away.

'You can't leave yet,' she says. 'You aren't well enough. You almost died, you know. You should be grateful.'

That's the second time she's said that: it almost sounds like a threat. Behind her the trapdoor is still open, and for a moment I consider making a run for it. Then reality kicks in: running isn't an option at the moment.

'I'd better get back,' she says.

The rocking horse nods violently as she stands up. Her jeans mould themselves around her as she bends to lift the heavy trapdoor. She makes more of a production of it than is strictly necessary, and the quick look she shoots my way as she straightens makes me think it isn't accidental.

'Can you leave the hatch open?' I ask. 'There's no air up here.'

Gretchen's laugh is light and girlish. 'Of course there is, or how could you breathe? You'd be dead.'

The trapdoor settles shut behind her. Even though I'm waiting for it, I still flinch when I hear the bolt slide home.

I don't remember falling asleep. When I wake the loft is dusky and full of shadows. Tilting my watch to catch the light, I see that it's after nine. I listen for some sounds of life outside, but there's nothing. Not a whisper, not so much as a bird or insect.

I feel like the last man on earth.

The tray of food that Gretchen brought is still by the bed. There's a wine bottle filled with water, a bowl of milk and two chunks of what looks to be home-made bread. I'm surprised to find that I'm famished. The milk is cool and thick, with a strong taste that makes me think it might be goat's. I dunk the bread in it, convinced it won't even scratch the surface of my hunger, but whoever prepared it knew better than I do. After a few mouthfuls my appetite withers and dies. I push away what's left and lie back.

Sated for the moment, I stare at the darkening roof beams as my foot throbs like a metronome. I can't decide if I'm a prisoner or a patient. I've obviously been well looked after, and if the farm's wood is full of illegal traps that explains why they didn't want to risk taking me to a hospital.

But after that my reasoning takes a darker track. I'm still locked in a barn, and nobody knows I'm here. What would have happened if I'd got worse? And what happens when I'm recovered? Are they just going to let me walk out of here?

Sweating and fretful, I toss and turn on the lumpy mattress, trying to get comfortable. At some point I drift off to sleep again. I'm back in the copse, scrubbing at the bloodstains on the seatbelt. They won't come off, and the belt is thumping against the seat. It's getting louder, and then I'm awake and in the loft, and the thumping is coming from the floor. There's time to realize that someone is coming up the steps, then there's the screech of the bolt being drawn and the trapdoor is flung open.

It falls back with a bang. A man stamps up the last few steps, carrying a lamp and a hunting rifle. He's in his fifties, thickset and barrel-bodied with iron-grey hair and a seamed, sun-dried face. Right now it's set in angry lines. The rifle isn't pointed at me but it's held in such a way I can see he's thinking about it.

I back up against the wall as he clomps over the boards. Mathilde hurries up the steps after him.

'Don't! Please!'

He ignores her. He stops at the foot of the bed and glares down at me. The yellow glow from the lamp forms a cavern of light around us, throwing the rest of the room into darkness.

'Get out,' he snarls. There's an aura of suppressed fury about him, a barely checked desire to drag me from the bed.

Mathilde takes hold of his arm. 'At least let him stay till the morning—'

He shrugs her off without taking his eyes from me. 'Get out,' he repeats.

I don't have much choice. I throw back the sheet, pretending to be unconcerned about my nakedness. Hobbling over to the commode, I sit down while I get dressed, trying not to wince as my jeans drag over my bandaged foot. There's no way I can force it into a boot, so I cram the damaged one into my rucksack with the rest of my things. That done, I precariously stand up.

The man – I'm guessing he's the father – jerks the stock of the rifle towards the trapdoor. 'Go on.'

'All right, I'm going,' I tell him, trying for a scrap of dignity.

And I want to; I'm just not sure I can make it across the loft. I pause, gathering all my strength for the long trek across the room. Mathilde's face is expressionless, as if she's isolated herself from what's going on.

He takes a step towards me. 'Move.'

I'm in no condition to argue. Gripping the aluminium frame of my rucksack with both hands, I push it in front of me, using it for support. The distance to the trapdoor is covered in a series of slow, painful hops. Mathilde and her father follow. In the light from his lamp I see Gretchen standing on the steps with the baby. Amazingly, it's still asleep, slumped bonelessly across her shoulder. But her eyes are wide, and she looks scared as she moves out of my way.

I push the rucksack right up to the trapdoor's edge. Anger and humiliation have got me this far, but I don't know how I'm going to get any further. The clean clothes are already sticking to me. I can smell my own body, the stink of illness in my sweat. Lowering myself carefully, I sit on the edge of the trapdoor and slip my arms through the rucksack's straps. Then, sliding forwards, I grope with my good foot for a step and put my weight on it. Holding onto the lip of the trapdoor, I feel a sense of triumph as I hop to the next step down. I've barely chance to register the quick footfalls behind me before something thumps into my back and I fly into the darkness.

The breath bursts from me as I tumble to the bottom of the steps. I crash into bottles, scattering them across the floor in a tuneless jangle. I lie where I've fallen, stunned and breathless. The rucksack's dead weight pins me down. I try to push myself up, and then someone is there helping me.

'Are you all right?'

It's Mathilde. Before I can answer her father comes down the steps, the light from his lamp glinting off the scattered bottles. Behind him I can make out Gretchen in the shadows. The baby has woken and started crying, but no one seems to notice. We're on a wooden gallery, a platform midway between the loft and what I guess, beneath the shadows, is the ground. I shrug free of Mathilde's hands and grab a bottle by its neck, struggling to my feet to face him.

'Keep back!' I yell in English, my French deserting me. I raise the bottle warningly, my injured foot clamouring as I totter for balance.

The man reaches the bottom of the steps, the centre of the yellow aura thrown by the lamp. His hands tighten on the rifle as he gives the bottle a contemptuous glance, then starts forward again. Mathilde steps between us.

'Don't. Please.'

I'm not sure which of us she's talking to. But her father stops, glaring at me with silent venom.

'I was trying to leave!' I shout.

My voice is unsteady. The adrenalin has left me weak and trembling. All at once I'm aware of the cool heft of the bottle in my hand. I sway, nauseous, and for an instant I'm back on a dark street, with another scene of blood and violence about to replay itself.

I let the bottle drop. It rolls slowly across the dusty floor-boards and bumps against the others with a muted chink. The baby is still howling, struggling in Gretchen's arms, but no one says anything as I lurch towards the next flight of steps. Almost immediately my legs give way and I collapse to my knees. I'm nearly weeping with frustration but I don't have the strength to get up. Then Mathilde is there again, sliding her arm under mine.

'I can manage,' I say petulantly. She doesn't take any notice. She eases me back against a wooden beam before turning to her father.

'He's in no condition to go anywhere.'

His face is made hard by the lamplight. 'That's not my problem. I don't want him here.'

If not for your trap I wouldn't be, I want to say, but nothing comes out. I feel dizzy. I close my eyes and put my head back against the beam, letting their voices swirl around me.

'He's a stranger, he wasn't to know.'

'I don't care, he's not staying.'

'Would you rather the police pick him up?'

The mention of the police makes me lift my head, but the warning doesn't seem to have anything to do with me. In my febrile state it seems that they're locked in some private contest, adults talking over the head of a child who won't understand. Probably they don't want the police to know about the traps, I think, but I'm too tired to wonder about it for long.

'Just let him stay for a few days,' Mathilde's voice pleads. 'Until he's got his strength back.'

Her father's answer is a long time coming. He glares at me, then turns away with a contemptuous snort. 'Do what you like. Just keep him out of my sight.'

He goes to the steps. 'The lamp,' Mathilde says, when he reaches them. He pauses, and I can see him contemplating taking it and leaving us without light. Then he sets the lamp down and descends into the darkness below without another word.

Mathilde fetches it and crouches next to me. 'Can you stand?'

When I don't respond she repeats it in English. I still don't say anything, but begin to heave myself up. Without asking, she takes the rucksack from my shoulders.

'Lean on me.'

I don't want to, but I've no option. Beneath the thin cotton, her shoulder is firm and warm. She puts an arm around my waist. Her head comes to my chin.

Gretchen moves out of the shadows as we reach the bottom of the steps. The baby is still red-faced and teary, but more curious now than upset.

'I told you to stay in the house with Michel,' Mathilde says. There's the slightest edge to her voice.

'I only wanted to help.'

'I can manage. Take him back to the house.'

'Why should I have to look after him all the time? He's your baby.'

'Please, just do as you're told.'

Gretchen's face hardens. She brushes past us, her flip–flops slapping angrily on the steps. I feel rather than hear Mathilde's sigh.

'Come on,' she says, wearily.

She supports most of my weight as we go up the steps and over to the bed. It takes for ever. I collapse onto the mattress, barely aware of her going away again. A minute later she's back, carrying the rucksack and lamp. She sets both by the bed.

'Your father didn't know I was here, did he?' I say. 'You didn't tell him.'

Mathilde is outside the lamp's circle of light. I can't make out her face, don't know if she's looking at me or not.

'We'll talk tomorrow,' she says, and leaves me alone in the loft.

London

THE RUCKSACK BOUNCES ON my back as I run to where the car waits on the slip road, its engine ticking over. It's a yellow VW Beetle, battered and rust-pitted but right now the most beautiful car in the world as far as I'm concerned. It's going dark and I'm numb from standing in the cold for the past two hours, cursing the drivers who've whipped past me onto the motorway without a glance.

I open the passenger door, surprised to see that the driver is a lone girl.

'Where are you going?' she asks.

'London, but the next services will do,' I tell her, desperate to get out of the bitter wind.

'I'm going to Earl's Court, if that's any good?'

'Thanks, that's fantastic.' I can catch a tube from there. I'm staying in Kilburn, renting the spare room in a flat whose owner is away for a month. After that I haven't a clue what I'll do.

But that's a problem for another day. I dump my rucksack on the back seat, careful to avoid the large artist's portfolio lying there, and then sit up front. She has the window wound down slightly on her side but turns the heating up full blast to compensate.

'I've got to have the window open because the exhaust leaks in,' she explains. 'I mean to get it fixed, but . . .'

Her shrug eloquently suggests a combination of what-can-
you-do and can't-be-bothered.

'I'm Sean.' I have to raise my voice over the competing roar of
the open window and hot air blowing from the heater.

She gives me a quick smile. 'Chloe.'

She's maybe a year or two younger than me, slender, with
pale-blonde cropped hair and deep-blue eyes. Pretty.

'Are you warm enough now?' she asks. 'If I leave the heater on
full for too long it overheats.'

I tell her I'm fine. She reaches out to the dash and adjusts the
temperature. Her hand is long-fingered and fine-boned. A thin
silver band encircles her wrist.

'I'm surprised you stopped. You don't often find girls taking a
chance on hitch-hikers. Not that I'm complaining,' I add.

'You've got to take some chances. Besides, you looked harmless enough.'

'Thanks,' I laugh.

She smiles. 'What are you going to London for?'

'Looking for work.'

'So it's a permanent move?'

'If I can find a job, yeah.' Although just the word *permanent*
makes me feel uneasy.

'What sort of work are you looking for?'

'Whatever's going. Bar work, labouring. Anything that pays.'

She glances over. 'You a graduate?'

'I was, a while back. But I wanted to travel, so I took some
time out.' *Some time* is deliberately vague: I'm uncomfortably
aware of how it's slipped by. Most of my peers have settled into
careers by now, but I've drifted from one job to the next without
any real direction.

'Good for you,' Chloe says. 'I went backpacking to Thailand
for six months. God, absolutely brilliant! Where'd you go?'

'Uh . . . just to France.'

'Oh.'

'I plan to go back,' I add, defensively. 'You know, when I've got enough money together.'

That's not likely to be any time soon. Even though I've stopped smoking, the casual jobs I've been doing don't pay much. She nods, but isn't really listening. I grip my seat as she suddenly switches lanes to overtake a van, pulling out in front of a speeding Jaguar that's forced to brake. It flashes its lights indignantly, jammed right up to our rear bumper. The VW's engine becomes shrill, gathering just enough speed to draw alongside the van without being able to pass.

'Come on, dickhead,' Chloe mutters, glaring past me at the van driver. I watch anxiously as she keeps her foot down until we're just ahead before darting back into lane. The van blares its horn and drops back, putting space between itself and the mad young woman in the VW. I let go of the seat, my hands aching from the pressure.

'So what did you study?' Chloe continues, unperturbed.

'Film.'

'Making or theory?'

'Theory.' I realize I'm sounding defensive.

She grinned. 'Ah, now I get it. *That's* why you went to France. Don't tell me – Truffaut's your hero. No, Godard.'

'No,' I say, stung. 'Well . . .'

'I knew it!'

I can't keep from grinning as well, happy to find someone to argue with. 'You don't like French cinema?'

'I don't *dis*like it, I just think the whole New Wave thing was overrated. It's just *dull*. Give me the Americans any day. Scorsese. *Taxi Driver.*' She turns one hand palm up in a there-you-are gesture. 'And he didn't have to use black and white to make his point.'

'What about *Raging Bull*?'

'That was a deliberate reference to the boxing footage of the forties and fifties. And it made the blood in the fight scenes more effective. What has Truffaut done to compare with that?'

'Oh, come *on* . . . !'

The argument runs on, both of us warming to it, until she has to stop at a services for petrol. I'm surprised to see from a road sign that London is only twenty miles away; the journey has passed too quickly. Chloe waves away my offer of a contribution towards the fuel, but as we set off again she seems distracted.

'So what about you?' I ask after a while. I motion towards the portfolio on the back seat. 'Are you an artist?'

'That's what I tell myself.' She smiles, but there's something sad about it. 'For a day job I work as a waitress and try to sell the odd illustration to advertising agencies. I'm on my way back from a pitch now. A big-eyed little kitten for a cat-food manufacturer.'

I'm not sure what to say. 'Congratulations.'

'They didn't go for it.' A shrug. 'It was rubbish anyway.'

The conversation dies after that. Suburbs have sprung up around us, and it isn't long before we reach the outskirts of London. She taps her fingers on the wheel in frustration with the slow-moving traffic. When we get to Earl's Court she pulls up by the tube station, leaving the engine running. I look for an excuse to delay the moment, but she's waiting for me to go.

'Well . . . thanks for the lift.'

'No problem.'

I'd made up my mind to ask for her phone number, but she seems miles away already. I climb out and start to pull my rucksack from the back seat.

'I know some people at a private language school,' she says abruptly. 'The place is short of an English teacher. I could put a word in for you, if you like.'

The offer takes me by surprise. 'I don't have any teaching qualifications.'

She shrugs this away. 'You can do a TEFL course easily enough. Do you speak French?'

'Yes, but . . .'

'Well, there you go. They get a lot of French students.'

I've never taught a thing in my life, never even considered it as a possibility. Still, it isn't as though I've any other plans.

'Thanks, that'd be great.' I take a deep breath. 'How about, I don't know . . . going for a drink sometime?'

3

I'M BY THE STREAM where I left the car. The water is clear and fast-running, but when I immerse my hands I can't feel it. It's warm, the same temperature as my body. I try to clean the clotted blood from beneath my nails, but the more I try the more there seems to be. The water is stained by it, a dark viscous red that now flows above my wrists. I know my own blood is somehow leaching into it but that only makes me scrub harder. When I take my arms from the stream they're red and dripping up to the elbows.

I'm about to put them back in when I feel a cramp in my foot.

I turn to look at it, and I'm lying in bed. Sunlight fills the loft. This time there's no lapse, no confusion. I know straight away where I am. I lie staring up at the roof, waiting until the last vestiges of the dream have faded and my heart rate has returned to normal.

The dream might have passed but my foot still hurts. And now other aches announce themselves throughout my body in a roll-call of abuse. Remembering, I look at my rucksack.

A boot print is clearly stamped on it.

Seeing it brings a rush of feeling. *Jesus. What was all that about?* I feel angry and shamed, and more confused than ever, but beneath all that is a sense of relief.

At least I'm not a prisoner.

The black rocking horse regards me evilly from one rolling eye as I take my morning painkillers, washing them down with lukewarm water from one of the wine bottles by the bed. According to my watch, it's eight o'clock, but there's no sign of breakfast. I'm hungry again, which I take to be a good sign. I'm still weak, but not with the will-sapping fatigue of yesterday. Apart from a few grazes and a lump where I hit my head, even the tumble downstairs doesn't seem to have damaged anything. Except my pride.

A distant sound disrupts the morning quiet: the whiplash of a shot, quickly followed by another. Probably Mathilde's father out venting his aggression on the local wildlife, I think, remembering the hunting rifle the old bastard was carrying. I stare up at the cobwebbed ceiling, trying to make sense of everything that's happened. I've got to get out of this place, that much is certain. Yet as soon as I start to think beyond the immediate future, despair overwhelms me. I was in enough trouble before I stepped in the trap. No matter what happens here, that won't have changed.

But I can't let myself dwell on that. First things first. Pain spears my bandaged foot when I try putting my weight on it, ending any hope of walking. Keeping it off the ground, I hop over to the window. The glass is dirty and hung with cobwebs that resemble rotting muslin. One of them, suspended from a rafter, strokes almost imperceptibly across my eyes. I wipe it off and look outside. Below me is a sunlit field striped with rows of grapevines. They run down to a wood, beyond which is a small lake. It must be the same one I saw just before I stepped in the trap, but from here its surface looks mirror smooth, coloured pale blue with reflected sky.

There's another unemphatic report of a rifle, this time followed by the excited barking of a dog. I can't see anyone, but just thinking of the man I met last night knots my stomach. Careful to avoid the photograph this time, I rummage in my rucksack for the pack of Camels I took from the car. The cigarette tastes foul but I need something to calm my nerves. I smoke it sitting propped up on the bed, legs stretched out and my back against the rough wall. The pack is half empty now; I'll need to ration what's left.

I don't know how long they'll have to last.

After I finish the cigarette I dig out a pair of boxer shorts, a psychological prop in case Papa comes calling again. I've only just pulled them on when I hear someone on the steps. I tense before realizing the footsteps aren't heavy enough to be his.

The trapdoor swings open to reveal Mathilde. I look past her, and relax when I see she's alone. Her face is unreadable as she approaches the bed.

'Good morning.'

She's carrying a tray on which is my breakfast and a bowl of water. There's also a roll of bandage and an old first-aid tin, and she has a worn towel folded over one arm.

'I've brought a clean dressing for your foot,' she says. 'It needs changing.'

She puts the tray, down on the mattress and perches on the edge beside it. Tucking her hair behind her ear, she turns her attention to my foot.

'How is it?' she asks, unwrapping the bandage.

'No better for being kicked downstairs.'

I don't mean to snap, but I can't help it. My nerves are ragged as Mathilde continues to remove the soiled bandage. Underneath, my foot is covered with clotted pads of surgical dressing, glued to my flesh with dried blood. One sticks when she tries to peel it away, making me suck in my breath.

'Sorry.'

Taking a wad of cotton wool from the tin, she dips it in the water and begins to soak the dressings. One by one they come away, pulling only slightly. Her shoulder obscures my view as she works.

'I heard someone shooting earlier,' I say.

'My father. He goes hunting.'

'I assume that was him last night?'

'Yes.' She pushes a wisp of hair behind her ear. It's always the same side, I notice; her left. 'I'm sorry. My father's a private man. He's doesn't like strangers.'

'So I gathered.' There's no point taking it out on her, though. She's not responsible for her father, and she's evidently created problems for herself by helping me. 'Why didn't you take me to a hospital? Because you knew he'd get in trouble over the traps?'

She looks up at me, the grey eyes solemn. 'I thought it was best to treat you myself. But if you'd needed urgent attention I would have made sure you had it.'

Bizarrely enough, I believe her. She looks at me for a moment longer, then continues removing the dressings.

'So I'm free to leave whenever I want?'

'Of course.'

'Then why was the trapdoor locked?'

'You were delirious. I didn't want you to fall down the steps and hurt yourself.'

The irony of that almost makes me laugh. 'Or risk your father seeing me?'

Her silence confirms it. I can't imagine how she hoped to keep my presence a secret, but having met the man I can understand why she didn't want him to know. I'm just glad it was his daughters who stumbled across me in the wood.

'How did you get me up here without him knowing about it?' I ask.

'My father has a bad back and sleeps most afternoons. We used a blanket to carry you from the woods. And we rested a lot.' Mathilde gently works at the last dressing, which doesn't want to come off. 'The barn's basic but it's dry and comfortable. You're welcome to stay as long as you want. At least until you're stronger.'

'Aren't you worried I'll tell the police what happened?'

'That's up to you.'

Again, I find myself wanting to believe her. Until I remember the plastic package hidden in my rucksack. Maybe she has a reason for thinking I won't go to the police, I think, suddenly clammy. But then Mathilde removes the last dressing, and when I see what's underneath I forget everything else.

'Oh shit!'

My entire foot is swollen and discoloured. The toenails look like tiny mother-of-pearl buttons against the purple skin, and matching arcs of puncture wounds march from above my ankle to my instep. They're puffy and inflamed; ugly little mouths crusted with dried blood and yellow pus. The black bristles of stitches protrude from them like the legs of dead spiders.

'Is it all right?' I ask anxiously.

Mathilde's face is expressionless as she soaks another piece of cotton wool and begins cleaning the puncture wounds. 'It's healing.'

'Healing?' I stare at my foot. The throbbing seems to grow worse now I can see it. 'Don't you think a doctor should take a look?'

She continues to dab away calmly. 'I told you there was an infection. That's what the antibiotics are for. But if you'd rather I fetched a doctor . . .'

The sight of the deformed thing on the end of my leg makes me tempted. But a doctor would mean questions, for me as well as them. And there's something about Mathilde that instils trust.

'So long as you think it's OK . . .'

She gives a nod of assent. Picking up a clean piece of cotton wool, she resumes her gentle wiping. The skin of her hands is rough, her fingernails cut short and square. No rings, I notice.

When the last wound is clean she exchanges the cotton wool for a tube of ointment. 'This will sting.'

It does. But by the time she's finished my foot doesn't look nearly so bad, more like a limb than a piece of chopped meat. Mathilde puts on clean dressing pads and winds the fresh bandage around them. Her movements are deft and economical. The tip of a white ear pokes through her dark hair. The shadows beneath her eyes seem more distinct than I've noticed before. There's a vulnerability about her, and yet an air of inviolability too, a self-containment that's not easily breached. Even though there's been no real apology over what's happened, I somehow feel that I'm the one who's been unreasonable.

I clear my throat when she finishes binding my foot. 'Thanks.'

Mathilde begins putting the first-aid things back in the tin. 'I'll bring hot water later, so you can wash. Would you like something to read? I can pick out some books if you like.'

I'm too restless to read. 'No thanks. How long before I can get out of here?'

'It depends on how soon you feel able to walk.' Mathilde looks around the junk stacked against the loft's walls. 'There should be a pair of crutches in here somewhere. I can try to find them later.'

'Whose were they?' I ask, suddenly worried that I might not be the first person confined here.

'My mother's.'

Picking up the tray, she goes to the trapdoor. I watch her descend through the hatch, half-expecting to see it swing shut behind her. But this time she leaves it open.

Breakfast is more substantial today, soft-boiled eggs broken up with butter and black pepper, a piece of bread, a glass of milk.

I'm famished, but I eat slowly, wanting to make it last. When I've finished I look at my watch. Hardly any time seems to have passed since I last checked. The loft is already growing hot, filling with a resinous scent of warm wood and dust. I've started to sweat already. The stubble on my jaw – several days' worth – has begun to itch and I'm conscious that I smell, a rank odour born of illness and heat. No wonder Mathilde wanted me to wash. I run my tongue over my teeth, aware also of how bad my mouth tastes. I didn't need the bottle last night: I could have knocked Papa out just by breathing on him.

I take my toothbrush and paste from my rucksack and scrub my teeth till my gums hurt. That done, I lie back down on the bed. But I'm too fretful to sleep, and with nothing to occupy it my mind starts to swarm.

Supporting myself against the wall, I hop across to the maze of old furniture to look for the crutches. Mathilde said she'd find them but I can't see any reason to wait. Everything up here seems maimed or incomplete, covered by a grey blanket of dust. There are three-legged chairs and mildewed suitcases, dressers with gaping drawers like missing teeth. Stacked behind a topless bureau I come across half a dozen old picture frames, ornate but empty of canvas or glass. Without thinking I begin sorting through the pile before remembering I don't know anyone now who'd use them. The thought brings a dull ache of guilt.

Pushing the frames out of sight, I carry on searching for the crutches.

I find one thrust under a tangle of broken chairs, but there's no sign of its twin. Still, one is better than nothing. The crutch is made of scuffed and battered aluminium. Once I've brushed it free of cobwebs and adjusted its height, I practise clumping up and down the loft. The effort soon tires me, but it feels good to be mobile again.

Sweating and out of breath, I take my prize back to the

mattress. But as soon as I lie down my thoughts start buzzing. I need a distraction. Most of my music library was on my phone, but I keep my old MP3 player in my rucksack. There's a decent selection of tracks on it, and thankfully its batteries aren't dead. Slipping in the earphones, I set it on shuffle and close my eyes as the music wraps around my head.

I don't know if it's a change in the pressure of air brushing my bare skin or movement against the light from the window that tells me someone else is in the room. At the same time something bumps against the bed. I jerk upright, opening my eyes to see someone standing next to it.

'God!'

Gretchen gives a start, almost dropping the bucket she's carrying. She hurriedly sets it down as I stop the music and take off the earphones. The sudden silence is like the lights coming up mid-film in a cinema.

'Sorry. I thought you were asleep,' she mumbles.

'How long have you been there?' I ask. She looks blank, and I realize I've spoken in English. I repeat it in French.

'Not long.' Her reply is so faint it's almost not there. 'Mathilde's sent water so you can wash.'

Gretchen keeps her head bowed, as if she's embarrassed to look at me. She's flushed from carrying the bucket up to the loft, sweating enough to make her cotton dress cling. Her eyes go to the earphones hanging from my neck.

'What are you listening to?'

It's an English band that's popular in Europe as well, but when I tell her the name I can see she hasn't heard of them. I offer her the earphones. 'Here, see what you think.'

Her face lights up, then she shakes her head. 'I'd better not. I'm not supposed to talk to you.'

'Is that what your father says?' Her face is answer enough. 'You're talking to me now.'

'That's different. Mathilde's busy with Michel. And Papa's with Georges.'

Meaning he doesn't know she's here. I put the earphones down. I don't want any more trouble, either for her or for me. 'Who's Georges? Mathilde's husband?'

Gretchen's mentioned him before, but the suggestion makes her laugh. 'No, Georges is *old*! He just helps Papa.' Still smiling, her eyes go to the earphones again. 'Maybe I can have a quick listen . . .'

She perches on the edge of the mattress and puts them on. Her eyes widen when I start the music.

'IT'S LOUD!'

I turn the volume down but she shakes her head.

'NO, IT'S ALL RIGHT, I LIKE IT!'

I wince and put my finger to my lips.

'SOR— sorry.'

She listens with a childlike expression of delight, nodding her head to the beat. Her face is flawless except for the slight bump on her nose, but without it her prettiness would be bland. I let the music run on to the next track as well. When it stops she can't hide her disappointment. Self-conscious again, she takes off the earphones.

'Thank you.'

'You can copy the album if you like.'

She looks at her lap. 'I can't. We don't have a computer. We don't even have a CD player any more, not since it broke.'

It's like they live in a different era. It doesn't seem much of a life for her. Or her sister, come to that. Even so, part of me isn't sorry the farm is so cut off. 'So what do you do for entertainment?'

She hitches a shoulder. 'There's TV. Or I take Michel out for walks.'

'How old are you?'

'Eighteen.'

It's older than I expect. Not because she doesn't look it, but there's an immaturity about her that suggests a younger girl. 'What about friends?'

'There are some local boys . . .' A smile curves her mouth as she winds the wire from the earphones around a finger. It turns into a moue of disappointment. 'But Papa doesn't like me seeing anyone from town. He says they're all idiots and I shouldn't waste my time.'

Somehow that doesn't surprise me. 'Don't you get bored?'

'Sometimes. This is Papa's farm, though. If you live here you have to obey his rules. Most of the time, anyway.'

It's said with a sly glance towards me. I know I'm supposed to ask what she means but I don't. 'Is that why he was angry last night? Because you'd broken his rules?'

The pretty features sour. 'That was Mathilde's fault. She should have told him about you. She'd no right to keep it a secret.'

'So you decided to tell him?'

'Why shouldn't I?' She raises her chin defiantly, for a moment looking disconcertingly like her father. 'Mathilde's always bossing me around, telling me what I can and can't do. But once you were awake it was only fair to Papa. It's his farm, not hers.'

I'm not going to argue. I've enough problems of my own without getting embroiled in a family dispute. And I'm suddenly aware that Gretchen seems to be sitting nearer to me than she was before. Close enough to feel the heat radiating off her bare arms.

'You'd better get back before you're missed.' I take the earphones from her and set them aside, in the process putting a little more space between us. She looks surprised but gets to her feet.

'Can I listen again sometime?'

'What about your father?'

She shrugs. 'He won't know.'

So much for obeying Papa's rules. But I get the feeling that Gretchen only obeys the ones she wants to. There's a self-conscious swing to her hips as she gets up and crosses to the trapdoor. I look away, pretending to be busy with the earphones. When her footsteps have receded down the steps I sigh and put them down again. I feel sorry for Gretchen, but the last thing I need is a bored eighteen-year-old stirring things up. Especially one with a psychotic father. I just want to get away from here, the sooner the better.

And then what?

The loft seems hotter and more airless than usual. I light a cigarette and lean back against the stone wall, blowing smoke at the ceiling. As I watch the blue haze disperse, I think about what Mathilde and Gretchen have said. In all the talk about the farm there's one person no one's mentioned.

The father of Mathilde's baby.

4

I GO OUTSIDE FOR the first time next morning.
    After Gretchen's visit, I slept for most of the previous day, rousing at one point to find a tray of food beside the bed. I managed to keep awake long enough to eat the clear chicken broth and bread, and then fell asleep again, still intending to get up and practise some more on the crutch.

But when I wake in the morning the food and rest have done their work. I feel much better. The loft is brightly sunlit but not yet hot, and there's a blessed freshness I know won't last until midday. Yesterday's supper tray has been replaced with one containing breakfast – eggs and butter again. I didn't hear anybody, but I'm growing used to the idea of someone coming here while I'm asleep.

I eat ravenously, wiping the last of the yolk up with bread and wishing there was more. The bucket of water Gretchen brought is still by the mattress, so I wash the dried sweat off myself as best I can and then take out my razor to shave. By my reckoning there's almost a week's worth of stubble to hack off, but at the last second I change my mind. There's no mirror in the loft, not even a broken one, but the bristles feel strange under my fingers. Not quite a beard but not like my own face either. It doesn't feel like me any more.

I decide that's no bad thing.

For a few minutes I feel deliciously clean, then I start to sweat again. The loft's small window is open, but all that achieves is to stir the air slightly without cooling it. The heat is already building up, and with it my restlessness. I get up, intending to practise with the crutch, and then see the trapdoor standing open. I hobble over to it and look down into the barn.

Nobody said I had to stay up here.

Negotiating the steps is much easier this time. Tucking the crutch under one arm, I go down backwards, using them like a ladder. My foot gives a warning throb every now and then, but by leaning my knee on each step I can keep my weight off it.

I stop to rest on the small landing I fell onto when Mathilde's father pushed me down the steps. The empty bottles I knocked over have been stood upright again, but even in daylight the barn is dank and gloomy. The stone walls are windowless, with the only light coming from the large open entrance. The air is cooler, and as I descend the last few steps I notice a scent of stale wine mixed in with the musty odour of stone and wood. At some time in the past the barn has been a small winery. There's an empty metal vat and the cobbles are scarred from where other equipment has been removed. One section of them has been torn up and replaced with concrete, new-looking but already starting to crack.

There's a tap jutting from one wall. Water spatters out onto the cobbles when I turn it and cup my hand underneath to take a few mouthfuls. It's teeth-achingly cold but tastes wonderfully fresh. Splashing a little onto my face, I go to the tall wine rack that stands nearby. It's half full of unlabelled bottles, but a good number of their corks are stained where the wine has seeped through. I sniff at one of them, wrinkling my nose at the sour taint, before going to the barn's entrance.

Sunlight pours in from outside. I stand for a moment, taking in the scene through the open doors. The world outside is framed between them, a vivid picture set against the dark walls. Like a cinema screen.

Squinting against the brightness, I lean on my crutch and walk into it.

It's like stepping into Technicolor. I breathe deeply, enjoying the scents of wild flowers and herbs. My legs are shaky, but after the smothering loft it's good to feel sun on my face. Careful of my bandaged foot, I lower myself to the dusty ground to take in the view.

Directly in front of the barn is the vine field I saw from the loft's window. It's bordered by woods, and further off I can just make out the blue of the lake through the trees. Beyond that is the pale gold of surrounding fields, stretching as far as I can see. Whatever else the farm might be, it's certainly peaceful. The air simmers with the drone of crickets and the occasional bleating of unseen goats, but nothing else disturbs the quiet. No cars, no machinery, no people.

I close my eyes and soak it up.

Gradually, another noise makes itself known. A rhythmic metallic creaking. I look up to see an old man walking towards me on a track through the grapevines. He's a bandy-legged, wiry old thing, and the creaking is caused by the galvanized buckets he carries swinging slightly on their handles. His sparse hair is almost white, his face baked the colour of old oak. He barely seems taller than me even though I'm sitting down. But there's a sinewy strength about him, and the forearms below his rolled shirtsleeves are thick with knotted muscle.

This must be the Georges Gretchen mentioned, I guess. I give him a nod. 'Morning.'

There's no acknowledgement. He continues unhurriedly towards the barn, walking right past me as though I'm not there. Unsettled, I turn my head to see what he's doing as he goes inside. There's the clatter of the buckets being set down, and a moment later I hear the tinny drumming of water as they're filled at the tap. After a few minutes the sound of water cuts off and he re-emerges. He doesn't so much as glance at me as he heads back down the track, forearms bulging as though they're stuffed with walnuts under the weight of the buckets.

'Nice to meet you, too,' I say to his back.

I watch him trudge across the vine field and into the wood at the far side. He's soon out of sight, and I wonder what he needs the buckets of water for down there. The farm doesn't seem to have any livestock except for chickens and the goats I've heard bleating, and no visible crops except for the grapes. Judging from the sour-smelling corks and the spaces where wine-making equipment used to be in the barn, it hardly seems to be making a success as a vineyard, either.

I wonder how they survive.

I've rested enough, and my exposed skin is starting to sting and redden. Struggling to my feet, I settle the crutch under my arm and shuffle around the corner of the barn. There's a roofless outhouse with an old hole-in-the-ground privy, and beyond that is the courtyard I remember from before. It's even hotter here. Heat shimmers off the cobbles, and the scaffolded house where I asked for water looks bleached in the sun. A weathervane shaped like a cockerel leans precariously on its sway-backed roof, waiting for the air to move.

A few hens peck lazily at the dirt but there's no one about. Thinking about water has made me thirsty again. There's the tap in the barn, but after the old man's indifference I feel a need to see another human face, if only briefly. I limp towards the house, the crutch slipping on the smooth cobbles. Off to one side, the broken clock on the stable block is still caught in its frozen sweep, single hand poised at twenty to nothing. The farm vehicles parked below it don't seem to have moved since the last time I was here. A dusty van and trailer sit outside the stable block as though they've died there, while the radiator of a decrepit tractor pokes from one of the arched stalls like the muzzle of a sleeping dog. Another stall is occupied by an old blacksmith's forge. Strips of iron are propped against it, but it isn't until I see the crude triangular teeth on one that I realize what I'm looking at.

Feeling a memory-ache in my foot, I carry on to the house.

It's even more run-down than I remember. The scaffold covers half of it, and unpainted shutters hang from the windows like the wings of dead moths. The ground at the foot of the wall is speckled with pieces of mortar that have fallen out, hardly any more cohesive than sand. A half-hearted attempt has been made to repair the crumbling stonework but it's obviously been abandoned. And not recently: the scaffolding is rusted in places, and so is a chisel that lies on the ground under it. When I nudge it with my crutch it leaves a perfect imprint of itself on the cobbles.

The kitchen door stands open. Wiping the sweat from my eyes, I knock on it. 'Hello?'

There's no answer. As I turn away I notice another door further down, unpainted and warped. Labouring over on my crutch, I knock again, then tentatively push it open. It creaks back on unoiled hinges. Inside is dark, and even from the door-way I can feel the damp chill that spills out.

'What are you doing?'

I spin round, performing an intricate dance with my crutch and good foot to keep my balance. Mathilde's father has materialized from behind the stable block. There's a canvas bag slung over his shoulder, from which the bloodied leg of a rabbit protrudes. More worrying is the rifle he carries, which is pointing right at me.

'Are you deaf? I said what are you doing?'

In the daylight he's older than I'd thought, nearer sixty than fifty, with brown melanomas of sun and age freckling his forehead. He isn't particularly tall, short in the legs and long in the body, but he's still a bull of a man.

I take a second to steady myself on the crutch, trying not to look at the rifle. 'Nothing.'

He glances at the open door behind me. 'Why are you prowling around?'

'I wanted a drink of water.'

'There's a tap in the barn.'

'I know, but I needed some fresh air.'

'I thought you said you wanted water?' Against the weathered skin his pale-grey eyes look like chips of dirty ice. They go to the crutch and harden even more. 'Where'd you get that from?'

'I found it in the loft.'

'And who said you could use it?'

'No one.'

I'm not sure why I'm protecting Mathilde but it doesn't seem right to lay the blame on her. I'm acutely aware of the rifle as her father's chin juts aggressively.

'So you thought you'd just help yourself? What else were you planning on stealing?'

'I wasn't . . .' All at once I'm too exhausted to argue. The sun seems to be pressing down on me, sapping what little strength I have left. 'Look, I didn't think anyone would mind. I'll put it back.'

I start to go past him back to the barn, but he's blocking my way. He makes no attempt to move, keeping the rifle pointed at me. Until now I'd thought he was just posturing, but looking into the hard eyes I feel a sudden doubt. I'm past caring though. I stare back at him, and as the moment drags on a rhythmic creaking gradually impinges on the silence. Looking across the courtyard, I see Georges unhurriedly walking towards us, a rusted bucket swinging from one hand.

If he's surprised to find his employer holding someone at

gunpoint he doesn't show it. 'I've repaired the fence as best I can, M'sieur Arnaud. It'll do for now but it still needs replacing.'

I might as well be invisible for all the notice he takes of me. Arnaud – I'd forgotten the name on the mailbox at the gate until now – has flushed deeper than ever.

'All right.'

It's a dismissal, but the old man doesn't take the hint. 'Will you be coming down to have a look?'

Arnaud huffs in irritation. 'Yes, in a while.'

Georges gives a satisfied nod and goes back across the courtyard, still without reacting to my presence. I'm forced to lean on the crutch again as Arnaud regards me, jaw working as though he's chewing his words.

But before he can spit them out a dog bursts from behind the stables. It's a young springer spaniel, all lolling tongue and flapping ears. When it sees us it comes bounding past Arnaud and prances around me. I try not to show how much I'm shaking as I reach down to tousle its head.

'Here!' Arnaud's voice cracks out. The dog dithers, torn between obedience and enjoying the attention. 'Get here, damn you!'

Obedience wins. The spaniel slinks over, cowering and wagging its tail frantically. It would tie a white flag to it if it could, but as Arnaud raises his hand to cuff it a spasm contorts his features. He stiffens, one hand going to his back as he straightens in pain.

'Mathilde! *Mathilde!*' he bellows.

She hurries around the side of the house, the baby in one arm and a basket of soil-covered vegetables in the other. A flash of what could be dismay passes across her face when she sees us, then it's wiped clean of any emotion.

'What's he doing out here?' Arnaud demands. 'I told you to keep him out of my way!'

Mathilde tries to soothe the baby, who has started crying at his grandfather's raised voice. 'I'm sorry, I—'

'It's not her fault,' I say.

Arnaud turns back to me, his face livid. 'I wasn't talking to you!'

'I only came out for some fresh air,' I say wearily. 'I'll go back to the loft, OK?'

Arnaud sniffs. He looks at the baby, who is still howling, then reaches out for him.

'Give him to me.'

His hands look huge as he takes the child from Mathilde and holds him at eye level, gently rocking him from side to side. He still has the rifle tucked under his arm.

'Eh? What's this, Michel? You don't cry. Be a big boy for your grandfather.'

His voice is gruff but fond. The baby hiccups and beams toothlessly at him. Without taking his eyes from his grandson, Arnaud turns his head to speak to me over his shoulder.

'Get out of my sight.'

I spend the rest of the day sleeping. Or rather half-sleeping: in the airless loft I drift in and out between consciousness and dreaming. At one point I rouse to find a tray of food and a fresh bucket of water has been left beside the bed. By Mathilde, I guess: even though I said I didn't want a book there's an old card-bound copy of *Madame Bovary* on the tray as well.

Maybe it's by way of an apology for the run-in with her father.

The evening passes in a haze of heat and sweat. I lie in my boxers on top of the mattress, drugged by the spiced, cigar-box smell of the loft. For lack of anything else to do I make an attempt at *Madame Bovary*. But the archaic French is impenetrable, and I can't concentrate. The words blur and the book keeps falling from my hands, until eventually I give up and put it aside. I think it's too hot to sleep, but when I close my eyes I slide under so deeply it's like drowning.

I wake with a cry, images of blood on a darkened street stark in my mind. For a few seconds I can't remember where I am. The loft is in darkness, but a ghostly light spills through the open window. My hands are hot and sticky, and with the nightmare still vivid I expect to see them stained with blood. But it's only sweat.

The moon's light is bright enough for me to see my watch without turning on the lamp. It's just after midnight. I reach shakily for my cigarettes. Only three left: I've started smoking them a half at a time. I light the burned end of one I started earlier and draw the smoke into my lungs. A weight of despair refuses to lift. When I finish the cigarette, making it last right down to the filter, there's no question of going back to sleep.

The loft is humid and close, floodlit by the moon. A strip of light runs across the floor and hooks over the edge of the bed. I get out of bed and hop along its silver path to the window. The night has turned the landscape black and white. Beyond the shadows of the woods, the moon's twin shines from the mirrored lake. There's a metallic moistness to the air. I breathe it deeply, imagining submerging myself in the water, feeling its coolness lift even the weight of hair from my head.

An owl hoots. I realize I'm holding my breath and let it out. There isn't enough air. Suddenly claustrophobic, I seize the crutch and lamp and go to the trapdoor. I've left it open, and it looks like a hole into nothing. In the lamp's dull glow I lower myself down the steps.

I don't think about what I'm doing. The barn below is dark, but once outside the full moon is so bright I no longer need the lamp. I turn it off and leave it in the entrance. The night air soothes my bare skin, scented with trees and grass. I don't feel tired at all now, only a feverish desire to get to the lake.

I follow the track that Georges used earlier, limping past rows of vines. It's a monochrome world, all light and shadow. I pause at the edge of the woods to catch my breath. The trees form a solid wall of black at the edge of the vine field. The air is cooler here, dampening any sound. Moonlight drips indiscriminately through the branches. I shiver, wondering what I'm doing. I know I should turn back, but the lure of the lake is too strong.

This is the furthest I've walked on the crutch, and my breathing is laboured as I go through the wood. I trudge with my head down, so focused on what I'm doing that I don't notice the pale figure until it's right in front of me.

'Jesus!'

I stumble back. Now I see more of them, motionless shapes in the trees. My heart is thudding, but none of them move. As the shock of seeing them fades I realize why.

The wood is full of statues.

They crowd both sides of the track, stone men and women dappled by moonlight. I sag in relief, but still have to touch one to reassure myself that the lifelike limbs aren't, after all, flesh and blood. My fingers encounter only the roughness of lichen and smooth, hard stone.

I smile, shame-faced, and as I do the wood's quiet is shattered by a shriek. It's high-pitched and inhuman, seeming to go on and on before it abruptly stops. I stare into the blackness, gripping the flimsy crutch. Just a fox or owl, I tell myself. But I feel the hairs on the back of my neck prickle upright. I turn and look at the statues. They haven't moved, but now their blind scrutiny seems unnerving. Then the shriek comes again, and my nerve breaks.

All thoughts of the lake are forgotten as I lurch back up the shadowed track. My breath rasps in my ears, blood thumping as I struggle on the single crutch. Up ahead I can see the moonlit field through the trees, impossibly distant. Christ, have I really come so far? Then at last I'm out in the open, and orderly rows of vines replace the dark trees. I lumber on, panting for breath, until I reach the sanctuary of the barn once more. Gulping for air, I stop to retrieve the lamp and look back towards the wood. The track is empty, but I don't relax until I'm in my loft again with the trapdoor shut behind me.

I collapse onto the mattress, chest heaving and legs like jelly. I'm drenched with sweat, as wet as if I'd actually been in the lake. The idea of going down there, as if I could swim with my foot bandaged up, seems ridiculous now. I don't know what I was thinking. *Don't you? Really?*

All I want to do is sleep. But before I do I go back over to the trapdoor and slide a chest of drawers on top.

Feeling safe at last, I go to bed and sleep like the dead.

London

CALLUM WAS STILL RANTING when I came back from the bar. 'Oh, come *on*! Did we see the same film? Tell me, did we? I was watching *The Last Detail*, what were you watching?'

'All I'm saying is it's still reinforcing character stereotypes. You've got the, uh, the hardened wiseguy, the rookie, the token—'

'They're archetypes, not stereotypes! I can't believe you missed the entire fucking point of the—'

'I didn't miss anything, I just think it's, uh, I don't know—'

'Exactly!'

'Callum, why don't you shut up and let Jez finish?' Yasmin cuts in.

'I would if he wasn't talking shite!'

I put the drinks on the table. Beer for Callum, Yasmin and me, orange juice for Chloe, vodka for Jez. Chloe gives me a grin as I sit down.

Yasmin turns to me. 'Sean, tell Callum it's possible to object to aspects of a Jack Nicholson film without being burned at the stake for heresy.'

'Sean agrees with me,' Callum cuts in. Raw-boned and shaven-headed, his piercings add to the faintly pagan image he likes to cultivate. 'Nicholson is the finest actor of his generation, bar none!'

'He was a jobbing actor who got lucky,' Chloe says. She darts a quick look at me to show she's deliberately baiting Callum. As ever, he bites.

'Bollocks! I've got one thing to say to you, Chloe. *One Flew Over the Cuckoo's Nest*. That's it.' He sits back, crossing his arms as if the argument's won.

'That was a dream role. Any halfway decent actor could have run away with it,' Yasmin says, rolling her eyes. Her hair is tied back tonight, and she's wearing the loose dark clothes that Chloe once confided show she's feeling self-conscious about her weight.

'Oh, come on! What about *Chinatown*? Or *The Departed*?'

'What about them?' Chloe begins ticking off on her fingers. '*Witches of Eastwick*. *Mars Attacks*. *Batman*. Best actor of his generation? Sure.'

Jez furrows his brow. '*Batman* was OK. Not as good as *The Dark Knight*, though.'

No one takes any notice of him. He's been drinking all night and looks even more crumpled than usual, which is saying something. Like Callum, he's a teacher at the language school in Fulham where I've been working for the past few months. Yasmin, his girlfriend and Chloe's best friend from art college, used to work there as well before she got a better-paying job at the university.

I love Friday nights. Classes finish early, and afterwards a group of us will go for a drink before heading for one of the independent cinemas that are within a few tube stops of the school. Callum is passionate about film but blows hot and cold about his favourite actors, writers, directors. Not so many weeks before it was Terrence Malick he'd raved about. Recently, though, we'd seen a screening of *Carnal Knowledge*, so for the next few weeks Jack Nicholson was going to be It.

I take a drink of beer and stroke Chloe's thigh under the table.

She squeezes my hand and smiles, then stretches and pushes back her chair.

'I'd better be getting back.'

She bends and kisses me, her short hair momentarily touching my face, then goes over to the bar. The Domino is off the King's Road, close to one of our regular cinemas, but the main reason we go there is because it's where Chloe works. Dark and modern, with cool blue lights illuminating the bottles behind the black granite counter, we'd never be able to afford to come here if Chloe couldn't get us cheap drinks. She says her manager knows, so I suppose it must be OK. Still, I sometimes wonder if he realizes how generous he's being.

I watch her go behind the bar, laughing at something Tanja, one of the other girls, says as she begins serving.

'Chloe's doing all right, isn't she?' Yasmin says.

I turn to see that she's watching Chloe too. 'Sure. Why shouldn't she be?'

Yasmin smiles, throwing the comment away with a shrug. 'No reason. I was just thinking out loud.'

It seems an odd thing to say. But I'm distracted when I hear Callum begin rubbishing Kurosawa.

'Please, tell me you don't mean that,' I say, setting down my beer.

Five minutes later I've forgotten what Yasmin said.

But I remember again later that night. I have to wait until the last customers have gone, and Chloe has wiped down the bar and put away all the glasses, before we can go home.

Outside, Tanja is waiting for a lift from her boyfriend. We say goodnight and then set off back to the flat. It's too late for the tube and taxis are a rare luxury, but Earl's Court isn't too far to walk. It's cold, though. There's a full moon, and the beginnings of frost on the pavement glint like diamond chippings.

I open my coat and wrap it around us. Chloe puts her arm around me, a source of warmth against my chest. The shops we pass are shuttered and closed, the wire-clad placards for yesterday's *London Evening Standard* already old news. I suppose I should feel more nervous walking through this part of town at this time of night, but I never do. I've grown used to it, and with Chloe working at the bar it seems too familiar to harbour any threat.

We're laughing, quietly so as not to wake anyone, as we cross the road to the flat. Parked cars line the street, dark metal out-lines that radiate cold. Out of the corner of my eye I see a figure detach from the shadows and head for us.

I keep walking, my arm protectively around Chloe. The man is a tall and bulky shape in a thickly padded coat. He's wearing a beanie hat pulled down almost to his eyes.

'Got the time?' he asks.

His hands are in his coat pockets, but on the wrist of one I can see the gleam of a watch. My heart starts racing. We should have got a taxi.

'Ten past three,' I say, barely glancing at my own watch. It's a new one, a birthday present from Chloe. Without being obvious I try to put myself in front of her as he comes closer. One of his hands begins to slide from its pocket, and something metallic glints in the moonlight.

'Lenny?'

The man stops. From the way he sways he's either drunk or on something. Chloe steps forward.

'Lenny, it's me. Chloe.'

He looks at her for a moment, then gives the slightest of nods. His chin lifts in my direction. 'Who's this?'

'A friend.'

She's trying to hide it but I can hear the tightness in her voice. Whoever this man is, she's scared of him.

'A friend,' he echoes.

His hand is still halfway out of his pocket, as though he's not yet made a decision. I draw breath to speak, to ask who he is and what's going on. But Chloe clamps hold of my arm, squeezing it to silence me.

'Well . . . 'bye, Lenny.'

She pulls me away. Lenny stays where he is, but I can feel him staring after us. My legs move stiffly. When we reach the other side of the road I look back.

The street is empty.

'Who was that?'

I'm angry to realize I'm half-whispering. I feel Chloe shiver. Her face looks small and pale, whether from the cold or something else I can't tell.

'No one. I'm frozen, let's get inside.'

Our flat is on the top floor of a squat concrete block. We go up the stairwell that always smells of piss and unlock the door. The fumes of turpentine and oil paints settle thickly on the back of my tongue as soon as we enter. The place is hardly an ideal artist's studio, but the rent's affordable and the skylights set into the flat roof make it bright, if cold. Chloe's paintings are stacked against the living-room walls, white-edged rectangles whose images it's too dark to see. I'd been surprised at first by how representational her style is, expecting it to be bolder and more abstract. Instead there's an impressionistic quality and an almost chiaroscuro treatment of light that reminds me of film noir. I like it, although I have secret doubts about the unfinished portrait of me that stands on an easel by the window. Technically it's one of her best, but the expression on the face isn't one I recognize. Maybe I just don't know myself very well.

Neither of us makes any move to put on the light. I stand in the bedroom doorway, watching as Chloe switches on the electric fire. A faint hum comes from it as the elements begin to snap and glow yellow.

'So are you going to tell me what that was about?'

Chloe keeps her back to me as she begins to undress. 'Nothing. He's just someone I used to know.'

Something swells in my chest and throat. It takes me a moment to realize it's jealousy.

'You mean you used to go out with him?'

'With Lenny?' Her shock is unfeigned. 'God, no.'

'What, then?'

She comes over to me in her underwear. 'Sean . . .'

I move her arms from around me. I don't know whether I'm angry because I felt helpless outside, or because I suddenly feel I don't know her. She sighs.

'He used to be a customer in a bar I used to work at. OK? You get to meet all sorts. That's all.'

She looks up at me, eyes open and candid. In the familiar surroundings of the flat the memory of the encounter is already starting to fade. And I've no reason not to believe her.

'OK,' I say.

I undress and get into bed. We lie in the dark without touching, the air in the bedroom frigid even with the electric fire. Chloe stirs and moves over, kissing me, murmuring my name. We make love, but afterwards I lie awake, staring at the skylight.

'Yasmin said something weird tonight,' I tell her. 'That you were "doing all right". Why would she say that?'

'I don't know. That's Yasmin for you.'

'So there's nothing I should know?'

In the dark I can't see her face. But a glint of light from it tells me her eyes are open.

'Of course not,' she says. 'Why would there be?'

5

I'M PACKED AND READY to leave when Mathilde comes to the loft next morning. I know who it is before I see her, can already distinguish between her steady tread and the slap of Gretchen's flip-flops. Her eyes go to the fastened rucksack by the bed, but if she draws any conclusions she keeps them to herself. She's carrying a tray, on which is a plate of food and a roll of clean bandage. And also an extra treat this morning: a steaming bowl of coffee.

'I've brought your breakfast,' she says, setting down the tray. 'Can I change your dressing?'

I sit on the mattress and roll up the leg of my jeans. The bandage is frayed and filthy from my abortive night-time excursion. If not for that I could almost believe I'd dreamed the whole thing. In daylight, the memory of the silent assembly of statues seems unreal, and I've convinced myself the scream I heard was only a fox after all. Probably caught in one of Arnaud's traps.

I can sympathize.

'Will you drive me to the road later?' I ask, as Mathilde begins to unfasten the bandage. She makes no comment on its soiled condition.

'You're leaving?'

'Straight after breakfast. I'd like to make an early start.'

The decision was fully formed when I woke. If I can make

it down to the wood and back, then I'm fit enough to travel. I could walk to the road on my own, but there's no point in tiring myself before I start. I still don't know what I'll do or where I'll go, but my latest run-in with Arnaud has convinced me I'm better off taking my chances rather than staying here any longer.

Mathilde continues to unwrap the bandage. 'Are you sure?'

'If you can drive me as far as the road I can hitch from there.'

'As you wish.'

Even though I've no reason to, I feel disappointed by her lack of reaction. I watch as she removes the bandage and peels off the dressing pads. When the last covering comes away I'm relieved that my foot doesn't appear any worse. In fact it seems better; the swelling has gone down and the wounds themselves appear less livid.

'It doesn't look as bad, does it?' I say, hoping for confirmation.

Mathilde doesn't answer. She gently turns my foot this way and that, then lightly touches the lip of one wound.

'Does that hurt?'

'No.' I study her as she continues to examine it. 'Is it OK?'

She doesn't answer. Her face is impassive as she lays her hand on my forehead. 'Do you feel hot? Feverish?'

'No. Why?'

'You look a little flushed.'

She bends over my foot again. I put my hand on my forehead. I can't tell if it's hotter or not.

'Is the infection getting worse?'

There's the slightest of hesitations before she answers. 'I don't think so.'

The yellowish cast of the bruising around the wounds seems to take on a more sinister hue. I watch uneasily as she cleans my foot and begins to wrap it in the fresh bandage.

'Is something wrong?'

'I'm sure it's fine.' She keeps her head down, denying me her face. 'Sometimes these things need watching. But I understand if you're in a hurry to leave.'

I stare down at my foot, wrapped in pristine white again. Suddenly I'm aware of my aching muscles. It might just be from the exertion of the night before, but then again . . .

'Maybe I should give it another day?' I say.

'If you like. You're welcome to stay as long as you want.'

Mathilde's expression gives nothing away as she collects her things together and goes back down the steps. When she's gone I flex my foot, testing it. I don't *feel* feverish, but the last thing I need is to fall ill on some deserted French road. And it isn't as if I've anywhere specific to go, or a burning hurry to get there. Not any more. Another day won't make any difference.

It crosses my mind that maybe this is what Mathilde intended, but I dismiss the idea. My being here has caused her nothing but trouble. She's no more reason to want me to stay than I have.

At least, that's what I tell myself. But as I swallow the antibiotic and reach for my breakfast, I'm aware that what I feel more than anything is relief.

By midday the loft is unbearably hot, and the musty scent from the old wooden furniture makes my skin itch. I listen to music and then doze, waking to find my lunch waiting beside the open trapdoor. Rubbing my eyes, I decide to eat it outside. Arnaud warned me to keep out of his sight, but even he can't expect me to stay in the barn all day.

Going down the steps is tricky with the tray, but I manage by balancing it on them while I clamber down one at a time. Before I eat I use the outhouse and wash myself under the tap in the barn where Georges filled his buckets. The small act of self-sufficiency lifts my spirits, and I feel almost cheerful as I settle myself against the barn's wall. Even in the shade it's still stiflingly hot. As I chew the bread and cheese, I look over the vine field towards the lake. From where I sit, there's just the glimmer of water visible through the trees. There don't seem to be any ill effects from my stupid attempt to reach it last night. No fever has developed, no throb of renewed infection. Only an increasing tension that has nothing to do with my foot. God knows where I'll be this time tomorrow, but it'd be good to at least see the lake before I go.

Finishing my food, I settle myself on the crutch and set off down the track. In the daylight I can see that the vines look half dead. The leaves are mottled and curling at the edges, and the sparse clusters of grapes droop like tiny deflated balloons. No wonder the wine smells so bad.

The sun is merciless. I thought it would be easier walking on the track now I can see what I'm doing, but in the heat it seems longer than it did last night. It's rutted and uneven, with tyre marks set into it like concrete casts. The crutch skids and slips, and by the time I get to the end of the field I'm soaked with sweat. It's a relief to reach the shade of the wood. The trees don't seem remotely threatening in the daylight. Like the ones nearer the road, they're mainly chestnuts, and I'm grateful to be under their green canopy.

As I follow the track through them I find myself listening for a repetition of the scream I heard the night before. But there's nothing more sinister than the chirrup of crickets. The statues too have lost their menacing aspect. There are about a dozen of the stone figures by the track, clustered apparently at random in the thickest part of the wood. All are weathered and old, and now I see that most are damaged. A broken-hoofed Pan capers next to a featureless nymph, while nearby a noseless monk seems to raise his eyes in shock. Standing slightly apart from the others is a veiled woman, the stone artfully carved to resemble folds of cloth covering her face. A dark oil stain mars one of the hands clasped to her heart, staining it like blood.

I can't imagine what they're doing hidden away in the trees, but I decide I like the effect. Leaving them to their slow decay, I carry on down the track.

The lake isn't much further. Sunlight glints off it, dazzlingly bright. Edged with reeds, the water is so still it looks as though you could scoop a hole in its surface. Ducks, geese and water-birds glide across it, dragging V-shaped trails in their wake. I breathe in the scented air, feeling the knots of tension ease from my shoulders. I'm realistic enough this morning to know that I won't be going swimming, but the thought is no less seductive.

I walk up to the top of a bluff that overlooks the lake. A lone chestnut tree stands there, spreading its branches out over the water. It looks deep enough to dive into from here, but then I notice a murky shadow lurking like a basking shark a few yards out. A submerged rock, waiting for anyone careless enough to jump in from the bluff. I should have known, I think. Even the lake has traps in it.

I lower myself to the ground, leaning back against the tree as I gaze out over the water. Coming down here has been tiring but I'm glad I made the effort. I won't get another chance, and my foot doesn't seem any worse. The bandage Mathilde put on earlier is already grubby, but there are no fresh bloodstains and the ache is becoming more of an itch. My anxiety's cost me an-other day, but there'll be nothing to stop me leaving tomorrow. *And then what?*

I don't know.

If there's an upside to having stepped in the trap, it's that it's taken my mind off everything else. While I've been here I've been too preoccupied to worry about past or future, but that's about to end. One more night and then I'll be back where I started. On the run in a foreign country, with no idea what I'm going to do.

My hands are trembling as I reach for my cigarettes, but before

I can light one the springer spaniel erupts from the woods. The ducks on the edge of the lake scatter noisily as it charges after them. Arnaud, I think, stiffening, but it isn't Papa who follows. It's Gretchen and the baby.

The spaniel notices me first. It runs up to where I'm sitting under the tree, stubby tail thrashing.

'Good girl.'

Glad of the distraction, I fuss over it and try to keep it from trampling on my foot. Gretchen stops now that she's seen me. She's wearing a sleeveless cotton dress, a pale blue that accentuates her colouring. It's thin and faded, and her legs are bare except for flip-flops. But she'd still turn heads in any city street.

She carries the baby, Michel, perched on one hip like an undeveloped Siamese twin. A faded red cloth, corners knotted to form a bag, dangles from her free hand.

'Sorry if I startled you,' I say.

She glances towards the track, as if debating whether she should go back. Then her dimples make a fleeting appearance.

'You didn't.' She hoists the baby to a more comfortable position, flushed from carrying him in the heat. She raises the red cloth. 'We've come to feed the ducks.'

'I thought it was only people in towns who did things like that.'

'Michel likes it. And if they know they're going to be fed they'll stay here, so we can take one every now and then.'

'Take' being a euphemism for 'kill', of course. So much for sentiment. Gretchen unfastens the cloth and tips out the bread, sending the birds into a frenzy of splashing. Their raucous cries are joined by the dog's barks as it prances at the edge of the water.

'Lulu! Here, girl!'

She throws a stone for the spaniel. As it chases after it she comes up to the top of the bluff and sits down nearby, setting the baby down beside her. He finds a twig and starts playing with it.

I look back at the track, half-expecting to see Arnaud there with his rifle. But the wood is empty. I'm starting to feel uneasy, although I'm not sure if that's the thought of her father or if it's just being around Gretchen. She seems in no hurry to get back. The only sound is the dog chewing on the stone and Michel blowing spit bubbles. Apart from the ducks and geese, we're the only living souls here.

Giving a theatrical sigh, Gretchen takes hold of the front of her dress and wafts it back and forth.

'I'm too hot,' she says, glancing to see if I'm looking. 'I thought it might be cooler by the lake.'

I keep my eyes fixed on the water. 'Do you ever swim here?'

Gretchen stops fanning herself. 'No, Papa says it isn't safe. Anyway, I can't swim.'

She begins picking the tiny yellow flowers that grow in the grass and making them into a chain. The silence doesn't seem to bother her, though I can't say the same. Suddenly it's shattered by the same scream I heard last night. It comes from the woods behind us, not as unsettling in daylight but sounding no less agonized.

'What was that?' I ask, staring into the trees.

Neither Gretchen nor Michel seems concerned. Even the dog only pricks up its ears before resuming its gnawing. 'It's just the sanglochons.'

'The what?' She's mentioned them before, I remember.

'Sanglochons,' she repeats, as if I'm an idiot. 'They're a cross between wild boars and pigs. Papa breeds them, but they smell bad so we keep them in the wood. They're always squabbling over food.'

I'm relieved that's all it was. 'So this is a pig farm?'

'No, of course not!' Gretchen says, giving me a reproving

75

glance. 'The sanglochons are just Papa's hobby. And it's not a farm, it's a chateau. We own the lake and all of the woods round here. We've nearly a hundred hectares of chestnut trees we harvest every autumn.'

She sounds proud, so I assume that must be a lot of chestnuts. 'I've seen that you make your own wine as well.'

'We used to. Papa wanted to call it Château Arnaud. He got a good deal on some vines and dug up our beet fields, but the grapes weren't hardy enough for our soil. They got some sort of blight, so we only produced one vintage. We've still got hundreds of bottles, though, and Papa says we'll be able to sell them once they've matured.'

I think about the sour-smelling bottles in the barn and hope they aren't planning on selling them any time soon. Gretchen picks another flower and works it into the plait. She looks at me over the top of it.

'You don't talk about yourself very much, do you?'

'There's not much to say.'

'I don't believe you. You're just trying to be mysterious.' She gives a smile that shows off her dimples. 'Come on, tell me something. Where are you from?'

'England.'

She gives my arm a playful slap. It hurts. 'I mean where-abouts?'

'I've been living in London.'

'What do you do there? You must have a job.'

'Nothing permanent. Bars, building sites.' I shrug. 'A bit of English teaching.'

There's no clap of thunder, and the ground doesn't split. Gretchen picks another flower and seems about to ask something else, but the dog chooses that moment to drop the stone it's been chewing on my lap.

'Oh, thanks a lot.'

I gingerly lift the saliva-coated offering and fling it away. The dog tears down the bluff and slows to a confused stop when the stone splashes into the water. It stares after it then back at me, heartbroken.

Gretchen laughs. 'She's so stupid.'

I find another stone and call the dog. It's still distracted by the loss of the first, which was evidently its favourite, but catches on when I throw the substitute into the trees. Happy again, it sprints after it.

'Gretchen's a German name, isn't it?' I ask, glad of the chance to change the subject.

She adds another flower to the chain. 'Papa's family were from Alsace. I'm named after my grandmother. And Michel here has Papa's middle name. It's important to keep the family traditions going.'

'Who's Mathilde called after?'

Gretchen's expression turns hard. 'How should I know?'

She plucks a flower so forcefully its roots come up with the stem. Discarding it, she picks another. I try to lighten the atmosphere. 'So, how old's Michel?'

'He'll be one in autumn.'

'I haven't seen his father. Is he from around here?'

I'm only trying to make conversation but Gretchen's face hardens even more. 'We don't talk about him.'

'Sorry, I didn't mean to pry.'

After a moment she gives a shrug. 'It's no secret. He left before Michel was born. He let us all down. We welcomed him into our family, and he betrayed us.'

That sounds like her father talking, but I keep any more comments to myself. Threading one last flower onto the link, Gretchen connects the two ends and loops the chain around Michel's neck. He grins, then snaps it in his small fist.

A blankness comes over Gretchen's features, as if someone's

taken hold of the skin and pulled it back. She slaps his arm, harder than she hit mine.

'Bad boy!' Her nephew starts to howl. I'm not surprised: her hand has left a red imprint on his chubby little arm. 'Bad, *bad* boy!'

'It was only an accident,' I say, worried she's going to slap him again.

For a second I think she might hit me instead. Then, as suddenly as it came, the mood passes. 'He's always doing things like that,' she says, throwing the broken flower chain aside. She picks up her nephew and cuddles him. 'Come on, Michel, don't cry. Gretchen didn't mean it.'

I'd say she did, but the baby is more easily persuaded. His howls subside to hiccups and soon he's chuckling again. After Gretchen's wiped his eyes and nose the entire incident is forgotten.

'I'd better take him back,' she says, climbing to her feet. 'Are you coming?'

I hesitate. I'd rather stay by the lake, and then there's her father to consider. 'No, I'd better not.'

'Why, are you scared of Papa?' She grins.

I don't know how to answer that. The man's already threatened me with a rifle and kicked me downstairs, and I'm in no rush to provoke him any further. But the accusation still rankles.

'I think it's better if I keep out of his way, that's all.'

'Don't worry. He has a bad back so he goes to bed after lunch. And Georges goes home for his, so there's no one to tell.'

She's waiting for me to go with them. It doesn't seem as though I've got much choice, so with a last look at the lake I manoeuvre myself inelegantly to my feet. Gretchen slows to allow me to keep up as we walk back through the woods, hip thrust out to support the baby's weight, legs long and tanned below the pale-blue dress. Her flip-flops scuff on the dirt track, beating out a counterpoint to the scrape of my crutch. A late-afternoon hush has settled. It seems even more pronounced when we reach the statues, the stone figures lending it the quiet of a church nave.

'What are these doing here?' I ask, pausing to catch my breath.

Gretchen barely glances at them. 'Papa's going to sell them. He started collecting them years ago. You'd be surprised what old châteaux have in their gardens.'

'You mean he stole them?'

'Of course not! Papa isn't a thief!' she retorts. 'They're only old statues, and the places they're from were all empty. How could it be stealing if no one lived there?'

I doubt the owners would see it that way, but I've upset Gretchen enough for one afternoon. And the walk has taken more out of me than I thought. The dog runs on ahead as we emerge from the woods and start across the dry vine field. The sun is still hot but lower now, so our shadows stretch ahead of us like spindly giants. I labour along with my head down, too tired to talk. By the time we've reached the barn I'm slick with sweat and my leg muscles are twitching with fatigue.

Gretchen pushes her hair back behind her ear as we stop by the doorway, an unconscious echo of her sister. 'You're all sweaty,' she says, dimpling a smile. 'You should practise on your crutch more. I take Michel for a walk most afternoons. If you like I could meet you at the lake again tomorrow.'

'I won't be here,' I tell her. 'I'm leaving in the morning.'

Saying the words makes it more real. Just the thought of it feels like stepping off a cliff.

Gretchen stares. 'You can't leave! What about your foot?'

'I'll manage.'

Her face hardens. 'This is Mathilde's fault, isn't it?'

'Mathilde? No, of course not.'

'She's always spoiling things. I hate her!'

The sudden venom takes me aback. 'It's nothing to do with Mathilde. I need to go, that's all.'

'Fine. Go then.'

She walks away, leaving me standing there. I sigh, staring into the dark interior of the barn. I wait till I've caught my breath, then begin the long haul back up the wooden steps to the loft.

I sleep for a few hours and wake to find that the sun has gone from the loft. It's still hot and close but there's a dusky quality to the light that suggests it's getting late. When I look at my watch I see it's after eight. No sign of dinner yet. I wonder whether it's delayed or if I've upset Arnaud or Gretchen enough not to get anything.

I'm not sure I could eat anyway.

I go downstairs and wash under the barn's tap. The icy water takes my breath away but makes me feel a little better. Then I sit down outside to watch the sun's slow descent. As it slides behind the chestnut wood I light up a cigarette. It's my last, but finding a supermarket or a tabac can be my first objective tomorrow. After that . . .

I've no idea.

The glowing tip of my cigarette is almost down to my fingers when I hear footsteps coming from the courtyard. It's Mathilde, carrying a tray on which I'm surprised to see is a bottle of wine as well as a plate of steaming food.

I start to climb awkwardly to my feet. 'Don't get up,' she says, setting the tray down beside me. 'I'm sorry dinner's late. Michel has gripe and wouldn't settle.'

Even though I'd told myself it didn't matter, I'm glad there's a mundane reason. Though I daresay Michel is less pleased.

'Smells great,' I tell her. And it does: pork and chestnuts, with sautéed potatoes and a green salad. It's a pity I'm not hungry.

'I thought you might like some wine tonight. It's only our own, but it's not too bad with food.'

'What's the occasion?' I wonder if it's meant to mark my de-
parture.

'No occasion. It's just wine.' She pours the water glass half full
of dark liquid. 'Are you still intending to leave tomorrow?'

I wonder what Gretchen's told her. Maybe nothing, and I'm
just flattering myself. 'Yes.'

'What are your plans?'

'Nothing concrete.'

It doesn't sound so bad when I say it like that. Mathilde tucks
her hair behind one ear.

'You could always stay here. We could use some help on the
farm.'

It's so far from anything I expect that I think I've misunder-
stood. 'Sorry, what?'

'If you don't have to go straight away then there's work here
that needs doing. If you're interested.'

'You're offering me a *job*?'

'Apart from Georges, there are only the three of us. We could
use an extra pair of hands, and Gretchen told me you've been a
builder.' Her hand goes to tuck her hair back again. 'You must have
seen the condition of the house. The walls badly need repairing.'

'I've worked on building sites but that isn't the same thing.
Why don't you hire a local builder?'

'We can't afford to,' she says simply. 'We won't be able to pay
you very much, but you'd be living here free. You'd have your
meals. And we wouldn't expect you to start straight away. You
can wait until you're stronger and then work at your own pace.
Whatever you feel you can do.'

I pass my hand across my face, trying to think. 'What about
your father?'

'Don't worry about him.'

Right. 'He does *know* about this, doesn't he?'

The grey eyes are unreadable. 'I wouldn't ask you if not. My father can be stubborn but he's a realist. The work needs doing and since Providence has brought you here . . . It would be good for all of us.'

Providence. Nothing to do with her father's traps, then. 'I don't know . . .'

'You don't have to decide now. Take your time. I just wanted you to know that you don't have to leave tomorrow.'

She rises gracefully to her feet. In the dusk her features are solemn and more indecipherable than ever.

'Goodnight. I'll see you in the morning.'

I watch her walk out of sight around the corner of the barn. Stunned, I take a drink of wine and grimace.

'God . . .'

It won't win any prizes but it's strong. I risk another sip, trying to collect my thoughts. Even though I've no idea what I'll do or where I'll go, I've been psyching myself up to leave because I didn't think I had a choice. Now I have. Staying here won't solve anything, but it'll give me breathing space to think things through. I can at least wait until my foot's healed before making any major decisions.

God knows, the last thing I need is to rush into anything else.

The sun has almost set, leaving only its last golden shout to echo on the horizon. I fork up some of the pork. It's strong and gamy, cooked with garlic and so tender it falls apart. I take another drink of wine and refill my glass. Mathilde's right: it is better with food, though that isn't saying much. Still, the alcohol and powerful flavours give me a pleasant buzz.

At some point I realize that the depression that's been hanging over me has lifted. I pour myself another glass of wine and look out over the wood to the distant fields. The only sound is the evening chorus of crickets. There are no cars, no people. The peace is absolute.

It's a perfect place to hide.

London

WE GO TO BRIGHTON on the money Chloe gets for a painting. The buyer is an art dealer who's opening a gallery in Notting Hill. He wants the painting, a cold still life of blues and purples that I privately find too sombre, for himself, and commissions another six to hang in the gallery when it opens.

'It's happening!' Chloe whoops after she's taken his call. She throws herself on me, arms and legs wrapping around mine. 'At last, it's really happening!'

That night we celebrate at the Domino. Chloe's working but finishes early, bringing over a couple of bottles of cava she says are from the manager.

'Tight bastard,' Yasmin grumbles. 'It wouldn't hurt him to have given you champagne.'

Chloe's high even without the alcohol, fizzing with plans and excitement.

'God, I can't believe it! He's got contacts in Paris and New York that he says are coming for the opening! And the art critic for the *Daily Mail* is going to be there!'

'I didn't know the *Daily Mail* had an art critic,' Jez mutters. Yasmin elbows him and gives him a look.

Chloe either doesn't hear or doesn't care. She's swigging cava like water. 'God, I'll finally be able to leave this place! Paint full time and tell all the ad agencies to shove it!'

Callum has brought a gram of coke as his contribution to the party. At our table in a darkened booth, he chops out lines on the back of a magazine with the edge of a credit card.

'What the fuck are you doing?' Yasmin hisses.

'It's all right, it's only a bit of blow. No one can see. Sean, you want some?'

'No, thanks.'

I've never been into coke. As far as I know, neither has Chloe, so I expect her to decline as well. To my surprise, she doesn't.

'You sure?' I ask.

'Why not?' She grins. 'It's a celebration, isn't it?'

'Chloe . . .' Yasmin warns.

'It's OK, don't worry,' she says, accepting Callum's offer of a second line. 'It's just this once.'

Yasmin leans over to me as I refill my glass from the bottle. 'Don't let her have any more.'

'She's just enjoying herself,' I tell her. Yasmin is OK but sometimes she can be too intense. 'Why shouldn't she? She deserves this.'

'And what if it doesn't work out? She doesn't deal well with disappointment.'

'Oh, come on, Yasmin. Lighten up.'

She glares at me. 'Are you really this stupid?'

I stare after her, surprised and stung, as she pushes back her chair and walks away. Well, somebody's jealous, I think.

Brighton is Chloe's idea. She's so on edge the week before the gallery opening that her fingernails are bitten to the quick. She works at her paintings all day, literally until she has to run out of the door to take her shift at the Dom.

'Let's go away,' she says, when they've been delivered to the gallery.

'Suits me. After the opening we can—'

'No, now. The waiting's driving me mad. I need to get away *now.*'

The resort town is dazzling white, all sunshine and brightness after the dour sprawl of London. We hitch down rather than trust Chloe's car, which is only good now for increasingly short distances. Buying a new one is a priority if all goes well with her paintings. She's full of plans and ideas, convinced that the turning point in her career has been reached. In some of the wilder moments I remember Yasmin's warning, but Chloe's new optimism is so contagious it sweeps aside any doubts.

We stop in a seafront pub and pay a ridiculous price for beers, reckless on the promise of Chloe's success and being on holiday. Afterwards we trawl charity and second-hand shops for picture frames that she can re-use for her own work. We don't find any, but buy an old instant camera that comes with half a dozen peel-apart films. We use them all on the seafront, counting down out loud as we wait for them to develop, only to find blank squares of emulsion underneath. Just one picture takes, of Chloe standing in front of the pier grinning as she poses like a model. She hates it but I hold it out of her reach when she laughingly tries to snatch it away. At her insistence, we book into a B&B that's well above our budget and eat a garlic-laden dinner in an Italian restaurant. We're more than a little drunk when we go back to the hotel, shushing each other in a fit of giggles as we unlock our room, and then make even more noise making love.

After three days we catch the train back to London, an indulgence Chloe grandly insists we can now afford. We arrive back in the late afternoon, to the news that the gallery owner has been declared bankrupt, the gallery's opening cancelled and all its assets seized. Including Chloe's paintings.

'They can't do that! The bastards, they can't just do that!'

I try to tell her she'll get the paintings back eventually, but I know it isn't just them. It's the opportunity they represented.

'Leave me alone,' she says flatly when I try to console her.

'Chloe . . .'

'I mean it! Just leave me alone!'

So I do. I'm glad for the excuse to go out. I want some time to come to terms with this myself, not so much the disappointment as the shameful sense of relief I felt when I heard. Nothing is going to change after all.

I consider calling Callum but I don't really want to talk to anyone. There's a retrospective season of French film at an art-house cinema in Camden. Along with half a dozen people I sit through a back-to-back screening of Alain Resnais's *Muriel* and *Hiroshima, Mon Amour*. Then the lights go up and I'm back in the here and now, in a world that seems so much less vivid than the monochrome ones I've just been watching.

It's raining outside, and the buses are full of commuters on their way home. When I get back the flat is in darkness. I switch on the lights. Chloe is sitting on the floor, the torn and broken canvases of her art scattered around her. Tubes of oil paint have been squeezed and discarded, smearing everything in a rainbow frenzy. The easel holding my unfinished portrait has been knocked over, the painting stamped on.

Chloe doesn't acknowledge me. Her face is streaked where she's dragged her oil-coated fingers across it. I pick my way gingerly through the littered canvases, slipping a little on a patch of paint. When I sit beside her and pull her to me she doesn't resist.

'It'll be all right,' I tell her, emptily.

'Yeah,' she says. Her voice is the only thing in the paint-smeared room that's dull. 'Of course it will.'

6

THE SCAFFOLD CREAKS AND sways like a tired ship. I climb the ladder one rung at a time, resting my knee on the wooden bars rather than using my injured foot. It's not much harder than going into the loft. At the top I test the rickety-looking platform before cautiously stepping onto it, gripping the horizontal scaffolding bars for support.

The scaffold feels dizzingly high. Still, the view from up here is even better than from the loft window. Resting to catch my breath, I can see the lake down in the woods and beyond that the surrounding fields and hills. It brings home more than ever just how cut off the farm is. I spend a few more minutes enjoying that fact, then I turn to see what I've let myself in for.

Half of the front of the house and one of its sides is covered with scaffold. Mortar has been hacked out from between the stones, and some of them have been completely removed and left on the platform. A lump hammer and chisel lie nearby. They're both rusted and the hammer is as heavy as a brick, its wooden handle worn smooth with use. The chisel is angled like a knife rather than having a flat blade like the one lying in the cobbles below. When I prod at the wall with it, the mortar crumbles easily. If the entire house is like this it's a miracle it's still standing.

Suddenly I'm convinced I'm making a mistake. I know how to mix mortar and I've tried my hand at laying bricks, but that was years ago. My few months spent as a labourer on a building site hardly prepared me for anything like this.

I step blindly away from the wall and catch my crutch on one of the stones scattered on the platform. I stumble against the horizontal scaffolding bar that acts as a railing, and for an instant I'm teetering out into space with nothing between me and the courtyard thirty feet below. Then I haul myself back, causing the tower to squeak and sway in protest.

Slowly, the motion subsides. I rest my head against the pole.

'What's happening?'

I look down. Gretchen has come out of the house and is standing in the courtyard with Michel.

'Nothing. I'm just . . . checking the scaffold.'

She shields her eyes with a hand, tilting her head to look at me. 'It sounded like it was collapsing.'

I wipe my damp palms on my jeans. 'Not yet.'

She smiles. She's hardly spoken to me since the afternoon I told her I was leaving, but it seems she's finally decided to forgive me. I wait till she's gone back inside, then sink onto the platform with unsteady legs. *Christ, what am I doing?*

It's two days since Mathilde offered me the job. At first I was content just to rest and get my strength back, carried along by relief at finding an unexpected refuge. I spent most of yesterday down by the lake, making a half-hearted attempt to read *Madame Bovary* under the old chestnut tree on the bluff. Sometimes I was able to forget the reason I was there. Then I'd remember, and it would be like falling. Before long my thoughts were gnawing away at me again. Last night was the worst. The few times I managed to drift off to sleep I woke gasping, my heart racing. This morning, as I watched the small window in my loft gradually grey and lighten, I knew I couldn't stand another idle day.

I'd hoped that physical work might help. Now I'm up here,

though, the sheer scale of the task terrifies me. I've no idea where to start. *Come on, you can do this. It's only a wall.*

I get to my feet and confront the house again. Nearby, two windows face out onto the platform. One of them is hidden behind wooden shutters, but the other is uncovered. On the other side of the dusty glass is an empty bedroom. There are bare floorboards and peeling wallpaper, an old wardrobe and an iron bedstead with a striped mattress. On the back wall is a dresser on which stands a framed picture. It looks like a wedding photograph; the man in a dark suit, the woman in white. It's too far away to make out any detail, but I guess it's Arnaud and his wife. The period looks about right, and shutting his wedding photo in a disused bedroom is about what I'd expect of him.

Careful where I put the crutch, I shuffle along the scaffold to look around the side of the house. There's the same air of incompleteness as there was at the front, a sense of interruption. Halfway along the platform a large cup rests on a folded tabloid newspaper, empty except for a dead fly lying in the dried brown crust at the bottom. The newspaper is as brittle as parchment when I pick it up. The date on it is eighteen months ago. I wonder if anyone has been up here since the unknown builder drained his coffee cup, put it down on his newspaper and didn't bother to come back. Maybe he had the right idea, I think, looking at how much work there's still to be done.

There's a commotion from behind the house. I limp to the end of the scaffold and find myself looking down on a kitchen garden. Neat rows of vegetables and cane tepees of beans form an oasis of order, beyond which is a paddock with a few goats, fruit trees and a hen house.

Mathilde is feeding chickens. As I watch she scatters a last handful of seed for them to squabble and cluck over and sets down her empty bucket. Unaware she's being observed, her unguarded face looks tired and sad as she goes to a corner of the garden. Hidden away there is a tiny flowerbed, a bright splash of colour amongst the more practical vegetables. Kneeling down, she begins tugging up the weeds growing between them. A soft sound drifts up to me and I realize she's humming to herself. Something slow and melodic; I don't know the tune.

I quietly move away. Back around the front of the house, the sun is blinding. At this time of day there's no shade on the scaffold, and my skin is already prickling where it's uncovered. I check my watch and see it's past noon; if I stay up here any longer I'll fry. The metal scaffolding poles burn my hands as I transfer myself onto the ladder and slowly make my way down. As I reach the bottom Mathilde comes around the corner of the house, wiping her hands on a cloth.

'You've taken a look?' she asks. The sadness I saw on her face in the garden has gone, concealed behind the usual calm. 'What do you think?'

'It's, uh, a bigger job than I thought.'

Mathilde looks up at the scaffold, shielding her eyes from the sun as Gretchen did earlier. In the sun her hair isn't so very much darker than her sister's. It just looks as though all the light's been taken from it.

'You don't have to start just yet. Not if you don't feel up to it.'

It isn't my health that worries me. Trying to keep my weight off my foot isn't easy, and the climb down has set it throbbing again. But it's bearable, and anything's better than inactivity.

I shrug. 'Only one way to find out.'

'I'll show you where everything is.'

She goes to the doorway where Arnaud confronted me a few days earlier. The warped door's hinges creak as she opens it, letting light into what I now see is a small, windowless store-room. A wave of cold, damp air rolls out from it, and as my eyes adjust I make out an untidy sprawl of building equipment with bags of sand and cement. Like the platform at the top of the scaffold, there's a touch of the *Marie Celeste* about the way everything's been left. A trail of cement spills from a slash in a paper sack in which a trowel still stands, while a spade protrudes from a mound of rock-hard mortar like a builder's Excalibur. Judging by the cobwebs clinging to it all, nothing in here has been disturbed in months.

There's a groan from the hinges as the door starts to swing shut behind us, cutting off the light. I turn to stop it, and jump as I see someone standing there. But it's only a pair of overalls hanging from a nail. At least Mathilde hasn't noticed my nerves. She stands to one side of the doorway, as though reluctant to come any further.

'Everything should be in here. There's cement and sand, and a tap for water. Use whatever you need.'

I look at the mess in the small room. 'Was your father doing the work before?'

'No, a local man.'

Whoever he was, he left in a hurry. I give the spade handle a tug. It quivers but doesn't budge, stuck fast in the solidified mortar.

'Why didn't he finish?'

'There was a disagreement.'

She doesn't enlarge. I go to examine the cement. Damp has made the grey powder from the split bag clump together, and when I prod the unopened bags they're hard as stone.

'I'll need more cement.'

Mathilde's standing with her arms wrapped tightly across her chest. 'Do you need it straight away? Isn't there something else you can be doing?'

I consider the piled bags, knowing I'm just stalling for time. 'I suppose I can hack out more of the old mortar . . .'

'Fine,' she says, and goes back out into the courtyard.

I take a last look around the dark room with its abandoned

tools, then follow her into the sunlight. Mathilde is waiting in the courtyard, and though her face is as hard to read as ever she looks pale.

'Everything OK?' I ask.

'Of course.' Her hand goes to her hair, absently tucking it back. 'Is there anything else you need for now?'

'Well, I'm out of cigarettes. Is there somewhere nearby I can buy some?'

She considers this new difficulty. 'There's a tabac at the garage, but it's too far to—'

The front door opens and Gretchen comes out. She's carrying Michel on one hip, and her lips tighten when she sees us. Ignoring me, she gives her sister a sullen stare.

'Papa wants to see him.' She lifts her chin with malicious satisfaction. 'Alone.'

It's the first time I've been inside since I asked for water. The kitchen is low-ceilinged and dark, with thick walls and small windows built to stay cool in the summer heat. There's a smell of beeswax, cooked meat and coffee. An old range dominates one wall, and the heavy wooden furniture looks as though it's stood here for generations. The scratched white boxes of the refrigerator and freezer look gratingly modern in this setting.

Arnaud is cleaning his rifle at a scarred wooden table. The half-moon glasses perched on his nose give him an incongruously bookish air, difficult to reconcile with the man who kicked me down the steps. He doesn't look up, continuing to work on the rifle as though I'm not there. I catch a whiff of gun oil and what I guess is cordite as he threads a long wire brush, like a miniature chimney sweep's, into the rifle barrel. It makes a fluted whisper as he pulls it through.

I shift my weight on the crutch. 'You wanted to see me?'

He unhurriedly squints down the barrel's length before

lowering it. Folding his glasses, he puts them in his breast pocket then sits back in his chair. Only now does he look at me.

'Mathilde says you're looking for a job.'

That's not how I remember it, but I don't bother correcting him. 'If there's one going.'

'That's the question, isn't it?' Arnaud's jaw works as if he's trying to crack a nut. Below it, the flesh of his throat has loosened with age, like an ageing weightlifter's. 'My daughter can tell you what she likes, but I'm the one who'll decide who works here. Ever worked on a farm?'

'No.'

'Any building experience?'

'Not much.'

'Then why should I take a chance on you?'

I can't actually think of a reason. So I remain silent, trying not to look at the rifle. Arnaud sniffs.

'Why are you here?'

It's on the tip of my tongue to say it's because of his traps, but that would only provoke him. Even if I'm no longer quite so worried that he'll shoot me, I'm uncomfortably aware that any job offer depends on his good graces.

'What do you mean?'

'I *mean* what are you doing wandering around a foreign country like a tramp? You're too old to be a student. What do you do for a living?'

I can tell from his manner that Gretchen's been talking. 'This and that. I've had a few jobs.'

'This and that,' he mocks. 'You don't give much away, do you? Got something to hide?'

There's a moment when I feel weightless. I'm aware of my colouring betraying me as blood rushes to my cheeks, but I make myself stare back.

'No. Why should I?'

Arnaud's mouth works, either ruminating or chewing some titbit he's found between his teeth. 'I expect people to respect my privacy,' he says at last. 'You'll have to stay down at the barn. You can eat your meals down there. I don't want to see you any more than necessary. I'll pay you fifty euros a week, if I think you've earned it. Take it or leave it.'

'OK.'

It's a pittance but I don't care about the money. Still, the glint in Arnaud's eyes makes me regret rolling over so easily. Showing him any weakness is a mistake.

He looks me up and down, weighing me up. 'This is Mathilde's idea, not mine. I don't like it, but there's work needs doing and since she seems to think we should hire some English deadbeat I'll let her. I'll be watching you, though. Cross me so much as once and you'll regret it. Is that clear?'

It is. He stares at me for a few moments more, letting his words sink in, then reaches for the rifle.

'Go on, get out.' He begins wiping it with an oily cloth. I limp to the door, angry and humiliated. 'One more thing.'

Arnaud's eyes are glacial as he stares at me over the rifle.

'Keep away from my daughters.'

7

I T'S TOO HOT TO even consider going back up the scaffold after my audience with Arnaud. Besides, it's lunch time, so when Mathilde comes back I wait outside the kitchen until the food's ready and then take my plate down to the shade of the barn. I need to cool off, in every sense. I'm still smarting, already questioning whether I wouldn't be better taking my chances out on the road. But my own reluctance at the prospect is all the answer I need. The only thing waiting for me beyond the farm's borders is uncertainty. I need time to work out what I'm going to do, and if that means abiding by Arnaud's rules then I can live with that.

I've put up with worse.

Lunch today is bread and tomatoes, with a chunk of dark and heavily spiced sausage I guess is home-made. There's also what on examination I find are pickled chestnuts, and to finish a small yellow apricot. I don't think I've eaten anything since I've been here that hasn't been grown or produced on the farm.

I eat it all, leaving only the apricot's stone and stalk, then sit back and pine for a cigarette. The spicy food has made me thirsty, so I go to the tap inside the barn. The faintly sweet air around the disused wine vats smells better than the wine itself. Crossing the rectangular patch of concrete in the cobbles, I catch my crutch on a deep crack running across its surface.

Not enough cement, I think, prodding at the crumbling edges with my crutch. If this was the same builder who worked on the house, he made an equally bad job of it.

I run the tap water and drink from my cupped hands. It's cold and clean, and I splash some on my face and neck as well. Wiping it from my eyes, I come out of the barn and almost bump into Gretchen.

'Sorry,' I say.

She smiles. She's wearing a short T-shirt and cut-down denim shorts I'm surprised Arnaud lets her get away with. She's carrying a bucket, this one plastic rather than metal like the ones I saw Georges using. The springer spaniel accompanying her fusses around me, tail wagging. I scratch behind its ears.

'I'm taking some scraps down for the sanglochons. But I think I overfilled the bucket.' She holds it in both hands, making hard work of it. 'You could help me, if you're not doing anything.'

I try to think of an excuse. Her father's warning is still fresh in my mind, and I'm not sure how I'll carry the bucket that far with my crutch anyway. Gretchen's smile widens, emphasizing her dimples.

'Please? It's really heavy.'

At her insistence, we carry it between us to start with, each of us with one hand on the bucket handle. After we've struggled for a few yards, Gretchen giggling all the time, I lose patience and carry it by myself. It's nowhere near as heavy as she made it look, but it's too late to change my mind now. Hopefully even Arnaud can't object to my helping feed his pigs.

'Are you growing a beard?' Gretchen asks as we follow the track through the vines.

I self-consciously feel the bristles on my chin. 'Not really. I just haven't shaved.'

Gretchen tilts her head, smiling as she considers. 'Can I touch it?'

Before I can say anything she reaches to stroke my cheek. The burnt-caramel smell of sun-heated skin comes from her bare arm. Her dimples are deeper than ever as she lowers her hand.

'It suits you. I like it.'

The dog bounds ahead of us as we walk through the chestnut wood. Gretchen takes a dirt path that forks off from the main track. It leads through the trees to a clearing, in which a large pen has been built from wire and rough planks. Standing off by itself is an unlovely cinderblock hut, but Gretchen passes that without comment as she heads for the pen.

The air in the clearing hums with flies. The ammoniac stink is so strong it hurts my sinuses. A dozen or so animals are lying prostrate on the churned-up ground, the only sign of life the occasional bass grunt or flap of an ear. They aren't like any pigs I've seen before. They're vast, darkly mottled, with a coarse, bristly pelt. Slumped in the shade of corrugated-iron shelters, they look as if they've been dropped into the mud like un-exploded bombs.

Gretchen opens a gate in the fence and goes in. 'Where's Georges?' I ask, looking uneasily at the basking creatures. There's no sign of the old pig-man.

'He goes home for lunch in the afternoon.' She holds the gate open for me. 'Aren't you coming in?'

'I think I'll wait here.'

She laughs. 'They won't hurt you.'

'I'll still wait.'

I'm still a little uneasy about being here, but limping all this way with the bucket has winded me. I need to catch my breath before heading back up the track. Taking the bucket – she doesn't seem to find it heavy now – Gretchen pushes back the dog as it tries to dart through the gate, and goes to the trough. Some of the pigs lift their heads and make inquisitive grunts when she empties the bucket into it, but only one or two can be bothered to get up and come over. I'm struck again by how big they are, sacks of flesh balanced precariously on ridiculously dainty legs, a horse's body on cocktail sticks.

Gretchen comes out again, closing the gate behind her.

'What did you say they are?' I ask.

'Sanglochons. Wild boars crossed with black pigs. Papa's been breeding them for years, and Georges sells the meat for us in town. It's very popular. Much better than ordinary pork.'

One of the creatures has ambled over. Gretchen picks up a wizened turnip that's rolled under the fence and drops it back over. The pig crunches it easily in its jaws. It makes my foot hurt again just seeing it.

But Gretchen isn't concerned. She scratches behind the sanglochon's ears as it noses hopefully for more food. The curve of its mouth gives it the appearance of a sweet smile.

'Doesn't it bother you?' I ask. 'Having to kill them, I mean?'

'Why should it?' She sounds genuinely bemused. Her hand rasps on the heavy bristles as she rubs its head. 'You can stroke it if you want.'

'No thanks.'

'It won't bite.'

'I'll take your word for it.' I've noticed there's a smaller fenced-off area at one side of the main pen. It looks empty, except for a solitary corrugated shelter. 'What's in there?'

Gretchen straightens, wiping her hands together as she goes over to it. Some of the fence panels here look new, the wood pale and fresh compared to the older sections.

'This is where Papa keeps his boar.'

'You make it sound like a pet.'

She pulls a face. 'It's not a pet. It's horrible. I hate it.'

'Why?'

'It's got a bad personality. Georges is the only one who can do anything with it. It bit me once.' She extends a tanned leg, twisting it slightly to reveal where the smooth skin of her calf is marred by a white scar. She smiles. 'Feel it. It's all rough.'

'So I see.' I keep my hands to myself. I'm not interested in flirting. Even if she weren't Arnaud's youngest daughter, there's something about Gretchen that makes me want to keep my distance. 'If it's that bad why doesn't your father kill it?'

She lowers her leg. 'He needs it for breeding.'

'Can't he get another?'

'They're expensive. Besides, Papa likes this one. He says it does what it's supposed to.'

As if on cue a sudden noise comes from the pen. Gretchen turns towards it.

'He's heard us.'

For a second I think she means Arnaud before I realize she's talking about the boar. There's a movement inside the shelter, a shifting of shadows. The tip of a snout emerges. Gretchen picks up a handful of soil and throws it to clatter on the corrugated roof.

'Pig! Come out, pig!'

No wonder it's bad-tempered, I think. Another handful of dirt follows. There's an angry grunt from inside, and then the boar bursts out.

It's even bigger than the sanglochons. And uglier. Small tusks jut from its lower jaw, and ears big as dock leaves flap over its eyes as it peers around myopically, trying to see where we are. Then it charges.

'Christ!' I say, hopping backwards as the boar slams into the fence. My crutch slips and I sit down, hard, in a patch of dried mud. I scramble to get the crutch under me again as the fence shudders. Gretchen hasn't budged. She's found a length of stick, and as the boar shoves at the fence she jabs at it over the top.

'Go on, pig! Pig! Go on!'

The boar squeals, enraged. The spaniel sets up its own com-motion as Gretchen lashes at the pig's back with the stick, the impacts meaty but insignificant against its bulk.

'I wouldn't do that,' I tell her.

'I'm only teasing it.'

'I don't think it sees the joke.' The boar is battering at the fence in an attempt to get at the barking dog, making the planks creak and shudder. No wonder Georges had to repair it. 'Come on, leave it alone.'

Gretchen regards me haughtily, out of breath. 'What's it got to do with you? It's not your pig.'

'No, but I don't think your father would want you to beat up his prize boar.'

She glares, still clutching the stick. For a moment I think she might use it on me, but then a rusty old 2CV bumps into the clearing. It stops by the pens and Georges climbs out. He doesn't seem any taller now he's standing than when he was in the car. His face is rigid with disapproval as he comes over.

He takes in the boar, still attacking the fence. This time I merit a cursory glance before he addresses Gretchen. 'What's going on?'

She looks sullenly at the floor. 'Nothing.'

'Then why is the boar upset? What was the dog doing by his fence?'

Gretchen shrugs. 'Just playing.'

His mouth tightens. 'You shouldn't bring the dog down here.'

'We didn't. She ran off.'

Georges just looks at her. I'm not happy that she's making me complicit in the lie, but I don't contradict her. Not that he seems interested in me anyway.

'You shouldn't bring the dog down here,' he says again. He goes past us to the pen. The boar snaps at him when he reaches over the fence, but then subsides and lets him scratch its head. I can hear him talking to it, soothingly, but can't hear what he's saying.

Gretchen pulls a face at his back. 'Come on. We mustn't upset Georges's precious pigs.'

She takes angry swipes with the stick as we leave the clearing. 'He's such an old woman! All he cares about are the stupid pigs. He even smells like them, did you notice?'

'Not really.' I did, but I'm not going to side with her. This was a bad idea in the first place: all I want now is to get back before Arnaud sees us together.

'It's the vinegar he rubs on them,' she goes on, oblivious. 'He says it toughens their skin against the sun but it makes him stink as bad as they do.'

Not just Georges. As we near the barn it becomes apparent that something of the sanglochons has accompanied us from the pens.

'What's that smell?' Gretchen asks, sniffing.

I look down at the muddy smears on my jeans and hands. 'Oh, shit . . .'

'You smell worse than Georges!' she laughs, backing away.

She's right, but at least it's encouraged her not to hang around any longer. I wait until she's out of sight before I strip off my T-shirt. Grimacing, I go inside the barn to clean myself up.

The sanglochon stink is still in my nose as I cross the courtyard to the scaffold. The sun has lost some of its bite since Gretchen and I came back, but the cobbles still shimmer with heat. It doesn't seem to have any effect on the storeroom's dank interior, though. After the dazzling brightness of the courtyard, it's like stepping into a crypt. I block open the door with a bag of sand, waiting until the shadows take on individual shapes before I go inside.

There's something eerie about the way everything has been

left. The spade in its petrified mortar, the scatter of tools and materials; it all reminds me of a preserved archaeological scene. As my eyes adjust, I grope behind the door and take down what I'm looking for.

The overalls are red, or rather they were once. Now they're crusted with dried mortar, dirt and oil. I'd remembered seeing them in here, and Mathilde told me to use whatever I needed. My skin creeps at the thought of wearing them, but they'll protect me from the sun. And, filthy as they are, they don't smell of pig shit.

Leaning my crutch against the wall, I strip to my shorts and pull the overalls on. The damp cotton feels unpleasantly clammy and gives off a stale whiff of old sweat. Still, they're not a bad fit so I guess they belonged to the previous builder. They're too long in the leg for Arnaud, and Georges could fit in one of the pockets.

I search through them as I go back outside. There's a pair of leather work gloves in the side pockets, so stiff and curled they look like amputated hands. I discard them along with a pencil stub and a small notepad that's filled with scrawled measurements. That seems to be about it, but then as I pat down the pockets for a last time I find something else.

A condom, still sealed in its wrapper.

It's not the sort of thing I was expecting to find in a pair of work overalls. I look back at the storeroom as something occurs to me. I haven't given it much thought, but now I wonder if there's a connection between the unfinished house and Michel's absent father. That would explain Mathilde's strange behaviour earlier, and also Gretchen's reaction down by the lake. She told me that Michel's father had betrayed them and let them down.

Maybe in more ways than one.

Leaving the condom in a corner of the storeroom, I wedge the crutch under my arm and climb up the scaffold. The ladder rungs are hot enough to sting my hands, and the platform at the top is like a kiln. There's no shade, and I'm already thankful for the overall's long sleeves. My doubts start to return as I consider the crumbling wall, so I pick up the lump hammer and chisel before I've chance to think about it.

'OK, then,' I say to myself, and take my first swing.

There's something Zen-like about hacking out the old mortar. The work is hard and repetitive, but hypnotic. Each steel-on-steel strike produces a clear musical note. With the right rhythm the chisel seems to sing, each new note sounding before the last has died.

It's actually relaxing.

I have to keep stopping to rest, but I soon find a pace I can maintain. I get around the problem of my injured foot by stacking two or three of the big rectangular stones left on the platform and using them as a rest for my knee. Sometimes for a change I sit on them and work that way. It doesn't keep the bandage from getting dirty, but there's no helping that.

I don't intend to work for long on my first day, but I lose track of time. It's only when I break off to blink away a fragment of mortar from my eye that I see how low the sun is. The afternoon has passed without my noticing.

Now I've stopped various discomforts begin to announce themselves. My arms and shoulders are aching and sore, and I've an impressive collection of blisters from gripping the hammer. There's also a livid bruise forming on the back of my hand, evidence of the times when I've missed the chisel.

I don't mind: it feels like honest pain. But I must have caught my watch as well, because there's a crack running across its face. The sight of it cuts through my mood like a slap. It's still working but I take it off and slip it into my pocket anyway. I don't want to damage it any more, and the watch is an uncomfortable reminder of things I'd rather forget.

Besides, I don't need to know the time while I'm here: the farm operates to its own rhythm. Taking off the cap from my sweat-damp hair, I look at what I've achieved. The newly hacked-out mortar is paler than the older areas, but also dispiritingly small seen against the expanse of wall that remains. Still, I've made a start, and that feels surprisingly good.

Leaving the hammer and chisel on the platform, I climb slowly down the ladder. The sun-heated rungs sting my blisters, and each step is an effort. I'd kill for a beer, I think, limping into the storeroom to collect my clothes. A bottle – no, a glass. Tall and amber and misted with condensation. I can almost taste it.

Tormenting myself with the thought, I go back into the courtyard. I don't notice Mathilde until I hear a crash of breaking crockery. I look round and see her in the doorway with Michel on one arm. At her feet is a shattered bowl of eggs, the bright yellow yolks smearing the cobbles.

She's staring at me, white-faced.

'Sorry, I didn't mean to surprise you,' I say.

'No, I . . . I didn't realize you were there.'

Her eyes stray to the red overalls I'm wearing, and suddenly I think I understand. 'There's no shade up there so I put these on. I hope that's OK?'

'Of course,' she says, too quickly.

I feel bad for giving her a shock but I wasn't to know wearing the overalls would upset her. Her reaction makes me think I'm right about Michel's father, but she's already recovered her poise. The baby contentedly gums a piece of bread as she moves him to a more comfortable position.

'How's the work gone?'

'Good. Well, OK.' I shrug, trying to see where I've hacked out. It's hardly visible from down here. 'I've made a start, anyway.'

Mathilde holds out her hand for my bundled-up clothes. 'Would you like me to wash those?'

'Thanks.' I don't argue. The freezing water in the barn won't get rid of the sanglochon smell, and I don't relish washing in it myself. I'm tempted to ask if I can take a shower or a bath, but I can imagine what Arnaud would say to that. Well, if I can't have a hot bath or a cold beer, there's one thing I'd like at least.

'You said earlier there was somewhere I could buy cigarettes. How far away is it?'

'A couple of kilometres. Too far for you to walk.'

'I don't mind. I can take my time.'

It isn't as if I've anything else to do. Now I've stopped working the endorphin high is starting to fade and my nerves are already beginning to jangle. It'll be worse knowing I can't calm them with a cigarette.

Mathilde glances back at the house, as though debating something. She pushes a strand of hair behind her ear.

'Give me half an hour.'

8

YELLOW DUST BILLOWS UP around the van as it bounces over the track's potholed surface. Mathilde is driving with the windows down, trying to dissipate some of the heat that's built up inside during the day. The vinyl of the seats is torn, white wadding showing through in places. Mine has been mended, if it can be called that, with black electrical tape. Despite the open windows, the van smells of diesel, dog and stale pipe tobacco.

When I went back to the house after getting washed and changed Mathilde and Gretchen were arguing in the doorway. I stopped at the corner of the courtyard, not wanting to interrupt.

'But it doesn't need doing!' Gretchen was insisting.

'Yes, it does.'

'Georges cleaned it yesterday! They're only pigs, they don't mind what they eat!'

'Please, just do as you're told.'

'Papa didn't say I had to. Why do I always have to do what you say? You're just trying to get me out of the way so you can go into town with him—'

'Just do it!'

It was the first time I'd heard Mathilde raise her voice. Gretchen flounced away, not so much as pausing when she saw me at the bottom of the courtyard.

'I hope you enjoy yourselves!' she snapped, flip-flops cuffing the cobbles as she marched past.

I watched her stomp off down the track towards the woods, then looked back at Mathilde. She was staring at the cobblestones, her posture tired. Then, realizing I was there, she straightened. Wordlessly, she went to the van, leaving me to follow her.

She doesn't speak a word as she drives up the track to the road. When we reach the closed gate she stops, leaving the ignition running as she climbs out.

'I'll do it,' I offer.

'It's all right.'

The padlock is obviously stiff, but eventually she manages to unlock it. She swings the gate open, lifting it up the last few feet to keep it from dragging on the ground. Returning to the van, she drives out onto the road, then gets out again to shut the gate. In the wing mirror I see her fastening the padlock, securing the farm behind us.

'Why do you keep it locked?' I ask when she gets back in, re-membering how I'd found the gate open when I came for water.

'My father prefers it.'

She seems to think that's all the explanation that's needed. Maybe it is, but as she sets off I still wonder who'd left the gate open before.

Being outside again is like re-entering a world I'd forgotten exists. I'm not prepared for how exposed I feel, how used I've become to the farm's insular universe. But I'm soon lulled by the warm evening, and the steady note of the van's engine. Begin-ning to enjoy myself, I rest my arm on the open window and let the slipstream buffet my face. The air has a warm, summer smell of pollen and tarmac. Mathilde, though, is less relaxed. And in a hurry to get back, judging by how fast she's driving.

The old van vibrates under the sustained speed. The grey strip of road stretches ahead of us. Wheat fields come right to the roadside, broken up with tall and feathery poplars and fatter trees that look like broccoli florets.

Mathilde's hand brushes my arm as she shifts down a gear when the van begins to grumble on an incline. It's accidental, but suddenly I'm aware of her rather than our surroundings. She's wearing a white shirt, cotton sleeves rolled just below her elbows. Her hands look weathered on the steering wheel. Against the brown skin her chipped fingernails are pink with health.

The silence, which until then I haven't noticed, begins to feel uncomfortable.

'Where did you learn to speak English?' I ask to break it.

She blinks as though her thoughts are far away. 'I'm sorry?'

'You spoke English when I first woke in the loft. Did you learn it at school?'

'My mother taught me. She was a teacher, before she got married. Languages. English, German and Italian.'

'So do you speak all of those?'

'Not really. A little Italian, but I've forgotten most of that now.'

'How about Gretchen?' I ask, remembering her sister's blank face when I lapsed into English.

'No. My mother died before Gretchen was old enough to learn,' Mathilde says flatly, and then: 'We're here.'

She pulls into the forecourt of a dirty white building. It's little more than a shack with a garage at one side and a bar-tabac at the other. A rusted sign for Stella Artois hangs outside, and a few battered tables and chairs stand under a faded awning.

Mathilde pulls up by one of the pumps. She seems calm enough, but there's a tiny pulse visible in the open neck of her shirt, fluttering like a trip hammer. For some reason I feel sorry for her, and what I say next surprises me as much as her.

'Do you want to come in for a drink?'

She looks at me, and for a second there's a flash of what could be alarm. Then it's gone. 'No, thank you. But I need fuel, so there's time if you want one.'

My face is red as I unfasten my seatbelt. As it slithers over me I have a sudden flashback to the bloodstained seatbelt in the Audi, and quickly climb out. The hum of the pump starts from behind me as I settle the crutch under my arm and go across the dusty concrete to the bar.

Inside it's dark, unlit except by the window and open doorway. There aren't many customers: three or four men at the tables and an older one sitting at the bar. The barman is drawing a beer as I enter, expertly flipping up the tap to stop the flow, then whisking the foam from the top with a wooden spatula. He sets it down for the old man, who doesn't look up from his newspaper. I get one or two glances as I limp in, but it feels so good to be in a bar again, back in society, that I almost commit the unforgivable sin of smiling.

Instead, keeping my face acceptably deadpan, I go and sit on one of the high stools.

'Six packs of Camels and a beer,' I say, in response to the enquiring lift of the barman's chin.

He's a thin man in his fifties, receding hair brushed sideways to hide a balding crown. I know how John Mills felt in *Ice Cold in Alex* as I watch him pour the beer, angling the stemmed glass so that the foam doesn't become too thick. I've worked in enough bars myself to appreciate the practised way he does it, but the associations that accompany the memory are unwelcome. I put them from my mind as he sets the beer down in front of me.

The glass is cold and beaded with condensation. Slowly, I raise it to my lips and drink. The beer is icy and clean, with a faint flavour of hops. I make myself stop before I empty the glass completely, lower it, and breathe a sigh.

The barman is watching me. 'Good?'

'Very.'

'Another?'

I'm tempted, but I don't want to keep Mathilde waiting. From where I am I can see the van through the window, but she's out of sight around the far side. 'Better not.'

The barman wipes the counter. 'Travelled far?'

'No, I'm staying round here.'

'Whereabouts?'

I'm already regretting saying anything. But he's looking at me, waiting. 'A farm, just up the road.'

'The Dubreuil place?'

'No.' I tell myself it hardly matters: no one here knows me. 'They're called Arnaud.'

The barman pauses his wiping to stare at me. Then he calls to someone behind me at the tables. 'Hey, Jean-Claude, this guy's staying at Arnaud's farm!'

Conversations stop. There's a rustle as the old man reading the newspaper lowers it to watch. Bewildered, I look around. Everyone's attention is on a burly character in dust-covered bib-and-brace overalls. He's around forty, with a dark growth of stubble and black eyebrows that form a single line across the bridge of his nose. He puts down his beer glass and looks at me, taking in my red hair, bandaged foot and the crutch.

'English?' His voice is brusque but not hostile.

'That's right.'

'So you're working for Arnaud?'

I give what I hope is a nonchalant shrug. 'Just passing through.'

'Passing through his daughters, you mean,' someone from another table comments. He's younger than me, with oil-stained jeans and a nasty grin. There's a general chuckling from the group he's with, but the burly man doesn't join in.

'Watch your mouth, Didier.'

The laughter dies away. I finish my beer without tasting it. I glance outside to see if Mathilde's finished filling up. I can't see her.

'What happened to your foot?' the man asks.

'I trod on a nail.' It's the first thing that comes to mind.

'Must have been a big nail.'

'It was.'

The barman puts my cigarettes down. My face is flaming as I cram them in my pockets and fumble for the money. He half-drops my change so the coins roll on the counter. As I gather it up the door opens.

It's Mathilde.

Her footsteps are the only sound as she comes over to the bar. Her face is composed, but there's a flush to her throat and cheeks.

'I'd like to pay for the fuel.'

The barman looks over at the burly individual in bib and braces, then rings in the sale. Only then does Mathilde acknowledge the other man's presence, although the way she turns to face him tells me she's known he's there all along.

'Jean-Claude.'

'Mathilde.'

It's agonizingly formal. Nothing else is said as the barman hands her the change. More politely than he did mine, I notice. He even inclines his head slightly as she takes it.

'Thank you.'

I can feel them all watching us as we walk to the door. I let her go out first, so I'm not sure if she hears the quick pig-grunt from the one called Didier or the stifled laughter that follows it. I close the door without looking back and limp after her as quickly as I can. Neither of us speaks as we get into the van. I wait for her to say something, but she starts the engine and pulls out without a word.

'Nice neighbours,' I comment.

Mathilde stares through the insect-flecked windscreen. 'They're not used to strangers.'

I don't think it was my being a stranger that was the problem. I want to ask why Arnaud's name prompted such a reaction, and who Jean-Claude is. But Mathilde's manner makes it clear she doesn't want to talk about it.

As we drive back to the farm in silence, I wonder if I've just met Michel's father.

It's a relief to be inside the farm's borders again. A fragile sense of security returns as Mathilde closes the gate behind us and re-fastens the padlock. She's filled fuel cans as well as the van's tank, but declines my offer to help unload them. 'I'll bring your dinner later,' is all she says.

The beautiful evening is lost on me as I go back down to the barn. I know I can't stay hidden on the farm for ever but I wish I'd never let Mathilde take me to the bar. I've drawn attention to myself needlessly, all for the sake of a beer and a few packs of cigarettes. And I don't even know why. I'm not surprised that there's no love lost between Arnaud and his neighbours – God knows, it's hard to imagine him getting on with anybody. Even so, the atmosphere in the bar seemed about more than the usual small-town feud.

He must have really pissed someone off.

I take the cigarettes up to the loft. I'm getting adept at handling the steps, and when I stop when I reach the first-floor gallery it isn't because I'm out of breath.

The trapdoor is open.

I remember closing it when I left. I pause, listening, but there's no noise coming from inside. I go up the rest of the steps as quietly as I can, although anyone up there must have heard me by now. Then I look through the open hatchway.

Gretchen is sitting on the bed. Her back is to me and my

rucksack is beside her, half its contents scattered on the mattress. I don't see the polythene package, but it was buried right at the bottom. Gretchen evidently found what she wanted before she got that far. She's moving her head rhythmically, the earphones almost hidden in her thick hair. I can hear the tinny whisper of music from them as I go up the rest of the steps and walk up behind her, no longer trying to be silent.

She opens her eyes in surprise as I lean down and switch off the MP3 player. 'Oh! I didn't hear you.'

'What are you doing?'

I try not to sound angry but it comes out accusing. Gretchen looks instantly guilty.

'Nothing. I was only listening to some music.'

I grab a handful of clothes and begin stuffing them back into the rucksack. As I do I feel to make sure the package is in there. Some of the tension leaves me when I touch the plastic wrapper, but my hands are still shaking.

'You should ask.'

'I did! You said I could!'

Now she mentions it, I can vaguely recall saying something. It was when I thought I was leaving the next day, though, and I'd forgotten all about it. Gretchen obviously hasn't. 'I meant when I was here,' I say, less heatedly.

'It's our barn. I don't need your permission.'

'That doesn't mean you can go through my things.'

'You think I'm interested in your old socks and T-shirts?' She's becoming angry herself. 'I don't like your stupid music anyway! And if Papa knew I was here you'd be in trouble!'

There seems a flaw in that logic, but I don't have the energy to argue. 'Look, I'm sorry I snapped. I just wasn't expecting anyone up here.'

Gretchen seems mollified. Showing no sign of wanting to leave, she leans against the rocking horse, stroking its mane as I

113

take the cigarettes and lighter from my pockets and drop them on the mattress.

'Can I try one?'

'Do you smoke?'

'No.'

'Then you shouldn't start.'

I know I'm being hypocritical but I can't help it. Gretchen pouts. 'Why are you in such a bad mood?'

'I'm just tired. It's been a busy day.'

She considers that, fingers twirling a hank of black horse-hair. 'How long are you going to stay? Until you've finished the whole house?'

'I don't know.' I'm trying hard not to think that far ahead.

'Papa says you're running away from something.'

'Papa doesn't know everything.'

'He knows more than you. I'm not sure he even likes you. But if you're nice to me I'll put in a good word.'

I don't say anything to that. Hoping she'll take the hint and leave, I gather up another T-shirt from the bed. Something falls from it.

It's the photograph.

'Who's that?' Gretchen asks.

'No one.'

I go to pick it up but Gretchen beats me to it. She holds the photograph away from me, teasingly.

'I thought you didn't have a girlfriend?'

'I don't.'

'Then why are you carrying her picture around with you?'

'I forgot to throw it away.'

'Then you won't care what happens to it.' Grinning, she picks up the cigarette lighter from the mattress and holds it under the photograph.

'Don't,' I say, reaching for it.

She twists away, still holding the photograph poised over the lighter. 'Ah–ah, I thought you weren't bothered?'

'Look, just give it to me.'

'Not until you tell me who it is.' She flicks a flame from the lighter. 'You'll have to be quick . . .'

I make a grab for the photograph. Gretchen gives a delighted laugh and snatches it away, and as she does one corner dips into the flame. There's a bloom of yellow as the glossy card ignites. Gretchen squeals and drops it. I knock the burning photograph away from the mattress, trying to put it out as the image blackens and curls. But it's fully alight, and the loft is a tinderbox of dry wood. Snatching up the bottle of water from by the bed I quickly douse the flames.

There's a hiss as the fire is snuffed out.

A burnt smell fills the loft. I stare at the puddle of ash and water on the floor.

'You made me burn my fingers,' Gretchen pouts.

I set the bottle down. 'You'd better go.'

'It wasn't my fault. You shouldn't have grabbed for it.'

'Your father will wonder where you are.'

She hesitates, but mention of Arnaud does the trick. I don't look round as she goes through the trapdoor. When her footsteps have died away I bend down and pick through the wet ash. There's nothing left of the photograph except a small piece of white border, blackened at the edges.

I let it drop back onto the floor and go to find something to clean up.

London

CHLOE GOES MISSING ONE night after work. I've been out with Callum and a couple of students after the last class. Not to the Domino, though: not any more. Where I used to enjoy being able to look up and see Chloe working behind the bar, anticipating the quiet moments when she'd be able to join us, now there's no pleasure in it.

'Do you feel you have to check on me?' she asked one night, when I'd said I'd see her there later.

'No,' I'd said, surprised. 'If you don't want me to come, just say so.'

She'd shrugged, turning away. 'It's up to you.'

It's almost one o'clock by the time I leave Callum and walk back to the flat. The smell of oil and turpentine is less strong now. Chloe hasn't painted since before we went to Brighton, but that's something we don't talk about.

She won't finish at the bar till two at the earliest, so I make myself a coffee and pick out a DVD. I settle on *L'Été meurtrier*, which like all the others in my collection I've seen several times. Chloe claims I like it because Isabelle Adjani spends virtually the entire film naked. She has a point, but the film's cinematography is beautiful even without that.

I watch the cycle of passion and tragedy run its inevitable

course. Only when the film ends do I realize how late it is: Chloe should have been back an hour ago.

No one answers when I phone the bar. I wait it out for another half-hour, then leave a note in case she comes back and set off for the Domino. The streets are empty. I follow the same route to the King's Road that Chloe and I used to walk, although since I've stopped meeting her she usually gets either a lift or a taxi. The doors of the bar are locked, no lights showing from inside, but I bang on them anyway. When the echoes have died down the building remains dark and silent.

I don't know what to do. I stand on the pavement and look up and down the deserted street, as if I might see her walking towards me. I've no idea where most of the bar staff live, but I once went with Chloe to a party at Tanja's. I don't even know if she's been working tonight, but it's all I can think of.

Even though I walk quickly it's nearly five o'clock when I reach her flat in Shepherd's Bush. The entrance is unlit and I have to use the light from my phone to read the names on the intercom. I press hers and wait. It's cold, but that isn't why I'm shivering. When she doesn't answer I press again, and this time keep on pressing.

'All right, all right, who is it?' The voice crackles through the intercom, angry and distorted.

'Tanja, it's Sean,' I interrupt, putting my mouth close to the speaker grille. 'Do you know where—'

'Sean who?'

'Chloe's boyfriend. She—'

'Jesus, do you know what *time* it is?'

'I know, I'm sorry, but Chloe didn't come home from work. Do you know where she is?'

'No, why should I?' She sounds tired and irritable.

My heart sinks. I'd hoped she'd say Chloe was there, that she'd gone to a party. Anything.

'Did you see her leave?'

'Yeah, she . . . Oh, no, that's right, I left before her tonight. She was still talking to this guy who came in. She said for me to go.'

'A guy? What guy? Who was he?'

'Just some guy. Look, I've got to get up early tomorrow—'

'Had you seen him before?'

'No, I've told you, he was just some guy! Flashy, but Chloe seemed to know him. Now can I get back to bed?'

The early-morning workers are beginning to filter onto the streets as I walk back to the flat. The note is still on the kitchen table where I left it. I look in the bedroom to check anyway, but the bed is empty.

At eight o'clock I call Yasmin. I don't really expect Chloe to be there. She isn't.

'Have you called the police?' Yasmin asks, instantly matter-of-fact.

'No, not yet.' That's a last resort I've been putting off. 'Do you think I should?'

'Give it till noon,' she says at last.

It's nearly eleven o'clock when I hear someone unlocking the door. I'm at the kitchen table, my mouth foul from coffee and fatigue. When Chloe walks in there's a moment's breathless relief. She pauses on seeing me, then closes the door.

'Jesus, where've you been? Are you all right?'

'Yeah.' She makes a vague gesture. 'I stayed at a friend's.'

'I've been worried sick! Why didn't you call?'

'It was getting late. I didn't want to disturb you.'

Chloe won't look at me. Her face is pale, blue shadows marking the skin under her eyes. The relief I felt has already gone, replaced by something else.

'What friend?'

'No one you know.' She starts moving towards the bathroom. 'I've got to—'

'What *friend*?'

Chloe stops with her back to me. 'Someone I used to know, that's all.'

'Tanja told me you saw some man in the bar last night. Was it him?'

Her head jerks in surprise. Then she gives a quick nod.

'Is he an ex-boyfriend?'

Again, a nod. The breath seems to be squeezed from my chest. 'Did you sleep with him?'

She's turned towards me now, her face drawn. 'Don't, please—'

'Did you *sleep* with him?'

'No!' she shouts, suddenly angry. 'Nothing happened, all right? Now leave me alone!'

'Leave you *alone*? You stay out all night with another man and expect me to just *ignore* it?'

'Yes! It's none of your business!'

Stunned, I stare at her. My anger's still there, but I know if I give in to it there'll be no going back. 'You really mean that?'

'No. I don't know.' Quietly, she starts to cry. 'I'm sorry, OK?'

She rushes into the bathroom and locks the door. I sit there feeling nothing, absolutely nothing at all.

9

I'M ALREADY UP WHEN Mathilde brings my breakfast next morning, woken by a hangover and the repetitive crowing of a cockerel outside. I drank another bottle of wine with dinner, and whatever else can be said about Château Arnaud, it's strong. I go down to the outhouse and put my head under the tap, washing away the last vestiges of sleep. Water dripping from my hair, I sit outside the barn in just my jeans, enjoying the early cool on my bare flesh.

It's a beautiful morning, like every other morning since I arrived here. The sky is an endless blue, not yet burned white by the heat that will come later. On the horizon there's a dark strip of cloud, but it seems too distant to be threatening.

I flick my foot at the rust-coloured hen which seems intent on pecking around it and look up as I hear Mathilde approach.

'Good morning,' she says.

Her face, as ever, gives little away. She sets the tray with my breakfast on the ground beside me. An almost invisible whorl of steam curls up from the coffee, and the bread smells freshly made. The two peeled eggs lie together in the dish like a pair of white buttocks.

'I made this,' Mathilde says, producing something she's been carrying under one arm. 'For your foot.'

It's the sole of a rubber boot, from which most of the upper has been cut away except for the heel. Trailing laces hang from holes punched on either side.

'Right.' I'm not sure what to say. 'Thanks.'

'It's to protect the bandage. I thought it might help while you work.' She pushes her hair back. It's the closest to nervous that I've seen her. 'I have a favour to ask. Gretchen told me you used to teach English.'

'Only privately,' I say warily. 'Not in a proper school.'

'Would you teach her?'

'Uh, I'm not sure that's—'

'I'd pay you myself,' she goes on, quickly. 'Not much. But you wouldn't have to give formal lessons. Just . . . while you're talking to her.'

I want to say no. After yesterday evening I've come to the conclusion that the less I have to do with her sister the better. 'Couldn't you teach her yourself?'

'My English isn't good enough.' She gives an apologetic shrug. 'And she doesn't like me telling her what to do.'

'What does your father say?'

'He won't be a problem.'

Which isn't quite the same as saying he approves, but Mathilde knows him better than I do. She's waiting for my answer, and try as I might I can't think of a good excuse to refuse.

'I suppose I could give her a few lessons . . .'

Mathilde's smile is an altogether more sober thing than her sister's, but while it lasts it makes her look years younger. 'Thank you.'

I watch her walk back to the courtyard, then examine the shoe. It smells of old rubber and probably only took a few minutes to make. Still, I'm touched: I can't remember the last time anyone did anything for me. And it does make life easier. When I put it on after breakfast I find I can actually set my foot down, even put enough weight on it to take a couple of hobbling steps.

On the scaffolding it gives me a feeling of stability and con-fidence I haven't had before. Taking up the hammer, I do my best to ignore my headache, which forms a syncopated throb with each blow, hoping the exertion will help me to sweat out my hangover. The blisters on my palm are sore but I can't bring myself to wear the sweat-stained gloves that were in the overall pockets.

Gradually, the stiffness begins to ease out of my muscles. I finish off the area I've been working on and start on the wall by the unshuttered bedroom window. Several stones underneath the gutter are loose, and there's nothing for it but to take them out altogether. Before I know it there's a hole in the wall big enough to crawl into, exposing the rough internal stonework underneath. I'm slightly awed by the damage I've caused, uncomfortably aware that I don't really know what I'm doing.

But there's still something satisfying about the focused violence of hammer and chisel. I pound away, fragments of mortar stinging my face like shrapnel. It doesn't even hurt so much when I hit my hand any more. The flesh and bone have become deadened, numbed by repeated blows. It's only when I stop long enough for it to start to recover that I can feel it.

I'm soon lost in the hammer's rhythm. My world shrinks to a thin strip of wall above the bedroom window, so that I'm slow to react when something inside the room catches my eye. Then it comes again, a flicker at the edge of my vision. I look up and see a face on the other side of the dusty glass.

'Jesus!'

The chisel clatters over the edge of the boards, bouncing between the wall and the scaffolding to ring onto the cobbles below. Gretchen opens the window, laughing.

'Did I frighten you?'

'No,' I say, but my heart is still thudding. 'Well, maybe a little.'

'I brought you a coffee.' She hands me a large cup. She sounds pleased with herself. 'I thought it would save you climbing all the way down.'

'Thanks.'

I'll have to go down anyway for the chisel, but I don't point that out. This is the first I've seen of Gretchen since she set fire to the photograph yesterday evening, although she doesn't seem too bothered about that now. She stays in the bedroom, leaning through the open window while I sit on the ledge.

'Mathilde says you're going to give me English lessons.' There's an archness to the way she says it.

'If you want them.'

'It was her idea,' she says, her face momentarily darkening. Then it clears. 'You could teach me in the afternoons. Papa'll be asleep, and Mathilde looks after Michel. We won't be disturbed.'

She's grinning, waiting to see how I'll react. I sip my coffee with a nonchalance I don't feel. It's strong and black, threatening to burn my tongue. 'Whatever.'

'What's that on your foot?' Gretchen asks, noticing the improvised rubber shoe.

'Mathilde made it.'

'Mathilde?' Her smile's gone. 'It looks stupid.'

I let that pass. A musty smell, not quite unpleasant, comes from the open window. Without the veil of dirty glass the peeling wallpaper and cracked plaster of the bedroom are more obvious. The iron bedstead with its lumpy mattress and bolster looks ready to collapse onto the bare floorboards.

'Whose room was this?' I ask.

'Maman's.'

I notice she doesn't say it was Arnaud's as well. I point to the photograph on the dresser. 'Is that her with your father?'

She nods. 'Their wedding.'

'How old were you when she died?'

'Just a baby. I can't really remember her.' Gretchen sounds

bored. 'I used to play in her wheelchair after she'd died. But then I fell out and hurt myself so Papa smashed it up.'

Just as well she never had a pony, I think. But, like a lot of things where Gretchen's concerned, I keep that to myself. She's gone quiet, and I swear I can feel what she's going to say next.

'Why don't you come inside?'

'No, thanks.'

She's moved to make room for me to climb in. 'It'll be OK, nobody comes up to this room any more.'

The coffee's still too hot but I take a drink anyway. 'I'll stay out here.'

'What's wrong?'

'Nothing.'

'So why won't you come in? Don't you want to?'

'I'm working.'

'No, you aren't. You're drinking coffee.'

Her smile is both teasing and confident. There's something about Gretchen that puts me in mind of a cat: sinuous and purring to be stroked, but capable of raking you with its claws if the mood takes it.

I've never been comfortable with cats.

'I'm still working,' I say. My head is thumping, the hangover back full force.

She goes to sit on the bed, one leg swinging. 'Are you gay?'

'No.'

'Are you sure? Saying no to a pretty girl's invitation, I think perhaps you are gay.'

'OK, I'm gay.'

She seems to have forgotten all about the scene with the photograph, but I'm not going to mention it if she isn't. Her smile is mischievous as she lies back on the bed, crooking one knee and propping herself up on her elbows.

'I don't believe you. I think you're just shy and need to relax.'

Gretchen leans further back on the bed. She raises an eyebrow, still smiling. 'Well?'

'*Hey! You up there!*'

Gretchen's smile vanishes as Arnaud's shout comes from the courtyard. Hoping she has the sense to stay quiet, I look down over the scaffold. Arnaud is glaring up at me from the cobbles. The spaniel is by his feet, ears cocked as it looks up as well.

'What are you doing?'

I don't know how much he can see or hear from where he's standing. I resist the impulse to look over my shoulder.

'Taking a break.'

'You've only just started.' He fixes me with an unfriendly stare and motions with his head. 'Get down here.'

'Why?'

'I've got another job for you.'

I don't know whether to be relieved or not. 'What sort of job?'

'Slaughtering a pig. Unless you're too squeamish?'

I hope he's joking. But his eyes are bright and watchful, daring me to refuse. And I don't want to stand around up here any longer than I have to: I don't trust Gretchen not to do something stupid.

'I'll catch you up.'

I turn away before he can say anything else. In the instant before I look in the bedroom I have an image of Gretchen still lying on the bed, so vivid that I can almost see her tan skin against the faded blue stripes of the mattress.

The bed is empty. So is the room. On the floorboards is a faint tracery where her feet have disturbed the dust, running to and from the door.

I close the window as best I can and make my way over to the ladder.

★

Arnaud and Georges have already singled out one of the sanglochons. I can hear squeals and gruff shouts as I go along the path to the pens. When I reach the clearing Georges is herding the condemned animal towards the gate of the sows' pen, which Arnaud is holding open. The rest of the pigs have, sensibly, made themselves scarce. They're at the far end of the pen, milling about as far from the two men as they can get. In the smaller pen nearby the dark shape of the boar is stalking up and down along the fence, grunting excitedly.

The sow Georges is driving towards the gate is comparatively small, not much bigger than a Labrador, but still looks big enough to bowl him over. He clearly knows what he's doing, though. He keeps it moving by slapping at it with a thin stick, steering it with a square of wooden board that he holds against its head. Neither he nor Arnaud acknowledges me as the pig is driven out of the pen. Arnaud follows closely behind as Georges directs the animal towards the small cinderblock hut that stands – ominously, it now seems – by itself.

'Close that,' he tells me, gesturing to the open gate.

He walks off without waiting to see if I do. The remaining pigs are starting to drift over to the gate, so I quickly shut and fasten it with a loop of wire that hooks over the fence post. There's a curse from Arnaud. I look around to see him sending the spaniel away with a kick as it gets too close. The dog yelps and runs off down the path.

They get the sanglochon to the entrance of the hut before it baulks. Its squeals become frantic, as though something about the place has panicked it. Georges has his full weight behind the board, pressing against the terrified animal, while Arnaud is trying to block it from escaping with his legs.

'Are you just going to watch?' he hollers at me.

I go across, standing opposite Arnaud so that, with Georges behind, the sanglochon has nowhere to run. I put my hand on its back and push. Its hide is rough and bristly. Solid, like a leather sandbag. Georges whacks it with the stick and the sow darts through the doorway.

Its squeals are amplified inside, pitching off the unyielding walls and concrete floor. I stay in the entrance, reluctant to go any further.

'Get in here and shut the door,' Arnaud snaps. 'Leave the top open.'

I do as I'm told. It's a stable door, split into two halves. There are no windows in the small hut, so the open top section is the only source of light. Flies buzz excitedly inside, and I try not to recoil from the stink of dried blood and faeces. In the centre of the shed is a waist-high stone slab. A rail is attached to the ceiling above it, from which hangs a pulley with a chain and hook. I stay close to the door as Georges picks up a long-handled lump hammer from the slab. It's bigger than the one I've been using, but the old man hefts it easily, his oversized forearms corded with tendons and veins.

The sanglochon is blundering from side to side in the corner, although it seems to realize there's no way out. Georges goes over to it and takes something from his pocket. Scraps of vegetables. He scatters them on the floor in front of the pig, scratching it behind the ears and muttering reassuringly. After a moment the animal calms down enough to get their scent. Still agitated, it sniffs at them. Georges waits until it puts its head down to eat and then hits it between the eyes with the hammer.

I flinch at the meaty thud. The pig drops, twitching on the floor like a sleeping dog chasing rabbits. While Georges takes hold of its back legs, Arnaud pulls the chain down from the pulley with a swift rattle. The routine seems almost choreographed, suggesting they've done it many times. Arnaud winds the chain around the pig's legs and slips the hook through a link higher up to hold it in place. As he straightens he winces and rubs his back.

'Give me a hand.'

I don't move.

'Come on, don't just stand there!'

I make myself go forward. He shoves a length of chain in my hand. Georges comes and takes hold of it with me. I still have the crutch under my arm. I hesitate, unable to think what to do with it, then lean it against the wall. Arnaud moves clear, walking stiffly.

'Pull.'

The chain is cold and rough. It moves easily for a few inches, and then checks as it takes up the pig's weight. There's a stench as the animal voids its bowels. The chain tugs at my arms as Georges heaves on it. I do the same. I've lost all volition. When he pulls, I pull. I feel the strain in my back, my arms. The pig's rear end lifts off the floor, and then it's hanging clear. It's still twitching, still alive. We pull it higher.

'OK.'

Arnaud puts a brake on the chain to stop it running out. We let go. The pulley squeaks on the rail as Arnaud drags it until the pig is suspended over the stone slab. It swings like a pendulum. Georges has put on a leather butcher's apron from a hook on the wall, stiff and crusted with black splashes. As he ties it, Arnaud fetches a wide aluminium bucket from a corner. He positions it under the pig's head, steadying its swinging with one hand. Georges goes to the slab again, this time picking up a long-bladed butchering knife. I'm watching it all as if I'm not really there, and then, as Georges goes to the pig, Arnaud turns to me with a sly smile.

'Do you want to do it?'

I grab for my crutch as Georges puts the knife to the sow's throat. From behind me there's a sound of something splashing into the aluminium tub, and then I'm outside. I make it a few yards before doubling over, the eggs I ate earlier rising on a wave of bile into my throat. There's a rushing in my ears as the bright clearing darkens. I hear the hollow *thud* of the hammer again, see the pig's skull squirt blood. Other images tumble over it, one falling body blurring with another: *someone screaming, blood shining black under the sick glow of a streetlight . . .*

The rushing in my head becomes the indifferent buzzing of flies. The clearing re-forms around me, restoring me to the here and now. I hear someone come out of the shed.

'No stomach for it, eh?'

There's pleasure in Arnaud's voice. I straighten, taking a last, steadying breath. 'I'm fine.'

'You don't look it. What's wrong? Frightened of a little blood?'

He holds up his hands. They glisten wetly, and panic flutters up in me again. I force it down. 'I thought you needed some sort of licence to slaughter animals? EU rules, or something?'

'No one tells me what to do on my own farm. Least of all a bunch of suited bureaucrats.' Arnaud regards me sourly as he takes a rag from his pocket and wipes his hands. 'Remind me again why you're here?'

My hangover has returned. I try to clear my head as Arnaud puts the bloodstained rag away. 'What do you mean?'

'There's got to be a good reason for a city boy like you to hide himself away. Won't anyone wonder where you are?'

'No.'

'Don't you have any friends?'

'None who'll stay up nights worrying where I am.'

'Family, then.'

'My mother left when I was a kid and my father's dead.'

'What did he die of? Shame?' Arnaud's grin is savage. 'You still haven't explained why you want to bury yourself away in the middle of nowhere.'

'Maybe that's my own business.'

'And what if I decide to make it mine? Give the police a little call?'

Strangely, the threat doesn't bother me. 'Then I'm sure they'll be interested in the statues and traps in the woods.'

The smile vanishes. The pale-grey eyes turn hard, then he grins. 'So you do have a set of balls on you after all. About time; I was starting to wonder.'

There's a banging from the pens at the other side of the shed. Still grinning, Arnaud tips his head towards it.

'Old Bayard's scented the blood,' he says, almost fondly.

'Bayard?'

'The boar.' There's the sound of wood breaking. Arnaud's expression changes. 'He's getting out.'

Bad back or not, he outpaces me as he sets off around the shed to the boar's pen. The fence is visibly bending as the boar batters at it, squealing furiously. One of the planks has a jagged split. As we get there another crack sounds out and the spilt widens, showing fresh white wood.

Arnaud yells at the boar, clapping his hands as he reaches the fence. It answers with a shriek of its own, intensifying its attack. Snatching up a stick, Arnaud jabs at it through the slats.

'Go on, you bugger! Get back!'

The animal is enraged. Moving more quickly than I would have believed given its bulk, it snaps at the stick. Arnaud pulls it back and jabs again, and there's a crunch as the stick breaks.

Arnaud throws it down. 'Georges!' he shouts over his shoulder. 'He's nearly out! Get a plank!'

Georges is already hurrying from the shed, throwing off the butcher's apron. But the boar becomes even more frenzied as it catches the scent of fresh blood on him. The broken spar gives way and Arnaud jumps back as the animal rams its head through the gap. The massive block of its shoulders crashes into the next spar up, bending it outwards.

'The board! Quick!' Arnaud tells me, pointing.

There's a thick square of plywood nearby, similar to the one Georges used with the smaller pig. I offer it to Arnaud but he waves me away.

'Give me your crutch!'

'What?'

'Your bloody crutch!' He beckons with his hand. 'Come on!'

I hesitate, but another crack from the fence decides me. I hand it over. Arnaud thrusts the padded end in the boar's face. It squeals and snaps at it, tearing the pad off with one of its tusks. Turning the crutch around, he jabs with the shaft. The rubber foot connects with the pig's snout. Arnaud puts all his weight behind it and pushes.

'Get ready with the board!' he grunts as the boar draws back. He gives another jab. 'Now!'

I shove the board against the gap in the fence. A moment later I'm almost bowled over as the boar rams it. I brace myself as best I can but I'm still knocked back until Arnaud stands beside me. He puts his leg against the board next to mine while he thrusts over the fence with the crutch. Even then, it's like trying to stop a bulldozer.

Georges appears again, carrying a long plank in one hand and a steaming bucket in the other. Without stopping, he drops the plank to the ground and goes to the pen several feet away. Leaning over the fence, he slaps his hand on it and calls to the boar, making clicking noises with his tongue. For a moment the animal is too enraged to notice, but then it charges this new annoyance. Before it reaches him Georges tips some of the bucket's contents into the pen. The sweetly rank smell of offal comes from it. The boar slows, snuffling uncertainly at the offering. Then, still grunting bad-temperedly to itself, it buries its snout in it.

Arnaud breathes a sigh of relief and steps away from the board. I begin to do the same.

'Keep it there!'

Walking stiffly, he goes over to Georges. His attention still on the boar, the old man pulls a hammer and several nails from his trouser pocket and gives them to him.

'It needs a new fence,' he tells Arnaud.

'It'll do for now.'

It has the sound of an old argument. Georges's silence makes his disapproval plain.

'Take him out of the way,' Arnaud says.

Georges picks up the bucket and clicks his tongue again. The boar trots after him like a dog as he walks around the pen. When he reaches the opposite side he tips out more slops from the bucket. The boar eagerly begins to eat.

Arnaud picks up the plank Georges dropped, bending with obvious effort. 'All right, you can move.'

My legs are shaking. I hop to one side and lean against the fence, hoping he won't notice. The crutch is lying on the floor. Arnaud kicks it and grins.

'Not much good now, is it?'

He's right. The pad lies in shreds and the metal shaft is bent and buckled. I lean on it experimentally. Useless. I'm surprised how lost I feel, but I'm not about to let Arnaud see that.

'What does he eat when he can't get aluminium?' I ask.

Arnaud chuckles. The incident seems to have put him in a good mood. 'Pigs eat anything. And old Bayard will take a chew of whatever he can get hold of. Think yourself lucky it wasn't his jaws you stepped in. You'd have one foot less if it was.'

I look uneasily over at the boar as Arnaud holds the plank in place and hammers a nail into it. But it's still eating, placid enough as Georges scrubs it with a long-handled brush. It seems quiet now, although I notice that the old man has stayed on the other side of the fence. As I watch he pours something from a bottle onto its back before continuing the rub. Vinegar, I guess, remembering what Gretchen told me.

'Does it always go berserk when you kill another pig?' I ask.

Arnaud speaks around a mouthful of nails. 'If the wind carries the blood to him.'

'Why don't you get one that's less vicious?'

He gives me a sour look as he hits the nail the rest of the way home and goes to the other end of the plank.

'He's a good boar. He only has to cover most sows once or twice to get the job done.' There's pride in his voice. He takes another nail from his mouth and hammers it into place with three blows. 'You don't get rid of prime breeding stock because of a bit of temper.'

'What about the pig you just slaughtered?'

'She was barren. I tried Bayard with her enough times for it to take if it was going to. If they're not going to litter they're no use to me.'

'No wonder he's mad if you're butchering his sows.'

Arnaud laughs. 'Bayard doesn't care about that. He's just impatient for the offal.'

He stands up, wincing. Massaging his back, he thrusts the hammer and nails at me. 'Here. Make yourself useful.'

Leaving me to finish off, he walks out of the clearing without a backward glance.

London

FOR A TIME AFTER Chloe's one-night disappearance, things settle almost back to normal. The fact of it hasn't gone away, but it's something both of us have avoided confronting. I've chosen to accept that she was telling the truth when she said nothing happened, and Chloe appears to have made an effort to put her temporary lapse behind her. If I don't think about it I can almost pretend things between us haven't changed.

But they have.

I've started meeting her at the bar again sometimes when she finishes work. Neither of us has acknowledged the implication behind this, which is that I no longer trust her. It's just part of the unspoken deal we've reached.

One night when I arrive she's at the bar with a man. She's standing next to him while he sits on a tall stool, and at first I think it's a customer. Then I take in the way they lean towards each other, the sombreness of Chloe's expression as she listens to whatever he's saying. I have to pause to steady myself, then I walk over.

Chloe looks up and sees me as I approach. Her eyes widen a little, in either shock or apprehension. The man also looks around now, but I take no notice of him. I force my mouth into the semblance of a smile.

'Hi. You ready to go?'

Chloe's face is alive with nervousness. 'You're early.'

Her eyes flick to the man. He's been staring at me and now I turn to face him. Chloe grows even more flustered.

'Sean . . . this is Jules.'

'Hello, Sean,' he says.

He's about thirty. Good-looking, with a stubbled jawline and gym-honed physique that suggest he's overcompensating for his almost femininely long-lashed eyes. The leather jacket and carefully distressed jeans are too obviously expensive to pull off the street look he's attempting.

I know straight away who he is. He regards me with a slyly condescending smile, as if he knows who I am as well.

I turn to Chloe. 'How long will you be?'

She can't look at me. 'Ten minutes.'

Head down, she hurries off to serve someone. I can feel the man she called Jules watching me. Right then I wish I hadn't given up smoking: it would give me something to do with my hands.

'So you're a teacher,' he says.

'For now.' I hate the thought of Chloe talking to him about me.

He smiles into his vodka. 'For now, eh? Sounds like you've got big plans.'

I don't let myself respond. He sits easily on the high stool, letting his expensive jacket and clothes speak for themselves. I don't ask what he does: I don't want to know.

'So, you and Chloe,' he says.

'What about us?'

'Nothing.' He seems amused again. 'I hear you met a friend of mine a while back.'

'News to me.'

'Guy by the name of Lenny.'

The name doesn't register. And then it does. The scary bastard who stopped us in the street that night. Chloe called him Lenny.

Jules slides off the bar stool. 'Got to go. Tell Chloe I'll be seeing her.'

I don't trust myself to answer. I unclench my hands as I wait for Chloe to finish. We go out and walk along the street. I wait for her to say something, but she doesn't. Not a word.

'Who was that?' I ask at last.

'Who?'

'Jules.'

'Oh, just a customer.'

I stop. Chloe continues a couple of paces, high heels rapping on the pavement, before she stops and turns. This is the first time she's looked me in the eye since I walked in the bar.

'Don't, Chloe.'

'Don't what?

'Treat me like an idiot. That was him, wasn't it?'

'If you already know why bother asking?'

'What did he want?'

'Nothing.'

'So why was he there?'

'He came for a drink. People do, you know.'

'Are you seeing him again?'

'No! I can't help who comes in the fucking bar, can I?'

She hurries away from me. I catch up and stand in front of her, blocking her path. Our breath steams luminously under a streetlight.

'Chloe . . .' Words clog in my throat. 'What's going on? For Christ's sake, just talk to me.'

'There's nothing to talk about.'

'Then why are you being like this?'

'I'm not being like anything. Christ, get off my back, you don't own me!'

'*Own* you? Jesus, I feel like I don't even *know* you!'

'Perhaps you don't!'

Her eyes are bright, with either tears or anger. It feeds my own. 'OK, you know what? Forget it. I'll pack my things and move out.'

It's my turn to walk off. I've not gone far when I hear her footsteps hurrying after me. 'Sean!'

I stop and turn. She puts her arms around me and rests her head on my chest. 'Don't go.'

My relief is so strong it scares me. 'I can't handle you seeing somebody else. If you are, tell me now. Just don't play games with me.'

'I won't,' she says, her voice muffled. 'I'm sorry. I won't, I promise.'

The pressure of her body snuggled against me feels warm and right. I stare over her head at the bleak chain of yellow lights running up the street. The frigid air carries an acrid tang from the unseen river. I stroke the familiar contours of Chloe's back, feeling cold and remote with the certainty that she's lying.

10

'I NEED CEMENT.'

Mathilde looks up at me. The kitchen was empty when I returned my breakfast tray, so I guessed she'd be here in the vegetable garden. There's a plastic bowl of freshly picked beans beside her, but at the moment she's kneeling by the small flower-bed. She turns back to it, plucking out one of the weeds that have snaked up between the plants.

'Isn't there anything else you could be doing?'

'Not really. I've hacked out as much as I can get to, and I better repoint that before I start anywhere else.'

The work's gone quickly this past week. But I've had to remove so many loose stones that the upper level of the house looks ready to collapse. I hope that's only superficial, and there was no option if I was going to do the job properly. Even so, I'd rather not leave the wall in this state for too long.

I've known this was coming for a few days, although I've been putting off telling Mathilde. After what happened at the road-side bar I'm not looking forward to venturing outside the farm again, and I doubt that she is either.

Whatever she's feeling, though, she keeps it to herself. She plucks another weed from the soil. 'When do you want to go?'

That was easier than I expected. I shrug. 'I'll have to make a list of what I need. But that won't take long.'

She doesn't look up from her flowerbed. 'Come up to the house when you're done.'

I realize I've been hoping she'd find an excuse not to go. But there's nothing more to say. Leaving her to her weeding, I limp back round to the courtyard, leaning on the old walking stick Mathilde gave me to replace the crutch eaten by the boar. Its dark wood has teeth marks where one of Lulu's predecessors chewed it, but it's thick and substantial, with a tarnished silver collar on the handle.

I look quite the dandy.

I try to disregard my nerves as I block open the storeroom door so I can see what I'll need to buy. Cement, for a start, but there seems to be plenty of sand. Another bucket and trowel, though, to replace the rusting ones. And a spade, I think, prodding the one frozen in the pile of mortar. It vibrates, twanging like a giant tuning fork. I search around until I find the grubby notepad and pencil stub I discarded from the overall's pocket. I leaf through the pages for a clean one to make a shopping list. It's full of scribbled measurements for old building projects, but one page catches my attention. It's a crude drawing of a naked woman, and talentless as the artist was there's one telling detail.

The woman's hair is tucked behind an ear.

My first thought is that it's Mathilde, that this is further confirmation of who Michel's father is. Then I look again and I'm not so sure. There's a dot on one cheek that could be a dimple, and I've occasionally seen Gretchen tuck her hair back in an unconscious echo of her sister. But the drawing is so primitive it's impossible to tell who it's supposed to be. If anybody: for all I know it could be a random doodle.

I guiltily snap the notebook shut when a noise comes from outside. It's only Georges, though. The old man is trudging across the bottom of the courtyard, a clanking bucket in each hand. I smile ruefully at my reaction. *That'll teach you*. Turning to a clean page, I begin jotting down what I need.

When I've finished I go back to the house. The door is open and Mathilde is busy dissecting a skinned rabbit. The bowl of freshly picked beans is beside her as she cuts and twists, deftly separating a leg joint.

'I'm ready when you are,' I say.

There's a snort from the other side of the room, which is hidden behind the open door. 'About time. It's taken you long enough.'

I didn't realize Arnaud was there. I push the door further back so I can see him. He's sitting at the scarred dining table with a large cup of coffee, Michel on his knee gnawing at a crust of bread.

'It's a big house,' I say, stung despite myself.

'Not that big. Makes me wonder what you do up on that scaffold all day.'

'Oh, you know. Sunbathe, read. Watch TV.'

'It wouldn't surprise me. You're certainly not doing much work.'

There's no real heat in the exchange. The bickering between us has become almost routine. It doesn't mean we like each other.

Arnaud feeds a coffee-soaked crust to Michel. 'He shouldn't have that,' Mathilde tells him.

Her father chuckles as his grandson crams the soggy mulch into his mouth. 'He likes it. He knows what's good for him.'

'He's too young.'

Arnaud is already dipping another piece. 'It's only coffee.'

'I don't want—'

The flat of Arnaud's hand cracks on the table.

'Are you *deaf*?'

Michel jumps at the shout, his face puckering. Arnaud gives Mathilde a final glare.

'Now look what you've done!' He bounces the baby up and down on his knee, his voice and expression softening as soon as he turns to his grandson again. 'Shh, there's a man. Here, there's plenty more.'

Michel grasps the soggy piece of bread he offers and smears it around his mouth. Mathilde silently finishes disassembling the rabbit. The stiff line of her back and the red flush on her neck are her only protest.

A door at the back of the kitchen opens and Gretchen enters. She smiles when she sees me, which is enough to spoil Arnaud's good humour.

'What are you grinning at?' he demands as she saunters across the room.

'Nothing.'

'Doesn't look like nothing to me.'

'I can smile if I want to, can't I?'

'It depends what at.'

His eyes go from his younger daughter to me, sharp and suspicious. There's a world of difference between the posturing grumpiness of a moment ago and the hostility I'm confronted with now. The atmosphere in the kitchen is suddenly charged; even Michel falls silent as he looks up at his grandfather.

Then Mathilde comes and stands between us. It's done so casually it could be accidental.

'You wait by the van while I get the keys,' she says.

I'm not sorry to go. I close the door behind me but I've gone only a few steps when there's the muffled sound of breaking crockery, followed by the siren of Michel's crying. I carry on across the courtyard to the van.

Just another day *chez* Arnauds.

Mathilde's face gives nothing of her feelings away when she emerges from the house. She comes over and holds out a set of keys.

141

'The big key is for the padlock on the gate. You'll need to lock it behind you.'

'You're not coming?'

'No.' Her usual inscrutability seems strained. 'You can drive?'

'Yes, but . . .' I wasn't expecting this. I wasn't looking forward to going, but thought at least Mathilde would be coming with me. 'I don't know where to go.'

'The builders' yard isn't far from the garage. Keep following the road until you reach the town square. It's on your right just after that.'

She's still holding out the keys. I take them reluctantly, still searching for objections. 'What about my foot?'

'The pedals are well spaced. You should be able to manage.' She opens the wallet-like purse and pulls out a few notes. 'That should be enough for cement and whatever else you need. I'd give you an advance on your wages, but my father . . .'

'It doesn't matter.'

I'm too taken aback by this new development to care. Mathilde seems uncomfortable as well. As she turns away, she pushes her hair behind her ear. I'm reminded briefly of the drawing, but I've more pressing worries than Mathilde's private life.

Even though it's still early the inside of the van is stale and hot. I prop my walking stick on the passenger side, then slide behind the wheel and try my bandaged foot on the pedal. Provided I don't snag the home-made shoe, it should be OK. Fastening the seatbelt prompts an unwelcome flare of memory, so I distract myself by checking the controls. I try the pedals again, then waste some more time adjusting the seat before I accept I'm only putting things off.

I turn the key.

The engine catches on the third attempt, rattling and roaring as I pump the accelerator to keep it from dying. When it's settled to a steady grumble I lower the window and slowly drive out of the courtyard. The gears are stubborn. I bump along the track's uneven surface in second. When I reach the gate I go through the time-wasting routine of opening it and driving through, then getting out of the van again to padlock it behind me. I climb back into the van and sit with the engine running, looking at the open road. Get on with it, I tell myself.

There are a few other cars about but not many. The old Renault is reluctant to come out of second. The gear lever is a fiddly thing that juts out from the dashboard, and the engine roars as I force it into third then up to fourth. There's no fifth gear, but the old van cruises along happily enough once it's got used to the idea. I point it straight down the grey strip of tarmac, heading into the heat-haze that retreats as fast as I head towards it. Already I can't understand what I was so anxious about. I relax into the seat, beginning to enjoy myself.

My sunglasses give the parched countryside on either side a blue tint, deepening the sky to an improbable sapphire. I lean my arm out of the window, enjoying the breeze as the wheat fields whip past, until I realize how fast I'm going. Reluctantly, I slow down: the last thing I want is to be stopped for speeding.

Some of my tension returns as I near the garage and bar where Mathilde and I stopped. But there's no one outside, and it's gone in a flash. Given the evident tensions between her father and his neighbours, I can't blame her for not wanting to come into town with me. Although calling it a town is flattering it, I see as I drive into it. It's not much more than a village. There are a few houses and shops that open directly onto the narrow pavement, and then I'm at the main square. It's small but pleasant enough, with plenty of trees for shade and a fountain in front of a boules court, on which two old men are already tossing steel balls at a tiny jack.

The open-fronted builders' yard is down a side street but still visible from the road. I park by the piles of sand, bricks and timber outside a corrugated, hangar-like building and go inside. Pallets of cement and plaster are stacked head-high against the walls. I buy what I need and then awkwardly load the heavy bags of cement into the back of the van. It's tricky, since I can't use my stick, and no one working there seems in any hurry to help. But I don't mind. My earlier anxiety has gone. In its wake comes a glow of confidence, born from relief as much as anything. As I drive back to the square I'm actually sorry to be returning to the farm so soon. When I see a parking space up ahead it occurs to me that I don't have to.

On impulse I pull in and stop.

The town has woken up during the time I've been buying supplies. I sit outside one of the cafés set around the square, enjoying the sense of freedom. The metal table rocks slightly on the uneven pavement when I hang my walking stick on its edge. After a few moments the waiter comes out, pad in hand.

'Coffee and a croissant.'

I sit back, content to wait. The street is still wet from its morning hosing. Water beads the aluminium legs of the chairs. There's a fresh, early-morning feel about the place that will have gone in another hour. Glad to have caught it, I look over the narrow road that separates the shops from the square. The ornate fountain is the grandest thing about it, hinting at a now forgotten pre-war opulence. The clack of balls from the boules court carries over the whine of the occasional moped or deeper engine noise of a car. The two old players have been joined by a third, equally decrepit, who for now just watches. They laugh and smoke, exclaiming at bad shots and slapping each other's shoulders at the good ones. One of them sees me watching and raises a hand in casual greeting. I nod back, feeling absurdly pleased at the acceptance.

After weeks of nothing but eggs for breakfast, the croissant tastes wonderful. The coffee is thick and dark with a finish of brown froth. I take my time over both, until there's only a broken carapace of crumbs left on the plate. Sitting back with a sigh, I order another coffee and light a cigarette.

Two young men walk past as I'm smoking. They're in their late teens or early twenties, both in jeans and trainers. I don't pay them any attention until I feel one of them staring at me. He turns away when I look up, but the small flare of disquiet grows when I catch them both glancing back again as they turn off the square.

I tell myself it's nothing. I'm a strange face in a small town, and my red hair marks me out as a foreigner. But it sours my mood, and when I see a yellow VW Beetle go by I don't feel like staying at the café any longer. Leaving the money in the saucer, I go to a tabac on the opposite side of the square to stock up on cigarettes. A boulangerie is open next to it, and when I come out the sweet aroma of its baking is too much to resist. The woman behind the high glass counter is buxom, with a cast in one eye. But she smiles as warmly as the bread smells when she finishes serving an old woman and turns to me.

'Six croissants, please.'

She picks out the sickle-shaped pastries from a tray behind her and drops them into a paper bag. I pay for them out of my own money. I daresay Mathilde and Gretchen will appreciate a change from eggs as much as I do. Arnaud can buy his own.

'You sound foreign,' the woman says as she hands me my change.

I'm starting to feel uncomfortable, but it's an innocent enough comment. 'I'm English.'

'Are you staying around here?'

'Just passing through,' I tell her, and leave before she can ask anything else.

It's time to go. I cut across the square to where I've left the van. All three old men are playing boules now, holding the silver balls in a backward grip and flipping them underhand. They land almost dead, hardly rolling on the gritty soil. One of the players, the newcomer, succeeds in knocking another ball away from the small wooden jack. There's laughter and expostulations. Watching them, I'm not aware of the footsteps behind me until I hear a shout.

'Hey, wait up!'

I look back. Three men are walking towards me across the square. Two of them are the ones who went past my table earlier. The third is also familiar, and I feel my stomach knot when I recognize him.

It's the loudmouth from the roadside bar.

I resist the temptation to glance towards the van, knowing I won't be able to reach it in time. Gripping the walking stick, I stop by the fountain. Spray tickles the back of my neck in an icy spatter as the three of them face me, the loudmouth slightly in front.

'How's it going? Still at the Arnauds' place?'

He's smiling, but it's a mugger's smile. I just nod. I remember his name now: Didier. He's in his early twenties, muscular and wearing oil-stained jeans and a T-shirt. His scuffed work boots look as though they could be steel-capped.

'So, what brings you to town?'

'I had to buy a few things.'

'Errands, eh?' I can see him weighing me up; an unknown quantity but with a bad leg. And outnumbered. He points to the bag from the boulangerie. 'What have you got there?'

'Croissants.'

He grins. 'Arnaud's daughters come cheap, eh? Although Gretchen never charges me for a fuck.'

There's laughter from the other two. I start to turn away but Didier moves to block me.

'What's the matter, can't take a joke?'

'I've got work to do.'

'For Arnaud?' He's stopped pretending to smile. 'What sort of work? Cleaning up pig shit? Or are you too busy fucking his daughters?'

One of the others starts making pig-squealing noises. I look past them but the town square is empty. There's no one except the old boules players. The day suddenly seems too bright. The soft splashing of the water in the fountain is crystal clear, the droplets shining in the sunlight.

'What's wrong? Pig got your tongue?' Didier's expression is ugly. 'Tell Arnaud if he wants anything here he should come for it himself, not send his fucking English errand boy. Tell him he's a fucking coward! Does he think he's safe out there behind his barbed wire?'

'I don't—'

'Shut your fucking mouth!'

He swipes the bag of croissants from my hand, knocking it into the water. I grip the walking stick more tightly as the other two step to either side, backing me towards the fountain. The boules players have finally noticed what's going on. There are cries of 'Eh, eh, eh!' and 'Stop that!' from the old men, all of which are ignored.

'I know you, Didier Marchant, I know who you are!' one shouts, as another of them speaks into a phone.

'Fuck off and die,' Didier calls back without looking round.

He's been pumping himself up, getting ready to start. Suddenly he feints a punch, snapping his fist out and drawing back at the last second. They laugh as I step back against the edge of the fountain. I instinctively raise the walking stick but my arms feel cumbersome and heavy.

'Yeah?' Didier says. 'You going to hit me with that? Come on, then!'

He doesn't really believe I will, and there's an instant when

I have a chance. The end of the walking stick is weighted and thick, and I can imagine the impact as it strikes his head. I can hear the crack of bone again as Georges brings the hammer down onto the pig's skull, the thud of a falling body. For a heartbeat I'm back in a dark street, seeing blood black and sticky under a streetlight. It makes me hesitate, but Didier doesn't.

He hits me in the face.

There's a burst of light. I stagger sideways, swinging the stick blindly. It's knocked from my hand. As it clatters to the ground something drives into my stomach, forcing the breath from me. I double up, raising my hands in a futile attempt to protect my head.

'What's going on?'

The voice is deeper and authoritative. Gasping, I look up as someone shoulders my attackers aside. Still bent over, all I can make out is a pair of bib-and-braces overalls. I raise my head further and see the brawny man from the roadside bar, the one Mathilde called Jean-Claude. Behind him is the boules player who was on the phone earlier, standing well back as the newcomer confronts the three younger men.

'I said what's going on?'

Didier answers sullenly. 'Nothing.'

'This is nothing, is it? And does Philippe know one of his mechanics is bumming off work doing this sort of "nothing" in the town square?'

'Keep out of it, Jean-Claude.'

'Why? So you stupid shits can beat someone up in the middle of town?'

'It's none of your business.'

'None of my business? Whose business is it if it isn't mine? Yours?'

'He's working for Arnaud. He's got no right to be here.'

'And you have?' The man's stubbled face is growing darker.

'OK, if you're going to beat anyone up you can start with me.'

'Jean-Claude—'

'What are you waiting for?' He spreads his hands, looking capable of snapping all three younger men in half. 'Come on, hero, I'm waiting.'

Didier looks down at his feet.

'No? Lost your taste for it?' The man shakes his head, disgusted. 'Go on, fuck off, all of you.'

They don't move.

'I said go!'

Reluctantly, they begin to drift away. Didier pauses long enough to point at me.

'Don't think this is over.'

The man watches them stalk off. 'You all right?'

I nod, but I have to lean against the fountain to hide my shaking. My cheek hurts from Didier's punch and my stomach feels bruised, but there's nothing serious.

I raise a hand in acknowledgement as the old boules player goes back to the game, then retrieve my walking stick and straighten to face the man who's just saved me. I don't blame my attackers for backing down. He's about my height, but there's the solidness of a rock about him, and the thick hands are so calloused they look incapable of bleeding.

'Thanks,' I say.

'Forget it. I should be the one apologizing.' He shakes his head in disgust. 'Didier's my cousin. When he screws up it always comes back on the family.'

'I appreciate it, anyway.' I lift the dripping bag of croissants from the fountain. Water streams from the sodden pastries as I drop them in a bin. 'What's his problem with Arnaud?'

The big man glances at my overalls. I get the impression he's been trying hard not to. 'You're working on the house?'

'I just came in for building supplies.'

I notice he's avoided answering my question. For the first time it occurs to me that, if I'm right about him being Michel's father, then I might have taken his job. But his next statement rules that out.

'I manage the builders' yard. I must have missed you.' Again, his eyes go to the overalls I'm wearing. 'How did you wind up at Arnaud's?'

'I was hitching and injured my foot in their woods. Mathilde patched me up.'

'I thought you said you trod on a nail?'

It's my turn to be evasive. I don't want to lie to him, but I don't want to stir up trouble either.

'Why is everyone so worked up about Arnaud? What's he done?' I ask instead.

Jean-Claude's face closes down. 'Nothing that concerns you.'

'That isn't what Didier thought.'

'Didier's a prick. But if you want my advice, stay clear of town. Or better still, find somewhere else to work.'

'Why? Come on, you can't just leave it at that,' I say, as he starts to go.

For a second or two I can see he's torn. He rubs at his chin, turning over some point in his mind. Then he shakes his head, more to himself than to me.

'Tell Mathilde that Jean-Claude was asking after his nephew.'

Leaving me by the fountain, he walks out of the square.

11

IN THE HEAT OF the sun the drying mortar gives off a smell as evocative as freshly baked bread. I mix the sand and cement together in the metal tub, then carry a bucketful up to the top of the scaffold. I transfer a small pile onto a wooden board, about a foot square, that I found in the storeroom, then trowel it into the grooves I've hacked out between the stones.

Pointing the wall is slow work yet oddly restful. There's something pleasurable about the soft hiss the trowel makes as I run the flat of its blade along the wet mortar to smooth it. Foot by foot, the wall is being remade. I replace the loose stones as I come to them, easing each heavy block into place and then mortaring around it until it's indistinguishable from the rest. In the days since I visited the town, the upper level of the house has begun to look solid and whole rather than a ruin on the verge of collapse. Each evening when I stop work I get a small charge when I look at what I've accomplished. It's a long time since I've done anything constructive.

It's longer since I've done anything I've felt proud of.

I finish the last of the mortar and take the bucket down to the storeroom to refill. The afternoon sun is blinding overhead, whiting out the blue of the sky with its mindless heat. When it's like this it's impossible to imagine the same landscape in winter, made brown and brittle or hidden under a skim of frost. But I know it'll come, all the same.

What little mortar is left in the galvanized tub has set. I scrape it out onto the pile outside the storeroom and decide I've earned a rest before I mix another batch. I sit in the shade and light up a cigarette. From down here it's apparent just how much there is still to do. The knowledge is somehow comforting. I take another drag on the cigarette, contemplating it.

'I'm not paying you to sit on your arse.'

Arnaud has appeared around the corner of the house. I take an unhurried drag of the cigarette.

'You've not paid me for anything yet.'

'What do you call three meals a day and a roof over your head? You'll get the rest when you've earned it.' He squints up at the house. The completed section seems even smaller than it did a moment ago. 'Not done much, have you?'

'I want to do it properly.'

'It's a wall, not the Venus de Milo.'

It's on the tip of my tongue to say he's welcome to get some-one from town to do it instead, but I stop myself. Although we haven't spoken about what happened in town with Didier and his friends, I'm sure Arnaud will have heard about it from Mathilde or Gretchen. Mathilde had asked about the bruise on my face from where Didier punched me. Predictably, she didn't pass any comment, although she'd looked shaken when I gave her Jean-Claude's message. Equally predictably, Gretchen was delighted to hear that I'd been in a fight, especially when she discovered who it was with.

'What did Didier say? Did he mention me?'

'Not really.' She'd be less pleased if she knew what he'd been boasting. 'Who is he, an old boyfriend?'

'Oh no. Just someone I see sometimes.' She'd shrugged, archly.

'I haven't seen him for a while, though. He's probably jealous. That's why he picked a fight with you.'

I doubted that, but I was starting to guess why the gate was unlocked when I first came to the farm. It couldn't be easy for Gretchen to meet any local boys with Arnaud watching over her.

'I got the impression it was more to do with your father. What's he done to upset everyone?' I asked.

'Papa hasn't done anything. It's them,' she'd said, and retreated into one of her sulks.

Since then there's been no further mention of the incident; if not for the new bruise on my face it might never have happened. But I've come to understand that the farm has a way of absorbing events, closing over them like the stones I toss into the lake.

A few ripples to mark their passing, then they're gone.

Arnaud regards the wall for a moment longer then jerks his head at me. 'That can wait. Come on.'

'Where?'

But he's already walking away. I'm tempted to stay where I am, then I give in and go after him. He crosses the courtyard to the stable block and goes behind the tractor occupying one of the archways. By the time I've squeezed past it myself he's already lifting something down from the back wall.

'Does this thing ever move?' I ask, rubbing my elbow where I've skinned it on the tractor's bodywork.

His voice comes from the back of the stables. 'Not since someone put sugar in its tank.'

'Who?'

'They didn't leave a business card.'

I think about Didier, and wonder if this could be the reason for the traps. 'Can't you drain it?'

Arnaud reappears. He's carrying something but it's too dark to make out what it is. 'Do you know anything about engines?'

'Not really.'

'Then don't ask stupid questions.'

He comes nearer and I see he's holding a chainsaw. It's bulky and grimed with oil, its long blade lined with snaggled teeth. I step back, but he's only going to a petrol canister. Unscrewing the fuel cap on the chainsaw, he begins to fill its tank.

'What are you going to do with that?' I ask, as the air sweetens with petrol.

'We need to stock up with firewood.'

'In summer?'

'Green wood takes a long time to dry out.'

I glance through the stable's archway at the house. 'What about the wall?'

'It'll still be there when you get back.' He adds oil from another container, then reseals the fuel cap and lifts the chainsaw in one hand. 'Get the barrow.'

There's a wheelbarrow beside a workbench. I struggle with it past the tractor, then set it down while Arnaud unceremoniously dumps the chainsaw into it. I've got a bad feeling about what's coming next, and he doesn't disappoint.

'Bring that with you.'

With that he sets off out of the stable block, leaving me to follow. Laying my walking stick in the barrow, I take hold of the handles. The heavy chainsaw unbalances it when I take the weight, almost upending the whole thing. I hurriedly set the barrow down again and shift the saw into its centre. Then, hobbling awkwardly, I wheel it after Arnaud.

He walks ahead of me, across the courtyard and through the grapevines to the woods. I only catch up with him when he stops in a semi-cleared area near the statues, where smaller tree stumps stand among the bigger trunks like broken teeth.

Kneading his lower back, he goes to a tree as I set the barrow down.

'Here,' he says, slapping it. 'This one.'

It's a young silver birch that's found space to grow among the bulkier chestnuts. I look blankly at Arnaud as he takes his pipe out of his pocket and begins filling it. 'What am I supposed to do?'

'Cut it down, what do you think?'

'You want *me* to do it?'

'I didn't bring you down here to watch. What's wrong? Don't tell me you've never used a chainsaw before.'

'Yes. No, I mean.'

'So now you get to learn. Just remember that it'll cut through bone as easily as wood, so if you're not careful it'll take you apart instead of the tree.' He gives a smirk. 'Wouldn't want any more accidents, would we?'

I clutch at the first excuse I can think of. 'Aren't we too close to the statues?'

'They haven't been hit yet, and they won't be now if you do it right.' He kicks the tree trunk about eighteen inches off the ground. 'Cut a notch about here, then saw through to it from the other side. That's all there is to it. Even you should be able to manage that.'

With that he goes and settles himself on a tree stump. The chainsaw sits in the wheelbarrow between us, waiting. My walking stick lies next to it, but if I was going to use my foot as an excuse I should have done it before I pushed the barrow down here. Arnaud gestures irritably.

'Well, what are you waiting for? It won't bite.'

I don't want to go anywhere near the thing, but pride won't allow me to refuse. I bend down and lift the chainsaw out. It's as heavy as it looks, old and ugly and stained with oil. I hold it warily, half-expecting it to roar into life by itself. There don't seem to be any guards or safety features, and what I assume is the starter cord is dangling from it. Conscious of Arnaud watching me, I brace myself and pull. Nothing happens.

'Try turning it on. And you might want to put it down first,' Arnaud says. He's enjoying this.

There's a toggle on the side of the machine. I flick it, then take hold of the cord again. This time when I pull it the engine chuckles and dies.

'Are you sure it works?' I ask.

'It works.'

Gripping the cord tightly, I yank as hard as I can. The chainsaw shakes as it flares into life, then settles into a buzzing roar.

The noise is deafening. The saw shudders in my hands as I approach the tree. It's a slender thing, the delicate leaves like translucent green coins against the silver bark. I lower the blade to where Arnaud indicated but can't bring myself to cut.

'Get on with it!' Arnaud shouts against the din.

I set myself so I'm balanced without putting too much weight on my bad foot, take a deep breath and touch the teeth to the tree.

The saw's buzzing rises to a scream. Fragments of raw white wood and bark spray out, and I instinctively draw back. The saw subsides to a growl. Imagining Arnaud's smile, I put it to the tree again.

The saw judders as it tears through the wood. I brace myself against it, squinting against the splinters and chips it spits into my face. I cut a V-shaped notch as Arnaud instructed, then knock out the wedge of wood and begin to saw through the other side of the trunk. I hope I'm doing it right, but I'm not going to ask. I'm almost all the way through when the tree creaks and begins to lean.

I quickly step back. There's a sound of cracking, then the silver birch topples and crashes down, bouncing once before settling to rest in a snapping of branches. As Arnaud predicted, it's well clear of the statues. I'm impressed, despite myself.

He motions towards the saw. The engine noise drops as I let it idle.

'There now,' Arnaud smirks. 'That wasn't so bad, was it?'

I trim the branches from the tree and then set about carving the trunk into manageable segments. The clearing soon begins to look like a lumber yard, shards of white wood scattered around like confetti. While I'm attacking the trunk Arnaud gathers the lopped branches together, arranging them roughly by size so that all but the smallest can be used for kindling.

It's hot work. Soon I'm stripped to my waist, the overalls rolled down and tied by their arms around my hips. Even Arnaud is forced to open his shirt, exposing a torso that's hairless and pallid as milk against the nut brown of his face and neck. A waft of acrid sweat comes off him. What communication there is between us is reduced to gestures and signs. The whining of the chainsaw fills the woods as we go about dismembering the tree.

Finally, it's done. When I switch the machine off, the sudden silence feels too heavy for the woods to support. Every noise seems amplified in the hush.

'Let's take a rest,' Arnaud says.

I flop down with my back against the plinth of a statue. My skin is spattered with oil and woodchips. Arnaud grimaces in pain as he lowers himself onto the same stump he sat on earlier.

'What's wrong with your back?' I ask.

'I fell down the stairs.' He gives a humourless smile. 'Same as you.'

I hope it hurt, I think, reaching for my cigarettes. He begins to refill his pipe, pressing down the tobacco with his thumb as I search for my lighter. With my overalls rolled to my waist, it's hard to get into the pockets.

'Light?'

Arnaud tosses me a box of matches. I catch them, surprised. 'Thanks.'

I light up, luxuriating in the nicotine hit as my muscles slowly uncramp. I can hear the faint tamp of Arnaud's mouth on the pipe stem, the faint whistle of air through its bowl. The first bird risks a tentative call. Gradually, the life of the woods returns to normal. I feel no urge to disturb it as I enjoy my cigarette. When it's finished I stub it out and put my head back.

I hear Arnaud chuckle. 'What?' I ask.

'I was just admiring your choice of backrest.'

I turn to find that I'm propped against the statue of Pan. The pagan god's crotch is right behind my head.

I settle back again. 'If he doesn't mind, neither do I.'

Arnaud snorts, but seems amused. He takes the pipe from his mouth and raps the bowl smartly against the heel of his boot to empty it. He grinds the ash into the soil but doesn't put the pipe away.

'How much do you think they're worth?' he asks abruptly.

For a moment I think he means the trees, before I realize he's talking about the statues.

'No idea.'

'No? You're so smart, I thought you knew everything.'

'Not when it comes to stolen statues.'

Arnaud takes out a short-bladed pocketknife. He begins scraping out the bowl of the pipe. 'Who said they were stolen?'

'You wouldn't have hidden them down here if they weren't.' I'm not going to admit it was Gretchen. 'Why haven't you sold them?'

'Why don't you mind your own business?' He grinds the knife into the pipe, but lowers it again after a moment, the task forgotten. 'It isn't that simple. You have to be careful who you approach.'

Very careful, judging by the grass growing around them. They've obviously been here for some time. 'If you didn't already have buyers, why did you get so many?'

'I had a . . . business associate. He said he knew a dealer who would take them off our hands.'

I stub out my cigarette. 'What happened?'

Arnaud's mouth is clamped into a bitter line. 'He let me down. Betrayed my trust.'

It's almost the same phrase Gretchen used about Michel's father. I'd put money on him and this 'associate' being the same man: the man whose dirty overalls I'm currently wearing. One way or another, Jean-Claude's nameless brother certainly left a mess in his wake. No wonder they don't want to talk about him.

'So why don't you just get rid of them?' I ask.

He snorts. 'If you want to try lifting them, go ahead.'

'You managed to get them down here.'

'We had lifting gear.'

'You mean your associate did.'

Arnaud gives an angry nod. He considers the pipe bowl again. 'I thought you might have some ideas. Contacts.'

'What sort of contacts?'

'The sort who wouldn't be too interested in where the statues came from. There must be plenty of rich English bastards who'd pay for this sort of thing.' When he looks at me there's a shrewd glint in his eye. 'There'd be something in it for you.'

'Sorry, but I don't know anyone.'

His scowl deepens. 'I should have known you wouldn't be any use.'

I can't help myself. 'This "business associate". Did he suggest making your own wine as well?'

Arnaud's look is answer enough. Snapping the knife shut, he rams it in his pocket as he pushes himself awkwardly to his feet.

'You can start taking the wood back.'

'By myself? How?' I look at the pile of cut timber. It was hard enough bringing the wheelbarrow down here with just the chainsaw in it.

He gives me a grim smile. 'Smart-arse like you, you'll think of something.'

It's early evening before I finish taking the sawn-up tree to the house. I make trip after trip, limping up and down the track until I'm aching all over. I keep telling myself that each trip is the last, that Arnaud can do the rest himself. But I don't want to give him the satisfaction of sneering that I couldn't manage. And leaving the silver birch to litter the woods seems too wasteful, no better than vandalism after I've cut it down.

So I carry on until all the logs are stacked under a lean-to at the back of the house. Only when I've put the wheelbarrow away do I remember I've left my walking stick in the woods. I almost don't bother going back: I've coped without it all after-noon, and the wounds on my foot are healing nicely. But just thinking about it makes them hurt again.

Besides, I've grown used to having something to lean on.

After I've stripped off my overalls I try to wash myself at the tap in the barn. Water runs between the cobbles, pooling in the rough concrete depression before draining into the deepening crack in its surface. As I try to scrub myself clean I make a note to bring some mortar down here to patch it. The cold water takes away my breath, but not even the block of caustic home-made soap can cut through the coating of oil and tree-bark.

I persevere until my skin is raw and wrinkled, then throw down the soap in disgust. Turning off the tap, I put my overalls back on and collect clean clothes from the loft. Then I go to the house and knock on the kitchen door.

Mathilde opens it.

'I could really use a bath,' I tell her wearily.

I'm ready for an argument, and if Arnaud was there I'd probably get one. But there's no protest from inside the room. Mathilde just takes in my oil-spattered state and steps back.

'Come in.'

The kitchen is full of cooking smells. Pans are bubbling on the range, but the kitchen is empty except for her.

'Where is everyone?'

'My father's with Georges and Gretchen's taken Michel out. He's teething again. The bathroom's this way.'

She leads me through the door at the back of the room and into a hallway. It's gloomy, unlit at this time of day by either natural or electric light. The stairs are steep and narrow, tarnished brass rods gripping the worn carpet. I follow her up them, taking hold of the painted wooden banister for support and keeping my eyes on the stairs instead of Mathilde's legs.

This is the first time I've been beyond the kitchen. It feels strange. The house is threadbare but clean. The stairs end at a long corridor that runs off in both directions. There are doors on either side, all closed. I guess one of those on my left must open onto the unused bedroom that I look into from the scaffold. But I'm not sure which it is, and there's no way of knowing what's behind any of them.

Mathilde goes down the corridor and pushes open a door at the far end. 'Here.'

The bathroom is so big that the ancient bath and washbasin look lost in it. The floor is bare boards except for a small rug beside the bath. But the room is bright and airy, even though the single window faces away from the sun this late in the afternoon.

'You have to run the hot water first, then add the cold. The pipes don't work properly if you try to run both at once. Be careful. It gets very hot.' She tucks her hair behind her ear, not quite looking at me. 'You'll need a clean towel.'

'That's OK.'

'It's no problem.'

She goes out, quietly closing the door behind her. I could be imagining it, but there seems to be a subtle change in her since I gave her Jean-Claude's message. A slight reserve towards me. It's hardly surprising: God knows, I wouldn't like strangers knowing about my private life. But I regret it, even so.

The bath is a deep iron tub, the chipped white enamel discoloured by twin ferrous streaks where the taps have dripped. The hot one creaks as I turn it, producing nothing for a moment except a groaning shudder that seems to stem from the heart of the house. Then a bolt of water spatters out, followed by a thick gush. I put in the plug and find that the water is as scalding as Mathilde warned.

The bathroom quickly fills with steam. When I turn off the tap the metal burns my fingers. I spin it closed, touching it as little as possible, and run the cold water. Deep as the tub is, it's nearly three-quarters full before it's cool enough to bear.

I go to lock the door, not wanting Arnaud – or Gretchen, God forbid – to walk in. But while there are screw holes from a missing bolt, there's no way of locking it. Hoping that Mathilde won't let anyone disturb me, I undress and lower myself into the bath. The heat soaks through my aching muscles and joints. Resting my foot on the side to keep the bandage dry, I slide down until I'm submerged up to my chin.

Bliss.

I'm drifting away when there's a knock on the door. Mathilde's muffled voice comes from behind it.

'I've brought you a towel.'

I sit up. The water has developed a limestone scum, making it opaque. 'You can come in.'

There's a delay before she opens the door. A towel is folded over one arm. Without looking over at the bath, she puts it on an old bentwood chair that stands against the wall.

'Can you reach it there?'

'That's fine.'

There's an awkwardness. She turns to go.

'I thought I'd take off the bandage,' I say. 'Bathe the wounds.'

'All right.'

She looks at where my foot dangles over the side of the bath. I wait, knowing what's coming next.

'Here,' she says. 'I'll do it.'

Mathilde sits on the edge of the bath while I raise my foot so she can unwind the bandage. The only sound is the faint rustle of cotton and the occasional drip of a tap. My exposed foot looks white and thin, as unfamiliar as a stranger's. The wounds caused by the trap have closed up, like scabbed and puckered mouths. They're still ugly but no longer inflamed. I've long since finished with the antibiotics, and the last painkiller I took was for a hangover.

Mathilde's hands are gentle as she bends closer to examine the wounds. The cotton of her shirt whispers over my toes.

'Are the stitches ready to come out?' I ask.

'Not yet.'

They look it to me, but I accept her verdict. 'How much longer?'

'Soon. But you can take the bandage off at night. It will do the wounds good to get some air.'

I lower my foot into the water as Mathilde gets up from the bath. I'm conscious of her standing beside me. My arm, resting on the edge, is only inches from her leg. Neither of us looks at the other, but suddenly I'm certain that she's as aware of me as I am of her.

'I have to see to dinner,' she says, but doesn't act on the words. The steam seems to close around us, veiling us from the rest of the house. I've only to move my hand and I'll touch her. Mathilde's head is still averted but her lips are parted ever so slightly, her cheeks rouged with a flush not wholly due to the heat. I begin to lift my arm, and as though there's an invisible connection between us Mathilde reacts at the same time.

She steps away.

'I'll put a clean bandage on tomorrow,' she says.

I grip the edge of the bath and push myself up slightly in the water, as if that was what I intended all the time.

'OK. Thanks.'

The steam swirls, agitated by the opening and closing of the door as she goes out. After she's gone it still carries the scent of her. I slide down in the bath and put my head under the water. The house's quiet is replaced by a submarine echo of bangs and clicks. Eyes closed, I think that Mathilde has come back in. I visualize her standing above me. Or Gretchen.

Or Arnaud.

I jerk upright, streaming water. The bathroom is still empty except for the vapour demons that twist in the invisible currents. The water isn't the only thing that's overheated, I think.

Taking up the bar of soap, I begin to wash myself.

London

'WHO'S JULES?'

Jez freezes in the act of raising his bacon sandwich to his mouth. He sneaks a quick look at me, then sets it back down on the plate.

'Jules who?'

We're at the café next door to the language school, which is actually no more than a cluster of first-floor rooms above an insurance broker's. The café is small and smells of fried food and stewed tea, and there's a main road noisily running outside its front window. But it's convenient, and Jez doesn't care about the aesthetics provided the food's cheap.

'Jules as in Chloe.'

He tries to assemble his crumpled features into something like puzzlement. 'Er . . . no, I don't think . . .'

He's a bad liar. I'd still held out some hope that I might be wrong, but it dies now. 'Who is he?'

'What makes you think I know?'

'Because you live with Yasmin and she's Chloe's best friend.'

'You should ask Chloe.'

'Chloe won't tell me anything. Come on, Jez.'

He rubs the back of his neck unhappily. 'Yasmin made me promise not to say anything.'

'I won't tell her. This is between you and me.' Jez doesn't look convinced. 'Please.'

He sighs. 'He's Chloe's ex. A real shit, but she split up with him ages ago, so it's past history now.'

I look down at my own coffee. 'I think she might be seeing him again.'

Jez winces. 'Fuck. I'm sorry, man.'

'Does Yasmin know?'

'That Chloe's seeing him again? I doubt it. If she does she hasn't said anything to me. And she hated Jules's guts.'

Some students from the class I'm due to take pass by outside and wave through the window. I raise my hand, relieved when they don't come in.

'Tell me what happened,' I say.

Jez plays uneasily with his cup. 'The man's a real bastard. He'd got some upmarket gym in Docklands, but he calls himself an entrepreneur. Flash sort, but hard as nails, you know?'

I nod. 'I've met him.'

'So I don't need to tell you. He gave Chloe a really bad time. She was sort of a trophy for him. You know, good-looking, an artist. Different from his normal type. He bought some of her paintings, that's how they met. But he was a real control freak, the sort who gets a kick from putting people down, you know? He's the one who got her onto coke and thrown out of art college.'

'*What*?'

Jez looks crestfallen. 'Shit, I thought you knew.'

This is all news to me. It's like I've stepped into a parallel world. 'Go on.'

'Oh, man, Yasmin's going to kill me.' He sighs, rubbing his hand over his face. 'Jules was into that whole drug scene. VIP lounges, clubs, parties. And it wasn't just steroids you could get at his gym, if you know what I mean. There was this big guy who used to supply him with stuff. Evil bastard, you wouldn't mess with him.'

That sounds like Lenny. I feel numb. Jez is looking at me worriedly.

'You sure you want to hear this?'

'Just tell me.'

'Yasmin tried to help, but Chloe was . . . well, you know. Then one night she OD'd on some shit Jules had given her. Yas found her and got her to hospital, then into rehab. She made Chloe change her phone number and move in with her until she was up to getting her own place. Completely cut Jules out of the loop, which pissed him off no end. He made all sorts of threats, trying to find out where Chloe was, but Yas wouldn't budge. And once Chloe was away from him she got herself straightened out. Started painting again, met you.' He shrugs. 'That's it.'

It's as if he's talking about a different person. Now I understand why Yasmin was so angry when Callum produced the coke at Chloe's celebration. Why she didn't want her hopes building up over the gallery. Painting was Chloe's prop, a new addiction to replace the old. And it had been pulled away from her.

The chair scrapes on the floor tiles as I stand up. 'Sean? Where are you going? Sean!' Jez shouts after me as I walk out.

I take no notice. I feel as though I'm already too late as I catch a tube back to Earl's Court. Chloe isn't at the flat so I search each room, scattering clothes, books and DVD cases. I find it under a loose panel in the bathroom. An innocent plastic box with an airtight lid.

Inside is a small bag of white powder, razor blade and make-up mirror.

I'm sitting at the kitchen table when she comes home from work. She pauses when she sees the box in front of me, then closes the door and begins to take off her coat.

'Aren't you going to say anything?' I ask.

'I'm tired. Can we do this some other time?'

'Like when? When you're in rehab again?'

She hesitates, then turns her back and starts filling the kettle. 'Who told you? Yasmin?'

'It doesn't matter who told me – why didn't you?'

'Why should I? It was a long time ago.'

'And what about this?' I push the plastic box across the table. 'Is that from a long time ago as well?'

'I'm a big girl, I can do what I like.'

'So what happened to "I'm sorry, I won't play any more games"?'

She gives a humourless laugh. 'You call this a game?'

I want to yell at her, but if I give in to it I'm scared I won't be able to stop. 'Where did you get it?'

'Where do you think?'

Even though I've known, it still feels like I've been punched. I can't bring myself to say Jules's name. 'Jesus Christ, Chloe, why?'

'*Why?*' She bangs down the kettle, water slopping onto the worktop. 'Because I can't stand feeling this *shit* all the time! Because I hate being such a fucking failure! And I'm sick of pretending I'm not! What are we even *doing* here? I'm working in a bar and you don't even live in the real world!'

'What are you talking about?'

'You don't even *know*, do you? You think watching films is real life? You don't even make your own, you just watch other people's! Other people's films, other people's lives, that's all you know about! Christ, you rave about French films and fucking France, but you never actually *go* there! When was the last time you even *went*?'

I sweep the plastic box onto the floor and jump to my feet. Blood pulses behind my eyes.

'Come on, then!' she shouts. 'Just for once in your life, why don't you *do* something!'

But I'm already moving past her. I walk out blindly, leaving the sound of Chloe's sobbing behind me.

12

'I'M BORED.'

Gretchen throws down what's left of the small yellow flower she's been steadily denuding of petals. I try not to sigh.

'Come on, try to remember.' I hold up my fork. 'What's the English word for this?'

'I don't know.'

'Yes, you do. We've done it before.'

She doesn't even look up. 'Knife.'

I put the fork back down on my plate. My attempts to teach Gretchen English haven't exactly been a success, although I admit I'm no more enthusiastic than she is. Conversation with Arnaud's youngest daughter is hard work at the best of times, and if I push her too much she subsides into her default state of sulk. Still, I promised Mathilde I'd try.

I hadn't planned on teaching her today, though. I'd gone down to the barn to wash before going to collect my lunch from the house. All morning I've been thinking about what happened in the bathroom yesterday, whether I misread the tension between Mathilde and me. Or even imagined it. I've wondered if I'd detect any difference in her today, but so far I haven't had much chance to find out. My breakfast was once again left on the loft steps this morning, and there was no sign of Mathilde in the kitchen when I took the dishes back.

170

I hoped I'd see her when I went for my lunch, if nothing else.

But as I was coming out of the barn, Gretchen arrived with a plate of food. Mathilde had asked her to bring it, she told me with a coy smile, and I knew then that any hope I'd had of a peaceful lunch was gone. If nothing else, trying to teach her English would cover the awkward silences. Not that they ever seem to bother Gretchen.

She lies on her stomach, idly kicking her legs as she plucks another flower from between the overgrown cobbles. She's wearing a yellow vest top and the faded cut-downs, legs long and tanned, the pink flip-flops hanging from her soiled feet. I draw a circle in the dirt with my finger, then add two lines in its centre pointing to twelve and nine.

'What time is that?'

'Boring o'clock.'

'You're not even trying.'

'Why should I? It's dull.'

'At least make an effort.' I sound like the sort of teacher I always used to hate, but Gretchen brings out the worst in me.

She gives me a petulant look. 'What for? I'm never going to go to England.'

'You might.'

'Why, are you going to take me?'

I think – hope – she's joking. Even so, just talking about going back makes something tighten in my chest. 'I don't think your father would like that.'

The mention of Arnaud sobers her, as it usually does. 'Good. I don't want to go anyway.'

'Maybe not, but it doesn't hurt to learn. You don't plan on staying on the farm all your life, do you?'

'Why shouldn't I?'

There's a warning in her voice. 'No reason. But don't you want to move out or get married eventually?'

'How do you know what I want to do? And if I do get married it won't be to anyone English, so what's the point of learning the stupid language? There's plenty of boys round here who'd want to marry me.'

And look how well that's going, I think. But it's time to back off. 'OK. I just thought you were bored.'

'I am.' She props herself up on an elbow, giving me a look. 'I can think of better things to do, though.'

I busy myself with the food and pretend not to hear. Today there's a thick hunk of bread and a bowl of cassoulet, with pale beans and chunks of sausage. It's almost black, with nebulae of white fat suspended in it. Gretchen pulls a face as I fork up a piece.

'I don't know how you can eat that stuff.'

'What's wrong with it?'

'Nothing's *wrong* with it. I just don't like blood sausage.'

'Blood sausage?'

She grins at my expression. 'Didn't you know?'

No, I didn't. I look at the dark paste and globules of fat. An image comes to mind of the stunned pig hanging by its hind legs while Georges puts the knife to its throat. I remember the sound of the blood splashing into the metal bucket. And behind that are other images, even less welcome.

I put the sausage down and set my plate aside.

'Have I put you off?' Gretchen asks.

'I wasn't hungry.'

I take a drink of water to rinse away the taste. There's a distracting tickle on my arm. An ant is questing inquisitively on my skin. Brushing it off, I see there are dozens milling around in the grass, ferrying breadcrumbs into a hole between the cobbles.

Gretchen cranes her head to see what's caught my attention. 'What is it?'

'Just ants.'

She moves closer to examine them. Picking up a handful of soil, she begins to trickle it in their path. The ants dash around in circles, antennae waving, then form a new line that bypasses the obstacle.

'Don't do that.'

'Why? They're only ants.'

She follows them with the soil. I turn away, annoyed by the casual cruelty, which is probably why I say what I do.

'Who was your father's business partner?'

Gretchen carries on sifting soil through her fist, letting it fall onto the ants. 'Papa didn't have a business partner.'

'He says he did. The one who helped him with the statues.'

'Louis worked for us. He wasn't Papa's partner.'

It's the first time I've heard his name. 'OK. But he's Michel's father, isn't he?'

'What's it got to do with you?'

'Nothing. Forget I asked.'

Gretchen picks up another handful of soil and drops it onto the mouth of the ants' hole. 'It was Mathilde's fault.'

'What was?'

'Everything. She got pregnant and caused a row, and that's why Louis left. He'd still be here if not for her.'

'I thought you said he'd let you all down?'

'He did, but it wasn't all his fault.' She shrugs. Her eyes have a far-away look, as though something inside her has switched off. 'He was good-looking. And fun. He was always teasing Georges, asking him if he was married to one of the sows, things like that.'

'Sounds hilarious.'

Gretchen takes the comment at face value. 'He was. There was this one time he took a piglet and dressed it up in his old handkerchief, like a nappy. Georges was furious when he found out, because Louis dropped it and broke its leg. He was going to tell Papa until Mathilde made him promise to say it was an accident. It would only have made Papa angry. And the sanglochons aren't Georges's anyway, so he'd no right to make a fuss.'

'What happened to the piglet?'

'Georges had to slaughter it. But it was a sucker, so we got a good price.'

The more I hear about this Louis, the less I like him. I can't imagine Mathilde with someone like that, but as soon as I think it I realize how ridiculous I'm being. It isn't as if I really know anything about her.

'So where's Louis now?'

'I told you, Mathilde made him go away.'

'But is he still living in town?'

Gretchen's face has hardened; she looks every inch her father's daughter. She throws the last of the dirt down onto the ants. 'Why are you so interested?'

'I only wondered if Mathilde—'

'Stop going on about Mathilde! Why are you always asking about her?'

'I'm not—'

'Yes you are! Mathilde, Mathilde, Mathilde! I hate her! She spoils everything! She's jealous of me because she's old and droopy and she knows men want me more than her!'

I raise my hands, trying to placate her. 'OK, calm down.'

But Gretchen is far from calm. The skin around her nose has turned white. 'You want to screw her, don't you? Or are you fucking her already?'

This is getting out of hand. I climb to my feet.

'Where are you going?'

'To work on the house.'

'To see Mathilde, you mean?' I don't bother to respond. I reach down to pick up the plate but she dashes it from my hands. 'Don't ignore me! I said *don't ignore me!*'

She snatches up the fork and lashes out. I jerk back but the tines snag my arm, tearing the flesh.

'Jesus . . . !'

I grab the fork from her and fling it away. A dark trickle of blood runs down my arm as I clamp my hand to the wound. I stare at Gretchen, more shocked than anything. She's blinking as though she's just woken up.

'I'm sorry. I – I didn't mean to . . .'

'Just go.' My voice is unsteady.

'I said I'm sorry.'

I don't trust myself to speak. After a moment Gretchen contritely gathers up the plate and cutlery, her hair hanging like a curtain over her face. Without another word she takes them around to the courtyard and disappears.

I stay where I am, waiting for my heart to slow down. The fork has left four parallel cuts in my bicep. Bloody, but not deep. I press my hand over them again. At my feet, the ants are swarming over the spilled food in an orgy of activity. The ones Gretchen killed have already been forgotten: all that counts is survival.

Leaving them to their feast, I go into the barn to clean my arm.

The sunset is spectacular. The dragonflies, bees and wasps that patrol the lake during the day have been replaced by midges and mosquitoes. Sitting with my back against the chestnut tree, I blow cigarette smoke into the air. I read somewhere that insects don't like it, but these don't seem to know that. I'm bitten already, but I won't really feel them until the morning. Tomorrow can take care of itself.

I've brought Mathilde's book with me. The peace is absolute, but I've no stomach for *Madame Bovary* tonight. The novel lies beside me, unopened, as I watch the last rays of sun turn the lake's surface into a dark mirror.

My arm is sore where the fork tore it, but the cuts are only superficial. I washed them under the tap, letting the frigid water sluice away the blood. It ran in pink trails across the cobbles, draining into the widening crack in the patch of concrete. Another of my predecessor's legacies. I told Mathilde I'd caught it on the scaffold and asked for cotton wool and sticking plaster. I thought it better to dress it myself than explain how I'd come by equidistant cuts. *Your sister stabbed me with a fork because she hasn't forgiven you for splitting up with Michel's father. Who she seems to have liked a little too much.*

No, that's one conversation I'd rather avoid. Still, if Gretchen had a crush on Louis it would explain some of the tension between her and Mathilde. And maybe it was more than a crush, I think, remembering the crude drawing I found in his notebook. The naked woman could have been either of them, and Louis doesn't sound the sort of man who'd have qualms about sleeping with both sisters.

Now who's jealous?

The chestnut tree is full of spiny globes. They aren't fully grown, but one of them has dropped prematurely and lies in the grass nearby. I pick it up, feeling the prickle of its spines in my palm. The sun has dipped below the trees now, and a dusky twilight has descended on the lake. I get to my feet and stand at the edge of the bluff. The chestnut makes a tiny splash when I throw it into the water. It floats like a miniature mine, bobbing above the darker shadow that marks the submerged rock.

Restless, I go down from the bluff and walk along the lakeside. I haven't been this far before, never felt any desire to go any further. Now, though, I feel compelled to plot the extent of the farm's boundaries.

The track ends at the bluff, and a little further along the woods come right to the water's edge. I pick my way along it to the far bank of the lake, then carry on until I reach the end of the farm's land. Strands of rusty barbed wire weave along the edge of the tree line, nailed into the trunks. There isn't much to see on the other side except wheat fields. There are no paths or tracks down here, and if there's any reason for the barbed wire I can't see it. The wheat is hardly likely to trespass, but that isn't the point.

Arnaud's marking his territory.

If I needed more proof it comes only a few minutes later. I start to follow the fence, and only at the last second notice a hard-edged shape nestled in a tuft of grass. It's one of Arnaud's traps, jaws spread wide and waiting. I didn't think he'd have bothered to put them all the way down here, but he obviously isn't taking any chances. Neither am I: I look around until I find a stick and thrust it into the trap's jaws. They snap shut hard enough to splinter the wood.

The thought of more of them hidden away snuffs any desire to explore further. In the fading light I use my walking stick to probe ahead of me as I head back to the lake. I come out on the opposite side to the bluff, and stand for a few moments to take it in from this new perspective. The banks of the lake are overgrown with reeds and bulrushes, but from here I can see a patch of shingle tucked behind a grassy hummock. I make my way over, my feet crunching as they sink into the thin covering of pebbles. The water shelves quickly, shading to dark green as it deepens. I crouch down and dip my hand in. It's cold, and a mist of sediment stirs when my fingers touch the bottom.

This would be a good place to swim from, I think. Most of the lakeside is muddy, but I could wade out from here. I swirl my fingers through the water, silvering the broken surface. The air hasn't lost its daytime heat, and the thought of stripping off and plunging into the cool lake is beguiling. Only my bandaged foot stops me, but I've waited this long. The stitches are almost ready to come out, and when they do I can celebrate with a long-overdue swim.

If I'm still here.

I stand up and flick the water from my hand, sending tiny ripples shivering across the lake. An insipid moon has come out as I return to the bluff for Mathilde's book, then head back through the woods. The sanglochons are quiet tonight, the statues silent as ever. It's only my mood that makes them seem watchful and sinister, but I'm still glad when I emerge from the trees.

The stars are scattered like powder across the darkening sky, a stark reminder of our insignificance. When I reach the barn I linger outside, not yet ready to go up to the loft's airless heat. I'm debating helping myself to another bottle of Arnaud's wine when the sound of breaking glass comes from the house.

It's followed by another. There's yelling and hysterical laughter as I hurry to the courtyard. As I reach it the kitchen door is flung open and Arnaud bursts out. In the spill of light I can see he's holding the rifle. I stop dead, certain that if he sees any movement in the darkness he'll shoot.

'No, don't!'

Mathilde rushes after him. He ignores her, striding towards the track that leads to the road. Rowdy cheers follow another shattering of glass that I now realize is a window breaking. Mathilde tries to hold Arnaud back but he shakes her off, and then they're both out of sight. I hurry across the courtyard as Gretchen appears in the doorway. She's holding Michel, her face white and anxious.

'Stay there,' I tell her.

Without waiting to see what she does, I set off after Mathilde and Arnaud, crossing the cobbles in an awkward half-run, half-hop. The shouting is coming from the woods behind the house.

There are several voices, whooping and jeering, and now I can make out what they're saying.

'*Here, piggy! Send your daughters out, Arnaud!*'

'*There's one of your little piggies here, come and say hello!*'

There are grunts and squeals, a high-pitched burst of raucous laughter. Ahead of me I can make out the shadowy figures of Arnaud and Mathilde against the lighter background of the track. Mathilde has hold of Arnaud's arm, struggling with him.

'Don't! Leave them, they'll go!'

'Get in the house!'

He pushes her away and in the same movement brings the rifle up and fires. His features are lit up as it cracks out, and the jeers are abruptly cut off. There's cursing and yells of alarm, followed by the crashing of undergrowth. Arnaud aims the long barrel into the blackness of the woods as he shoots again and again, working the bolt so quickly that the snap of one discharge merges with the next. Only when the commotion has died away does he stop, lowering the rifle with what could be reluctance.

In the distance a car engine roars into life and quickly recedes. Quiet settles like a blanket over the night.

Arnaud doesn't move. Mathilde stands with her back to him, hands over her ears. They're two featureless black shapes, no more human in the darkness than the trees themselves. She remains immobile as Arnaud finally turns back towards the house. His footsteps crunch on the track. He passes me as if I'm not there. I wait, watching Mathilde. Eventually she drops her arms. I hear a soft snuffle. One hand comes up to her face, makes a wiping motion. Slowly, she begins to make her way down the track.

'Are you OK?' I ask.

My voice makes her start. I can pick out her features now, pale and scared against the dark framing of her hair. She gives a nod.

Head down, she goes past, so close she almost brushes against me. She vanishes around the corner of the house, and a moment later I hear a faint click as the kitchen door is closed.

I stay on the track, looking up towards the now silent woods. My heart is racing. Gradually, the whisper of crickets resumes.

Accompanied by their music, I go back to the barn.

London

THE SKYLIGHT IS FOGGED with condensation. Rain sweeps against it with a noise like a drum roll. Our smudged reflections hang above us as we lie on the bed, misted doppelgangers trapped in the glass.

Chloe has gone distant again. I know her moods well enough not to push, to leave her to herself until she returns of her own accord. She stares up through the skylight, blond hair catching the glow from the seashell-lamp she bought from a flea market. Her eyes are blue and unblinking. I feel, as I always do, that I could pass my hand over them without any reaction from her. I want to ask what she's thinking, but I don't. I'm frightened she might tell me.

The air is cold and damp on my bare chest. At the other side of the room a blank canvas stands untouched on Chloe's easel. It's been blank for weeks now. The reek of oil and turpentine, for so long the smell I've associated with the small flat, has faded until it's barely noticeable.

I feel her stir beside me.

'Do you ever think about dying?' she asks.

I don't know what to say. The atmosphere between us has been strung taut since I found the coke. Chloe swears it was an isolated mistake she won't repeat, and I'm trying to believe her.

Neither of us talks about Jules. Each day is a delicate balancing act that could fall and shatter if we don't maintain it.

Yet I've noticed she's become more withdrawn lately. There's nothing specific, but a few days ago I searched the flat again while she was out. When I didn't find anything I told myself I'd been imagining things. But it could just mean she's found a better hiding place.

'What sort of question's that?'

'Does it scare you?'

'Jesus, Chloe . . .'

'It doesn't scare me. It used to, but it doesn't any more.'

The muscles in the back of my neck are knotted and clenched. I push myself up so I can look at her. 'Where's this going?'

She's staring up through the skylight, her eyes bright points in the shadowed paleness of her face. Just when I think she isn't going to answer, she does.

'I'm pregnant.'

At first I don't know what I feel. Of all the things I've expected, all the scenarios I've imagined, this wasn't one of them. Then everything's swept away by euphoria and relief. So that's what's been wrong.

'God, Chloe, that's great!' I say, starting to put my arms around her.

But she lies stiff and unresponsive. She's still staring through the skylight, and now I see the brightness from her eyes spill and run down her cheeks. I pull back from her as a coldness begins to spread through me.

'What?' I ask, though I already know.

Chloe's voice is level, unaffected by the tears on her face.

'It isn't yours.'

13

THE POLICE ARRIVE NEXT morning. I'm climbing down from the scaffold when I hear footsteps in the courtyard. I glance around, expecting it to be Mathilde or Gretchen, and the sight of two uniformed gendarmes shocks me motionless. Only the fact that I have one arm hooked over a ladder rung stops me from falling.

Oh, Jesus Christ, I think.

Their white shirts are dazzling in the sun. The dark lenses of their sunglasses rob them of expression as they look at me, caught halfway down the ladder like a fly in a web. The smaller of the two, who has the look of seniority about him, speaks first.

'Where's Arnaud?'

The words don't communicate anything to me. I stare at him stupidly.

'We're looking for Jacques Arnaud,' he repeats, irritably. 'Where is he?'

The bigger gendarme takes off his peaked cap and wipes the sweat from his brow. The armpits of his shirt are stained with wet rings. For some reason, that frees me enough to dredge up a sentence.

'Try the house.'

Without thanking me they walk up to the door. I'm still immobile on the ladder so I force myself to continue down to the courtyard. My legs feel sluggish, as though I've forgotten how to use them.

Arnaud might be out hunting for all I know, but the door opens before they can knock. He confronts them with silent belligerence. When the smaller gendarme asks, 'M'sieur Arnaud?' he gives only the barest nod of confirmation. The gendarme is unimpressed.

'We've had a report of shooting here last night.'

His partner with the sweat-stained shirt notices me watching. I quickly turn away and go around the side of the house. As soon as I'm out of sight I sink to the ground.

They aren't here for me. I let my head hang and take deep breaths. The murmur of voices still drifts from the courtyard, but I can't make out what's being said. I quickly pull myself up the inside of the scaffold like it's a giant climbing-frame, hardly noticing the way it sways and creaks. Once I've hauled myself onto the platform I creep along it to the end nearest the kitchen. The voices become audible again.

'. . . no formal complaint has been made,' Arnaud is saying below. 'I was defending my property. If you know who it was you should be arresting them, not me.'

'We aren't arresting anyone, we're just—'

'Then you should be. Someone attacks my home, but I'm the one you harass because I fire a few shots in the air to scare them off? Where's the justice in that?'

'We've heard the shots weren't in the air.'

'No? Was anyone hurt?'

'No, but—'

'There you are then. Besides, I don't know how they can say what I was aiming at, they took off so fast.'

'Can we talk inside?'

'I don't see that there's anything to talk about.'

'We won't take up much of your time.'

The gendarme's voice has a touch of steel in it. I can't hear Arnaud's answer, but there's the sound of footsteps going into the house. The door closes. All I can think about is the plastic-wrapped package in my rucksack. It seems like madness not to have got rid of it, let alone leave it hidden under a few old clothes.

Too late now.

I become aware I'm biting at a torn piece of thumbnail and make myself stop. From where I'm crouching I can just see the lake over the tops of the trees. I could hide down there until the police have left. Perhaps even climb over the barbed wire and head across the wheat fields until I reach another road. If I'm lucky I could be miles away before anyone knew I'd gone.

But that's panic talking. The gendarmes aren't interested in me; they've only come to warn Arnaud about firing his rifle last night. At least, that's what I hope. If I run I'll only be drawing attention to myself.

Besides, where would I go?

I chop the trowel worriedly at the mortar drying on the board. Without giving any thought to what I'm doing I scoop a little out and press it into the wall. Then I do it again. The soft scrape of the metal on the stone has a tranquillizing effect, quieting the tremor in my hands. After a while I stand up. I work mechanically, moving the trowel from the board to the wall and back without conscious thought. With each stroke I forget about Arnaud, forget about the police. Forget about everything.

I don't even hear the kitchen door opening again.

'How's it going up there?'

I stop and look down. The big gendarme is standing in the courtyard squinting up at me. He isn't wearing his sunglasses, and without them his eyes are small and piggish.

'Looks like hot work,' he calls up.

I make a show of carrying on working. 'Yeah.'

He plucks his damp shirt away from his chest. 'Bitch of a day. We had to leave the car and walk from the road, as well. The gate's locked.'

'Right.'

'Can't stand the sun. Never could. From April till October, it's just hell as far as I'm concerned.'

'I know what you mean.'

'Yeah, with your colouring you must feel it pretty bad too.'

The mortar slips off the trowel and spatters onto the platform. The gendarme studies the house, taking off his cap and running his fingers through his hair before replacing it. His thick moustache all but obscures his mouth.

'Been at it long?'

'Oh . . . since about nine.'

He smiles. 'I don't mean today.'

'Right. A few weeks.'

My board is empty. The mortar left in the bucket has become too dry to work with, but I scoop a pile out anyway. It's either that or go back down. I can hear the gendarme's boots creak as he shifts his weight.

'You're English, aren't you?'

I nod.

'You speak good French. Where did you learn?'

'I just picked it up.'

'Really? You must have a knack.'

'I got a good grounding at school.'

'Ah. That'll be it.' He takes out a handkerchief and mops his face. 'What's your name?'

I'm tempted to invent one, but that will only make things worse if he wants to see my passport. There's no reaction when I tell him.

'So what brings you to France, Sean?' he asks.

I run the trowel blade across the wall, needlessly smoothing the mortar. 'Just travelling.'

'If you're a tourist you shouldn't be working.' My face burns as blood rushes to it. After a pause he laughs. 'Don't worry, I'm only joking. So were you here last night, for the trouble?'

'Some of it.'

'Some of it?'

'I heard the commotion. I didn't really see it.'

'But you knew something was going on.'

'It was hard to miss.'

He wipes the back of his neck with the handkerchief. 'Tell me what happened.'

'I heard some windows smash. There was shouting. From the woods. It sounded like there were quite a few of them in there.'

'What were they shouting?'

'Things about Arnaud and his daughters.'

'Pretty nasty, eh?'

'It wasn't nice.'

'So how many times did Arnaud fire the rifle?'

'Oh . . .' I frown as though I'm trying to remember. 'I don't know.'

'Once, twice? Six times?'

'I'm not sure. It was all a bit confused.'

'Was he aiming into the wood?'

'I couldn't say.'

'Where were you when all this was going on?'

'At the end of the house.'

'But you couldn't see what was happening?'

'It was dark. By the time I got there it was all over.'

'Didn't you run up to see what was going on?'

I hold up my foot so he can see the bandage. 'Not with this.'

Even as I'm doing it I know it's a mistake. He looks at it without surprise. 'What did you do?'

'Trod on a nail,' I say, wishing I'd kept my mouth shut.

'A nail. Right.'

There's a harder look on his face now, replacing the superficial friendliness. I turn away, pretending to point the wall with the too dry mortar.

'Do you know who it was?' I ask, trying to sound casual. 'Last night, I mean?'

'Probably just local youths.' He sounds indifferent. I get the impression no one's going to be arresting Didier and his friends for throwing a few stones. The gendarme puts on his sunglasses, hiding his small eyes. 'How long will you be staying?'

'Until the house is finished, I suppose.'

'And then you'll be moving on.'

I'm not sure if that's a question or not. 'I expect so.'

The sunglasses continue to stare up at me. I think he might say something else, but then the kitchen door opens again and the other gendarme comes out. The two of them talk, their voices too low to make out, but the smaller one shakes his head in obvious annoyance. Then the big gendarme says something and they both look at me.

I turn away again. After a second I hear them walk across the courtyard. I continue pretending to work, daubing almost dry mortar onto the stones until I'm sure they've gone.

My legs are weak as I sink down onto the platform. I put my head between my knees and try not to throw up.

'Are you up there?'

It's Mathilde. I take a deep breath and get to my feet. She's at the foot of the scaffold, holding a plate of food. The spaniel stands next to her, eyeing it hopefully.

'I've brought your lunch.'

'OK. Thanks.'

I've no appetite but I don't want to stay up here any longer. Not where everyone can see me. I take my time climbing down the ladder, expecting Mathilde to have left the plate on the window-ledge as usual. But when I get to the bottom she's still there. Her face is pale, the shadows under her eyes more pronounced than usual.

'The police were here. About last night.'

'I know. One of them was asking me about it.'

She gives me a quick glance, then looks away. Her hand goes up to push her hair back in what I've come to recognize as her habitual expression of unease.

'Are they going to press charges?' I ask.

'No. They warned him about firing his rifle in future. That's all.'

I try to sound indifferent. 'So will they be coming back?'

'They didn't say. I don't think so.'

She almost seems to be reassuring me.

When she's gone I set off across the courtyard. Slowly at first, trying to seem normal, but by the time I reach the barn I'm almost running, jabbing the walking stick into the earth like a third leg. It's only when I get to the steps that I realize I'm still holding the plate. Bread and meat spill from it as I put it down and rush up to the loft. I drag my rucksack onto the bed and start tugging at the drawstring. I've kept it fastened since Gretchen went in it for the MP3 player, and now I swear as I struggle to untie the knot, listening for any footsteps that might announce the return of the police.

There's a bitter taste in the back of my throat as I reach in and grab the package. Its smooth weight is a reminder of everything I'd rather forget. I've had plenty of time to decide what to do, but it was easier to avoid thinking about it altogether. Now I don't have any choice. I look wildly around the piled junk in the loft for somewhere to hide it, but everywhere seems too obvious. I need a place where it'll be safe from a casual search, where it won't be found by accident.

It takes a while, but eventually I think of one.

A bee grumbles over the vines, droning like a crippled plane. There's a half-heard thrum in the air, as though the sun is making even the silence vibrate. The heat seems to have a physical weight, sapping will and energy alike.

I gaze out at the day through the barn entrance. I'm sitting on the concrete strip with my back against one of the old wine vats. It's much cooler down here than in the loft, although 'cool' is still a relative term. My lunch was still on the step where I'd left it when I came back from hiding the package. Or rather the plate was: Lulu had discovered it in my absence.

I wasn't hungry anyway.

The springer spaniel lolls next to me, digesting my lunch and enjoying the shade. I should get back to work, but I can't find the motivation. The morning's events have left me hollowed out. The gendarmes' visit has unsettled me even more than the violence in the square. At least then I'd been able to return to the farm's sanctuary, to shut myself away behind its gate. Now the outside world has followed me inside, reminding me that any sense of refuge is no more than an illusion. I can't hide here indefinitely.

The question is where do I go?

Cocooned in shade, I stare through the barn entrance at the sunlit vines, absently picking at the crack in the concrete surface. The broken edge crumbles away easily. There's something hypnotic about letting the grains sift through my fingers, like sand at a beach. *Not enough mortar in the mix.* The crack has grown bigger, worn away by my walking over it to the steps. At its widest point it's maybe an inch across, and as I run my fingertips along it they touch something that rustles.

Too lethargic to move, I turn my head to look. There isn't enough light in the barn to make out what it is, but it feels like a scrap of cloth. Probably something that was mixed in with the concrete; yet another example of Louis's less than stellar workmanship. I give it a half-hearted tug, but there's not enough of it to grip.

Losing interest, I brush the sand from my hands and leave the scrap where it is. The barn's cavernous interior is spicy with old wood and grape musk. I wouldn't have thought it was possible to feel tired after what's happened, but heat and reaction are a potent combination. Resting my head against the rough vat, I stare at the sunlit day beyond the barn entrance, a rectangle of light in the darkness . . .

Something hits my foot, and for an instant I think I'm caught in the trap again. Then the last vestiges of sleep drop away and I see a blurred figure looming over me.

'What?' I gasp, scrambling to sit up.

I don't know if I'm relieved or not to find it's Arnaud. He stares at me coldly, foot cocked ready to kick me again. Lulu is frantically wagging her tail at him, managing to seem both cowed and guilty.

'What are you doing?' he demands.

I rub the sleep from my eyes. 'It's my lunch break.'

'It's after four.'

Looking past him, I see that the light outside has changed. A high haze, like a sheet of muslin, has turned the sky a uniform white, reducing the sun to a formless glare.

But I'm not in the mood to apologize. 'Don't worry, I'll make up for it.'

I expect Arnaud to make some comment, but he isn't really listening. There's a preoccupied scowl on his face.

'Mathilde said the gendarmes spoke to you.'

'One of them did.'

191

'What about?'

'He wanted to know what happened last night.'

'And?'

'And what?'

'What did you tell him?'

I'm tempted to let him sweat, but my heart isn't in it. 'That it was too dark for me to see anything.'

Arnaud scans my face, looking for signs that I'm lying. 'Was that all they wanted to know?'

'He asked what I'd done to my foot.'

His smile is bitter. 'So you told him about the traps, eh?'

'I said I'd stepped on a nail.'

'Did he believe you?'

I shrug.

His jaw works as though he's chewing that over, then he turns and walks away. *Don't mention it*, I think, staring at his back. I don't want the police sniffing round here any more than he does, but a simple thank you wouldn't kill him. Arnaud's only gone a few paces, though, before he pauses.

'Mathilde's cooking something special tonight,' he says grudgingly. 'You can eat with us.'

Before I can answer, he's gone.

14

THE COURTYARD IS IN shadow as I limp across it towards the house. A lone hen refuses to get out of my way, so I usher it aside with my walking stick. The bird clucks and flaps before settling down to resume picking at some invisible speck. My freshly washed hair and beard are still damp, and I've even dressed for the occasion, putting on a fresh T-shirt and my cleanest pair of jeans. I feel uncomfortable, the familiar setting made strange by the occasion.

I keep reminding myself it's only dinner.

Lulu has been banished to the courtyard. She lingers hopefully outside the kitchen, fussing over me briefly when I walk up but more concerned with getting back inside. The windows are open, letting out the smell of roasting meat. I raise my hand, catch myself hesitating, and knock on the door.

Gretchen opens it. She stands back to let me in, blocking the dog's attempt to dart past with a terse 'No, Lulu!'

The kitchen is warm and humid with cooking. Saucepans are simmering on the old range. Mathilde is stirring one briskly with a spoon. She gives me a perfunctory smile.

'Sit down.'

I go to the table, which is set with four places, and pull out one of the unmatching chairs.

'That's Papa's,' says Gretchen.

She lingers by the table while I move to another seat. Except for when I told her to stay in the house last night, we haven't spoken since her tantrum – I don't know what else to call it – outside the barn. There's nothing in her manner now to indicate either embarrassment or hostility. She acts as though nothing's happened.

'Ask him if he'd like an aperitif,' Mathilde tells her.

'I know, I was going to,' Gretchen snaps. She turns to me, awkwardly. 'Would you like an aperitif?'

'That sounds good.'

I'm going to need a drink to help me get through this evening; I'm on edge enough as it is. I expect Gretchen to tell me what they have, but she looks enquiringly at her sister. Mathilde keeps her eyes on her saucepans.

'There's pastis.'

I wait, but that seems to be it.

'Pastis is fine,' I say.

Arnaud comes in as Gretchen's taking the bottle from a cupboard. He's carrying Michel, who looks sleepy and fractious.

'What's this?' he asks, frowning when he sees what she's doing.

Gretchen pauses in unscrewing the cap from a bottle of Ricard. 'Mathilde told me to get him an aperitif.'

Arnaud looks over at me for the first time. I'm sure he's going to tell her to put the bottle away, but he only shrugs.

'If he wants to rot his gut with that stuff it's up to him.'

Gretchen pours a big measure into a small glass and fills another with water. She sets them both on the table in front of me. I smile thanks and pour a little water into the clear amber liquid. It swirls, turning opaque and milky. I take a drink and feel the liquorice warmth burn down my throat.

Arnaud is watching me as I lower the glass. 'Gut rot,' he says again.

I raise the glass in an ironic toast. Gut rot or not, it tastes better than his wine. Michel begins squirming irritably. Arnaud jogs him up and down.

'Hey, hey, none of that, eh?'

'He should be in bed,' Mathilde says, glancing over from the saucepan she's stirring.

'He didn't want to go.'

'He's tired. If you put him down he'll—'

'I said he didn't want to go.'

The sound of saucepans bubbling is suddenly the only noise in the room. Mathilde keeps her head down. The flush on her cheeks could be from the heat of the range, but it wasn't there a moment ago. Arnaud stares at her, then holds out Michel to Gretchen.

'Here. He needs changing.'

'But Papa—!'

'Do as you're told.'

Mathilde puts down the spoon.

'I'll take him.'

'You're cooking. Gretchen can do it.'

'I'd rather—'

Arnaud silences her with a raised finger, levelling it at her like a gun until she lowers her head and turns back to the pan. He motions to Gretchen.

'Take him.'

Gretchen flounces out of the kitchen with the baby. Arnaud wanders over to the range and sniffs at the steaming pans. He takes the spoon from Mathilde and tastes the sauce.

'More pepper.'

As she obediently grinds peppercorns he sits at the table, lowering himself with a sigh that's almost a grunt into the chair. His chair, of course.

'I see the top section of wall's nearly done,' he says, settling.

I take a sip of Ricard. 'It's getting there.'

'How much longer do you think it'll take?'

I put down my glass. I don't want to think about the future. 'To finish the entire wall? I don't know, a few weeks maybe.'

'And the rest of the house?'

'Longer than that. Why?'

'Just so I know.'

As we're talking Mathilde takes the saucepan from the heat and quietly slips out. If Arnaud notices he doesn't object. He picks up the opened bottle of wine from the centre of the table and pours himself a glass. He takes a sip and grimaces. There's a basket of bread next to the bottle. He breaks off a chunk and chews it as he drinks.

We sit at the table in a silence that's broken only by the bubbling pans. I still don't know why I've been invited. I'd assumed it was because I'd covered for him with the police, but now I'm starting to suspect there's another reason. Arnaud isn't the grateful sort.

Gretchen comes back into the kitchen. Without fuss, she goes straight to the range and puts the sauce back on the heat. Arnaud doesn't spare her a glance, either unaware of the subtle collusion between his daughters or choosing to overlook it. Mathilde and Gretchen can evidently co-operate when they need to, despite the tension between them.

I've finished my pastis. Arnaud sees the empty glass and slides the bottle of wine over. 'Here. Make yourself at home.'

I'm not sure if he's being facetious or not.

The 'something special' is a boneless pork loin, rolled and rubbed with salt and rosemary and roasted with unpeeled cloves of garlic. The kitchen fills with its heavy scent when Mathilde lifts it steaming from the oven. She carves it by the range, cutting off oozing slices and laying them on plates that Gretchen then brings to the table. There are dishes of shallots, puréed chestnuts, chard and sautéed potatoes already set out, all of which Arnaud helps himself to first.

Gretchen brings her own plate over to the table. As she sits down she catches my eye and smiles. I pretend not to notice, hoping her father won't either. It's a vain hope.

'What are you smirking at?'

'Nothing.'

Arnaud glares at her. 'Is there something I'm missing here? Some joke?'

'No.'

'Then why are you grinning like a donkey?'

'I'm not.'

'You think I'm blind?' Arnaud's face is growing darker, but as he's about to say something else Mathilde puts a dish on the table and knocks over the wine.

'Oh, I'm sorry!'

She quickly rights it, but not in time to stop the crimson stream spreading. Arnaud pulls back his chair to keep it from dripping on him as the spill runs off the table edge, and Mathilde runs for a cloth.

'Watch what you're doing,' he snaps as she mops it up.

But it's diverted him. Mathilde brings another bottle, filling mine and Arnaud's glasses before pouring smaller measures for herself and Gretchen. Gretchen frowns.

'Is that all?'

'For now,' Mathilde says, setting down the bottle.

'Papa!' Gretchen protests.

Arnaud gives a short nod of indulgence. Shooting her sister a triumphant look, Gretchen fills her glass to the brim.

Mathilde quietly takes her seat.

Arnaud is at the table's head, facing me, with Gretchen and Mathilde on either side. He's already started eating, but I wait for Mathilde. The sauce is mustard and cream, not too hot and cooked with the meat's juices. The pork is delicious.

'This is great,' I say.

The praise is aimed at Mathilde, but Arnaud intercepts it.

'It should be. You won't find better pork than this.'

He stabs up a piece of meat. His jaws work as he chews, muscles bunching below his ears. He swallows, looking at me.

'Recognize it?'

I haven't a clue what he's talking about. He forks up another piece of meat and waves it at me.

'This. Don't you recognize it? You should; you helped kill it.'

I pause as I cut into a slice, but only for a second. I'm not going to give him the satisfaction. 'I thought it looked familiar.'

'Makes it taste better, eh? Gives it a certain flavour, knowing where it came from.' Arnaud refills his glass without offering the bottle to anyone else. 'Of course, Mathilde doesn't agree. She thinks pork is "unclean". Don't you, Mathilde?'

For the first time I notice that Mathilde's plate holds only vegetables. She keeps her eyes downcast.

'I just don't like it,' she says quietly.

'She just doesn't like it.' Arnaud consumes half his glass of wine at one go. His expression is mean. 'Chicken is fine, or duck, or rabbit. But not pork. Why is that, do you think, eh?'

'People like different things,' I say.

I wasn't intending to defend her. All I want to do is get the meal out of the way and go back to my loft. He looks at me, thoughtfully.

'Is that right,' he says dryly, and drains the rest of his wine.

The remainder of the bottle quickly goes the same way. Arnaud eats and drinks with bellicose concentration, dominating the table like a hair trigger waiting to go off. But the main course passes without explosion. Afterwards there's goat's cheese, the usual strong, half-set stuff that Mathilde makes. I decline, but Arnaud smears it thickly on pieces of bread with his knife.

It's grown dark inside the kitchen. When Mathilde switches on a tall floor lamp the twilight outside becomes full night. I get up with my plate as she and Gretchen begin to clear the table, but Arnaud waves me back down.

'They can manage.'

He finishes one last scallop of bread and cheese, brushing his mouth with his fingertips. But despite the relaxed pose there's a restlessness about him. Abruptly, he pushes back his chair.

'Come on. We'll go into the sitting room.'

Both Mathilde and Gretchen stare after him in surprise as he leaves the kitchen. Now what? I wonder, reluctantly following him.

Arnaud goes through a doorway at the far end of the hallway. It's a long, narrow room that looks like it runs the whole width of the house. As I go in he's kneeling by the fireplace, holding a match to a balled piece of newspaper under half-burned logs. Once it's caught he tosses the match into the grate and straightens, knees cracking like gunfire.

He motions brusquely to one of the chairs.

'Sit.'

I do, but not where he indicates. There's a sofa and several chairs more or less facing the fire. I pick an old wooden chair with curved arms that's deceptively comfortable. Despite the warm night it's cold in the room, which has a fusty smell of old furniture. A television set that looks old enough to be black and white stands in a corner. I notice one of the windows is boarded up: a reminder of Didier's visit the night before.

Arnaud switches on a lamp and goes to the bureau. On either side of its roll-top are two small cupboards. He opens one and takes out a bottle and two glasses.

'You like cognac?'

I overcome my surprise to say yes. He pours a little into each of the glasses and puts the bottle away. Handing one to me, he sits at the opposite side of the fire in a high-backed armchair and takes a sip of cognac.

'Ahh.'

He settles contentedly into the chair. I take a drink myself. The pale-gold liquor is smooth and seems to evaporate before it reaches the back of my throat.

'Thirty years old,' Arnaud says.

'Very nice.'

Better than his wine, at least. But I'm too ill at ease to enjoy it, certain that the bill for all this is still to be presented. An awkward silence descends. Whatever's on Arnaud's mind, I'm far from certain I want to hear it. I take another drink of cognac and look around the room. Several framed photographs are on a small gate-legged table by the fireplace. The more recent are of Gretchen when she was little. The biggest, visible even though it's at the back, is of a dark-haired woman and a young girl.

Arnaud sees me looking. 'My wife and Mathilde.'

'They look alike.'

He nods, staring at the photograph. 'Gretchen takes more after my side.'

'Your wife was a teacher, wasn't she?'

It's meant innocuously enough, but he looks at me sharply. Wondering how I know, although he doesn't pursue it. He takes his pipe from his shirt pocket and begins filling it.

'When I met her Marie was a teacher, yes. But she gave it up. There was plenty of work for her to do here.'

'She still taught Mathilde, though.'

That earns me another look. 'She wanted to. English, German, Italian, she thought Mathilde should learn them all. Especially Italian. Because of its culture.' He lights the pipe and draws on it scornfully. 'There's no place for *culture* on a farm. She learned that soon enough.'

His mouth clamps down on the pipe's stem. There's no hint

of sympathy or affection. I think about the wedding photograph left in the disused bedroom and feel sorry for the woman.

I nod towards the photograph of his wife and daughter. 'How old was Mathilde there?'

'Ten or eleven. It was taken before Marie became ill.' He takes the pipe from his mouth and points the stem at me accusingly. Blue smoke meanders up from its bowl, filling the room with a thick, sweet smell. 'Have you heard about that as well, eh?'

'I know she died.'

'Oh, she died, all right. Eventually. Some wasting disease. The last six months she couldn't get out of bed. Left me trying to run a farm with an invalid wife and two young daughters. The doctors said it might be this, it might be that, but never got around to putting a name to it. Small wonder they couldn't cure her. Officious bastards.'

Arnaud angrily knocks back the rest of his cognac and stands up. He takes my glass without asking and goes to the bureau.

'The world's full of people who think they know better than you,' he says, refilling both glasses. He hands me mine and returns to his seat, taking the bottle with him. His expression is broody as he jams the pipe back into his mouth. 'There's always someone who thinks they have a right to tell you what to do. Doctors. Neighbours. Police.'

He shoots me a quick glance.

'All these people who prattle on about rights and freedom, and being part of society. Society! Ha! Society isn't about freedom, it's about doing as you're told!'

He takes a gulp and slams his glass down on the chair arm so hard some of the thirty-year-old spirit slops over the lip.

'A man has the right to live his own life as he sees fit. Take you. You're not even French. You're a foreigner. English, but I don't hold that against you. Other than that, what do I know? Nothing. Except that you've got something to hide.'

I try to keep a poker face, wishing I'd not had so much to drink. He grins.

'Don't worry, that's your business. Whatever it is, I don't care. You keep yourself to yourself, and I like that. But whatever it is you're hiding, or running away from, you're no more a part of society than I am.'

Arnaud takes another drink, watching me all the while.

'Why did you lie to the police?'

The abrupt change takes me unawares. 'Would you rather I hadn't?'

'That's not the point. You could have caused trouble over the traps, but you didn't. Why not?'

I try to think of something bland and non-committal, but it's too much effort. I just shrug, letting him read into it what he wants.

He smiles. 'Me and you, we're more alike than you think. What do you know about Louis?'

I take a drink of cognac, not sure where this is leading. 'Not much.'

'But you've wondered, eh? Why we don't like to talk about him. And why those cattle in the town treat us as they do.'

I shrug again, liking this even less.

'Don't worry, I don't blame you.' Arnaud grimaces, taking the pipe out of his mouth as though it's left a bad taste. 'Louis was a time-waster. Made his living doing odd bits of building work, but he was full of big ideas. Always had some scheme or another on the go. Like the vines he knew of going cheap. Or the statues. He had the lifting gear and a pick-up truck, I had the space to keep them until they were sold. Of course, I didn't know then he was getting into my eldest daughter's pants.'

Arnaud glowers at his pipe.

'I can't blame Mathilde. Louis could charm the flies off a cow's arse. She should have known better than let herself get pregnant, but when she did Louis saw his big chance. He asked her to marry him. Not because he wanted to do the right thing, you understand. He just saw it as a way he could get his hands on all this . . .'

He gestures around him, taking in the house and land beyond it.

'What he didn't know was that when I die everything will pass to Michel. Gretchen and Mathilde will be looked after, of course, but they won't get the farm. And neither will any-one they marry, I've made damn sure of that. My big mistake was telling Louis. Oh, he showed his true colours then, right enough. Told me he'd got a buyer lined up for the statues, and that he knew of someone in Lyon who'd more to sell. Said we'd get double the return on them, and like a fool I believed him. So I stumped up the cash – plus extra for his expenses – and that was the last we saw of him. He stole my money and abandoned the mother of his child like she was so much garbage!'

Poor Mathilde, I think. I'd already guessed the story's broad strokes, but even allowing that Arnaud's version of events is probably biased, it must have been a humiliating experience for her.

'Of course, then all the back-stabbing and gossip started,' Arnaud goes on bitterly. 'I could hardly tell anyone about the statues, but it wouldn't have made any difference anyway. Louis was popular in town, one of their own. So whatever made him leave couldn't be his fault, could it? Never mind that he'd fucked my daughter and betrayed my trust. Oh, no, they weren't about to blame *him*! No, it was *our* fault he'd left, we'd obviously *driven* him to it!'

The bottle rattles against his glass as he pours himself another cognac. He almost bites a drink from it.

'It gave the small-minded bastards the excuse they'd been waiting for. My daughters, even Gretchen, were harassed when-ever they went into town. When we stopped going they came out here. There were obscene phone calls; one night someone tried to set fire to the barn. The tractor's petrol tank was spiked with sugar. So I had the phone taken out and put up barbed wire. I made no secret about setting the traps, so the bastards knew what they could expect if they came on my land.'

Or anyone else, I think. But any irony is lost on Arnaud. 'Why are you telling me all this?'

'So you know what the position is. Because you kept your mouth shut when the police talked to you.'

I don't believe him. There's another agenda here, but whatever it is I'm not going to find out now. Arnaud gets to his feet, signalling that the audience is over.

'That's enough talk for tonight. We've got an early start to-morrow.'

'Doing what?'

'Taking up the traps. The police were asking about them. Those bastards from last night must have said something.' He looks at me with sudden suspicion. 'You sure you didn't tell any-one?'

'I've already said I didn't.'

I told Jean-Claude I'd injured my foot in the wood, but nothing more than that. It doesn't seem to occur to Arnaud that the neighbours he has such contempt for might not feel obliged to keep his secret, especially not after being shot at. But contradictions like that evidently don't count for much with him.

'That fat pig of a gendarme lectured me about traps being illegal. Illegal! On my own land!' Fury makes his voice quaver. 'I told them what I did here was my business, and unless they came back with a search warrant I didn't want to hear anything about it.'

That sends a chill through me. 'Do you think they will?'

'How should I know? But I'm not about to give the bastards the satisfaction of finding anything if they do.'

'And you want me to help you?'

'That's right.'

Arnaud throws back his head to drain his cognac, the tendons standing out either side of his throat like a rungless ladder. Smacking his lips with pleasure, he lowers his glass and grins. It gives him a crafty expression in the firelight, but his eyes are as hard as ever.

'Unless you'd rather explain to the police why you lied to them as well?'

Arnaud's cognac hums in my head as I go back to the barn. The night seems unnaturally clear, contrasting with the muzziness in my head. I meander a little across the courtyard, the walking stick skidding off the rounded tops of the cobbles. It's dark in the recesses of the barn and I've left the lamp upstairs. I pick out an empty wine bottle by touch, knocking over several others. Icy slivers of water spatter on the floor as I fill it at the tap, then cup my hands and splash my face.

Better.

I haul myself up the steps, glad to reach the familiarity of the loft. It's too much effort to close the trapdoor, so I leave it open. My walking stick slides to the floor when I try to lean it against the wall, but I can't be bothered to pick it up. I manage to pull off my T-shirt before I flop down onto the bed still in my jeans. I want to take them off, I really do, but the rich food and alcohol are like lead weights on my eyelids. I close them, just for a few seconds. In a moment I'll get up and finish undressing.

In a moment . . .

I'm back in the old room, the old bed. I feel the shift of the mattress and then the warmth of her next to me. Her lips brush my mouth, feather against my cheek. There's a glow of happiness in my chest that she's here, that everything's back to normal. But even as I start to respond I know something's wrong. The feeling grows as she presses against me, the scents and contours different. Soft hair drapes across my skin as a hand strokes me, and then I open my eyes and I'm back in the loft, and Gretchen's face is only inches from mine.

There's a second or two when instinct almost takes over. Then I'm wide awake as shock kicks in. I sit up, tumbling her off me onto the mattress.

She giggles. 'Did I frighten you?'

My head and heart are both thumping. I push myself away from her a little more. 'What are you doing?'

'What do you think?' Her teeth and eyes shine in the darkness. She's wearing a short white T-shirt and nothing else. 'Aren't you pleased to see me?'

'You shouldn't be here.'

'Why not? Everyone's asleep. And you are pleased, I can feel.'

Her hand reaches for my jeans. I move it away. 'You need to go.'

'You don't mean that.'

'Yes, I do.'

I swing my feet off the mattress and stand up. The last thing I want is any entanglement with Gretchen, but that's easier to remember if I'm not lying next to her.

Even in the moonlight I can see her confusion. 'What's wrong? Don't you like me?'

'Look . . .' I stop myself before I say anything I'll regret. 'It's not that. I just think you should go.'

There's a silence. I try to think of something else to say, some way of getting her out of here without prompting another tantrum. If she starts on about Mathilde now, things could turn ugly. Then I see her smile, teeth white in the darkness.

'Are you scared of Papa? You are, aren't you?'

I stay quiet, let her draw her own conclusions. It's easier to let her believe that, and it isn't as if there isn't some truth in it. She kneels up on the bed.

'What did he want to talk to you about earlier? He can't have been too cross if he gave you his best cognac. I know he did because I washed the glasses.'

'It was just about the farm.'

'Liar.' She laughs. 'Don't worry, I won't let him hurt you. Not unless you're mean to me, anyway.'

I don't know if she's joking or not. 'Look, he wants me to help him with the traps. I've got to be up in a few hours . . .'

'That's plenty of time.'

'Gretchen . . .'

'All right, I'll go. We don't want Papa kicking you downstairs again.' Her good humour's returned. I go to the trapdoor as she gets off the bed. Her hair catches the moonlight, and her legs are long and bare in the short T-shirt. She looks lovely, and for a moment I'm glad I fell asleep in my jeans.

She pauses in front of me, her smile impish as she strokes my arm.

'Don't I at least get a goodnight kiss?'

'Not tonight.'

'You're no fun.'

She pouts, not yet ready to let me off the hook. I feel her fingers stop when they encounter the plaster. I can see her frown as she examines it.

'What did you do to your arm?' she asks.

London

I'M CLEANING GLASSES BEHIND the counter at the Bar Zed when the customer walks in. There's something familiar about him, but not so much that I think anything of it. He shows no sign of recognizing me as Dee serves him a beer, which he takes to a table at the far side of the room.

I soon forget about him. The Zed's near Canary Wharf, and in the months I've been working here I've lost count of the number of faces I've served across the bar. I got the job when I handed in my notice at the language school. I wanted a clean break, and there were too many reminders there of my time with Chloe. After I moved out I stayed with Callum for a while, sleeping on his sofa until I found a tiny studio flat in Hackney. It isn't much, but it's somewhere to hang my film posters and store my DVDs. Besides, it's only temporary until I've saved enough money to go to France. That's my new plan, all part of making a fresh start.

I'm still here, though.

Somehow it's never seemed the right time to make the move. It's always next week, next month, next whenever. In the meantime the Zed isn't so bad. It's an upmarket place that by day attracts the city-types whose expense accounts can afford the lunch-time menu. The evening crowd are no less affluent and tend to appreciate the big mirrors behind the stainless-steel counter. Sergei, the owner, is OK. He and his boyfriend, Kai, help out when it's busy. There are worse places to work.

It isn't as though it's permanent.

The man who came in earlier approaches the bar for another beer. This time I serve him myself. I still can't place him. He's big, with a hardened look about him that sets him apart from the Zed's usual customers. As I'm pouring his beer he looks towards the door, then at his watch.

That's when I realize who he is.

I keep my head down as I hand him the change. He goes back to his table. While I serve other customers I keep watching him. He's obviously expecting someone, and not enjoying the wait.

It could be anyone. But I know, with a certainty that feels like vertigo, who it's going to be.

I'm bringing ice out of the kitchen when Jules arrives. He's with two gaudily attractive girls who teeter drunkenly, laughing as they head for the table where Lenny is sitting. The sight of him stops me in my tracks. I feel a breathless rush of feelings, a cocktail of fury, hate and dismay all combined, then I turn and go back into the kitchen.

'Shit, Sean, watch where you're going!' Sergei grumbles, trying not to spill what's on the tray he's carrying as I barge through the door.

'Sorry.' I move aside. My limbs feel stiff and unnatural. 'Uh, look, would it be OK if I took a break from the bar? Washed some dishes, or something?'

'You're joking, right? Perhaps you'd like to put your feet up while I bring you a coffee?'

Still muttering, he bumps the door open with his hip and goes into the bar.

'Shit,' I say, as the door swings shut.

'Problem?' Dee looks up from where she's spooning olives onto small plates.

'No, it's all right.'

I manage to hold a smile until she turns away, then sag back against the wall. Jez had told me that Jules ran a gym in Docklands, but in the aftermath of breaking up with Chloe I'd forgotten all about it. I'd been so keen to get away from our old haunts in West London that it never occurred to me I'd be working in his territory.

I take a deep breath and go back out. The place is busy, and for a while it looks as though I'll get away with it. Lenny comes to the bar again but this time it's Dee who serves him. He pays me no more attention than before, and I start to think they might finish their drinks and go without noticing me.

It's as they're about to leave that my luck runs out. Through a gap in the crowd I look across and see the four of them getting up from their table. And at exactly the same moment, as if I've called to him, Jules looks up and sees me.

I turn away and start serving someone else. I'm trying to act as though nothing's happened, but as I snatch a glass from the shelf I knock off another two. They shatter on the floor.

'Shit!'

I've spoken too loudly, earning a cross look from Sergei, who's serving nearby. There's the usual lull in the noise level at the sound of breaking glass, then conversations resume. I take a dustpan from under the counter and duck down to sweep up the fragments, glad of the excuse to be out of sight.

When I stand up Jules is leaning on the bar.

I ignore him, emptying the broken glass into a bin before continuing to serve drinks. All the while I'm conscious of him watching me. Soon, there's no one left at my end of the bar except him. I can't pretend he isn't there any longer.

I face him across the stainless-steel counter. He looks fit and tanned, although as he moves his head the bar lighting exposes dark rings under his eyes, like bruises. But he has the same half-smile on his face I remember.

'Gave up teaching, eh?' He makes a show of looking around. 'Nice crowd you get in here. Do they tip well?'

'What do you want?'

'Oh, now you can do better than that. Aren't you supposed to ask what I'd like to drink? "Excuse me, sir, what can I get you?" Something like that?'

I'm clenching my jaw so tightly my teeth hurt. Jules smiles at me again. His pupils are like pin-pricks. I tell myself he's nothing to me, that I should let him say whatever he has to and then leave. But I'm not prepared for his next words.

'I'll tell Chloe I've seen you.' He raises his eyebrows. 'You did know she's living with me now?'

No, I didn't. I haven't seen Chloe since I moved out. I'd considered offering to stay until she'd had the abortion, but in the end I hadn't. What Chloe did with her life was no longer any of my business, she'd made that clear. I told myself a clean break was best for both of us.

But I'd no idea she'd gone back to Jules. As far as I knew, the abortion was purely her decision, and I'd assumed that meant she'd broken with him as well. My feelings must be written on my face.

'Oh, you obviously didn't know,' he grins.

'How is she?'

'Why should you care? You walked out on her, didn't you?'

My knuckles whiten on the glass I'm holding, but then Lenny comes over. Big as Jules is, the other man towers over him.

'You coming?'

'Just saying hello to an old friend of Chloe's. You remember Sean, don't you?'

Lenny gives me an uninterested glance, but before he can

say anything a smartly dressed man and a woman approach the bar. The man signals to me. 'I'd like a glass of Chablis and—'

'We're talking,' Lenny says without turning around.

'Well, I'd like serving, so—'

He breaks off as Lenny turns his head to stare at him. Although the big man's expression doesn't change the atmosphere is suddenly charged.

'Fuck off.'

The customer begins to bluster, but it's half-hearted. He allows the woman to lead him away. Lenny turns back to Jules as if I'm not there.

'Hurry it up.'

It's more an order than a request. Jules flushes as the other man goes back to where the two drunken girls are waiting.

'Business calls.' He gives a hard smile, attempting to regain face. 'I'll tell Chloe I've seen you. She'll be thrilled.'

I stay where I am after he's gone. A man waves his credit card at me.

'Hey, you serving or just standing there?'

I turn and walk into the kitchen. Sergei says something to me but I don't hear what. I go through the fire-escape door and out into the alleyway at the back. There's the sweet smell of garbage and urine.

Letting the door close behind me, I slide down the wall and close my eyes.

15

'YOU AWAKE UP THERE?'

The words are a towline to consciousness. I open my eyes as it drags me up, not knowing who called or even if I dreamed it. The thump of someone banging on the trapdoor convinces me that I haven't.

'Come on, wake up, you lazy bastard!'

It's Arnaud. My first thought is Gretchen. I jack-knife upright in bed, half-convinced she's still there. But I'm alone, thank God. The chest of drawers is still on the trapdoor, where I pushed it the night before. Overkill to keep out an eighteen-year-old girl maybe, but just as effective against her father. In a waking panic I think he must know his daughter was here, before I remember I'm supposed to be helping him with the traps.

'All right,' I call. My head is thumping from the rough wine and Arnaud's cognac, and the rude awakening hasn't helped.

'About bloody time!' I can hear the wooden steps creak under his weight. 'Hurry up and get your arse down here!'

'Give me five minutes.'

'Make it two!'

His footsteps clump away from the trapdoor. I groan, hanging my head. It can't be much past dawn. A grey early light filters into the loft. Wanting nothing more than to fall back onto the mattress and sleep for another hour, I pull on my overalls and go downstairs. I stop off at the tap to drink thirstily and splash water on my face and neck. Beads of it cling to my beard and its cold is a temporary salve for my headache.

Arnaud is waiting outside with Lulu, a canvas workman's bag slung over his shoulder. He carries the rifle broken over one arm. There's a hangover pallor, and the white stubble looks like a skim of frost against his brown face. He glowers at me.

'I told you to be ready early.'

'I didn't know you meant at the crack of dawn. What about breakfast?'

'What about it?'

He's already walking across the courtyard. Lulu fusses around me like a long-lost friend as I go after Arnaud. I expect him to follow the track towards the road, but instead he goes down the side of the stable block. I thought I knew the farm well by now, but there's a path here that I never knew existed. It makes me wonder what else there is here I don't know about.

I trudge along it behind him. There's a clamour of birdsong, bell clear in the chilled air and low-lying mist. Wishing I'd put on a T-shirt under the overalls, I rub my arms and feel the outline of the plaster. The morning feels momentarily colder as I remember Gretchen's amnesia of the night before. In some ways it's even more disturbing than her attacking me in the first place. It could have been an act; God knows she's certainly capable of histrionics. But this isn't the only time it's happened: I remember after she set fire to the photograph she never so much as mentioned it again. At the time I thought she'd just developed a convenient memory, choosing to ignore an awkward incident.

Now I wonder if it wasn't something more than that.

The path has taken us into the deep woods above the house, the buffer between the farm and the rest of the world. Trying to put Gretchen from my mind, I concentrate on not tripping over tree roots. Ahead of me, the back of Arnaud's neck is stiff and uncompromising, seamed with horizontal creases. Looking at the gun, I belatedly wonder if coming into these lonely woods with him is such a good idea. I don't know what Gretchen might have told him but Arnaud is hardly the type to give anyone the benefit of the doubt. The sound of a shot would pass unnoticed out here, and a body could lie undisturbed amongst the tree roots indefinitely.

I shake off the morbid thoughts. Arnaud is nothing if not direct: if he meant me any harm I'd know about it by now. Besides, the way my head is aching he'd only be putting me out of my misery.

There's a stillness to the woods, a sharp silence through which every sound seems heightened. Something rustles a few yards to one side. Lulu bristles and bounds after it, until Arnaud checks her with a sharp word. The dog reluctantly slinks back to him, casting regretful looks behind her.

At a bend in the path Arnaud leaves it and heads off into the trees. The grass is beaded with dew, darkening the bottoms of my overalls where they swish against it. Lulu begins to run ahead, but Arnaud again calls her, taking hold of her collar to thrust her behind him.

'Aren't you worried she'll get caught in a trap?' I ask.

'I don't let her near them.'

'What happens if she wanders into the woods by herself?'

'Then it'd be her own fault.' He scans the ground ahead of him. 'Here.'

There's an open trap concealed in the grass. Arnaud picks up a dead branch and jabs at the square plate at its centre, springing the jaws in a snap of breaking wood. He slips the knapsack from his shoulder and takes out what looks like an old army entrenching tool, folded in half. My first impulse is to back away, but he only opens it and hands it to me.

'Dig up the spike.'

215

I take the spade and lean my walking stick against a tree. I sometimes wonder how much I really need it any more, but I don't feel confident enough to do without. The trap is tethered to the buried spike by a length of chain. One end of the entrenching tool is a pointed spade, the other a pick. I hack with the pick until the ground is broken up, then prise out the spike in a shower of dark earth.

Arnaud is waiting with a sack. I drop the trap into it and hold out the entrenching tool.

'You can carry it,' he says, setting off back to the path.

We dig up another two traps before we come to an area of woodland that's familiar. I look at the scene below me. The view of farm, trees and lake is ingrained in my mind like a bad dream. Arnaud is waiting by a tree. Its exposed roots are gashed where a knife stabbed into them. Nearby an empty water bottle lies on its side. The trap is still sprung shut at the tree's base, the edges of its clamped jaws clotted with black.

'Well?' Arnaud demands. 'What are you waiting for?'

I put the entrenching tool down. 'You can do this one.'

There's a malicious spark in his eye. 'Brings back bad memories, does it? Don't worry, it can't hurt you now.'

I don't answer. His smile fades. Dumping the bag and rifle, he snatches the tool from me and begins chopping at the ground around the spike, gouging indiscriminately at earth and tree roots. He's a powerful man, but the spike is well buried, as I know from experience. It takes longer than the others to work loose and Arnaud is sweating before it's done. He opens his shirt, revealing his white and hairless torso. When he bends to pick up the trap he abruptly stops and presses a hand to the small of his back.

'Put it in the sack,' he says as he straightens, grey-faced. 'Or is that against your principles too?'

He stalks off, leaving me to finish up. I lift the trap by the spike. There are bright scratches still from where I tried to prise it open. It spins slowly on the chain, an ugly pendant of blood-stained metal.

I drop it in the sack.

There are traps all over the woods. Each time we fill one of the sacks Arnaud has brought we leave it by the side of the path to collect later. The traps are all well hidden, concealed among tree roots and clusters of grass, even, on one occasion, in a shallow hole skilfully camouflaged with twigs and branches.

Arnaud goes unerringly to each one, locating them without hesitation. The half-full sack bumps against my leg as I follow him to another. A thick growth of grass has sprung up around it, so that only the chain is visible. He searches for a stick to clear it.

'What's the point?' I ask.

'The point of what?'

I drop the sack of traps to the ground. 'Of these things.'

'To keep people out, what do you think?'

'It didn't work the other night.'

Arnaud's cheek muscles bunch. 'They were lucky.'

'And you weren't?'

'What's that supposed to mean?'

'You think the police would only have given you a warning if somebody had stepped in one?'

'You think I'd care?'

'Then why are we taking them up?'

'Because I won't give them the satisfaction of finding them. In a week or two, when this has blown over, I'll set them again.' He gives me an odd sideways glance. 'And if I catch somebody in one, what makes you think they'll be able to tell the police about it?'

He clears the last of the grass from the trap and gives a short laugh.

'No need to spring this.'

The remains of a rabbit hang from the trap's closed jaws. It must have been there for months. The flies and maggots have already done their work, leaving only a desiccated bundle of fur and bones.

Arnaud prods it with his foot.

'Take it up.'

The morning chill and mist have burned off by the time Arnaud eventually calls a break. The sun drips through the branches, not yet hot but intimating at the heat to come. We stop where a flat-topped rock breaks through the earth to form a natural seat. Leaning the rifle against it, Arnaud takes it himself. I lower myself to the ground, glad of the respite.

'How many more traps are left?'

'Plenty more in the woods down by the lake. Why? Getting tired?'

'No, I'm loving every minute.'

He snorts but doesn't deign to reply. I try not to think about how long it'll be before breakfast as Arnaud rummages in his knapsack and brings out a greaseproof-paper-wrapped parcel. Both Lulu and I watch him unwrap it. Inside are two cold chicken breasts. To my surprise he offers one to me.

'Here.'

I take it before he changes his mind. He rummages in the knapsack again, this time coming out with a plastic bottle of water and a length of bread.

'The bread's yesterday's,' he says disparagingly as he breaks it in half.

I don't care. We eat in silence, sharing water from the same bottle, although I notice we both wipe the neck before we drink. I throw occasional scraps to Lulu, who's convinced herself that she's starving. Arnaud ignores her.

When he's finished he takes out his pipe and fills it. I'd join him, but in my rush to get out of the loft I came without my cigarettes.

'How's your back?' I ask.

It's meant as a peace offering after the food. Arnaud bites on his pipe and stares through the smoke.

'No better for digging.'

We're silent after that. Arnaud seems as intransigent as the rock he's sitting on. I catch him watching me at one point, but he looks away again without speaking. There's a tension about him that rekindles my earlier paranoia. He picks up the rifle, sights along its length.

'So, are you enjoying my daughter's generosity?'

Oh shit, I think, wondering what Gretchen's said. 'What do you mean?'

He gives me an irritated glance. He sets down the rifle and fiddles with his pipe. 'Mathilde. She's been pampering you like a newborn. Cooking your meals, changing your bandage.'

'Right. Yes, she's been . . . very generous.'

He takes the pipe from his mouth, flicks an invisible mote from the bowl and replaces it. 'What do you think of her?'

'I'm not with you.'

'It's a simple enough question. What do you think of Mathilde? She's an attractive woman, no?'

Arnaud's capable of taking offence no matter what I say, so I opt for the truth. 'Yes, she is.'

That seems to be what he wants to hear. He pulls on his pipe. 'It's been hard on her. Running the house. Taking care of Gretchen when their mother died. Now being left to look after a baby by herself. Not easy.'

I haven't noticed him trying to make things any easier for her.

'It hasn't been any better for me, either, God knows,' he goes on. 'Bringing up two daughters. A place like this, a man needs a son. Someone who can work with him, take over eventually.

I always hoped Marie would give me a boy, but no. Only girls. I thanked Christ when Michel was born, I can tell you. It's no joke being surrounded by women.'

Arnaud taps out his pipe on the rock, looking at it instead of me.

'Still, it's worse for Mathilde. A good-looking woman, still young. She needs a man. A husband, ideally, but you've got to be realistic.' He purses his lips, still considering the pipe. 'You understand what I'm saying?'

I tip my head, non-committally.

'Trouble is, the men around here aren't worth much. Small minds, that's all they've got. Half of them would screw a cow if they could find a stool to stand on, but when it comes to an unmarried woman with another man's child . . .'

His sigh is a shade too theatrical.

'You'd think they'd have more sense than to let their preju-dices blind them. I'm not going to live for ever, and Mathilde's my eldest. Michel won't be old enough to take over for years, and there's no saying I'll still be around to help him when he does. I'm the first to admit this place needs work, but . . . Well, it doesn't take much to see the potential. You understand me?' he asks, looking at me directly for the first time.

'I think so.' I understand, all right. It's not so much that he'd make such a proposal that shocks me, as that he'd make it to me.

He nods, satisfied. 'I wouldn't expect anyone to make up his mind straight away. But, for the right sort of man, it's worth giving some thought, wouldn't you say?'

'What would you call the right sort of man?' I ask, keeping my voice neutral. But perhaps not as neutral as I intend, because Arnaud gives me a shrewd glance.

'Somebody who can recognize an opportunity when he sees one,' he retorts. And then, less tartly, 'Someone I can trust.'

'Like you trusted Louis?'

Arnaud's face closes like a trap. He thrusts his pipe into his pocket and stands up.

'Come on. We've wasted enough time.'

I get wearily to my feet and bend to pick up the sack. The snick of the rifle bolt being slid back is unmistakable in the quiet. I turn to find Arnaud standing with the barrel pointing at me.

I don't move. Then with relief I see that his attention is on Lulu. She's staring into the trees, ears cocked.

'What's she—?'

'Shh!'

He motions me to one side. The dog is so tense she's quivering. Arnaud raises the rifle stock to his shoulder, readying himself.

'Go.'

The word is little more than a whisper, but Lulu begins moving into the woods, stalking in a slow-motion walk. A little way off she halts, one forepaw poised in the air. I still can't see anything. Suddenly she hurls herself forward. At the same time two birds burst from the grass ahead of her, wheeling into the air in a clatter of wings.

The crack of Arnaud's rifle makes me jump. One of the birds tumbles from the sky. There's another crack. The remaining bird veers away, climbing higher. A third shot sounds, but the bird has already lost itself beyond the higher branches.

There's a muttered curse from Arnaud. He lowers the rifle, clicking his tongue in exasperation. Lulu comes trotting back with her head held high, the bird lolling from her mouth. Arnaud takes it from her and tousles her ears.

'Good girl.'

For all his disappointment, the shooting has put him in a better humour. He tucks the bird – a partridge, I think – into his knapsack.

'Time was I'd have got them both. My reactions aren't what they were. Aim and shoot automatically, that's what it comes down to. You've got to let instinct take over. Make the first shot count.' He gives me a cold glance. 'Stop to think about it and you miss your chance.'

I choose to take him literally. 'Why don't you use a shotgun?'

'Shotguns are for people who can't shoot.' He rubs the stock of the rifle. 'This is a 6mm Lebel. Used to be my grandfather's. Older than me and still fires .22 cartridges true to fifty yards. Here. Feel the weight.'

Reluctantly, I take it from him. It's surprisingly heavy. The wooden stock is polished a warm satin from use, marred by a crack that runs for half its length. A sulphurous, used-firework smell comes from it.

'Want to try?' he asks.

'No thanks.'

Arnaud's grin is infuriatingly cocksure as I hand it back. 'Squeamish again, or just frightened of loud noises?'

'Both.' I hoist the sack. 'Shall we get on?'

It's late morning when we return to the house. We've filled half a dozen sacks with traps, and haven't even started on the woods by the lake.

'We'll do them some other time,' Arnaud says, rubbing his back. 'If the police come again they'll look near the road first.'

The sacks are cumbersome and heavy, so we take one each and leave the rest in the woods. Arnaud dumps his with a clank in the courtyard and gruffly instructs me to fetch the others myself. No surprise there, I think sourly, as he goes into the house. It take me several trips to collect them, lugging one sack at a time over my shoulder like a scrap-iron Santa. By the time the last of them has been safely stowed in the stable block, I'm aching all over and dripping with sweat. Sucking a skinned knuckle, I stand in the courtyard to catch my breath. There's a movement in the kitchen doorway and Mathilde comes out.

'Is that the last of them?' she asks, shielding her eyes from the sun.

'For now. There's still the woods around the lake, but we've finished up here.'

I can't tell if she's pleased or not. 'Would you like a coffee?'

'Thanks.'

I follow her inside. Except for Michel, who's sitting in a wooden playpen, we're alone in the kitchen. I sit at the table, remembering at the last minute not to sit in Arnaud's chair.

'It's all right, he's gone to lie down,' Mathilde says, seeing me avoid it. 'His back.'

I can't find it in myself to be sympathetic. 'Where's Gretchen?'

'Collecting eggs. She won't be long.' Mathilde spoons ground coffee into the aluminium percolator and sets it on the range. 'How's her English progressing?'

It's the first time she's asked. I try to be diplomatic. 'Let's say I don't think she's very interested.'

Mathilde makes no comment to that. She occupies herself at the sink until the percolator begins making choking noises, then takes it from the heat and pours the black liquid into a cup.

'Aren't you having any?' I ask as she brings it over.

'Not right now.'

She hesitates by the table, though, and then surprises me by sitting down as well. She looks tired and I find myself remembering her father's proposal. To take my mind off it I sip at the scalding coffee, searching for something to say.

'Are you sorry the traps have gone?'

It isn't the best conversational opening, but Mathilde takes it in her stride. 'No. I never wanted them.'

'Your father seems to think the farm needs protection.'

223

She looks at me, then away. The grey eyes are unfathomable. 'No one can cut themselves off completely.'

For some reason that feels like a reproach. We both watch Michel in his pen, as though hoping he'll break the silence. He carries on playing, oblivious.

'Do you—' I begin, then stop myself.

'Yes?'

'It doesn't matter.'

She looks at Michel, as though guessing what I'm going to ask. 'Go on.'

'I just wondered . . . do you ever hear from his father?'

I half-expect her to grow angry. She only shakes her head, still watching Michel. 'No.'

'Where is he?'

There's the slightest of shrugs. 'I don't know.'

'Doesn't he want to see his own son?'

I regret it the moment it's out. Of all people, I've no right to ask something like that. There's a beat before Mathilde answers.

'Michel wasn't planned. And Louis never liked responsibility.'

I've already asked more than I should. Yet there's a sense of intimacy between us I'm sure I'm not imagining. Something about the way she sits there makes me want to reach out: instead I wrap both hands around the coffee cup.

'Haven't you ever thought about going away? Just you and Michel?'

She looks startled by my bluntness. So am I, but the more I see of her father and sister – even Georges – the more I think that Mathilde is the only sane person on this farm. She deserves better.

'This is my home,' she says quietly.

'People leave home all the time.'

'My father—' She breaks off. When she carries on I have the feeling that it isn't what she was going to say. 'My father dotes on Michel. I couldn't take him away.'

'He'd still have Gretchen.'

Mathilde looks out of the window. 'It's not the same. He always wanted a son. Daughters were always . . . a disappointment. Even Gretchen. Now he has a grandson, he expects him to be brought up on the farm.'

'That doesn't mean you have to go along with it. You've got your own life.'

Her chest silently rises and falls. The only sign of any agitation is the quick pulse in her throat. 'I couldn't leave Gretchen. And she wouldn't come with me.'

No, she probably wouldn't, I think, remembering what her sister has said about her. Still, Mathilde's acceptance is infuriating. I want to ask if she thinks Gretchen would do the same for her, to tell her she's wasting her life at the beck and call of a man who's just tried to barter her away like damaged goods. But I've already said more than I should, and at that moment the kitchen door opens and Gretchen walks in.

'The hen with the bad eye's getting worse,' she says, hugging a bowl of eggs to her stomach. 'I think we should—'

She stops when she sees us. Mathilde stands up and quickly moves away from the table. I feel myself colouring, as though we've been caught out.

'What's he doing here?' Gretchen asks.

'Just taking a break,' I say, getting to my feet.

Mathilde begins washing the percolator. 'What's that about the hen?'

Gretchen doesn't answer, but her face says it all.

'I'd better get back to work,' I say, going past her to the door. 'Thanks for the coffee.'

Mathilde gives a quick nod of acknowledgement but doesn't look round. Gretchen ignores me completely, her eyes locked on her sister's back. I go outside, but I've not gone far before raised voices come through the open kitchen window. They're indistinct at first, but then one of them – Gretchen's – gains in pitch and volume until the words themselves become audible.

'. . . *do what you say? Why do you always try to spoil everything!*'

I can't make out Mathilde's reply, only its placating tone. Gretchen's voice grows more strident.

'*Yes, you do! What gives you the right to tell me what to do? I'm sick of you acting like*—'

There's a sharp crack of flesh on flesh. A moment later the door is flung open and Gretchen bursts out. I quickly move into the stable block as Mathilde appears in the doorway.

'Gretchen!'

She sounds anguished. Gretchen spins around to face her, revealing a reddened imprint on her cheek.

'I *hate* you!'

She runs across the courtyard. Mathilde starts after her, but halts at the sound of Michel's crying. The unhappiness is written plain on her face before she notices me. Turning away, she goes back inside to her son.

I step out of the stable block's shelter, making sure first that Gretchen has gone. Whatever problem she has with Mathilde, I'd rather not be caught in the middle of it. The farm's usual quiet has returned. I head back for the barn, unsure what to do. There's no point in mixing up a batch of mortar; it must be nearly lunch time and after my early start I don't feel like clambering up the scaffold straight away. The coffee has left me thirstier than ever, so I go to the tap for a drink. As usual, the barn is cool and smells of old wood and sour wine. I turn the tap on, cupping my hands under the cold spatter. Over the top of its splashing I hear another noise. Turning off the tap, I go out of the barn, wiping my wet hands on my overalls. There's a ruckus coming from the woods down by the lake. It's too far away to make much out, but from the squeals it sounds like another sow is meeting its maker.

Then I hear the scream.

It's Gretchen.

I set off down the track, stabbing my walking stick down in a gait that's half-run, half-skip. The commotion becomes louder as I near the sanglochon pens. Shouts, barking, squealing. When I reach the clearing I see Georges, the boar and Lulu engaged in a complex dance. The old man is trying to herd the boar back into its pen while Lulu makes mad dashes at it. Enraged, the boar is wheeling round to try to get at her, thumping against the piece of board Georges is using to push it and almost barging the old man off his feet.

Nearby, Gretchen presses her hands to her mouth, transfixed.

'Get the dog!' Georges is shouting at her, struggling to block the boar and kick the spaniel away at the same time. 'Get hold of it!'

Gretchen doesn't move. I can see the old man is tiring. His attempts to keep the two animals apart are growing laboured. He glances around as I enter the clearing, and Lulu takes that moment to dart behind his legs. He staggers, losing his grip on the board, and as the dog tries to jink away the boar surges forward. There's a shrill cry and an audible crunch as its jaws close on the spaniel's hind leg.

I plough straight into the boar without slowing, hoping to knock it away from the dog. It's like running into a tree trunk. My momentum carries me over its back, the breath huffing from me as I pitch onto the ground on the other side. I scramble away, frantically kicking at the thing's tusks as it turns on me, and then Georges thrusts the board between us.

'Get the other one!' he shouts.

It's propped against the fence. I grab it and rush back, snatching up my walking stick from where it landed. Pushing my board next to Georges's, I bring the stick down on the boar's head.

'Not so hard!' Georges snaps.

The boar doesn't feel it anyway. It butts and thrusts at our boards as the spaniel crawls and flops away, her leg trailing behind her. Then Arnaud is there as well, adding his weight to ours. The three of us push and slap at the pig, using the boards to block its vision until at last we manage to steer it back inside its pen. It throws itself against the fence but Arnaud has already slammed and fastened the gate.

His face is grim as he turns to Georges, breathing heavily. 'How did he get out?'

'The gate was open,' Georges states flatly. He's the least winded of the three of us.

'Christ almighty, didn't you check it?'

The old man gives Arnaud a reproving look. 'Yes.'

'It couldn't have opened itself!'

'No,' Georges agrees.

Arnaud's face sets. 'Where's Gretchen?'

She's nowhere in sight. Mathilde is there, though, crouching by the spaniel. It's panting in shock, one hind paw hanging by threads of bloody tissue. Arnaud looks down at it, tight-mouthed.

'I'll fetch my rifle.'

Mathilde begins trying to lift the dog.

'What are you doing?' he asks.

'I'm taking her to the veterinarian.'

'No, you're not. A bullet's the best thing for her.'

Mathilde doesn't answer. She struggles to her feet, hugging Lulu to her chest. The dog screams as its leg flops against her.

'Didn't you hear what I said?' Arnaud demands.

'I heard.'

She takes a step forward. He's blocking her way.

'You're not going anywhere! Put her down and—'

'No!'

The refusal stops him dead. It's the first time I've seen her stand up to him. Arnaud glares at her, but Mathilde stares back, white-faced to his mottled anger.

'I'm not going to let you kill her.'

She doesn't raise her voice this time, but there's no doubting the purpose in it. For a moment I think Arnaud is going to hit her. Then he moves aside.

'Please yourself. Just don't expect me to pay for the vet.'

Mathilde goes past him, straining under the dog's dead weight.

'Let me,' I say.

'I can manage.'

But she doesn't resist. Lulu whimpers as she's passed over. I feel Arnaud watching me. I have a sudden intuition that he might think that I'm helping Mathilde because of what he said earlier, that I'm fulfilling my part of a tacit bargain. The thought angers me as I turn and find Gretchen standing behind us.

Her face is smeared with tears. She looks anywhere but at Lulu, although her eyes seem to be constantly drawn towards the dog's leg.

Arnaud pushes past me and seizes her arm.

'Did you open the gate?' Her head is down on her chest. He grabs her shoulders and shakes her. 'Answer me! Did you open the gate?'

'No!'

'Then how did the boar get out!'

'I don't know! Leave me alone.'

She tries to pull free but he twists her around to face the dog. 'Look! Look what you've done!'

'I didn't do anything! Get *off*!'

She wrenches free and runs into the wood. Arnaud stares after her, then turns on us.

'Go, if you're going!' he snaps, and stamps off towards the pens.

I do my best not to jolt the dog as I carry her back to the

courtyard, letting Mathilde bring my walking stick. My foot holds up well, considering. When we get to the van she spreads out an old blanket on the passenger seat. The spaniel is shivering but still licks my hand as I set her down. Her hind leg looks as though it's been minced. Splinters of white bone pierce the bloodied flesh, and for once I think Arnaud might be right. We're only prolonging her suffering. But she isn't my dog, and it isn't my place to say.

Mathilde shuts the door and goes around to the driver's side.

'Do you want me to take her?' I ask, knowing how she feels about going into town.

'It's all right.'

'Shall I come with you?'

'No, thank you. We'll be fine.'

She's like a stranger. I watch her drive up the track, easing over the bumps. The van reaches a bend and is lost in the trees, leaving behind a slowly settling trail of dust. When the sound of its engine fades it's just as though nothing has happened.

London

JULES COMES BACK TO the bar the following week. It's early and the bar is quiet. Kai, Sergei's boyfriend, has brought me a coffee and is chatting to Dee about the best way to cook a rice timbale. I'm half-listening, keeping an eye on the entrance. I'm about to take a drink of coffee when the door opens and Lenny walks in.

I put the coffee cup down. He's alone, but if he's here then there's a good chance Jules will be on his way as well. He looks over at me, indifferent but letting me see he knows who I am. He goes to where Dee is serving.

'Bottle of Stella,' he says to her, paying me no further attention. As he reaches out to take his change I see the gold watch on his wrist. It's a Rolex or a copy, chunky and jewelled. He notices me looking at it.

'What?'

'Just admiring your watch.'

I'm thinking about how he'd asked the time when Chloe and I encountered him in the dark street. I don't expect him to remember, or make the association if he does. But I've underestimated him. I feel a chill as the stubbled face stares at me.

'I don't give a fuck about you,' he says. 'If you've any sense you'll keep it that way.'

With a last look to make sure I've got the message, he takes his drink over to a table.

'What was that all about?' Dee asks, coming over.

'Private joke.'

There's nothing funny about this, though. You don't go out of your way to cross people like Lenny. I don't even know why I did it.

After that I'm waiting, knowing it's only a matter of time. The coffee I've drunk sours in my stomach. I think I'm ready, but my pulse still leaps when Jules comes through the door. When I see the girl with him my first emotion is relief, because it isn't Chloe. Then they walk into the light and I feel a physical shock. It *is* her; it just isn't the Chloe I knew. Her hair is styled and more obviously blonde, and she's wearing a short red dress that shows off her legs in the high heels. When I knew her she hardly wore any make-up at all; now she's almost unrecogniz-able behind the eyeliner and lipstick.

She walks slightly behind Jules as he goes over to greet Lenny. She hasn't seen me, and I'm certain from her distant expression that Jules hasn't told her I work here. I don't realize I'm staring until Sergei comes out of the kitchen with two unopened bottles of Absolut.

'Here, Sean, put these in the freezer,' he says, thrusting them at me. He glances at my face. 'And for God's sake, smile! You look like you're going to kill somebody.'

I take the vodka from him and go to the freezer beneath the bar. But I don't open it, because now Jules and Chloe are coming over.

Jules is looking straight at me, but Chloe hasn't noticed who he's steering her towards. As they get near he puts his arm around her shoulders. She looks up at him in surprise, and the grateful flicker that crosses her face breaks my heart.

Then she sees me and stops dead. Still smiling, Jules tightens his arm around her and forces her forward.

'Surprise. Look who's here,' he says.

I put the bottles down. Chloe is staring down at the counter. Her throat works, but no sound comes out. She's lost weight; she was always slim but now she's rake thin. One look is enough to tell me she's using again.

'Aren't you going to say hello?' Jules says, tightening his arm around her shoulders. 'Come on, there's a good girl.'

Obediently, she raises her head.

'Hello, Sean.' Her voice is so low it's almost a whisper. There's an unfocused look to her eyes that makes me think she's on more than just coke these days.

'Hi.'

My face feels turned to stone. Jules is watching, missing nothing. 'Quite the reunion, isn't it? Tell you what, I've got some business to sort out, so why don't you two catch up? I expect you've got lots to talk about.'

'Jules, no, I—'

'Oh, and we'll have two vodkas on the rocks. Bring mine over, will you?'

He gives me a wink, stroking Chloe's shoulder in a demonstration of possession before swaggering over to join Lenny. The silence is awful as Chloe and I face each other across the bar.

'So . . . how are things?' I make myself ask.

'Great. Really good.' She's nodding as if trying to convince herself. 'You?'

'Top of the world.' It's hard to look at her. I wish the bar were busy so at least I'd have other people to serve, but it's still perversely quiet. 'How's the painting going?'

It's a cruel question. There's a quick flare of satisfaction when I see the hurt on her face, and then I hate myself for it.

'Oh, I'm not really . . . I'm sort of helping Jules with his business now. He's a bit short-staffed, so . . . Anyway, he says he might want some of my work for his gym when things . . . you know . . .'

I'm not sure I do, but I nod. 'That's good.'

She's still smiling as her eyes start to brim. 'It's all right, I'm fine. Really,' she says. 'I just wish . . .'

I feel something give in me as she starts to cry. Pride wars with the instinct to reach out to her. Not for long, but long enough.

'Chloe! Get over here.'

The shout comes from Jules. She dashes the tears away with the heel of her hand, and the moment when I might have said or done something is gone.

'I'm sorry,' she says, averting her face as she hurries away.

I ask Dee to take their drinks over and go into the kitchen. When I come out again the place is starting to fill up. For a while I'm blessedly busy. The next time I look across, Chloe and the others are gone and another group of people are sitting at their table.

16

REPLACING THE STONES IS a slow business. The section of house I've started working on is in even worse condition than the rest, having faced directly into the teeth of the weather blowing up from the lake. I've had to remove a lot of stones completely, cleaning them of the old mortar before putting them back. They're big and heavy, squeezing out the wet mortar like coffee-coloured icing when I push them back into the gaps. Sometimes their weight makes them settle too far, so that they don't line up with the stones on either side. Whenever that happens I take them out and start again. I doubt anyone on the ground would notice, or care very much if they did.

I would, though.

I trowel mortar onto the top and sides of another stone and lift it up. The hole is at shoulder height, so I have to bench-press the stone into place. Bracing it on my chest, I ease it in, praying it will sit level this time, thankful when it does. I scrape off the surplus mortar and flex my sore shoulder muscles. I've made good progress this morning, which would normally be enough to make me feel pleased. Not today.

My bucket is empty. I take it back down the ladder and go into the dank storeroom. A pile of empty plastic sacks confronts me: I'm down to my last bag of sand.

I'm going to have to go into town again.

I swear and throw the bucket down. I've known this was coming for days. It's taken a lot of mortar to replace the stones, and while there's plenty of cement I've almost used up all the sand that was in the storeroom. If I'd known there wasn't enough I could have fetched more when I went for the cement, but I'd assumed my predecessor knew what he was doing. My mistake.

In addition to his other failings, Louis wasn't much of a builder either.

I find Mathilde in the vegetable garden at the back of the house. She's kneeling at the tiny bed of flowers, uprooting the weeds that have sprung up since last time. She looks up as I approach, and again I feel I've somehow disturbed her in a private moment.

'I need more sand.'

She doesn't question it this time. Her expression is resigned, as if there's no longer anyone who can do or say anything to surprise her. She only nods and silently gets to her feet.

I go with her and wait in the kitchen while she fetches her wallet. Gretchen is sitting at the table with Michel. She doesn't acknowledge me. Since the boar escaped she's withdrawn into herself. It isn't so much that she ignores me as that she no longer seems to register I'm even there.

If I'm honest, it's a relief.

'Will that be enough?' Mathilde asks, handing me a few notes. They're all small denomination.

'I think so.'

'The keys are in the van.'

She returns to her garden as I go to the Renault. It's greenhouse hot inside, but I don't bother waiting for it to cool. After I've gone through the usual rigmarole of unlocking and locking the gate, I stand for a moment, looking out at the road. A car shoots past, coming from the direction of the town and heading off towards its own destination. As I watch it go something uncurls at the back of my mind, so indistinct I don't recognize it for what it is at first.

Restlessness.

The feeling has been growing ever since the gendarmes came. I don't worry any more about them coming back: if they were going to they would have by now. But the disruption that arrived with them has never really left.

Without enthusiasm, I climb back into the van. The drive into town seems to take no time at all. The roadside bar hardly seems to flash by before I'm at the square. The boules players are already out, although I can't tell if they're the same ones. The fountain is still spraying gaily in the sunshine. My hands are clammy on the steering wheel as I pull into the builders' yard. The engine dies with a shudder. Taking a deep breath, I climb out.

There's no sign of Jean-Claude.

I allow myself to relax, though only a little. I reach into the van for my walking stick, then pause. My foot is all but healed. The stitches are almost ready to come out and I've started leaving off the bandage when I'm not working. I still use the rubber boot that Mathilde made, but that's only because my own chafes the wounds. The stick is starting to feel more like a habit than a necessity, and I know the time is coming when I'll have to stop relying on it.

But not yet. Picking it up, I lean on it and limp into the hangar-like building.

I order and pay for the sand and am directed back out into the yard. There are wide wooden bays filled with pebbles, grit and sand. No one's about, but there's a shovel sticking out of the sand and a pile of empty plastic sacks, so I begin filling them myself.

I work with my back to the yard, mechanically driving the shovel into the mound of sand, ignoring the impulse to keep looking behind me. When the sacks are full I bring the van over.

The blanket that Lulu was on is balled up in the back, the blood-stains on it dried black. I push it aside and start loading the sacks, stacking them upright so the sand doesn't spill. Now I've almost finished some of the nervous energy begins to bleed off. I pause to wipe the sweat from my forehead.

'Need any help?'

Jean-Claude is standing by the van, wearing the same bib-and-braces overalls as before. He moves quietly for such a big man.

'Thanks, I can manage.'

I turn away and continue with the loading. He takes hold of a sack anyway, effortlessly slinging it into the van and then hefting the next. The last few sacks are stacked away in a few seconds.

I give him a grudging nod of thanks and close the doors. Of course, he isn't about to let me go that easily.

'Someone told me Mathilde was in town a few days ago. Taking an injured dog to the vet's. What happened to it?'

'It got too close to a boar.'

'Ah. I thought it might have trodden on a nail. How is it?'

I choose to think he means Lulu. 'Not good.'

'Kinder to put it out of its misery. Mathilde always had a soft heart, but it doesn't always do anyone any favours. Will it live?'

'If it does it'll be with three legs. Thanks for the help.'

I climb into the van. Jean-Claude takes hold of the door, pre-venting me from closing it.

'I want to talk to you.'

Whatever he's got to say, I doubt I want to hear it. 'I've got to get back.'

'It won't take long. Anyway, it's lunch time. There's a café near here where the food is OK. On me.'

'No, thanks.'

'You have to eat, don't you? All I want is a few minutes of your time. But if that's too much to ask . . .'

He takes his hand away and gestures towards the gates. Much

as I'd like to shut the door and drive away, I owe him for intervening with Didier and his friends.

'Get in,' I say.

We sit at the back of the café, away from the other customers. I look at the small plastic menu without really seeing it.

'The omelettes are good,' Jean-Claude suggests.

They might be, but I've had enough eggs lately. I order the plat du jour and a beer; I need something to steady my nerves.

'So,' I say.

He sets down the plastic menu. 'I hear Arnaud had a visit from the police.'

'That's right.'

Jean-Claude waits a moment, then continues when I don't say anything else. 'I respect a man's right to protect his property as much as anyone, but Arnaud goes too far.'

I can't argue with that, but Arnaud wasn't the only one at fault. 'How's Didier? No unexplained gunshot wounds, I hope?'

'Didier's an idiot. He gets worse when he's had a few beers. Hopefully he'll outgrow it.'

'I wouldn't put money on that.'

That earns a wry smile. 'Don't worry, he won't cause any more trouble. I've had a word.'

The look on his face suggests it wasn't gentle. I take a drink of beer, to give myself something to do. Jean-Claude still hasn't touched his wine. He seems ill at ease as well, and despite myself I'm starting to feel curious.

'What do you know about my brother?' he asks.

Here it comes, I think. 'Not much. They don't really talk about him.'

'But you know he's Michel's father? And that he got involved in a few . . . well, let's say business schemes with Arnaud?'

'I've heard something about it.'

'Then did you know that Louis is missing?'

Bizarrely, my first thought is one of regret: I knew coming here was a mistake.

'No,' I say.

Reaching into his pocket for a leather wallet, he takes out a well-creased photograph and sets it in front of me on the table. In it he's standing beside a green pick-up truck with a younger man, taller and not so heavily built. Jean-Claude's hair is plastered to his head and his face and chest look wet. He's wearing a strained smile as the other man laughingly holds up an empty beer glass to show the camera.

'That's Louis. His sense of humour's rowdier than mine.' Jean-Claude's tone is somewhere between exasperated and fond. 'He disappeared eighteen months ago. Supposedly went off on some business trip to Lyon and never came back. No one's seen or heard from him since. Not me, none of his friends. Nobody.'

There's something about the other man with him in the picture that strikes a chord, but I can't place it. Then I do. He has on the red overalls that I'm wearing. I instinctively glance down at myself. Jean-Claude nods.

'They're an old pair he kept at Arnaud's. He said he didn't want to take the pig smell home with him.'

At another time I might take that as an insult. I slide the photograph back across the table. 'Why are you telling me all this?'

'Because I want to find out what's happened to him. And I think Arnaud knows more than he claims.'

He breaks off as the food arrives. Glad of the chance to collect my thoughts, I pick at the plate of steak and frites in front of me. Under other circumstances I'd welcome the change from pork, but I've lost my appetite.

'What makes you think Arnaud knows something?' I ask, far from certain I want to hear the answer.

Jean-Claude mops up the oil from his omelette with a piece of bread. Talking about his brother doesn't seem to have affected his appetite.

'The business trip was connected with one of the schemes he'd dreamed up with Arnaud. I don't know what, because Louis liked to play his cards close to his chest, but I'm certain he was involved. And Arnaud's story doesn't add up. Has he told you that Louis asked Mathilde to marry him because he got her pregnant?'

I nod, reluctant even now to give too much away.

'No disrespect to Mathilde, because she's a good woman. But I know my brother, and believe me he isn't the marrying kind. Most of the rest of it I could accept, but the idea of him suddenly doing the decent thing and proposing to Mathilde? No way. Louis puts Louis first, always has. If he was going to leave town because he got some girl into trouble, he'd have done it years ago.'

'Maybe he wanted the farm,' I say, repeating what Arnaud told me. Belatedly I remember that I wasn't going to say anything.

Jean-Claude snorts. 'Right, because it's such a goldmine. Look, all Louis wanted was to screw around and make money, the easier the better. He wasn't interested in owning a *farm*, and certainly not a struggling one that's mortgaged to death. If Arnaud wasn't so up his own arse he'd realize no one in his right mind would want anything to do with the place.'

'Then why would he lie?'

'That's the question, isn't it?' He looks across at me, chewing a piece of omelette. 'Maybe it suits him for people to think Louis shafted them and ran out on Mathilde. I don't know and Arnaud won't talk about it.'

'Have you asked him?'

'Of course I have. At least, I've tried. He ranted on about

Louis and warned me not to bother them again.' His expression darkens. 'Michel's my flesh and blood as well, but Arnaud won't even let me see my own nephew. He keeps them all buried away in that place, and what sort of life is that for a child? Or his daughters, come to that. He's always tried to keep them on a tight rein, especially Gretchen. Not that I blame him with that one. She's had half the town's boys sniffing after her at some time or another. I sometimes think . . .'

'What?' I ask, when he doesn't continue.

But he only shakes his head. 'It doesn't matter. The point is that ever since Louis went missing Arnaud's cut the farm off from town completely, and why do that if he doesn't have something to hide?'

'Maybe because of people like Didier.'

I don't mean to defend Arnaud, but the situation doesn't seem as one-sided to me as Jean-Claude makes out. He finishes his omelette and wipes his mouth with a paper napkin.

'Maybe. I'm not making excuses for Didier. But Arnaud acts like he's under siege. He's always had a chip on his shoulder, but barbed wire and man-traps?' Jean-Claude gestures at my foot with his knife. 'And please, don't insult us both by pretending that was an accident. I never actually believed the rumours about the traps before, but Christ! Why would you stay there after something like that?'

He seems genuinely puzzled, but that's a door I'm not about to open. 'I still don't see what you want from me.'

'Like I said, Arnaud knows more than he's saying or he wouldn't have bothered making up that bullshit story. You're living on the farm, you could look around, ask questions. Maybe see if the old guy, Georges, has seen or heard something he hasn't told anyone about. Find out what Arnaud's hiding.'

Spy on them, in other words. It puts me in an awkward position, but I'm more distracted by something else Jean-

Claude's said: *he keeps them all buried away.* He was talking about Arnaud's family, but it's another image entirely that comes to my mind.

The crumbling patch of concrete in the barn.

I push my plate away, the food almost untouched. 'If you're so convinced he's lying why don't you go to the police?'

'You think I haven't? I tried the local gendarmerie and the National Police in Lyon, for all the good it did. Without proof, they don't want to know. They said Louis is a grown man, he can do what he likes.'

It takes me a moment to realize what that implies. Rural areas of France like this come under the jurisdiction of the gendarmerie: the National Police only operate in cities. There's only one reason I can think of why Jean-Claude would have approached both, and I seize on it.

'Where did you say he was last seen?'

Jean-Claude hesitates. He lowers his eyes to his glass, turning it in both hands. 'There was a sighting of him at a garage on the outskirts of Lyon, two days after he left here. He was caught on the security camera when he stopped for fuel. But that doesn't prove anything.'

He's wrong. It proves his brother only went missing after he left town. From the way Jean-Claude's been talking I assumed Louis never actually made it to Lyon, that his disappearance must be directly linked to Arnaud and the farm. If the last sighting of him was in a city halfway across the country, that's something else entirely.

It feels like a weight's gone from my shoulders.

'Have you thought that the police could be right? Maybe he had a good reason for running away.' The irony of that only occurs to me as I'm saying it. It prompts a twinge of shame I deliberately ignore.

Jean-Claude stares at me, big arms resting on the table. I

have the uncomfortable feeling that he's weighing me up, reconsidering what to make of me.

'My wife and I, we haven't been blessed with children,' he says. 'Apart from her, Louis is my closest family. And I'm his. Whenever he fucks up, sooner or later he comes to me to sort it out. Because I'm his brother, that's what I do. Except this time.'

'Look—'

'Louis is dead. I don't need the police to tell me that. If he were still alive I'd have heard from him by now. And Arnaud's got something to do with it. I don't care where Louis was last seen, the old bastard's hiding *something*. So what I want to know is if you'll help me find out what happened to my brother?'

Despite his gruffness, the loss and frustration are plain. God knows I can sympathize with the need to find someone to blame, but it doesn't change anything. 'I still don't see what I can do. I don't even know how much longer I'll be staying there. I'm sorry.'

It sounds like I'm making excuses, even to me. Jean-Claude stands up, taking out his wallet and dropping a note onto the table to cover lunch.

'There's no need to—'

'I said it was on me. Thanks for your time.'

His broad shoulders briefly block the doorway as he turns his back and walks out.

The cabin of the van is like an oven, stifling with the smell of hot plastic and oil. It drives sluggishly, the bags of sand in the back weighing it down like an anchor. I keep my foot on the accelerator, trying to force the speed from it. It's only when the van begins to rattle that I ease off, and then only slightly. The engine vibrates, complaining as I drive along the almost empty road.

I don't know why I'm so angry, or who at. Myself probably:

I should never have agreed to listen to Jean-Claude. Still, at least now I know the reason for the hostility towards Arnaud. The town's been given a juicy scandal to chew on, and someone as antisocial and belligerent as him would make a convenient target.

But I can't see how he can be held responsible for Louis going missing. From what I've heard, Michel's father seemed more than capable of antagonizing any number of people himself. Either he crossed the wrong person or decided to cut his losses and start afresh.

Good luck with that, I think bleakly.

My mood doesn't improve as I near the farm. The last time I ventured out I couldn't wait to get back: now I find myself slowing down as the gate comes into view. I pull up onto the verge alongside, sitting with the engine running instead of getting out. The road carries on past it into the distance, heading in the direction I first came. For the first time since I arrived, I find myself seriously contemplating the prospect of going back.

But back to what?

I climb out to unlock the gate, repeating the process again once I've driven through. I guide the van down the rutted track and park in the courtyard. Opening the back, I start transferring the bags of sand one at a time into the storeroom. There are a lot of them: I bought as many as I could fit in, not wanting to run out again.

It feels now that I've bought too many.

A sense of impatience begins to build up in me as I unload the van. At first I don't know its cause, but then some sand spills out onto the floor and I make the connection. There's no reason for the conversation with Jean-Claude to bother me, not now I know Louis got as far as Lyon.

But I can't stop thinking about the patch of concrete in the barn. And whatever it was I saw caught in it.

Mathilde comes from the house as I've almost finished empty-ing the van. She's carrying Michel astride her hip.

'Was there a problem?'

'No.' I slide the last bag of sand towards me across the van floor.

'You were a long time.'

'I stopped off for lunch.'

She watches me lift the sand, as though waiting for me to continue. 'My father says you can eat dinner in the house with us again tonight,' she says when I don't.

'OK.'

I walk past her, the heavy sack hugged to my body. Going into the cool storeroom, I drop it to the floor with the others, already regretting being abrupt. I'm not looking forward to spending another evening with Arnaud, but there's no use taking my bad mood out on Mathilde. If there's one victim in all of this, it's her.

I go back out, intending to apologize, but the courtyard's empty.

I close the van's doors and look up at the scaffold. But I already know I'm not going up it just yet. There's something I have to do first.

I set off across the courtyard to the barn.

The cavernous interior is cool and dark. I go inside and look down at the cracked scab of concrete. I've walked over it every day for weeks without really noticing it. It's rectangular, about five or six feet long and half that wide. Big enough to hold a body. I think again about what Jean-Claude said.

He keeps them all buried away.

An awful feeling is starting to form. I tell myself I'm being stupid, but I have to know. I glance around to make sure I'm alone, then crouch down. I can just make out the small scrap that's protruding from the crack. It could be anything. A sweet wrapper, a dirty rag. Anything at all.

So why don't you find out?

I squeeze my thumb and forefinger into the gap. The object is stiff but pliable, and held fast. Pinching hold, I work it backwards and forwards, skinning my fingers and causing more concrete to crumble away. Whatever's caught in there resists for a few more seconds, and then breaks free with a scatter of grit.

I climb to my feet and take my prize into the sunlight. It's a torn strip of cloth, the same dusty colour as the concrete. I examine it, turning it in the light, and then give a laugh as I realize what I'm holding. It isn't cloth, it's paper. Thick paper.

A piece of cement bag.

Chalk one up for an over-active imagination, I think, brushing sand off my scraped fingers.

I work later than usual that afternoon, making up for lost time and trying to exorcise some of the tension that still lingers. The sun is only just above the trees when I finally call it a day. My shoulders ache and my arms and legs are heavy as I lower myself down the ladder. I trudge back to the barn to wash under the freezing tap. Stripping off the overalls, I remember something else Jean-Claude said and pause to sniff them. Dirt and sweat, but if there's a smell of pig I can't detect it.

Maybe I don't notice any more.

I change into my own clothes and then head up to the house for dinner. The door is open so I go straight into the kitchen. The table has already been set for four. I take the same seat as last time. My seat. Arnaud sits at his usual place at the head. He opens a bottle of wine and silently pushes it towards me. Gretchen gives me a smile as she helps Mathilde serve the food, as if she's emerging from whatever distant place she's been. They join us and we begin to eat.

Just like a normal family.

London

I ONLY GO ON the date as a favour to Callum.

'Come on, why not? I've been trying to get Ilse out for a drink for ages, but she wants to bring her friend. You'll like her, Nikki's a great girl.'

'So you've met her?' We're standing at the bar in Callum's local, a packed pub with large-screen TV showing different sports. It's his idea of a quiet drink.

'Well, no, but Ilse says she is,' he admits. 'And she's Australian. Come on, Sean, it's like falling off a horse. If you don't get your feet back in the stirrups soon you're going to forget how to ride. Then when you finally do get in the saddle again you'll fall off, and we don't want that, do we?'

'What the hell are you talking about?' I say, but I'm laughing.

'I'm talking about going out and having a good time. What have you got to lose? God forbid, you might even enjoy yourself.'

'I don't know . . .'

He grins. 'That's settled then. I'll fix it up.'

We meet in a bar near Leicester Square. The plan is to have a drink before taking in an early screening of the latest Tarantino. It's Callum's suggestion, but I'm not a fan of Tarantino's newer work and I'm not sure blood and violence is the right sort of film for a first date. As we wait in the bar I'm nervous, already regretting agreeing to this. When the two girls arrive I'm even more convinced I've made a mistake. Nikki is a copywriter for an advertising agency, and it's soon obvious that she's as reluctant to be there as I am. Strangely, that makes things easier, and once we've established that neither of us expects anything from the other we're both able to relax.

One drink slides into two, and then three, so that we have to hurry to make the film. Callum's already bought the tickets, and as we cross the foyer I take my phone out to switch it off. I've no sooner got it in my hand than it rings.

The caller ID says it's Chloe.

I stare at the screen. I've not seen or heard anything from her since the night Jules brought her into the Zed. I've no idea why she might be calling now.

'We need to go in, Sean,' Callum says, giving me a look.

My thumb hovers above the *Answer* and *Ignore* keys. Before I can press either the ringing abruptly stops. *Chloe* glows up at me from the screen for a moment longer, then winks out.

I feel a stir of guilt as I turn the phone off and put it away. But the others are waiting for me, and Chloe made her choice. If it's anything important she'll leave a message or call back.

She doesn't.

17

M Y STITCHES COME OUT late one morning. The scabs from
the trap's metal teeth have hardened and healed since I've
left off the bandage, and the stitches perform no function any
more except to irritate me. They could probably have come out
sooner, yet Mathilde hasn't suggested it and I haven't pressed. For
some reason I'm reluctant to have the unsightly black whiskers
removed.

But this particular morning they're itching more than ever.
When I find myself furiously scratching at them, then tugging
at a loosening thread myself, I realize I can't ignore it any longer.

It's time.

I ask Mathilde when I collect my breakfast from the house.
Brushing back a strand of hair, she simply nods.

'I can do it later, if you like.'

I thank her and retreat back to the barn. Yet after breakfast
I still put it off. I mix a batch of mortar to take up the scaffold.
I've lost track of days, but I'm pretty certain this is a Sunday. Not
even Arnaud has suggested I should work seven days a week,
but I've fallen into the habit all the same. It keeps the time from
lying too heavily on my hands, something it seems to do more
and more lately.

I feel unsettled and out of sorts as I start trowelling the mortar
into the gaps. It isn't only the thought of having the stitches

taken out. I've been sleeping better than I have in years. Physical exertion, good food and sun have been an effective counter to insomnia, or at least they were. Since Gretchen's nocturnal visit I've taken to sliding the chest of drawers on top of the trapdoor again, but I can't blame her for my broken sleep.

The dreams about washing my hands in the copse have started again.

I ease another stone into place, scraping off and then smoothing the wet mortar until it's indistinguishable from its neighbours. The upper section of the house is almost done. A few more days and it'll be time to drop the scaffolding boards to a lower level and begin the cycle all over again. There's plenty of the big farmhouse left to hack out and repoint, enough work to keep me occupied for months.

If that's what I want.

Wiping a trickle of sweat from my forehead, I glance at my watch to check the time. But of course it's still in my ruck-sack, where it's been ever since I started working on the house. I haven't missed it, but now I'm nagged by an irrational feeling that I'm late for something.

I'm out of mortar, which makes this as good a time as any for a break. Carrying my empty bucket down the ladder, I leave it at the foot of the scaffold and go to the kitchen. The door is open, but when I knock it's Gretchen who answers.

'Is Mathilde around?' I ask.

Her smile vanishes. 'Why?'

'She said she'd take my stitches out this morning. But if she's not here it doesn't matter.'

I feel a sneaking sense of relief at the delay, but Gretchen is already moving to let me in. The thin cotton dress she's wearing shows off her tanned legs. 'She's upstairs with Michel.'

I hesitate, then step into the kitchen. The flagged floor, worn table and chairs are cosily familiar, yet the room doesn't seem

251

right without Mathilde. A chicken carcass lies next to the sink, plucked and naked.

'I'll come back later,' I say, turning to go.

'No, you can wait.'

It's more an instruction than a reassurance. I look through the doorway at the sunlit courtyard as Gretchen goes to the chicken and picks it up by its yellow feet. Its head flops as she splays it out on a chopping board. One of its eyes is milky and blind, I notice. I try not to flinch as she brings down a large cleaver, severing the outstretched neck.

'Why don't you sit down?'

'I'm OK, thanks.'

Scraping the decapitated head into the sink, she flips the chicken round and deftly cuts off both feet. 'It seems like I hardly see you any more.'

'I was here last night.' It's taken for granted now that I'll eat with them every evening. I'm free to enjoy the rest of my meals alone, but I've begun to miss my solitary dinners outside the barn. Watching Arnaud work his way through his sour wine, his volatility increasing as the bottles empty, soon becomes wearing.

Gretchen looks over her shoulder at me. 'That isn't what I mean. You're not avoiding me, are you?'

'No, of course not.'

'Good. I thought you might be cross about something.'

I don't have an answer to that. The thin scabs on my arm left by the fork tines are itching, and I only just stop myself from rubbing them. The kitchen's low ceiling and heavy furniture suddenly feel oppressive.

'We could have lunch together today,' Gretchen says, pulling something red from the chicken's gullet. 'You could teach me some more English.'

I look towards the doorway leading to the stairs, but there's no sign of Mathilde. 'I didn't think you were interested.'

'I will be, I promise.'

'Uh, well, I . . .'

I look round with relief as the door to the stairs opens and Mathilde comes into the kitchen with Michel. When she sees us she seems to pause slightly before continuing into the room.

'I didn't hear you come in,' she says, crossing to the high chair.

'He's been waiting to have his stitches taken out,' Gretchen tells her, shoving the chicken under the tap. Blood from its severed neck streaks the sink.

'I can come back,' I say.

'That's all right.' The baby struggles, howling as she tries to put him in the chair, his face red and wet. Mathilde turns to her sister. 'Gretchen, can you take Michel?'

'No, I'm busy.'

'Please. He won't settle in the chair while he's teething. I won't be long,' Mathilde says, trying to calm him.

'He's your son, I don't see why I've always got to take him everywhere with me,' Gretchen grumbles, but dries her hands as she goes for her nephew.

'I'll see to your stitches in the bathroom,' Mathilde says. She turns away, so misses the glare Gretchen shoots at her back.

I go around the table so as not to get too close to Gretchen while she's near a cleaver. Closing the door behind us, I follow Mathilde upstairs. I sit on the side of the bath while she takes what she needs from a cupboard: tweezers, a small dish, a towel. I peel off the sock, revealing my foot in all its pallid glory. The wounds are still crusted in places but there's also the raw pink of healing flesh from which the stitches sprout like bristles.

Mathilde crouches in front of me, using a cloth soaked in hot water to clean and soften the scabbed wounds. Then she spreads the towel on her lap and rests my foot on it. It feels awkwardly intimate.

'This shouldn't hurt too much.'

There's a tugging sensation, no more, as she teases at the end
of a stitch with a pair of tweezers. When it's out she drops it into
the dish and goes on to the next. Her hands are cool and gentle
as she eases out the recalcitrant strands. I watch her as she works,
wholly intent on what she's doing, and find myself remembering Arnaud's tacit offer. I shift my thoughts onto something else.

'How's Lulu?' I ask.

'There's no change. The veterinarian says the stump's infected.'

I try to think of something to say that won't sound like a
platitude but I can't. More than ever, I've started to agree with
Jean-Claude: Mathilde's sentimentality hasn't done any of them
any favours. Least of all the dog.

'Did you run into Jean-Claude the other day?' she asks, as
though reading my mind.

'Jean-Claude . . . ?'

'When you were in town.'

'Oh . . . Yes, he was at the builders' yard.' I feel like I've been
caught out. 'How did you know?'

'You were gone a long time. I thought it might be because
you'd seen him.'

I'm not sure if this is leading up to something, but she wouldn't
have brought it up if she didn't want to talk about it. 'He told me
Louis was missing,' I say.

It's impossible to read Mathilde's expression. When I asked
before about Michel's father she'd said only that she didn't know
where he was. But then she doesn't have to tell me anything.

She pushes back a strand of hair. 'Yes.'

'What happened?'

Her breath whispers against my foot. 'Louis said he had some
sort of business in Lyon. He persuaded my father to lend him
some money and then he left. That was eighteen months ago. I
haven't seen or heard from him since.'

Again, it seems she's waiting for me to say something. 'Couldn't he have just decided to steal the money and not come back?'

'I don't think so. If he were still alive he'd have been in touch with someone by now. Not me, perhaps, but Jean-Claude.'

It's only what his brother's already told me, but it seems to carry more weight coming from her. 'Jean-Claude thinks—'

'I know what Jean-Claude thinks.' Mathilde raises her head to look at me. The grey eyes are calm and sad. 'My father didn't kill Louis. If anyone's to blame, it's me. He was unhappy when he found out I was pregnant, and the last time I saw him we argued. If not for that, maybe things would have been different.'

'You can't blame yourself. Maybe if your father talked to Jean-Claude—'

'No.' She shakes her head. 'My father's a proud man. He won't change his mind.'

'Then couldn't you talk to Jean-Claude yourself?'

'It wouldn't do any good. He holds us responsible. Nothing I say can change that.'

Mathilde turns her attention back to the stitches, making it clear the conversation has ended. She drops another thread into the dish and repositions my foot. I can feel the warmth of her body through the towel.

'Just one more.'

There's a slight sting as the last stitch pulls free. She puts the tweezers in the saucer and dabs antiseptic on the holes where the stitches have been. Without them the foot has an unfinished look, like an unlaced shoe.

'How does that feel?' she asks.

'Not bad.'

My foot is still on her lap. Her hands rest on it, and all at once I'm very aware of the contact. The touch of her fingers on my bare skin is like an electric charge. From the flush that's risen to her throat, she's conscious of it too.

'*Mathilde, Michel won't stop crying!*'

Gretchen's shout comes from downstairs, petulant and demanding. Mathilde moves my foot and quickly rises from the chair.

'I'm coming,' she calls. The tiredness is back behind her eyes as she gathers up the tweezers and dish. 'It might be tender for a day or two where the stitches have been. You should still be careful.'

'I will. Thanks,' I say. But she's already gone.

As I stand I catch sight of my reflection in the mottled bathroom mirror over the washbasin. My face is thinner than I remember. It's sunburnt and peeling, with white lines radiating from the corners of my eyes where they've been screwed up against the light. The beard completes the transformation: it doesn't look like me any more.

I stare back at the stranger, then go back downstairs.

It feels weird to wear a boot on my injured foot again. The bloodstains on the leather have resisted several scrubbings and there are twin arcs of punctures on both sides. I'll need a new pair eventually, but for now it's enough to look down and see two feet that are more or less symmetrical.

The novelty is fading, though. I'm already beginning to forget what it was like to have my foot bound and strapped. I have the strange sensation that everything is reverting to how it was before I stepped in the trap, as though the thread of my life is trying to pick up from where it left off.

Even so, I'm reluctant to put too much weight on my foot, and when I take my afternoon walk down to the lake I still use my walking stick. I'm aware that it's become more of a psychological crutch than a physical one, but that's something I don't dwell on. Once my foot's fully recovered I'll have no more reason to stay, and I'm not ready for that.

Not yet.

I go up to my usual spot on the bluff and settle against the trunk of the chestnut tree. The lake is placid, the surface unruffled even by ducks at this time of day. But change is evident even here. The year's moved on without my noticing it. The leaves of the surrounding trees are a darker green than when I first arrived, and although it's still hot the sunlight seems subtly sharper. The season is approaching its turn, and so is the weather. I rub my wrist where my watch used to be, looking at a dark smudge of cloud on the horizon.

At one time I couldn't imagine winter touching here. Now I can.

The cloud bank has encroached further by the time I set off back up the track, obscuring the sun with a preliminary haze. There's even a threat of rain in the air as I walk through the woods, but the statues at least are unchanged. Pan still capers manically, and the veiled woman still stands bowed and remorseful. Under the darkening sky, the blood-like stain on her worn sandstone looks more livid than ever.

'Hello.'

I give a start. Gretchen is in the cleared patch of ground where Arnaud and I felled the silver birch. There's no Michel or Lulu with her this time. She's alone, making a daisy chain of the small white flowers that carpet the meadow grass. There's a pleased look about her that for some reason makes me feel like I've been ambushed.

'I didn't see you,' I say. 'What are you doing down here?'

'Looking for you.' She rises to her feet, tying off the strand of flowers into a circle. 'You promised me an English lesson this afternoon. Have you forgotten?'

I can remember her saying something in the kitchen but I'm pretty sure I didn't promise anything. 'Sorry, it'll have to be some other time. I need to get back to work.'

'You don't have to go straight away, do you?'

She walks towards me, still with the unsettling smile. For a moment I think she's going to put the daisy chain around my neck, and take an automatic step backwards. Instead she walks past, close enough for her thin dress to brush against me. Reaching up, she drapes it around the neck of a stone nymph.

'There,' she says. 'What do you think?'

'Very nice. Anyway, I should get back.'

But that's easier said than done. Gretchen is standing in my way, and when I try to move around her she sidesteps to block me. She grins.

'Where are you going?'

'I told you, I've got work to do.'

'Uh-uh.' She shakes her head. 'You owe me an English lesson.'

'Tomorrow, maybe.'

'Supposing I don't want to wait?'

Her grin is mischievous and vaguely threatening. Or maybe that's just my imagination. I have to resist the urge to move away from her again.

'Your father's going to wonder where I am,' I say. But this time invoking Arnaud doesn't work.

'Papa's asleep. He won't know if you're late.'

'Mathilde will.'

Mentioning her sister is a mistake. 'Why are you always so worried what Mathilde thinks?'

'I'm not,' I say hurriedly. 'Look, I need to get back.'

She glares at me sullenly for a moment, then pretend-pouts. 'All right, but on one condition. Bring me the necklace.'

She points at the flower chain hanging around the statue's neck. 'Why?'

'You'll see.'

With a sigh I go to the nymph and reach for the flowers.

There's a rustling from behind me, and I turn to see Gretchen's dress slither to the ground.

She's naked underneath.

'Well?' she says, smiling. The air in the woods suddenly seems closer than ever. She steps towards me. 'Mathilde doesn't look like this, does she?'

'Gretchen . . .' I begin, and then I hear the engine.

I look past her as Georges's old 2CV wheezes into view on the track. I'm too stunned to move, but it's too late anyway. I can see the old man sitting behind the steering wheel like a wrinkled schoolboy, and he can hardly miss us. But if he's surprised by the sight of Gretchen standing naked in the middle of the track he gives no sign. As the Citroën bumps nearer, his face displays no more expression than when he killed the sow. Then the car turns off where the track forks to the sanglochon pens and disappears into the trees.

The sound of its engine fades. Gretchen stares after it before turning to me, wide-eyed.

'Do you think he saw me?'

'Unless he's blind. Get dressed.'

Subdued, she does as she's told. I don't bother to wait. Leaving her in the woods, I head back to the farm, stabbing the walking stick into the rutted dirt of the track. The full impact of what's just happened is only now starting to sink in. Christ knows what Arnaud will do when he finds out. He certainly won't believe I didn't encourage Gretchen, or that nothing's happened between us. Yet as I walk through the grapevines it isn't his reaction I'm worried about.

It's Mathilde's.

I almost go straight to the house there and then. Better if she hears it from me than Georges or Arnaud. Or Gretchen, God forbid: I dread to think what sort of spin she'll put on this.

But by the time I've reached the barn I've talked myself out of it. If I tell Mathilde it'll look as if I'm trying to cause trouble. Besides, Georges is such an enigma I've no idea what he'll do. Maybe he's so uninterested in anything except his pigs he won't even say anything.

So instead I mix up a batch of mortar, angrily churning sand and cement together with a bucket of water. The beginning of a tension headache probes the back of my neck as I climb up the scaffold. I've no enthusiasm, and even the bucket seems heavier than usual. But I don't know what else to do, and I might as well finish more of the wall while I wait for the fallout.

Something else falls instead. As I mechanically smooth mortar into the gaps between the stones I feel a wet splash on my cheek. I look up and see that the sky has darkened to a muddy grey. With a sound of dropping pennies, raindrops begin to spatter down onto the scaffold.

The weather has finally broken.

London

I'M SPRAWLED ON THE sofa in my flat watching a DVD of *Les Diaboliques* one afternoon when my mobile rings. I've seen the film numerous times already but I was bored and there's nothing else to do before I'm due at the Zed. I've been telling myself I should do something more constructive with my free time, get my life moving again. But like most things these days it seems like too much effort.

I pause the film and pick up the phone. It's Callum.

'Sean, I've just read about it in the newspaper. I'm really sorry, man, I'd no idea.'

I haven't seen Callum for a while. Not since the double date, in fact. There was talk about doing it again, but it never happened. The truth is I've been trying to cut myself off from links to my old life, although 'cutting' is altogether too active a description for what I've been doing. It's more like letting them die away of their own accord.

I'm still looking at the frozen black and white image on the TV screen: Simone Signoret leaning over the suited body of Paul Meurisse in a bathtub. It's a great scene. 'No idea about what? What are you talking about?'

There's a pause. 'You mean you didn't know about Chloe?'

It's in the *London Evening Standard*. I don't have a copy but the report is on the website. It's brief, and there's no accompanying photograph. Presumably they didn't think the story merited it, or maybe they just didn't have time to locate one after Chloe's body was pulled from the Thames.

A former drug addict, is how the report describes her. Suicide or accident, no one seems sure, although she matches the description of a young woman seen falling off the guard rail of Waterloo Bridge two nights earlier. She'd been so stoned or drunk that none of the witnesses could say whether she stumbled or jumped. The story has only made the news because her body was found bumping against the pilings of a jetty by a group of schoolchildren on a boat trip. The report reserves most of its sympathy for them rather than Chloe.

She was just another addict.

Jez answers the phone when I call Yasmin. I haven't spoken to him since I left the language school. I've nothing against him but the fact he lives with Chloe's best friend made it awkward for both of us.

I don't care about that now, though. 'It's Sean,' I say.

'Sean.' His voice is even heavier than usual. 'You've heard?'

'Just now. Callum called.'

'You OK?'

I don't bother to answer that. 'Is Yasmin there?'

'Yeah, but . . . I don't think you should speak to her right now.'

I stare out of my window at a pigeon that's landed on the ledge. It cocks its head to look at me through the glass. 'What happened?'

'I don't know much. She'd been using again, though. Yasmin tried to get her to clean up, but you know how it is. She'd started doing some serious stuff.' There's a hesitation. 'You know Jules dumped her?'

I put my head against the wall. 'When?'

'A couple of weeks ago. Chloe told Yasmin that Jules was in

trouble. I told you he had a gym in Docklands? Well, by the sound of it he thought the old quay it was in was going to be redeveloped, so he bought the entire building. Hocked himself up to the hilt expecting to make a killing, and then the plug got pulled on the redevelopment. So now he owes Lenny, the big guy who's been supplying him with shit at the gym, as well as some people Lenny does business with. People you really don't want to owe money to. I don't know all the details, but Chloe . . . Look, I shouldn't be telling you this.'

'Go on.'

There's a sigh. 'Well, Chloe said that Jules was starting to deal more seriously, trying to pay off his debts. He'd got something set up and wanted her to courier for him. As in an all-expenses-paid trip to Thailand.'

'Jesus.' I close my eyes.

'She didn't, she said no,' Jez goes on hurriedly. 'But Jules lost it. Threw her out of his apartment, told her she was a parasite, stuff like that, and then cut her dead. Wouldn't have anything more to do with her. I think some of it was probably payback for her walking out on him last time, and it must have pushed Chloe over the edge. Yasmin did what she could, but—'

There's a sudden commotion on the other end of the line. I can hear muffled voices, one of them angry, and then Yasmin comes on.

'Are you happy now?' she shouts. She's crying. 'You fucking shit, why'd you let her go back to that bastard?'

I rub my temples. 'It was her choice, Yas.'

'You left her when she needed you! What did you think she was going to do?'

'I didn't ask her to sleep with him and get pregnant!' I shoot back.

'You should have given her some fucking support! It could have been yours, but you just walked out and abandoned her!'

'What?' My mind's racing. 'No, Chloe told me it was his—'

'And you *believed* her? Jesus, are you really that fucking stupid? She wanted to make it easy for you, and you let her, didn't you? You might as well have pushed her yourself, you selfish—'

There's the sound of a struggle as Jez tries to take the phone. I listen, numbly, as he comes back on, sounding flustered.

'Sorry, Sean. Yasmin's . . . well, you know.'

'What she said, is it . . . ?'

'I don't know anything about that,' he says quickly. 'Look, I've got to go. It's probably better if you don't call again. Just for a while. I'm sorry.'

The line goes dead. Yasmin's words feel like they're burrowing into me. *It could have been yours.* Christ, was that true? Coming on top of Chloe's death, it's too much to take in. But Yasmin wouldn't make up something like that. And the two of them were best friends; Chloe would confide things to her she'd never tell anyone else.

Including me.

Knowing I'm only tormenting myself, I scroll through my phone's logged calls. From what Jez said, Jules must have finished with Chloe around the same time she made that last call to me. And I'd ignored it because I was about to go into a film I didn't want to see, with people I didn't know. Her name is still there, close to the end. Seeing it on the glowing screen makes me insanely tempted to call it. Instead I check my voicemail in case I missed a message. But of course there's nothing.

I feel like I'm suffocating. I hurry out of my flat, pretending to myself that I'm walking aimlessly until, inevitably, I come to Waterloo Bridge. It's a utilitarian concrete span, streaming with traffic beside the pedestrian walkway. I go to the middle and lean over the parapet, looking down at the slow-moving river. I wonder what it must have felt like, stepping off into nothing.

If she was still conscious after she hit the dark water. If she was frightened.

If she thought about me.

I spend the rest of the day getting drunk. From time to time I take out my phone and stare at Chloe's logged call on the small glowing screen. Several times I'm on the verge of deleting it, but I can't bring myself to do it. The evening is warm and sunny, and I sit in a bubble of isolation from the other people sharing the pub's terrace. One moment I'm numb, the next I'm swamped by grief, guilt and anger. Anger is the easiest to bear, and at some point the decision takes hold in my mind as to what I have to do. As the light fades I get up and head unsteadily for the nearest tube station. Jules's gym is in Docklands. I don't have an address but it doesn't matter. I'll find it.

I'll find him.

18

Rain thrums on the roof like static from a broken radio. Outside, water streams and drips over the kitchen window in a steady cascade, like a curtain of glass beads. It's coming down so heavily that the door and windows are all closed, leaving the kitchen hot and stifling. The rain doesn't seem to have made it any cooler, and the airless room is claustrophobic and thick with cooking smells.

Mathilde has gone to town with dinner this evening, serving a rare first course of artichokes in butter.

'What's the special occasion?' Arnaud grumbles. Butter varnishes his mouth and chin.

'No occasion,' Mathilde tells him. 'I just thought you'd like a change.'

Her father grunts and goes back to gnawing at the artichoke, nuzzling obscenely at the centre of the splayed leaves. Gretchen all but ignores me as she sullenly helps her sister serve the food.

Georges evidently hasn't told Arnaud about seeing us in the woods earlier. So far, at least. Either he really does only care about his pigs, like Gretchen says, or he's learned to turn a blind eye to anything that doesn't concern him. Either way, I should be relieved.

Instead I feel almost disappointed.

I've been in a strange mood all afternoon. There was no question of doing any more work once the rain started. It quickly turned my mortar to sludge, and when the wind picked up as well, buffeting the scaffold with each squall, I'd no choice but to come down. Soaking wet, I went back to the barn and stripped off my wet overalls, then watched the storm through the loft's window. The landscape outside was transformed, the familiar pastoral scene replaced by a wilder persona. The fields beyond the wind-thrashed trees had been smeared from existence, while the lake was no more than a blur. As thunder rumbled in the distance I contemplated swimming in it now, with its surface shredded by the downpour.

Instead I stayed in the loft, listening to the drumming rain and waiting for the promised lightning. It never materialized, and before long the storm's novelty had worn thin. Smoking one of my last cigarettes without enjoyment, I tried to read another chapter of *Madame Bovary*. But my heart wasn't in it. As the day dragged into evening without any let-up in the downpour, I grew more restless. For the first time in weeks I put my watch back on, watching the seconds tick by to when I'd have to go to the house for dinner. As well as apprehension, there was also a strange sense of anticipation.

Now I'm finally here, though, it's an anticlimax. Everything carries on as normal. Mathilde comes around with the pan, serving a second artichoke to each of us. They're small but tender, the meaty flesh of the leaves succulent and soft. I don't have much appetite, but I accept another all the same. She pours a little hot butter from the pan onto it before moving away, as expressionless as ever.

As I tear a leaf from the choke and bite into it, I catch sight of my watch. It feels both familiar and strange on my wrist, and my stomach sinks to see that only a few minutes have passed since the last time I looked. The hands seem to be moving through honey, as though the farm is slowing the laws of relativity to suit its own rhythm. Or maybe I'm just waiting for something to happen.

'Going somewhere?' Arnaud says.

I lower my watch. 'Just lost track of time.'

'Why? Don't tell me you're tired.' He gives a wheezing laugh, waving a ruined artichoke at me. 'You've hardly done anything today. The rain's given you a holiday, what have you got to be tired for?'

There's a needle-gleam to his eyes. He's in a good mood, I realize. He's the only one in the room who is. Gretchen seems determined to out-sulk herself, while Mathilde is even quieter than usual. I wonder if her sister has said anything about this afternoon, and the possibility takes away what little inclination I have to make conversation.

Arnaud remains unaware of the undercurrents around the table, too intent for the moment on his appetite. As Mathilde and Gretchen serve the main course – thin strips of pork with a caper sauce – he speaks to me again.

'I hear the stitches are out of your foot.'

'Yes.'

'So there's nothing to slow you up any more, eh?'

'I suppose not.'

'Something to celebrate for both of us then.' He reaches for the wine bottle and makes to refill my glass.

'No, thanks.'

'Come on, you're empty. Here.'

I move my glass away. 'I don't want any more.'

He frowns, holding the bottle poised so the red liquid is close to spilling from its neck. 'Why not? Is something wrong with it?'

'I just don't feel like drinking.'

Arnaud's mouth is clamped into a disapproving line. He's had most of the bottle already, and I doubt it's his first. He pours himself more, splashing it onto the table. Over by the range, Mathilde flinches as the bottle bangs down.

'What?' he demands.

'Nothing.'

He stares at her, but she keeps her eyes downcast as she returns to her seat. Taking a swig of wine, he impales a piece of meat with his fork and glares around the table as he chews.

'What's the matter with everyone tonight?'

No one answers.

'It's like eating in a morgue! Is there something going on I don't know about? Eh?'

The question is met by silence. Across the table, I feel Gretchen's eyes on me but I pretend not to notice. Arnaud empties his glass. His good mood hasn't lasted very long. He reaches again for the bottle and sees Mathilde watching him.

'You want to say something?'

'No.'

'Are you sure?'

'Yes.'

He continues to stare, looking for something to criticize. Failing to find it, he takes up his knife and fork and resumes eating. The pork hardly needs chewing. It falls apart, the sauce piquant with garlic and the capers.

'Not enough seasoning,' Arnaud grumbles.

The comment goes unacknowledged.

'I said there's not enough seasoning.'

Mathilde wordlessly passes him the salt and pepper. He grinds pepper liberally over his food then douses it with salt.

'I've told you often enough to use more when you're cooking. It kills the flavour putting it on afterwards.'

'Then why do it?' I ask before I can stop myself.

Arnaud gives me a poisoned look. 'Because then at least it tastes of something.'

'It tastes fine to me,' I say to Mathilde. 'It's delicious.'

She flickers a nervous smile. Her father stares at me across the table, chewing slowly. He swallows, taking his time before answering.

'And you'd know, would you?'

'I know what I like.'

'Is that so? I didn't realize you were such a gourmand. All this time I thought it was just some no-hope hitch-hiker I'd got living in my barn.' Arnaud raises his glass in an ironic salute. 'I'm honoured to have your opinion rammed down my throat.'

The sound of the rain is loud in the sudden silence. Gretchen is watching us wide-eyed. Mathilde starts to get up.

'There's some sauce left in the pan—'

'Sit down.'

'It's no trouble. I can—'

'*I said sit down!*'

The plates jump as Arnaud's hand crashes onto the table. Even before the reverberations die away the sound of Michel's crying comes from upstairs. But no one makes a move to go to him.

'Why don't you leave her alone?' I hear myself say.

Arnaud slowly turns to stare at me. His face is already flushed from the wine, but now it darkens even more. 'What?'

It feels like I'm running downhill, knowing I'm heading for a fall but carried away by the rush. 'I said why don't you leave her alone?'

'Don't—' Mathilde begins, but Arnaud silences her with a raised hand.

'You hear that, Mathilde? You've got a champion!' He doesn't take his eyes off me, his voice becoming dangerously low. 'You sit there, eating my food, drinking my wine, and *question* me? In my own *home*?'

Mathilde's face has paled, while Gretchen's pretty features have developed an ugly twist. At any other time I might recognize that as a warning, but I'm too focused on Arnaud. His expression is murderous, and a vein beats rapid time on one temple. It makes me glad he doesn't have his gun to hand.

And then, suddenly, something changes. A glint of calculation comes into his eyes. He shrugs, unclamping his jaw enough to give a forced smile. 'Ah, to hell with it. I'm not going to argue about a plate of pork. A man's entitled to his own opinion.'

For a second I'm at a loss, then I get it. He thinks this is about the conversation we had in the woods; his suggestion that I should take Mathilde off his hands. The pent-up tension that's been building in me all day abruptly deflates.

Arnaud sets about his food again with gusto. 'So, you like Mathilde's cooking, eh? Good for you. Perhaps I was a little hasty. You know what they say, a woman who knows how to cook for a man knows how to keep him happy in other ways as well.'

Jesus. I look across at Mathilde, hoping she doesn't think I'm party to this. Her eyes are averted, but the same can't be said for her sister's. Gretchen is glaring at me with a fury that's drawn the skin of her face taut against its bones. The force of it slaps me like a physical jolt, and then she turns to her father.

'Papa, I've got something to tell you.'

Arnaud waves his fork indulgently, without looking up. 'Go on.'

I stare at her, not wanting to believe she's going to do this. But of course she does.

'I saw Georges in the woods this afternoon. Didn't he mention it?'

'No, why should he?'

She looks at me, angelic face dimpling in a vindictive smile. 'Sean can tell you.'

Arnaud lowers his knife and fork, suspicion replacing his earlier indulgence. 'Tell me what?'

'Gretchen, why don't you—' Mathilde tries to intervene, but their father isn't going to be put off.

'Tell me *what*?'

They're all staring at me. The three faces show differing expressions: Arnaud anger, Mathilde fearfulness and Gretchen growing uncertainty, as though she's belatedly regretting what she's started. Strangely enough, I feel calm. As though I've been trying to find my way to this moment but didn't realize it until now.

'I'm leaving.'

The announcement is met with silence. It's Arnaud who breaks it.

'What do you mean, leaving?'

'Just that. There's something I need to do.' Now I've said it all my indecision and uncertainty have gone. It's as though a weight's been lifted from me.

Arnaud's face has grown thunderous. 'You've been here all this time and you never mention this before? What's so urgent that it needs doing now?'

'It's personal. I know it's sudden, but I can't put it off any longer.'

'What about your obligations here? It's all right to put those off, I suppose?'

'The wall's in a better state than it was. But I can stay a few more days, at least until—'

'Don't bother!' Arnaud bellows. 'If you're going to desert us you're not spending another night under my roof! Go on, Judas! Pack your things and get out!'

'No!' Gretchen cries. She looks angry and upset, but that could just be frustration. 'No, he can't leave!'

Her father waves aside her objection. 'Yes, he can! And good riddance! We don't need him!'

Mathilde has been silent till now. She seems genuinely shaken. 'Wait, can't we—'

'No, let him go!' Arnaud roars. 'Didn't you hear me, you un-grateful bastard? I said get out!'

I push my chair back and head for the door. Mathilde hurries to stop me. 'At least let's wait until tomorrow to talk about it! Please!'

I'm not sure if the plea is aimed at me or her father. Arnaud glowers at her, jaw working as though he's gnawing a bone.

'Please!' she says again, and this time there's no question who she's addressing.

Arnaud throws up his hand in a dismissive gesture that ends with him grabbing the wine bottle. 'Let him do what he likes, I don't care. Stay or go, it's all the same to me.'

He sloshes wine into his glass. Mathilde takes hold of my arm and hurries me into the courtyard. Before she shuts the door after us, my last view is of Gretchen, staring after us with her face pinched and intent.

Outside, the rain has eased up but a fine drizzle still hangs in the air. It's cool and damp enough to make me shiver. Mathilde leads me across the slick cobbles until we're out of earshot.

'I'm sorry,' I say.

She shakes her head. Her hair is misted by the drizzle. 'You don't have to go.'

'Yes, I do.'

'My father's just angry. He didn't mean what he said.'

I'd beg to differ, but it doesn't matter anyway. 'It's not him. I've stayed too long as it is.'

She glances back at the house. I can't tell what she's thinking. 'Won't you change your mind?'

'I can't. I'm sorry.'

She's silent for a moment, then sighs. 'Where will you go? To England?'

I just nod. It's only now starting to sink in. Mathilde tucks rain-damp hair behind her ear.

'Will you come back? Here, I mean?'

'I don't know.' I'm surprised and moved that she's asked. I wish I could say, but the decision won't be mine to make.

'You should stay until morning, at least.'

'I'm not sure that's a good idea.'

'My father will calm down. Besides, there won't be many cars on the road this late.'

She has a point. If I go now I'll either be walking all night or still outside the gate come morning. I glance back at the house. 'I don't want to cause any more trouble . . .'

'You won't. And I have to talk to you before you go.'

'What about?'

'Not now.' She's standing close to me. Her grey eyes seem huge. 'Can I come to the loft later? After midnight?'

'I . . . OK. Sure.'

Her hand rests lightly on my chest. 'Thank you.'

I stare after her as she hurries back to the scaffolded house and disappears inside. Then I'm alone in the post-rain quiet. A breeze causes the old weathervane to twist and creak on top of the stables, carrying a rustle of the distant trees. Clouds slide across the not yet dark sky, fitfully obscuring a rising moon. My thoughts are in a tumult as I set off across the wet courtyard to the barn. Everything seemed so clear only minutes ago. Now I don't know what to think.

Or what Mathilde might want.

A sudden wave of doubt takes the strength from my legs. *Christ, what am I doing?* I lean against the barn wall, sucking in air, and it's only then I remember I've left my walking stick in the kitchen. There's a moment of panic, but it quickly passes. I'm not going back for it, and once I accept that I feel calm again. With a last deep breath, I straighten and carry on back to the loft to pack my things.

It's time to face up to what I've done.

London

I<small>T'S DARK WHEN I</small> arrive in Docklands. I've no idea what the time is – the numbers on my watch face seem part of an illegible code – but it's late. The bars and restaurants I pass are closed, and the only sound is the echo of my footsteps.

I've reached that stage of pseudo-clarity that feels like being sober. Jez said the gym was near an undeveloped quay, but after wandering at random all I've accomplished is to get myself completely lost. The area is a maze of unlit tower blocks, gentrified dock buildings and derelict warehouses overlooked by faltering regeneration.

It's beginning to sink in how stupid this is. Even if I find Jules, what would I do? Any idea of retribution now seems pathetic, an alcohol-fuelled fantasy to stave off my own guilt. As I walk the empty streets Yasmin's accusations play in my head like a looped recording. *You just walked out and abandoned her. She wanted to make it easy for you, and you let her, didn't you?* Did I? Is that really what happened? I don't know any more. The thought that the baby might have been mine leaves a physical ache under my breastbone. I've gone over and over everything Chloe said, trying to decipher the truth. I can't, but much as I want to believe that Yasmin was just hitting out I know it isn't only Jules who's to blame.

The beginning of a hangover is starting to throb in my

temples. I feel tired, sick with regret and self-disgust. All I want now is to go back to my flat, but I've no idea how to get there. The streets all look the same; tunnels of brick, chrome and glass that as often as not lead to dead-ends of dark water and silent boats.

Then I turn a corner and see light coming from an open doorway in a warehouse. A car is parked on the other side of the road, but other than that the street is deserted. I walk faster, hoping to find someone who can tell me where I am. I've wandered well away from the more affluent parts of Docklands. Apart from the warehouse, all the buildings around here are derelict. Beyond a fenced-off strip of wasteland is the black sheen of water and a run-down quayside. But it isn't until I notice the developer's board outside the warehouse and the skeletal frames of exercise machines through the ground-floor windows that I fit it all together. I slow down, still not quite believing this can be what I think, and then someone comes out of the doorway and crosses the road to the car.

The electronic squeal of it unlocking carries in the quiet street. I've stopped, watching as the man goes around to the back and opens the boot. I lose sight of him for a few moments, then the boot is slammed shut and the figure goes to the driver's side and gets in. I stand motionless, no more than twenty or thirty feet away, as Jules is revealed by the dim interior light. Whatever stomach I had for confrontation has gone as I watch him slumped at the steering wheel. There's nothing smug or arrogant about him now. The stubbled face looks tired and defeated, his eyes shadowed.

Not daring to move in case he sees me, I wait for him to go. Instead he rummages for something out of sight. I only realize what he's doing when he bends his head, pressing a finger to the side of his nose as he snorts something from the back of his hand. Suddenly more purposeful, he straightens and starts the car engine. A moment later the road is lit up by bright halogen headlights.

And so am I.

I shield my eyes from the glare, hoping even now he might not notice me. For a moment nothing happens. Then the engine and headlights are turned off. As I try to blink away their after-image I hear the car door open. It chunks shut as Jules comes to stand in front of the car.

'What the fuck are you doing here?'

Still dazzled, I try to make him out in the darkness. 'Chloe's dead.'

It's the only thing I can think of to say. There's a pause. For a second or two I actually hope we might be able to put aside any rivalry.

'And?'

'Did you know?'

'Yeah. So if that's what you came to tell me you can turn around and piss off.'

The anger that had drained away starts to seep back. 'What did you do to her?'

'*I* didn't do anything, she did it all herself. That's why they call it suicide. Now why don't you do us both a favour and fuck off, because I'm really not in the mood for a sermon.'

'You threw her out.'

'Big deal. I didn't ask her to jump off a bridge.' There's some-thing defensive behind his aggression. 'Anyway, what the fuck's it got to do with you? I can't remember you being so concerned when you walked out and left her. You want to blame anyone, look in a fucking mirror!'

It's close enough to what Yasmin said to make me want to hit out. 'Did you know she'd had an abortion?'

That's met with silence. My eyes have adjusted enough to see him shrug. 'So what?'

'She said it was yours.'

'Yeah? She should have been more careful. At least she had the sense to get rid of it.' The callousness sounds forced, but it's quickly replaced by rage. 'You want to know why I kicked her out? Because she'd got to be a fucking liability. An *embarrassment*! She was a fucking cokehead, it's not my fault she couldn't keep her shit together.'

'And who made her like that?'

This time the silence is threatening. 'You need to watch what you're saying.'

'You got her hooked and then dropped her when she wouldn't courier for you!'

'Last chance. Shut the fuck up and go. Now.'

'Why, so you can ruin someone else's life? You're just a fucking pimp!'

For a few seconds the only sound is our breathing. Then Jules turns back to his car. I think he's going to drive off but instead he goes around to the passenger side. He opens the door and leans inside, emerging with something long and slender.

'I warned you,' he says, walking towards me.

He's got a baseball bat.

The situation seems unreal. I take a step back, and as though that's the trigger he rushes forward. I try to dodge as he swings, gasping in shock as much as pain as the bat smacks into my raised arm. I stumble away as Jules flails wildly, missing more often than he connects, and there's a clatter of glass as I trip over a box of empty bottles. Off-balance, I only just get my arm up in time as the bat comes at my head. It glances off my shoulder and catches me on the cheek. There's a hot flash of light, then I'm falling. I land clumsily, sending bottles skittering over the pavement. Numb with panic, I try to scramble away as Jules raises the bat above me, his face contorted.

'The fuck's going on?'

The shout comes from across the road. A big figure blocks out the light from the same doorway Jules came from. As it steps into the street I recognize the broad shoulders of Lenny.

'It's the cunt from the Zed,' Jules pants. The bat is still poised ready to swing, but it's clear he's deferring to the other man.

The big head moves, trying to make me out in the darkness. 'What's he doing here?'

'He's heard about Chloe. He's trying to blame me for—'

'For fuck's sake,' Lenny mutters, and starts towards us.

There's something terrifying about his unhurried intent, and while Jules is still distracted I grab one of the bottles lying nearby and hurl it at his head. He sees it coming and ducks, and as it shatters behind him I make a run for it. There's a shout as I barge past, and I feel the bat whoosh past my head close enough to ruffle my hair. Then I'm pounding down the street as hard as I can. Jules's footsteps are just behind me as Lenny angles across the road to cut me off. There's nowhere to go, but Jules's car is dead ahead. Its passenger door is still open, so I throw myself inside. Jules grabs for me and cries out when I slam the door on his arm, trapping it. The baseball bat clatters to the pavement as I heave on the handle, keeping him pinned. His arm's bleeding where the edge of the door has gouged into it, and as he clutches for me across the seat I see that Lenny has almost reached the car. I can't keep them both out, so as Jules tries to wrench free I shove the door against him. He stumbles backwards, and as his arm clears the door I yank it shut.

There's a beautiful *clunk* as I hit the central-locking button and the bolts shoot home. Then the car shudders as Jules hurls himself against it.

'Open the fucking door!' he shouts, banging on the glass. 'You're dead, you hear me? Fucking dead!'

I'm sprawled across the front seats, gasping for breath. Pushing myself upright, I see why Jules hasn't used his key to unlock the car.

It's still in the ignition.

I scramble over to the driver's seat as he pounds on the passenger window. 'Don't you fucking dare!'

My hand shakes as I turn the key and jam my foot down. The car jerks forward and stalls. I flinch at a sudden bang on the door next to me as Lenny rams an elbow against the window. The car rocks as Jules wrenches at the door, yelling as I turn the key again.

'*No, wait! Don't—!*'

The engine drowns out his voice. Lenny has picked up the baseball bat but I'm already accelerating away. He jumps back but Jules runs alongside, still hammering on the glass. He's screaming at me now, but I stamp on the pedal and he abruptly disappears. There's time for a moment's relief, then the steering wheel is almost torn from my hands as the car bucks and judders. A clattering comes from the passenger side, as though something's snagged underneath. The juddering stops as I brake, jerking forward as the car screeches to a halt. I twist round, but there's no one nearby. In the rear-view mirror I can see Lenny standing motionless in the road behind me.

There's no sign of Jules.

The engine chugs softly. I look over at the passenger side. The seatbelt is trapped in the door, unspooled and twisted like a miniature noose. When I reach over and open it, the belt snakes sluggishly back inside as it tries to rewind. But the mechanism's damaged and it soon stops. I stare at the frayed fabric, thinking about Jules groping for me across the seat. How he banged on the window as I sped off.

Leaving the engine running, I climb out of the car.

Lenny is staring down at something lying in the gutter. It isn't moving, and in the glow from a streetlight I can see the back-to-front wrongness of its limbs. Something black and viscous pools around it, glistening like oil. Any doubts I might have are snuffed by Lenny's lack of urgency. I automatically take a step forward but stop when he raises his head and looks at me. He's still holding the baseball bat, and I back away as he starts walking towards me with a deliberation that's chilling. The driver's door bumps against my legs, then I'm scrambling into the car and grinding through the gears.

As I roar away, I glance in the rear-view mirror. Lenny has stopped in the middle of the road. My last view is of him staring after me, the baseball bat still gripped in one hand.

I drive until I feel I've gone far enough to be safe. Pulling over, I manage to open the door in time to throw up, hanging onto the door as I heave scalding bile into the road. When the spasm's passed I grope for my phone to call for an ambulance. It won't do Jules any good but I'm functioning automatically now, obeying the Pavlovian response of a good citizen. Besides, I can't think of anything else to do.

But my phone's broken. Its screen is cracked and the casing threatens to come apart in my hand. I don't know when it happened, but it's useless. I start driving again, intending to stop at the first public phone I come to. Except I don't see one. I turn on the windscreen wipers as a sudden downpour smears the glass, turning the world outside into an Impressionist blur. I feel like I'm trapped in a nightmare, but gradually my mind starts to work again. Soon I'm able to think clearly. At least, that's how it seems at the time.

It's still raining, but the first flush of a summer dawn is lightening the sky when I pull up outside my flat. Almost feverish with the need to hurry, I let myself in. I'm shaking, hurting all over, but I can't stay here. Lenny knows who I am, and it's only a matter of time before he or his business associates find me. I can't even hand myself in to the police, because I doubt I'd be any safer in prison. There's only one thing I can think of to do.

I cram clothes and what cash I have lying around into my rucksack, only remembering my passport at the last minute. I take a last look around the small flat, with its shelves of old DVDs and framed film posters. There's a rare reproduction from *Rififi*, and a print of Vadim's *Et Dieu . . . créa la femme* with a luridly breathy Bardot that nearly bankrupted me. None of it seems important now.

I close the door and hurry back out to where I've parked Jules's car. It's an Audi, sleek and expensive. I don't look like the sort of person to own an expensive car, but the urge to get away overwhelms everything else.

There's never any question of where I'm going to go.

I throw my rucksack into the boot and go to open the driver's door before I stop. I don't want to see what might be on the passenger side, but I can't leave without making sure. Checking that the street is still empty, I make myself go around the car. The black paintwork on the rear wheel arch is scraped and dented. But not so much that it will attract any attention, and the rain has washed off whatever blood was there.

There's nothing to show what I've done.

It's too early for much traffic, and I make good time to the Dover ferry terminal. By now reaction is setting in. I'm hung-over and exhausted, aching from the fight earlier. Nothing seems real, and it's only as I'm buying a ticket that it occurs to me that the car registration number might flag an alert. I'm stunned at my own stupidity for not having abandoned it and boarded as a foot passenger.

But there are no sirens, no alarms. I drive the dead man's car into the boat's cavernous metal belly, then go up on deck and watch the white cliffs slowly recede.

A few hours later I'm hitching on a dusty French road under a white sun.

19

I T DOESN'T TAKE LONG to pack. My few clothes and belongings are soon tucked away in the rucksack. I could have left it until morning, but it feels more like a statement of intent to do it now. I'm not going to change my mind this time.

If anything, that makes me even more nervous about Mathilde's visit.

After that, there's nothing to do but wait. It's fully dark outside, though it's not yet nine o'clock. Another sign that summer's almost over. Three hours till Mathilde comes. Her copy of *Madame Bovary* lies beside the mattress. Something else I'll be leaving unfinished. In the glow from the lamp, I look around the shadowed loft. Even with all its junk and cobwebs, it's come to feel like home. I'll be sorry to leave it.

I lie on the bed and light another of my last cigarettes. I flick off the flame from the lighter, remembering the photograph from Brighton curling to ash. I wish Gretchen hadn't burned it, but then I wish a lot of things. Maybe I couldn't have altered what happened to Chloe, but I'll always wonder. And even if I could somehow absolve myself of failing her, no one made me go to Docklands that night. Because I did a man is dead. Never mind that it was accidental, or that I was only trying to get away. I killed someone.

There's no escaping that.

I blow smoke at the ceiling. I have to go back, I know that now. The thought of what will happen is still terrifying, but for my own peace of mind I've got to take responsibility for what I've done. Yet whenever I think about Mathilde, and what she might want, I feel my resolve wavering.

Then there's another complication. The plastic package from Jules's car is still where I hid it after the gendarmes' visit. I can't leave it there, but I can hardly take a kilo of cocaine back into the UK with me.

So what do I do with it?

The loft is close and humid, too airless for me to think. I go to the open window. Beyond the grapevines and woods, I can just make out the lake, silver against the darkness. Seeing it gives me a sudden sense of purpose. Mathilde won't be here for a while yet, and I promised myself I'd swim in it once the stitches came out.

This is my last chance.

I don't bother with the lamp as I descend from the loft, trusting to familiarity to negotiate the wooden steps. Moonlight floods through the open barn doors, illuminating the crumbling concrete I became so paranoid about. I barely give it a thought as I pass by on my way outside.

The drizzle has stopped. The night smells unbelievably sweet, a fresh breeze stirring the vine leaves. There's a full moon, but the torn clouds that pass over it cast scurrying shadows on the field. There's a constant rustle of movement as I enter the woods. Water drips from the branches, darkening the statues hidden among the trees. The white flowers that Gretchen hung around the nymph's neck seem luminescent when the moonlight touches them, but fade away as another cloud crosses the moon.

Then I've left the stone figures behind and ahead of me is the lake. There's an iron tang to the air, and the black water is shivered by the breeze. A sudden movement makes me start, but it's only a duck ruffling its feathers. As the moon re-emerges I see there are more of them, dotted around the bank like stones. I make my way to the patch of shingle and strip off. My bare feet look mismatched, one of them unmarked and familiar, the other thin and white, criss-crossed with angry weals.

The frigid water takes away my breath when I walk out into the lake. I reflexively rise onto tiptoe as it laps up to my groin, then wade further out. I pause when the bottom abruptly shelves away, bracing myself before plunging in.

It's like diving into ice. Cold stabs into my ears as the water closes over my head, then I break into a clumsy crawl. I thrash out towards the centre of the lake, forcing blood into my sluggish limbs. Gasping, I tread water and look around. My wake has left a ragged tear across the surface. Everything seems different out here, strange and still. The water feels bottomless and deep. Below me there's a flicker of silver as a fish catches the moonlight. Looking down, I see my body suspended in blackness, so pale it looks bloodless.

God, it feels good. I start swimming again, this time in an easy breaststroke. The bluff where I've spent so many afternoons rises up in front of me, the sweeping branches of the chestnut tree spread like wings against the sky. Seeing it brings home that I've been there for the last time, and as quickly as that any pleasure is snuffed out.

I wanted to swim in the lake, and now I have. There's no point staying out any longer. I turn to head back, but as I kick out my foot touches something hard. I jerk away before realizing it's only the submerged rock I've seen from the bluff. Tentatively, I stretch out a foot again.

And quickly recoil.

The rock is smooth. Not with the expected slime of algae or weed, but a hard, polished smoothness. I lower one foot, then the other, until I'm standing on it. The water comes up to my chin. The surface below me is flat and slightly convex, pitted with tiny blisters of corrosion. But I don't need those to tell me it isn't rock I'm standing on.

It's a car roof.

I probe around with my toes, mapping its shape. One foot slips off the edge and suddenly there's nothing beneath me but water. I flail around as the lake closes over my head, coughing and choking as I stand on the roof again. At least I've established that it isn't a car. The roof's too narrow and truncated for that.

More like the cab of a truck.

Shivering, I look at the lake's banks. They're a long way off and too soft and muddy to drive across anyway. No, the only way anything could end up here is if it came off the bluff. I stare up at the overhanging edge, trying to imagine a truck rolling off by accident. It's too far away, though. For whatever I'm standing on to have got this far out it must have been driven off deliberately.

I badly want to swim back and get dressed. But I can't do that, not yet. Taking a deep breath, I dive down. The water slips ice-picks into my ears. Everything's dark. I can't see a thing, but then the moon comes out from behind a cloud and suddenly an otherworldly light filters down from the surface. The looming hulk of the truck takes form below me. My vision's blurred but I can see it's a pick-up. The open flatbed behind the cab is exposed and empty. I kick deeper as my chest starts to heave. Too many cigarettes. Fighting my body's buoyancy, I grab for the door handle and almost let go when it swings open in slow motion.

My heart's begun a timpani beat as I pull myself nearer. The interior of the cab is hazy and full of shadows. I peer inside for two or three heartbeats, and then the moon is covered and it's dark again. Letting go of the door, I push for the surface. I burst into the night air, gulping in breaths as the banging in my temples begins to subside.

Nothing.

The murky water made it hard to be certain, but I didn't see anything inside the cab; no bulky shadow or slow wave of limbs. I contemplate taking another look to make sure, but the thought makes my flesh crawl. I can't bring myself to dive down again.

Teeth chattering, I start swimming back. I force myself to go steadily, fighting the urge to rush. Then something – a trailing weed or twig – brushes against my ankle and my restraint shatters. I thrash towards the shore, splashing through the shallows until I'm back on the shingle. Shivering, I rub my arms and stare back at the lake. The ripples from my wake are already settling, leaving the water still and black once more. There's nothing to suggest what's hidden below its surface.

I begin dragging on my clothes. There's no doubt in my mind who the truck belongs to. It was impossible to see its colour, but I'm guessing it'll be dark green. The same as the one in the photograph Jean-Claude showed me. The last known sighting of Louis was in Lyon, so I'd assumed that whatever happened to him must have happened there. I was wrong.

He came back.

I struggle to pull my jeans over my wet skin. Try as I might, I can't think of an innocent explanation for why his pick-up is in the lake. Jean-Claude tried to tell me that Arnaud was responsible for his brother's disappearance and I wouldn't listen. I didn't want to. I can't believe even now that Mathilde knows anything about this, but I'm not going to stay and find out. The farm's been hiding at least one secret.

I don't want to become another.

My boots won't go on. The wood seems threatening and watchful as I struggle to force my feet into them. I keep looking around, half-expecting to see Arnaud materialize from the shadows with his rifle. But except for a lone statue in the trees, I'm alone. I'm reaching down to pull on my boot before

I remember there aren't any statues this close to the lake, and at that same moment it steps out of the woods.

Gretchen is alabaster pale in the moonlight, skin bleached white as stone. She stares at me without coming any closer.

'I went to the loft. You weren't there.'

I find my voice. 'No, I, uh . . . I needed some air.'

'I saw your rucksack. All your things are packed.'

I don't know what to say to that. Gretchen looks out at the water. Her earlier anger has been replaced by an eerie calm that's even more unsettling.

'You've been in the lake.'

'I was hot. I wanted to cool down.'

'You were underwater for a long time. What were you doing?'

'Just swimming.'

I'm trying to gauge how much she knows, if it's possible she isn't aware of what's in there. But I'm shivering so much it's hard to think straight.

'I told you, Papa says you shouldn't swim in there. It isn't safe.' *Safe for who?* 'If I tell him he'll be angry.'

'Then don't tell him.'

'Why shouldn't I? You're leaving tomorrow anyway.' Her gaze is cold and distant. 'You don't care about me or you wouldn't be abandoning us.'

'I'm not abandoning anybody.'

'Yes, you are. I thought you were different but you're not. We trusted you, and now you've betrayed us.'

She said the same about Louis. 'Look, I'm sorry if—'

'No, you're not. You led me on.'

'That's not true—'

'Then promise you'll stay.'

'Gretchen—'

'You have to promise. Or I'll tell Papa.'

Christ. I glance back at the water. Whether she knows about

the truck or not, I don't want her saying anything to Arnaud. Not until I'm well away from this place.

'OK,' I tell her. 'I'll stay.'

Gretchen stares at me. I can feel the hairs on the back of my neck start to stand on end.

'Liar.'

'No, I—'

'I don't like you any more.'

'Gretchen, wait—' I shout, but she's already running up the track. After a frozen second I set off after her. I've no idea what I'll do, I only know that I can't stay down here while she tells her father. But I'm out of shape, and with my boots unlaced and flapping it's like running in a bad dream. Gretchen races through the wood ahead of me, flickering in and out of the moonlight like a wraith. My chest and legs are burning as I pass the statues, and then one of my boots slips off and I'm tumbling onto the track. The breath explodes from me. Winded, I push myself up in time to see Gretchen's white figure running out of the wood and through the vines. A cloud obscures the moon, dimming her from sight, but it's obvious I'm not going to catch her now. Not before she reaches the house.

I bend double, wheezing for air. Shit, *shit*! I try to think clearly. Maybe I'm overreacting, and there's an innocent explanation. Maybe the truck's just an old one that was dumped. I desperately want to believe it but the memory of what I found in the lake is too strong. And I can't take the chance: if the pick-up is Louis's then Arnaud won't risk me telling anyone.

He isn't going to let me leave the farm.

As if on cue, his raised voice carries distantly from the court-yard, bellowing incoherently. I think I can hear Mathilde as well, a pleading counterpoint, then a door slams and there's silence.

He's on his way.

I look around for my missing boot, but the moon is still

overcast and all I can see are shadows. There's no more time. Stones and twigs stab into my bare foot – the newly healed one – as I hurry off the track to hide in the trees. Once Arnaud's gone past I can cut back to the road: I'll worry about my rucksack later.

I've not gone far when there's a sudden *snap* as I step on something sharp. I throw myself back, heart banging as I tense for the bite of iron jaws. It doesn't come: it's only a dead branch. But in my panic I'd forgotten the woods down here are still full of Arnaud's traps. I daren't go any further, not when it's too dark to see where I'm treading.

There's a flicker of movement off through the trees. I look back towards the vine field. The moon is obscured and for a moment all is shadows. Then it reappears, and I see the unmistakable figure of Arnaud hurrying down the track. He's carrying something that glints in the moonlight, and when I realize what it is any hope of reasoning with him vanishes.

It's his rifle.

The moon goes behind another cloud, cutting off my view as though a curtain's been drawn. But he's much closer than I expected. It's too late to retrace my steps and make a run for the lake. Even if I avoid the traps he'll be close enough to see me, and on the track I'll make an easy target. Desperate, I look around for somewhere to hide. I'm not far from where we cut down the silver birch, and most of the trees around me are either saplings or stumps. None are big enough to provide cover, but then a ripple of moonlight breaks through the branches and reveals the statues.

I run over before the brief light fades, hoping Arnaud won't have put traps near them. Throwing myself to the wet ground, I huddle behind the monk's stone robes. I'm out of breath and my bootless foot is throbbing. It feels sticky: I must have gashed it on the dead branch, or maybe the wounds have reopened. But that's the least of my problems. I peer round the statue. Without the moon the woods are made up of different depths of black. Nothing moves, and then I see a shadow coming down the track.

I duck back, pressing myself against the cold stone. Above me the sky is a patchwork of clouds and stars, but down here all is dark. I stare up through the trees, praying for the moon to stay hidden. I want to take another look but I'm afraid he'll see me. So I lie there, listening for his approach. The breeze stirs the leaves and branches, drowning out other sounds. I shut my eyes, trying to visualize where he'll be. I tell myself if I count to thirty he'll have gone past by then. But when the half-minute's passed I still don't move. What if I'm wrong, or he's stopped? I squeeze my hands into fists, trying to decide. I can't stay here indefinitely: my best chance of making it to the road is while Arnaud is down at the lake. He must have gone by now. I tense, getting ready to look again.

There's a muffled *crack* of a twig breaking.

I lie perfectly still. I'm holding my breath, not daring to breathe. I strain to hear past the rustling trees, willing the clouds to stay for a few moments longer. But the high wind is already dragging them clear, their black silhouettes becoming edged with an argent glow. I watch helplessly as the moon slides out from behind them, flooding the world with opal light. Then another twig snaps only a few feet away.

'Sean?'

Mathilde's voice is hushed. The release of tension takes the strength from me.

'Here.'

She's looking towards the other statues. She turns at my whisper and hurries over, glancing off through the trees towards the track as the Judas moon hides its face again, plunging the wood into shadows.

'You have to leave,' she says in a low voice, crouching down beside me. 'My father thinks you're still at the lake. You need to go before he comes back.'

Even now I'd been hoping she'd reassure me I'd nothing to worry about, that it was a misunderstanding. I start to get to my feet again but she pulls me back down. She's just a shadow herself, her face all but invisible in the dark.

'Not yet. Give him a little longer to get out of sight. Here, put this on.'

She pushes something at me. I can't see it but I recognize it by touch as my boot.

'I found it on the path,' she whispers. 'That's why I thought you'd be here.'

'Where's Gretchen?' I ask, blindly trying to pull on the boot. My foot is slick with blood but too swollen for it to fit.

'With Michel.'

'What did she tell your father?'

'Never mind. Take these.' Mathilde presses something else into my hands. Keys and what feels like a small roll of money. 'It's not much but it's all I have. And you'll need this.'

She passes me something thin and flat. It takes me a moment to realize it's my passport.

'You've been in my rucksack?' My thoughts are still sluggish, but I can't see how she'd have had time to go up to the loft.

'Not tonight. I took it the first time you went into town.'

I don't know which shocks me more, the fact she took my passport or that I never noticed it was missing. 'Why?'

'Because I didn't want you to leave without telling me. I have a favour to ask, but now we need to go. Are you ready?'

Favour? 'I can't get the boot on,' I say, more confused than ever.

'Do it later. We have to hurry.'

She's already ushering me from behind the statue. I've no

choice but to carry the boot, the rough ground gouging into my bare foot.

'Careful,' she says, steering me away from a patch of shadow. At first I don't know what she means, then I make out something hard-edged hidden in it.

So much for Arnaud not setting traps near his statues.

But Mathilde seems to know where to tread as she hurries me back to the track. I limp along as fast as I can, fresh hurt coming from my foot each time I set it down. The clouds covering the moon are shredded, allowing a sickly light to dapple through. I risk a glance towards the lake, but can't see Arnaud.

'What favour?' I ask, keeping my voice low.

There's enough light to see her tuck her hair behind her ear in the familiar gesture. I can't make out her face but I can sense her agitation.

'I want you to take Gretchen with you.'

'You *what*?'

'Shh, just listen.' Mathilde grips my arm, her voice low and hushed. 'I have to get her away from here, and she'll go with you. I know it's a lot to ask but I don't expect you to support her. I'll send more money, as much as I can.'

'Jesus, Mathilde . . .'

'Please! I could have told the police about the drugs in your rucksack.'

Of course she'd know, I think, too stunned to feel shocked. I was feverish for three days. A stranger: did I really expect her not to search my things to see who she was looking after? The only surprise is that she let me stay anyway.

Unless she had her own reasons.

The overhanging leaves cast a shadowplay on Mathilde's face as moonlight breaks through the clouds. The track comes to life around us. Past the wood, the vine field is thrown into sharp relief, the rutted track clearly etched on it like lines drawn in charcoal. I think I see a flicker of movement on it as Mathilde urges me to walk faster.

'Hurry, we—'

The sudden crack of a gunshot rings out. It comes from behind us, the direction of the lake, and we both flinch as it's followed by a second. Mathilde pulls me off the track.

'Down here!'

The trees close in like a tunnel as she leads me down the fork to the sanglochon pens. Branches whip at me as I run just behind her, favouring my cut foot, and then we're in the ammoniac stink of the clearing. The full moon shines overhead like a beacon, picking out the sows slumped asleep like hairy bolsters. Hoping they don't wake, I limp behind Mathilde. I expect her to head towards the wood at the far side, but instead she goes to the cinderblock hut.

'In here,' she pants, pushing open the door.

There's no time to argue. I hurry inside and the light is cut off as both halves of the stable door swing shut. The reek of offal and old blood closes in around us. It's pitch black and our laboured breathing sounds too loud in the enclosed space. There's no window, but as my eyes adjust I see chinks of light seeping through gaps in the mortar. Mathilde brushes past me and peers through one.

'Is he there?' I whisper.

'I don't know. I don't think so.'

I go to look for myself, and there's a muted clinking as my shoulder brushes something. I give a start before realizing it's the chain hanging from the pulley. Groping in the dark to quieten its swaying, I feel my way around the stone slab standing in the middle of the hut. I press my face against one of the chinks in the rough wall, blinking as my breath huffs away dirt and sand. The small crack doesn't allow much of a view, and the clearing is already darkening as another cloud covers the moon. But there's no sign of Arnaud.

'If he'd seen us he'd be here already,' Mathilde murmurs. At least the hut's walls won't let our voices carry: Arnaud would have to be right outside to hear us. 'He must have been shooting at shadows.'

'Then let's go.' I'm already regretting coming in here. I move towards the thin line of light leaking around the door, but Mathilde reaches out to stop me.

'Not yet.'

'Why? Shouldn't we go while he's still at the lake?'

'He could be on his way back by now. We could walk right into him.'

She's right, but I'm loath to stay where we are. The cinder-block walls might stop a small-calibre bullet, but if Arnaud guesses we're in here we'll be trapped.

'What about the woods on the other side of the clearing? Can we get out that way?'

'No, it's too dangerous. There's no path and my father laid traps in there as well.'

Oh Christ. I try to think. 'So what do we do now?'

'We wait. In a few minutes I'll go out and see if it's clear.'

'What if it isn't?'

'Then I'll tell him you slipped away while he was at the lake. Once he's gone to bed I'll come and get you.'

Mathilde sounds as calm as ever. For an instant I feel a sudden fear that she might bring her father here, but of course that's ridiculous. She wouldn't be doing all this if she meant me any harm. I have to trust her.

I lower myself to the floor as she takes another look outside, hoping I'll be able to get my boot on. My foot feels raw and swollen. I brush the dirt from it and give an involuntary gasp as I catch the torn flesh.

'Are you all right?' Mathilde asks.

I nod before I realize she can't see me. 'It's just my foot.'

'Here, let me.'

There's a rustle as she crouches down. Her hands are cool on my skin as she gently feels my foot in the darkness. I draw in a breath as she probes something tender.

'You've reopened some of the wounds and gashed your instep. Have you anything to bind it with?'

'No.'

'Never mind. I'll help you get your boot on.'

Her hair brushes against my arm as she starts to work the boot over my foot. 'Why do you want Gretchen to leave so badly?' I ask, trying to ignore the discomfort. 'Because of what's in the lake?'

There's the smallest of pauses. 'That's one reason.'

So she does know about it. I feel a sense of unreality that we're having this conversation. I wish I could see her but she's just another shape in the darkness.

'What happened to Louis, Mathilde?'

She continues trying to ease the boot onto my foot. For a moment I don't think she's going to answer. When she does her voice is quiet and resigned.

'I found out I was pregnant while he was in Lyon. I was going to tell him when he came back. I had a little money, so I hoped I could persuade him to take us away somewhere. Gretchen too. She was . . . fond of Louis. But I should have known she'd tell my father. There was a scene. He and Louis fought . . .'

I flinch as the boot slips home. 'So then your father drove his truck into the lake?'

'He wanted to get rid of everything that showed Louis had been at the farm. He came straight here from Lyon. It was night, so no one knew he was back. Afterwards . . . we just pretended nothing had happened.'

I feel her hands fall away from my boot as though her mind's already elsewhere. I reach down and start to fasten the laces as she gets to her feet.

'What about the body?' The truck's cab was empty, but now I can't help but think about the crumbling patch of concrete in the barn again.

'My father brought it down here.'

'Here?'

'For the sanglochons.'

It takes a moment for her meaning to sink in. *Jesus*. Horrified, I look around the blackness of the small hut, remembering the stunned sow being hauled off the floor, the sound of the blood spattering into the bucket. Something Arnaud said suddenly takes on an awful significance.

Pigs eat anything.

'How much does Gretchen know?' I ask.

'I don't know.' Mathilde sounds weary. 'She was dazed and hysterical afterwards, and she's never spoken about it. Ever since she was a little girl, Gretchen's been able to block out anything she doesn't want to think about. As though it never happened.'

I've seen that for myself. But the memory of Gretchen's bizarre amnesia is swept away by a far worse thought. I've been assuming that Arnaud killed Louis.

Maybe he didn't.

My foot hurts when I stand up, though not so much that I won't be able to run if I have to. I peer out through the chink in the wall. What I can see of the clearing in the leprous moonlight is empty.

'Your father didn't kill Louis, did he?' I ask, without turning round.

There's the briefest of pauses. 'No.'

'Gretchen's sick, Mathilde. She needs help.

'Sick?'

'You can't keep on protecting her. Even if she didn't mean to kill Louis, sooner or later she's going to hurt someone else. Or herself.'

'No, you don't understand,' she says, as though she's explaining to a child. 'Gretchen didn't kill Louis. I did.'

Something cold uncoils in my stomach. 'I don't believe you.'

'Louis was beating my father. Hurting him.' Her voice is flat, as though all the emotion has been drained out of it. 'When Gretchen tried to stop him he punched her. Hard, in her face. So I picked up a spade and hit him.'

The crook on Gretchen's nose, I think, numbly. I turn towards Mathilde. I can barely see her in the darkness, but she's so close we're almost touching.

'If it was an accident why didn't you go to the police?'

'I can't go to prison.' For the first time since I've known her she sounds scared. 'It'd be hard enough for Michel, but I couldn't leave Gretchen alone here. Not with my father.'

'Why not? I know she's your sister, but—'

'She isn't my sister. Gretchen's my daughter.'

There's a second when I think I must have got it wrong. Then I realize. *Arnaud?* The foul air in the hut seems to congeal around us.

There's a soft movement as Mathilde brushes at her cheeks.

'I was thirteen. My father told my mother the baby was some boy's from town. He said they had to pretend it was theirs to protect my reputation. Then he told the school I was ill and kept me at home until Gretchen was born. No one ever questioned it. After that it was as though she really was their daughter.'

'Couldn't you have *told* someone?' I say, appalled.

'Who? My mother must have known, but she wasn't strong enough to stand up to him. And when she died who else was I to tell? Georges?'

'Does Gretchen have any idea?'

'No!' Her sudden vehemence takes me aback. 'She mustn't, not ever. I won't let him destroy her life as well. I told him if he ever touched her I'd kill him. The only time he tried, I pushed him so hard downstairs he was bedridden for a month.'

She says it with cold satisfaction. It makes her sound like a different woman from the one I know. Or thought I did.

'What about Michel? Is he . . . ?'

'He's Louis's. But my father regards him as his own. He always wanted a son, an heir to leave the farm to. Daughters aren't the same, not even Gretchen. I think that's why . . .'

'Why what?' I ask, when she falls silent.

I hear her sigh, as though she's drawing breath from a long way away. 'After my mother died, there was another baby. A little girl. My father never let me see her. He told me she was stillborn, but I . . . I thought I heard her cry.'

The farm is like a macabre set of Russian dolls, I think. Each time I'm convinced I've reached the last secret there's another, even uglier, inside. 'For God's sake, how can you stay here? Why don't you leave?'

'It isn't that easy.'

'Yes, it is! You pack your things and go! He can't stop you!'

'I couldn't leave without Gretchen.'

'Then take her with you!'

'Haven't you been *listening*?' she flashes, again giving a glimpse of the emotion dammed up behind the façade. 'What do you think I was doing with Louis? She won't leave her father. At least, not with me.'

So now we're back where we started. I turn away and look outside again, as much to give myself time as anything. Torn clouds pass over the moon. The small section of clearing that's visible looks harmless and tranquil, but all around it the trees form a wall of impenetrable shadow.

'Now you see why I have to get Gretchen away from here,' Mathilde says from the darkness. 'I don't care how or where. Anything's better than this. She'll go with you.'

I'm grateful it's dark in the small hut so I don't have to face her. It's a sign of her desperation that she's still trying to persuade me to take her daughter after all this. Or maybe she hopes I'll feel obliged now she's confided in me. Either way it makes no difference.

'I can't. I'm sorry.'

I hear something behind me. Turning, I see the thin light around the door blocked out as Mathilde passes in front of it, and then there's another sound. Only faint, barely more than a whisper: the soft scrape of steel on stone. And I suddenly remember the butchering knife that Georges picked up from the slab.

'Will you reconsider?' Mathilde asks from the darkness.

The moment seems to hang. I remember the hammer that also sits on the slab. There's a muscle twitch that might be the start of my hand moving, then a noise comes from outside. It's quickly stifled, but there's no mistaking it.

A child's whimper.

There's a flurry of movement and moonlight floods into the hut as Mathilde wrenches open the door. As she rushes out I see her hands are empty. I hurry after her, half-expecting to find Arnaud waiting with his rifle.

But it isn't her father who's standing outside. It's Gretchen.

She's clutching Michel to her like a shield. Her hand is clamped across his mouth, pinning him as he struggles. There's no need to ask how much she's heard.

Mathilde falters. 'Gretchen . . .'

'It isn't true. You're not my mother.'

'No, of course not.' Mathilde tries to smile.

'Papa didn't do those things. I don't believe you, you're lying!'

'That's right. I was making it up.' Mathilde holds out her hands. 'You're hurting Michel. Here, let me—'

'Stay away!' Gretchen backs off. Michel twists his face away from her hand and begins to wail. Mathilde takes a step towards her.

'I only want to—'

'*Stay away from me!*'

Still holding Michel, she turns and runs. Ignoring the pain in my foot, I overtake Mathilde as she chases after her, but Gretchen has already reached the sanglochon pen. She hoists Michel into the air above the boar's enclosure.

'Get *away*! I *mean* it!'

Mathilde stumbles to a halt next to me as Gretchen holds Michel poised over the fence. The boar is nowhere in sight, but the baby's howling has disturbed the sows in the next pen. Their agitated grunts add to the commotion.

'Come on, Gretchen, you don't want to hurt him,' I say.

'*Shut up!*' she yells, her face blotched and wet with tears. 'You don't care about me, you're as bad as her!'

There's movement in the pen behind her. The boar's snout appears in the cave-like entrance of its shed. Small, mean eyes regard us from under the heavy flaps of its ears.

'Gretchen, please listen to me!' Even in the moonlight Mathilde's face is ashen. 'I'm sorry—'

'No, you're not! You're lying! Papa didn't do that! My mother's dead, you're not her!'

Behind her, the boar has emerged. It begins to pace, watching us.

'You're frightening Michel,' Mathilde says. 'Give him to me, and then—'

'No!' Gretchen shouts, and with a squeal the boar charges. It thuds into the fencing, and as Gretchen recoils I lunge forward.

But she sees me and thrusts Michel towards the enclosure again. 'Get *away*!'

I back off. The boar butts against the planks, enraged. The baby is wailing, legs kicking in the air.

'No!' Mathilde's hands have gone to her mouth. 'Don't, please! You don't want to hurt Michel, he's—'

'He's *what*? My *brother*?' Gretchen's face slowly crumples as Mathilde says nothing. 'It's not true! I don't believe you!'

Beginning to sob, she hugs Michel to her. Thank God. Beside me, I can feel the tension ebb from Mathilde.

'Come up to the house,' she says as she steps forward. 'Let me take Michel, and—'

Gretchen's head snaps up. '*Whore!*'

Her face is contorted as she lifts Michel again. The wooden planks buck and creak under the boar's attack. Oh God, I think, getting ready to launch myself forward, knowing neither Mathilde nor I can reach her in time.

Mathilde stands with her arms out. The moon clears a cloud, illuminating the scene like a floodlight. 'Please, just let me explain—'

'Whore! Lying *whore*!'

'Gretchen, please—'

'Shut up! I hate you, I HATE YOU!'

Gretchen pivots towards the pen, and there's a sound like a whip cracking. She staggers, losing her grip on Michel as her legs buckle. I run towards them as she collapses but Mathilde is there first. She snatches up Michel, quickly checking that he's unhurt before thrusting him at me and turning to her daughter.

There's a dark stain spreading on the front of Gretchen's T-shirt. Even now I don't understand what's happened, not until I hear a moan and turn to see Arnaud at the edge of the woods. The rifle stock is still set to his shoulder but as I watch the barrel drops to point harmlessly at the ground.

He stumbles into a run towards us as Mathilde kneels beside Gretchen. She's lying on her back, limbs moving spastically as she blinks up at the sky.

'Mathilde . . . ?' It's a small girl's voice, lost and confused. 'Mathilde, I don't . . .'

'Shh, it's all right, don't try to speak.'

Mathilde takes hold of one of her hands as Arnaud reaches us. He pauses to rest a hand on Michel, then drops down beside Gretchen.

'Oh, Jesus! God, no . . . !'

My mind seems stalled. I stand there helplessly, awkwardly holding Michel. I tell myself that the rifle is too small bore to do much damage, that it's only lethal for birds and rabbits. But blood is still soaking into Gretchen's T-shirt, and now she begins to cough black gouts of it.

'No,' Mathilde says, as if she's reproving her. 'No!'

Gretchen is staring up at her, eyes wide and scared. With her free hand Mathilde presses at the small hole in her chest. Gretchen tries to speak, but then an arterial gush bursts from her mouth and she starts to choke. Her back arches, feet kicking in the dirt as she spasms. For a moment she's rigid, straining against it. Then all the tension leaves her body, and it's over.

A stillness seems to descend, a bubble of quiet that neither Michel's crying nor the boar's squeals can break. Mathilde half-sits, half-slumps, so that one leg is pinned under her. She's still holding Gretchen's hand. She lowers it as Arnaud weeps and strokes his daughter's face.

'I'm sorry. She was going to throw him, I had to,' he keens. 'Oh God, no, I'm sorry.'

Mathilde stares at her father across Gretchen's body, then her hand cracks across his face louder than the rifle shot. He doesn't seem to notice, rocking backwards and forwards with the bloody print on his cheek.

Behind them, the boar hammers at the fence in a frenzy, goaded by the scent of blood. Mathilde gets unsteadily to her feet. She absently tucks her hair behind her ear, but the gesture is broken and automatic, accomplishing nothing except to leave a dark smear. She walks drunkenly to where Arnaud dropped the rifle.

'Mathilde,' I say, my voice a croak.

I might as well not have spoken. She picks up the rifle and comes back, no more steadily than before. Her hands and arms have red gloves to her elbows.

'Mathilde,' I repeat, struggling to hold onto Michel. But I'm no more than a spectator now. She stands over her father as he kneels by Gretchen. He doesn't look up when she chambers a round and raises the rifle to her shoulder.

I flinch away as the rifle fires. The report is followed by a shriek from the boar. When I look back Arnaud is still weeping beside his daughter. Mathilde fires again. This time I hear the bullet slap into the boar's flesh. It roars and spins around, then charges the fence once more. Mathilde calmly works the rifle bolt to reload. She walks closer until she's firing right down onto the animal's back. Each shot is accompanied by a frenzied squeal as the boar continues to attack the planking. Its dark-grey hide is black with blood as it shrieks its pain and rage.

Then Mathilde puts the barrel to its ear and pulls the trigger, and the screams are abruptly cut off.

Silence settles, shroud-like, around the pens. Only the soft weeping from Arnaud disturbs it, but gradually other sounds begin to filter in. The pigs' frightened squeals, Michel's cries, the rustle of the trees. As the land comes back to life around us, Mathilde lets the rifle drop from her hands. She stares off at nothing while her father kneels over Gretchen's body, and I stand apart from them both, convinced that this moment will go on for ever.

Epilogue

A MIST-LIKE DRIZZLE, TOO light to call rain, blurs the distinction between ground and low grey clouds. The trees by the roadside are displaying their skeletal nature, stark branches showing through the sparse leaves, while what were fields of wheat are now furrows of bare stubble waiting to be ploughed under.

I walk the last kilometre to the farm. After the car has pulled away it occurs to me that, by a vagary of the last few lifts, I'm following the same route as when I first arrived. I stop when I reach the barbed-wire-topped gate, looking past it at the familiar track disappearing into the trees. The mailbox stencilled with *Arnaud* is still nailed to the post. But the white lettering is more faded than I remember, and the rusty padlock that used to bar entry has been replaced by a severe construction of brass and steel. Pinned to the centre of the gate is a subtler form of warning: a printed notice announcing that this is now bank property.

I rub my hand along the gate's weathered grain, but make no attempt to climb over. Now I'm here I'm reluctant to go any further. I wait for a lone car to flash past before throwing my rucksack onto the other side and clambering across the corroded wire. The once-dusty track is puddled and muddy, and without the cover of leaves I can soon make out the farmhouse through the trees. Then the track emerges in the courtyard, revealing the changes a few months have made.

The place is abandoned. No hens scurry about as I cross the cobbles, and the van and trailer have been removed. But the stable block's dead clock still stands at twenty to nothing, and the ancient tractor remains; too broken and decrepit to move from its long-time home. The house is closed and shuttered, more dilapidated than ever under its rusting scaffold. The section of wall I repaired looks smaller than I remember, a cosmetic repair that doesn't conceal the fundamental rot.

I've been apprehensive about coming back. Now I'm here, though, I don't feel very much at all. The changed season and bleak landscape are too different from my memory, robbing the once familiar surroundings of their potency. Seeing them again feels surreal and strange, like revisiting a fever-dream.

In the days after Arnaud put a bullet into his youngest daughter's heart, I went through my story countless times with the French police. Eventually, once they were satisfied I'd told them everything I knew, I was allowed to return to the UK. I'd given my assurance that I'd return for the trial, which was true as far as it went.

I just didn't mention that the decision wouldn't be mine to make.

London seemed grey and dirty after the green lushness of the farm. The world had continued to turn in my absence: the streets still seethed, the traffic still crawled, and the Thames still flowed. My return was momentous only to me. I'd expected to find myself a wanted man, that there would be a warrant out for my arrest at the very least. The reality was less dramatic.

In my guilty imaginings I'd always assumed that the police would know what had happened in Docklands; that I'd killed a man and run away. It never occurred to me that the only person who could tell them might have chosen not to. Rather than draw that sort of attention to himself, Lenny had simply left Jules's body lying in the gutter, where it lay undiscovered until later that morning. Given the nature of his injuries, it was blamed on a hit and run, and with no evidence or witnesses his death had remained unsolved.

It might have stayed that way if I hadn't given myself up.

Of course, I knew that wouldn't be the end of it. There was still the threat of Lenny, and what he might do once he found out I was back. But by now Jules's former business partner had problems of his own. I learned from a coffee-breathed CID sergeant that the big man was in custody himself after being caught in a drugs raid. Lenny was facing ten years in prison, on charges that included assaulting police officers as well as supplying and distributing class A drugs.

I kept my expression neutral when I heard that.

There was another surprise to come. I'd taken it for granted that I'd be held in custody myself, at least until it was decided what I was going to be charged with. Instead, at the end of the interview I was told I was being released on bail. 'You came back from France to hand yourself in,' the CID officer shrugged. 'I don't think you're much of a flight risk.'

For want of anywhere else to go, I headed back to my old flat. I expected to find someone else living there, my belongings long since thrown away. But my keys still worked, and when I let myself in everything was as I'd left it. If not for the dust and accumulated post piled behind the door, I might never have been away. As indifferent to my absence as everything else, the rent had automatically continued to be taken from my bank account, eating up the money I'd been saving to go to France. The irony wasn't lost on me. Still, it meant I had somewhere to stay until my case came to trial.

There was no point thinking further ahead than that.

And so I stepped back into the husk of my old life. I even

returned to my old job at the Zed, after a contrite conversation with Sergei. I needed the money, but it was a bizarre feeling, as though the events of that summer had never happened. That was brought home to me when I bumped into Callum one day.

'Hey, Sean,' he said. 'Not seen you around lately. What've you been doing with yourself?'

It dawned on me that he'd no idea I'd even been away. People have their own lives, and it's vanity to think we play anything other than a bit-part in them.

'Got your tickets yet for the New Wave season at the Barbican?' Callum asked.

He looked surprised when I told him I hadn't even known about it. At one time I would have rushed to book, but now the news left me unmoved. Thinking about it, I realized I'd not been to the cinema or watched a film since my return. It wasn't even a conscious decision; I'd just had more important things to do.

Chloe would have appreciated that.

My trial was held in a busy courtroom, just one in a long line of proceedings held that day. After all my anxiety it was almost an anticlimax. For a while there was talk of charging me with involuntary manslaughter, but that had been quietly dropped. Jules's own history of drug dealing and violence, as well as his treatment of Chloe, weighed in my favour. Even the fact that I'd technically stolen his car was considered too much of a grey area to bother with. While it counted against me that I'd fled the country, my lawyer argued that I'd been acting in self-defence and justifiably scared for my life. And if it had taken me longer than it should have to turn myself in . . . Well, there were extenuating circumstances.

I was found guilty of failing to report an accident and of leaving the scene. The sentence was six months in prison, suspended for two years.

I was a free man.

I stayed in London long enough to hand in my notice and say a few goodbyes, then I left. There was nothing to keep me there, and I still had unfinished business to attend to.

And now here I am.

Slipping a little on the wet cobbles, I go over to the house. The storeroom door is closed. Water drips onto me from the scaffold as I stand outside, suddenly certain that it'll be locked. But it isn't: there's nothing in there anyone would want to steal. The warped door creaks open reluctantly. Inside seems darker than ever, the grey daylight from the courtyard barely illuminating the windowless room. The red overalls are missing, but everything else looks untouched since I left it. I go over to where the bags of sand are stacked. One of them is set a little apart from the others, though not so much that anyone would notice. Putting down my rucksack, I roll up my sleeve and push my hand and arm up to the elbow into the damp sand. I dig around slowly at first, then more urgently when I can't find anything. I plunge my arm deeper, spilling sand onto the floor. Just when I'm convinced there's nothing there my fingers encounter something hard. I pull it out.

The plastic-wrapped package looks just as it did when I hid it here, on the afternoon after the gendarmes' visit. I'd made no mention of it when I'd recounted my story to either the French or UK police, an omission of which I'm not particularly proud. But given everything else I had to tell them it would have been an unnecessary complication. Even if they'd believed I was unaware of what was in the boot of Jules's car, I'd be hard pressed to explain why I'd kept it.

I'm not sure I know myself.

The storeroom seemed a good hiding place at the time, but I'd not anticipated the package would be left for so long. Since then barely a day has gone by that I haven't fretted it would be found, that the storeroom would be searched or cleared out. But I needn't have worried.

Mathilde kept my secret, just as I kept hers.

News of Louis's murder and Gretchen's death was met with predictable outrage in the town. But while the facts surrounding the tragedy were soon widely known, the truth behind them was another matter. Before I left the farm to call for the police and an ambulance on the night of the shooting, Mathilde had begged me not to reveal that she was Gretchen's mother.

'Promise me!' she'd insisted, her face etched with grief. 'Promise me you won't tell them!'

I hadn't wanted to listen. I couldn't see what could be gained by further silence, and the idea of protecting Arnaud was repugnant. But Mathilde clutched my arm, grey eyes burning with intensity.

'It's not for me, it's for Michel. *Please!*'

I understood then. In everything she'd done, her first priority had always been her children. It would be hard enough for her son to grow up with his mother and grandfather branded as murderers, without having to endure an even worse stigma. I couldn't blame her for wanting to spare him that. And I thought there might also be another reason for her reticence. If the truth about Gretchen's parentage were to come out, it might easily raise questions about Michel's. Mathilde had told me he was Louis's son, but I wasn't sure she'd want that claim put to the test.

Some stones are better left unturned.

So I kept my silence, and Mathilde's secret. The only other person who might have thrown more light on the farm's murky history was Georges, and for a while I wondered how much the old pig handler might really know. But not even the police could breach his indifference. He maintained that in all the years he'd worked at the farm he'd seen nothing, heard nothing, knew

nothing. The only emotion he displayed came when the interview was over.

'What about the sanglochons?' he asked.

He'd broken down and wept when he learned they'd been
destroyed.

After all that had happened I thought the farm could hold no
more revelations, that it had exhausted its capacity to surprise.
It hadn't. Arnaud made no attempt to deny any of the charges
levelled against him, and his account matched Mathilde's in
every detail. Except one.

He claimed he'd killed Louis himself.

According to Arnaud, the younger man had only been
stunned by Mathilde's blow. Once in the cinderblock hut he'd
started to revive, so her father had finished the job himself before
dismembering Louis's body and feeding it to the sanglochons.
When the police asked why he hadn't tried to save him, the
reply was typically blunt:

'One pig's throat is the same as another.'

It's possible he was lying, trying to take the blame to protect
Mathilde. But I find that hard to believe. Given the sort of man
he was, it's more likely that he was simply content to let his
eldest daughter believe she'd killed her own lover. It would tie
her to him even more, and that sort of casual cruelty is more in
keeping with the Arnaud I knew. As for why he should confess
now, I think there was no longer any reason not to. He'd already
lost everything.

Mathilde saw to that when she asked Jean-Claude and his
wife to adopt Michel.

I was shocked when I first heard, but then it made a certain
kind of sense. Although I can't imagine what it must have cost
her to give up her son, even if the court was lenient she knew
Michel would barely know her by the time she was released. So,
as ever, she put his interests before her own. Jean-Claude will

give Michel a good home, and just as important a fresh start. And for Arnaud, having his beloved grandson brought up by Louis's brother will hurt far more than any prison sentence.

Like everything else about her, Mathilde's revenge was subtle.

I barely recognized the old and broken man who was led into court. The flesh hung from his bones like an ill-fitting suit, a wattle of loose skin sagging between chin and throat. But it was the eyes where the depth of the change was most evident. The steely gaze was gone, dulled by doubt and loss.

Only once was there a flash of the Arnaud I remembered. When the verdict was announced, his head came up to glare around the courtroom with something like his old contempt. Then his eyes met his daughter's. She stared back at him, implacable and calm, until he lowered his head.

If the condemnation heaped on Arnaud was inevitable, what I'd not anticipated was that Mathilde would be vilified almost as much. Even if she didn't deliver the fatal blow herself, she'd still helped conceal a murder. And without the background of a lifetime's abuse to provide a context, her role in Louis's death emerged in a cruelly harsh light. When her own verdict was announced she remained as outwardly controlled as ever, though I could see her hand trembling as it tucked her hair behind her ear. I watched, feeling helpless, as she was led out. As she reached the door, for a brief moment she looked directly at me.

Then the door closed and shut her from sight.

Brushing the sand off the package, I go back out of the storeroom. The drizzle has turned to rain as I head across the courtyard towards the barn. Water drips from its entrance as I prop my rucksack against the wall inside. The dark interior is as cold and damp as if it's never known a summer. I can make out the dull glint of wine bottles in the wooden rack on the back wall, too sour for anyone to want. The patch of concrete on the floor looks smaller than I recall, the crack in it still unrepaired.

I'd intended to go up to the loft one last time, but there doesn't seem any point. Instead, leaving my rucksack in the dry of the barn, I follow the track down to the lake.

The ground is muddy and churned, the leafless grapevines resembling rows of tangled wire. Even the wood is hardly recognizable as the green-canopied place I remember. The chestnut trees are bare, and underneath their dripping branches is a mat of dead leaves and bristling shells.

There'll be no harvest this year.

I walk straight past the fork leading to the sanglochon pens without slowing. I've no desire or reason to go there again. It's only when I come to the statues that I stop. I thought they might have been taken away, but they're still here. Unchanged and apparently unmissed. I try to recall how I felt hiding from Arnaud that night, to summon up something of the uncertainty and fear. I can't. In the grey daylight the statues are just mundane stone carvings. Turning away, I continue down to the lake.

The water is wind-shivered and grey. At the top of the bluff the ground is scarred and gouged with heavy tyre tracks. I stand under the empty branches of the old chestnut tree, staring down at the rain-pocked lake. I can't see below its surface, but there's nothing there any more. Louis's truck has long since been winched out and taken away.

The polythene package in my hand feels solid and heavy. My feelings towards it remain as ambiguous as when I first saw it hidden in the car boot. I had ample opportunities to dispose of it during the summer, yet I didn't. I could tell myself it was simple cowardice, insurance in case Lenny or any other of Jules's associates wanted it back, but that isn't entirely true. Like turning over a rock to see what lies underneath, now I'm here I finally acknowledge the real reason why I've kept it all this time.

I couldn't bring myself to get rid of it.

I've no idea how much it's worth, but it's more money than

I've ever had. Enough to start a new life. And with Jules dead and Lenny in prison, there's no one else to claim it. I was in London long enough for them to have found me if there were. I weigh the package in my palm, feeling the possibilities beneath the crinkle of plastic. Then, drawing back my arm, I throw it out over the lake as far as I can.

It arcs against the grey sky before landing in the water with a small, unemphatic splash.

I jam my hands in my pockets and watch the ripples flatten out until there's nothing left. Chloe didn't get a second chance, and neither did Gretchen. I'm not going to waste mine. Turning away, I retrace my steps through the woods. After stopping off at the barn for my rucksack, I head back to the house. I've done what I came here for, but there's one more thing I want to do before I go.

The kitchen garden is unrecognizable. The goats and chickens have gone, and the ordered rows of vegetables have either died or run amok. The tiny flowerbed has grown wild and straggled, but even this late in the year there are still a few splashes of colour. I stand looking down at it, thinking about the sadness I saw on Mathilde's face when she was tending this small patch of earth. As if she were tending a shrine.

Or a grave.

Mathilde never said what her father had done with the remains of her stillborn daughter, but I can guess what she chose to believe. The police were unaware of any transgression except Gretchen's death and Louis's murder, so the small bed of flowers remains undisturbed. Yet try as I might, I can't see Arnaud burying evidence of his other crime where it could so easily be found. Not when he had a much more permanent means of disposal, as he showed with Louis. I doubt he'd feel differently just because it was his own flesh and blood.

Especially not another daughter.

That's only speculation, but there are other unanswered questions. I still can't decide if what I heard in those last moments in the hut was really the sound of Mathilde lifting the knife from the stone slab. I don't want to believe it, but then I think about everything else she did to protect her family. Once I'd found Louis's truck in the lake, she'd nothing to lose by telling me the rest, hoping even then to persuade me to take Gretchen away. But after I'd refused would she really have allowed me to leave, knowing what I did?

In my more optimistic moods I tell myself she would. She'd saved my life once before, when I'd stepped in the trap. Except then I'd represented an opportunity rather than a threat. In my darker moments I wonder what would have happened if I'd got worse instead of better. Would she have seen I received proper medical attention as she'd said, with all the risk that implied? Or would I have ended up like Louis, another offering for her father's sanglochons?

I don't know. Maybe I've been so tainted by the farm's secrets that I'm seeing them where they don't exist. And my own actions don't give me the moral right to judge. That night in the hut when I thought Mathilde had taken the knife from the slab, my first thought was of the hammer that Georges had used to stun the sow. If Michel hadn't announced Gretchen's presence just then, would I have actually picked it up?

Used it?

Not so long ago I would have said no, but that was before Jules. Even though I didn't mean to kill him, I keep asking myself if that made any difference. If I'd known what would happen when I drove away, if it came down to a simple question of him or me, would I have acted any differently? There's no easy answer. Under the skin we're all still animals. That's what the society Arnaud so despised is meant to disguise, but the reality is that none of us know what we're truly capable of.

If we're lucky we never find out.

On impulse I crouch down and begin plucking weeds from the flowerbed. I'm not sure why, but it feels right. When a semblance of the former neatness has been restored, I stand up and take a last look around. Then, wiping the muddy soil from my hands, I go back to the courtyard and give a sharp whistle.

'Lulu! Here, girl!'

The spaniel lopes out from behind the stables where she's been sniffing. She's barely slowed by the single hind leg, and her enthusiasm makes me smile. I hadn't planned on claiming her, but no one else wanted to and the vet couldn't keep her indefinitely. It was either that or let her be destroyed, and I couldn't do that. Besides, it's surprising how much easier it is to hitch a lift when you've a three-legged dog as a travelling companion.

As we pass the house Lulu stops by the kitchen door and whines. But she doesn't stay long, and soon follows me out of the courtyard and back up the track. She slips under the gate while I climb over. Once we're on the other side I look up and down the road. There are no cars in sight. The spaniel watches me with her ears cocked, wobbling slightly as she waits for me to decide which way to go. It's only when she's standing still that balance becomes a problem.

So long as we keep moving she's fine.

Acknowledgements

Even by my standards, *Stone Bruises* has been a long time coming. People who've helped along the way include SCF, Ben Steiner, my agents Mic Cheetham and Simon Kavanagh and all at The Marsh Agency, my editor at Transworld, Simon Taylor, and my parents, Sheila and Frank Beckett.

As ever, a huge thanks to my wife, Hilary, without whose belief, help and support this would never have been written.

Simon Beckett, September 2013

Simon Beckett has worked as a freelance journalist, writing for national newspapers and colour supplements. He is the author of four international bestselling crime thrillers featuring his forensic anthropologist hero, Dr David Hunter: *The Chemistry of Death*, *Written in Bone*, *Whispers of the Dead* and *The Calling of the Grave*.

Simon is married and lives in Sheffield. To find out more, visit www.simonbeckett.com.